A Life of Secrets

By Margaret Kaine

The Black Silk Purse
A Life of Secrets

For my much-loved family

A Life of Secrets

MARGARET KAINE

Allison & Busby Limited
11 Wardour Mews
London W1F 8AN
allisonandbusby.com

First published in Great Britain by Allison & Busby in 2020.
This paperback edition published by Allison & Busby in 2020.

A CIP catalogue record for this book is available from
the British Library.

10 9 8 7 6 5 4 3 2 1

ISBN 978-0-7490-2500-7

Typeset in 11.5/16.5 pt Adobe Garamond Pro by
Allison & Busby Ltd.

The paper used for this Allison & Busby publication
has been produced from trees that have been legally sourced
from well-managed and credibly certified forests.

Printed and bound by
CPI Group (UK) Ltd, Croydon, CR0 4YY

'Love is not love that alters when it alteration finds'

WILLIAM SHAKESPEARE

Chapter One

Bloomsbury, London, 1926

'*You look so seductive with your hair loose, so beautiful,*' the husky and haunting voice crept into her mind and she found herself struggling to push the memory away. Yet she had to, it belonged to another life, one taken from her by the terrible war that had robbed England of the cream of her youth. And only too aware of the pitfalls of allowing such nostalgia to overwhelm her, it was a welcome distraction for Deborah when there came a timid tap on the door.

A pale and anxious face peered round, followed by the plainly dressed figure of a young woman.

'Please, do come in and take a seat.' Deborah indicated the chair opposite her desk and waited.

'Be you Miss Claremont?' The girl's voice was hesitant.

'Yes, that is my name.'

'And is it true that you find positions for such as I?'

Deborah studied her, trying to establish the girl's dialect. 'I shall certainly try to help you if I can.' She opened a file and on a blank sheet of paper wrote the date. 'Perhaps if you could tell me your name?'

'Boot.'

'And your Christian name?'

'Sarah.'

'Age?'

'I be nineteen this coming June.'

Again, that soft burr. 'And your current address?'

She named an East End area notorious for its poverty and crime, and Deborah frowned. 'May I ask how long you have been resident there?'

'A fortnight, miss.'

Deborah felt a surge of relief. Poverty in itself was not a crime, but dishonesty was, and it was essential that her agency's reputation for supplying staff with good character did not become tainted. Otherwise she would never be able to achieve what had become her only purpose in life.

'And before then?'

'Wiltshire, miss, then I come up to the London house when I were sixteen. Kitchen maid to start with, and finally parlourmaid.' The last word was spoken with pride.

'And your reason for leaving?' Deborah paused, seeing colour rise in the girl's face. 'If it was for an embarrassing reason, I can promise you that I won't be shocked, nor will I judge you. Not unless it was for theft. In that case I'm afraid I cannot help you.' Sarah's expression was one of horror. 'No, miss, I never stole nothing in me life.'

Deborah waited.

The words stumbled out. 'It was the master. Been after me for weeks, he had, ever since I went upstairs to work. And I knew it was only a matter of time afore he had his way, because we servants weren't allowed locks on our doors. He was a randy old—' She bit her lip. 'And I wouldn't have bin the first maid he'd ruined.' Sarah looked directly at her with eyes full of honesty. 'I was brought up respectable and I want to stay that way.'

'So you gave notice.'

She shook her head. 'No, I just packed me bags. I wasn't taking no chances.'

'Was that wise? To leave without a reference?'

'Better than leaving with something else, if you'll beg me pardon, miss.'

Deborah's lips twitched. But the situation didn't call for levity. The girl, like many before her, was now in a desperate situation and through no fault of her own. However, she did need to probe a little more. 'But you knew you had somewhere to go, to family perhaps?'

'I thought I had, miss. I went back to Wiltshire, but I found me auntie had taken up with a man at long last and I didn't fancy the way he looked at me either. Out of the frying pan, if you know what I mean. So I slung me hook and managed to find a cheap room here. You know, miss, it's a mixed blessing to be born with looks.'

Deborah's lips twitched again. She had no illusions about how she must appear to this young girl, older and dressed as soberly as she was.

'And how did you hear about my agency?'

'It was when I went to Mass at St Malachy's. The priest told me as how you had a charitable outlook on girls without references.'

'Deserving girls,' Deborah corrected.

'Yes, miss.'

'And you want to go back into service?'

'Even though things are changing, it's all I know.'

Deborah regarded her. It was true that since the war ended, increasing numbers of women were looking for different employment, but a position in a good household still offered advantages for girls without family support. A roof over one's head, warmth and food were benefits not to be underestimated. Deborah took great care in placing her applicants. 'And the name of your previous employer?' She made a note of it with an asterisk, 'Females – send only homely and middle-aged.'

She gazed at the young woman before her. Fair, with a good complexion and frank blue eyes, she seemed trustworthy and Deborah had great faith in her own judgement. 'If you would like to return the day after tomorrow, perhaps in the afternoon at three o'clock, I may have some news for you.'

'You mean you'll help me?'

Deborah smiled at her. 'I'll certainly try.'

Sarah rose. 'Oh, thank you, miss. I'll be here on the dot.'

Deborah watched her leave and then began to leaf through her card index, thankful that her father had not subscribed to the belief that education was wasted on women. Her private tutor, Mr Channing, had included administration in his teaching, peering at her over his half-rimmed spectacles.

'It is quite probable that you will marry a member of the aristocracy, or at least be the mistress of a large household, and you will find such knowledge useful.'

Deborah paused in reflection. Who could have possibly foreseen that at the age of twenty-six she would not only be a spinster, but while concealing her title, have an occupation that would have appalled her parents. A staff agency would have been regarded as 'trade', a term of disparagement used by her insular class to describe anyone who worked for a living other than in a profession. Even as a young girl she had inwardly rebelled against such narrow-minded snobbery.

But it was only when her heart was splintered, first by the news that the man she adored had been killed at the Battle of Amiens, and weeks later by the loss of her parents to the Spanish flu pandemic, that Deborah discovered within herself a core of steel. Her beloved mother, then within days, the gentle, intelligent man who had been her father, had succumbed to the airborne virus that had taken the lives of 228,000 people in Britain alone. And afterwards she'd had desperate need of that inner strength. Even more so when it was revealed that her brother Gerard had been appointed as her guardian.

That evening, Deborah sat before her walnut dressing table feeling impatient as Ellen began with firm strokes to brush her shining bob. 'I'm feeling rather tired tonight, I wish I hadn't accepted the invitation to go and dine with the Anstruthers. And Gerard expects me downstairs for drinks beforehand, more's the pity. I expect my new sister-in-law will have invited more of her boring friends.' She knew that her mother would have disapproved of such intimacies with one of the servants, but Deborah had little patience with such conventions. She had fought years ago for Ellen to be her personal maid, with Gerard's opposition only stiffening her resolve.

'You're mad. The girl is far too young and inexperienced!' Her brother's pale-blue eyes had been like flint. 'An older woman such as Olive would be a much more sensible choice.'

What you really mean, Deborah had thought, is that she would be a useful spy for you. She'd stood her ground. 'Ellen might be a parlourmaid now, but she is an intelligent girl and a quick learner. Besides, I had discussed the matter with Mama before she died. Naturally, her maid then attended me, but now that she's left . . .'

'I don't believe you.'

'I hope you are not accusing me of lying, Gerard. You should consult Fulton, because he was aware of the plan.'

It was a bold untruth but with relief she saw his expression of uncertainty and knew she had won. The Claremont household depended greatly on the efficient butler who had not only run their Grosvenor Square house for twenty-five years, but to whom their mother's word had been sacrosanct. Gerard would never dare to gainsay one of her instructions.

'Sadly, Mama died before she discovered how much you needed guidance.'

The barbed reminder had made Deborah, who then was at her most vulnerable, flinch, but over the years Ellen had not only repaid her support with fierce loyalty, she had become her trusted confidante.

Deborah smiled. 'I suppose I'm lucky that since she married Gerard – Julia shows little interest in my personal affairs. She knows I serve on various charity committees and enjoy shopping and lunching out with friends, but never asks for details.' She considered her reflection as Ellen teased her hair into its sleek shape.

Ellen said, 'But she might later, as she becomes more used to being the mistress here.'

The possibility had already occurred to Deborah, and it was not a welcome one. While she had been able to conceal her activities from her cold and distant brother, she suspected that Julia might become both curious and ultimately more perceptive.

'I shall tell her the same as I told Gerard at the beginning, that I just like to keep busy during the middle of the week. My habit of spending time away from the house on Tuesdays, Wednesdays and Thursdays has long been accepted. If she does ask further, I'm sure I'll cope with it.'

Ellen turned to the two couture gowns she had laid out on the rose silk eiderdown. 'Which one, Lady Deborah? The blue or the green?'

She gave them a cursory glance. 'You decide, Ellen.'

'I think the blue, it matches your eyes. And the sapphire earrings look lovely with it.'

Deborah tried to imagine how she would feel in Ellen's place, caring for beautiful clothes for another woman to wear, handling her exquisite jewellery, yet unless she was an excellent actress, she had never betrayed any jealousy. One Christmas, Deborah had offered her a string of seed pearls and with some reluctance Ellen had accepted, but she only ever wore them beneath her black dress, fearing being accused of theft, or even of causing jealousy. The revelation about the insecurity of servants was one that Deborah had never forgotten.

Ready at last and gazing at her reflection in the cheval mirror, she had to admit that her applicants, or even clients at the agency, would hardly recognise her. There, Deborah was careful to wear only layers in grey: dropped-waist dresses with pleated skirts and matching jersey cardigans. Or a plain skirt and white or ivory blouse. Her business outfits, as she thought of them, were completed not only by a small cameo brooch and black bar shoes, but plain lens spectacles. But now, the blue brocade dress not only revealed her bare shoulders but was cut on the bias to drape in sinuous folds over the contours of her slim figure. A body she was well aware that men found attractive. Knowing that her decision to remain single was a constant irritant to her brother, afforded her not a small amount of pleasure.

It was when Deborah paused at the foot of the sweeping staircase that she heard from the open door of the drawing room the tinkling sound of her sister-in-law's voice.

With a sigh Deborah paused in the doorway. The room held several small groups of people, while Julia, with Gerard by her side, was talking to a young woman with insipid features. Deborah remembered her as also being vacuous.

'Good evening, Deborah, you've joined us at last.' Julia's smile was thin. 'I believe you know Caroline Morton. You recall that she was one of my bridesmaids.'

Deborah wondered whether it was truly a coincidence that all of Julia's six bridesmaids had been less than beauties. The bride had shone like a lily in a field of dandelions. 'Yes, of course. How are you, Caroline?'

'I am exceedingly well, thank you, Lady Deborah.' She gave a complacent smile. 'Have you heard my news? I have just become engaged to be married.'

'My congratulations, and who is the lucky gentleman?'

'Unfortunately, my fiancé could not be here this evening.' She named an odious friend of Gerard's, who was florid of face with hard eyes and fleshy fingers. Deborah had to bite her lip to suppress an exclamation of dismay. He would eat this little mouse alive. And she had no doubt that he had chosen his bride in anticipation of her fortune. Deborah hated hypocrisy. Caroline might be glowing with pride at the prospect of having a wedding band on her finger, but Deborah suspected that she was more in love with the status of a married woman than she was with the man himself.

'Maybe one of these days you will have similar happy news to share,' Julia's tone was one of honey.

'Now why would I wish to marry,' Deborah's own voice was also sweet as she turned to her stony-faced brother, 'when I have such a welcoming and comfortable home here in Grosvenor Square?'

'But surely you would like to have your own establishment?' Caroline said. 'Every woman wishes for that.'

'But I am not like most other women.' She met Gerard's gaze in challenge, but he was looking towards the door where a tall man was hovering.

The butler announced, 'Mr Theodore Field.'

'I believe he's single,' Julia whispered, with an arch glance at Deborah, which only served to annoy her.

Gerard turned to greet him and made the necessary introductions, mentioning that the new guest was a Member of Parliament.

'And which political party do you favour, Mr Field?' Deborah said.

'Mr Field is a leading Conservative,' Gerard snapped. 'Something I would have expected you to know.' He turned to the MP. 'My sister professes an interest in politics.'

Deborah ignored him. 'I would imagine, Mr Field, that with the widespread unrest in the country, this is not an easy time to sit in the House.' He was by far the best-looking man she'd met for ages.

'Indeed it isn't, Lady Deborah. But of course, one has to do one's duty.'

Pompous prig, she thought. He's obviously not prepared to elaborate on a political point with a mere woman. She excused herself, relieved she would soon be leaving for her dinner engagement. But then what else had she expected? Only after a long and bitter struggle had women achieved the vote, and then only once they were thirty years of age. As for their political opinions being sought and valued, that was a rarity. Deborah glanced at Gerard's smug face, which epitomised the grim fact that it remained a man's world.

It was only by running the staff agency that Deborah had been brought into close contact with ordinary people, and she continued to be shocked to discover how many of the women had suffered hardship or abuse at the hands of their fathers or their brothers. Often innocent young girls sent out to service were a target for unscrupulous employers who, complacent in their innate superiority, managed to remain free from censure. But I can at least try to protect my own applicants, Deborah thought, while her fixed smile gave lip service to the idle gossip around her. And that, surely, was a worthwhile ambition. It also gave meaning to what would otherwise be a rather empty life.

Chapter Two

Gerard glanced up absently as the butler placed the salver with the morning's post on the small table beside him, then, once he had finished an article in *The Times*, idly picked up a paperknife. Bills he put aside to approve before being forwarded to his agent on his country estate. Invitations received only a cursory glance as he now left such things for Julia to attend to. Then his hand stilled. He stared down at the envelope. The uneducated scrawl wasn't familiar, but the postmark was. He hesitated, a creeping sense of dread rising from the pit of his stomach. Why now, after so much time had passed? His lips compressed into a thin line so tight it almost hurt before he forced himself to slit open the cheap envelope. All it contained was a single sheet of lined paper ripped from an exercise book. He looked down at the signature and found it different from the one he'd expected. The content was terse.

Dear Sir,
Myrtle Waters died last week and has today bin buried. I
carn't keep the child. She sed to write to you.
    Yours respecfully
    Annie Jones

Gerard swore, and leaning forward, clenched his hands on his knees. He'd never expected that blasted business to raise its head again, could hardly even recall the features of the woman who had died. He'd played his part by giving way to what had amounted to blackmail at his original suggestion that the brat should be sent to a workhouse, and had paid handsomely to keep the Claremont name free from any scandal. Hurriedly he glanced down at the envelope again, feeling relief that this Annie Jones had incorrectly addressed her note to G. Claremont, Esq., which meant that his true identity was unknown.

But the confounded problem would have to be taken care of, and with urgency. He toyed again with the workhouse option, but what if Myrtle had left an incriminating letter in case that circumstance ever arose? She had been vehement in her outrage at even the thought. He could never take such a risk. Leaning back in his chair, Gerard took a deep breath and steepled his fingers. This was going to need intensive thought, especially in finding the needed trustworthy accomplice. Whereas the right amount of money could buy most things, absolute discretion could not always be relied upon and that was paramount. He shuddered at the thought of the unsavoury truth emerging. That would be disastrous.

It was an hour later, having come to a decision, that he summoned Fulton. 'Is Her Ladyship in the morning room?'

'Yes, I believe so, sir.'

'Alone?'

The butler inclined his head.

'I shall join her. And although it's early, I'll take a glass of Madeira there.' Seconds later, Gerard went to join his wife.

'Darling,' she said from the Chesterfield sofa where she was flicking through the *Tatler*. 'I'm sorry I wasn't down for breakfast.'

'Didn't you sleep well?'

'Yes, I was just feeling lazy.' She patted the seat beside her.

Gerard, however, settled into an armchair opposite. 'Sweetheart, I have a matter to discuss with you.' He turned as the butler brought in his wine, then waited until he'd left.

'It is just a suggestion, my sweet, but I wondered whether you might enjoy several days in Paris, perhaps to choose some new clothes?'

Her face lit up. 'What woman could resist? You are so good to me, Gerard.'

'It gives me pleasure to indulge you. And you will need a companion, of course.'

'You mean you would not be accompanying me?' Her limpid blue eyes showed dismay.

He shook his head. 'Unfortunately, I can't. However, perhaps we should make the most of an opportunity . . .' he hesitated. 'Would this not be a chance to develop your relationship with Deborah?' Seeing her frown he continued, 'It would lead to a more harmonious atmosphere, don't you agree? Perhaps being in your company might soften her a little, bring out her more feminine side.'

'You think so? I don't find her easy, Gerard.'

'I know, neither do I. But it would oblige me, Julia.'

She sighed. 'In that case, I shall suggest it to her.'

'No sense in delay; perhaps quite soon, would you like that?'

'It sounds lovely. I'll talk to Deborah when she returns this afternoon.'

A little of Gerard's tension eased. Julia's nature meant that he could easily bend her to his will, and already her mind would be turning to fripperies. Also, he found her blonde prettiness and curvaceous body appealing, whilst her excellent lineage boded well for a suitable heir. Gerard had never considered that Julia might refuse his marriage proposal. Hadn't becoming the Countess of Anscombe been every debutante's ambition? But in view of the contents of the letter, he could do without any social distractions in the near future, inevitable if Julia were in residence. He may also need to bring unsuitable people to the house. And Deborah's presence? She was far too perceptive.

* * *

23

At the agency, Deborah's thoughts were of Sarah Boot. She would be coming that afternoon in the hope of being the recipient of good news. And Deborah had found something to offer her. However, she did find herself in something of a quandary. Yes, there was a request for a parlourmaid in Hampstead but where the position would be a quiet one. The mistress was an elderly spinster who led an almost reclusive life while the staff, small in number, were long established. That in itself was a recommendation, but Deborah couldn't help wondering whether such a lively spirit as Sarah's wouldn't feel confined. Frowning, she tapped her pencil on Sarah's file. There was another opening here in London that might suit the girl, a grand and busy household. But Deborah had occasionally dined there, and as always needed to be wary of taking any risk that might threaten her own anonymity. Her appearance might be different devoid of the plain lens spectacles she wore at the agency, but she could do nothing to alter her voice. It was unrealistic to hope that a parlourmaid waiting on table might not recognise her, and a servants' hall was always a hotbed of gossip. As Gerard was fond of lecturing her, no whisper of scandal must ever touch their family. And so most of her placements tended to be with middle-class families rather than with aristocracy.

Deborah made her decision. 'Elspeth?'

Her assistant came in from the small outer office. When she had first opened the agency in Bloomsbury, and held interviews, the stockily built Elspeth Reid with her greying hair, intelligent eyes and calm manner had convinced Deborah that she had found the ideal person. Not only because she was the widow of an Anglican minister, Deborah had known instinctively that her true identity would be safe in her hands. She had never had a moment's regret, indeed the two women, different in both age and background, had become firm friends.

Deborah smiled at her. 'I think the only sensible solution would be to place Sarah Boot with the elderly spinster in Hampstead.'

'Aye, from what you've told me about her, I agree. Although in this morning's post there is a request for a housemaid at Felchurch Manor.'

'Our last placement there worked well. You know, if Sarah proved willing to accept a lower status, that might suit her better. And isn't it in Wiltshire where she grew up? Thank you, Elspeth. I shall give her the two options and let her choose for herself.'

In the East End, Sarah was putting a few scraps of cheese into a small saucepan of milk. With a hunk of yesterday's bread, it would suffice to keep hunger at bay. Striking a match to light the gas, her gaze wandered over the mean basement room, with its grimy windows, limp curtains and cracked linoleum; she had even heard the scuttling of a rat last night. How she hoped that her days there would soon come to an end, and it was all because of her aunt's stupidity. It had been a cruel disappointment to knock on the door of her aunt's cottage and face the dark stubble of Joe Moffat, a local man Sarah had always detested.

'Oh, it's you,' he muttered then shouted over his shoulder. 'It's your Sarah!'

With a feeling of dread she had gone into what was once her home, and one glance at Lily's gold band was enough to confirm her fear. Sarah was both shocked and bewildered. Joe Moffat was well known to be an idle bugger so why on earth had Lily, who had always managed to support herself, taken such a coarse man to her bed? Within minutes of Sarah's arrival, he was patting her aunt's bottom as if to establish his ownership, and it wasn't long before his sly gaze flicked over Sarah. She flashed him a look of disdain and with a grin he ambled out to the tiny garden.

'Why didn't you tell me,' she hissed, 'at least invite me to the wedding?'

Lily, a thin wiry woman with a tired face, looked sheepish. 'It were a rush job, or rather I thought it was.'

Appalled, Sarah stared at her. 'Whatever got into you?'

Lily glanced uneasily over her shoulder. ''Twas the last Harvest Supper, there was somethin' in the punch.'

And Sarah could guess who put it there. Lily, with her cosy cottage would be a prime catch for a layabout like Joe. 'It was a false alarm, then?'

Lily nodded. 'I'd missed me monthly, but it must've been my age. I should have thought of that, but I just panicked.'

'But you're all right?' Sarah jerked her head towards the garden. 'With him, I mean?'

Lily shrugged her shoulders. 'He's not so bad.'

'But you're still paying the rent.' Sarah's tone was flat.

'No change there, I'm afraid.' Lily bustled to the kettle. 'Anyway, sit you down, you must be parched. Are you hungry?'

When Sarah nodded, Lily cut her a slice of fruit cake. 'What brings you back? You've not bin dismissed?'

Sarah told her what had happened or could have happened. 'I'd hoped to come back to live with you for a bit, but there's a fat chance of that happening now!'

'I could ask Joe if he'd mind. There's still your old room empty.'

Sarah wavered, but with her previous experience still fresh in her mind decided to trust her instincts. She'd shaken her head. 'No, I'll stay tonight and then go back to London. There'll be more chance of a live-in job.'

At precisely three o'clock that afternoon Elspeth ushered Sarah into Deborah's office. Sitting straight, wearing a straw hat and clutching her bag on her knee, she sat before the desk with a look that managed to be both anxious and hopeful.

Deborah gave a reassuring smile. 'I have good news for you, I have found you two possible positions.' She saw Sarah's face light up, and went on to give a full explanation of each post. 'Of course, they are both dependent upon a favourable interview, but it is rare that my recommendation is not accepted.'

Sarah was frowning and biting her lip in concentration. 'You say it'd be a very quiet household in Hampstead?'

Deborah nodded. 'And a small one where you would

probably be the youngest member of staff. The establishment in Wiltshire is much larger.'

'But the post is only of housemaid.'

'Yes, but I imagine you would have prospects of advancement.'

'And I could start right away at both of them?'

Deborah nodded.

'Well, miss, if you could see where I'm living now, you'd understand why I'll take either. But . . .' Again she bit her lip. 'What do you think, miss?'

Deborah surveyed her. There was spirit in the girl, it was apparent in her posture, her quick mind. She would hate to see that dimmed by monotony.

'If you don't mind the temporary demotion to housemaid, considering your age, I think you might be happier in Wiltshire.'

An expression of relief passed over Sarah's face. 'Oh, thank you, miss, I was wondering that myself.'

'Then if you go and see Mrs Reid in the outer office, she will give you all the details and arrange for you to travel down for interview. She will also advance your rail fare and expenses.'

'You'll get it back, though?'

Deborah smiled. She really did like this girl. 'Yes, we'll get it back.'

Sarah stood. 'Thank you very much, Miss Claremont.'

Deborah nodded, and smiled to herself seeing Sarah leave with a much lighter step. How old was she, nineteen? An age when a world of promise stretched ahead. Sarah's spirit had reminded her of herself at that age or even younger. And with that thought came the memory of her closest friend, Abigail. She missed her vivacious friend. Similar in age and intellect the two girls had grown up in Berkshire on nearby estates and had hoped to come out together as debutantes. But with the outbreak of war, all Court presentations were suspended. Abigail was now living in married bliss in Scotland, and Deborah reminded herself that she owed her a letter.

She thought again of Sarah. Please God, fate would be kind to her. As to her own fate, it was better to remind herself of the countless blessings her privileged birth had brought. But that didn't mean that deep in her soul there wasn't an emptiness, even if she had become adept at hiding it.

Chapter Three

Later that afternoon back at Grosvenor Square, Deborah went upstairs to remove her coat and to change into more suitable attire only to find Ellen hovering in the bedroom. 'Did all go well, my lady?'

'Indeed it did, Ellen. It was a most satisfactory day.'

'Only Fulton gave me a message for you from Her Ladyship. When you returned would you kindly join her in the drawing room.'

Deborah stared at her in surprise. 'Then I had better go down.'

Once changed into a fresh ivory crêpe de chine blouse and pearls to enhance her plain skirt, Deborah left her room and went thoughtfully down the stairs and across the black-and-white tiled hall to the drawing room, which had always been a favourite of hers, holding as it did memories of her parents' sophisticated evening soirées. Many times she had sat at the top of the stairs concealed by a turn in the bannister to listen to the clink of glasses and laughter. With the occasional glimpse of stylish evening gowns, it had seemed to her as a young girl to be the epitome of glamour.

But now, intrigued by the summons from Julia, she went into the room to see her seated on one of the deep cushions of a cream sofa. She was browsing through a magazine, her sole occupation it seemed to Deborah, who had yet to see her reading an actual book. Then she chided herself for being uncharitable. Her sister-in-law was merely a product of her background, in the same way that the florid middle-aged woman Deborah had just interviewed was a product of hers. It had been a pity that the latter had been too rough round the edges for Deborah to find her a suitable position. But she had at least been able to give her the name of another agency whose standards were not as exacting as her own.

Pushing such thoughts away, Deborah greeted the young woman who was now mistress not only of the Grosvenor Square house, but also of their country seat in Berkshire.

'I'm so pleased to see you, Deborah.' Julia put down her magazine. 'Please, do come and share tea with me.' She rose and went to the silken bell pull at the side of the marble fireplace.

'Of course.' Deborah chose an armchair opposite the sofa, a Queen Anne coffee table between them.

They chatted about the weather, a new hat that Julia had bought, and then after the refreshments had arrived and tea had been poured she said, 'Deborah, as I plan to go to Paris quite soon for the latest fashions, I was wondering whether you would care to accompany me?'

Deborah stared at her in astonishment. Julia had made no secret of her disdain for her sister-in-law's spinsterhood, and in the nine months since her wedding had shown little inclination for friendship.

'Only Gerard thought,' Julia added, 'and naturally I agree with him, that it would be rather nice if we could become friends. After all, we do live in the same house.'

Deborah searched her sister-in-law's eyes for any sign of sarcasm, but Julia's gaze remained frank. 'It was his suggestion about Paris?'

'Yes.'

Deborah, careful to keep her features expressionless, was immediately suspicious. Even as a boy her brother had always been plotting something, often lying to get his own way.

'For how long, Julia?'

She shrugged. 'I'm not sure, but at least several days. Do say you'll come.'

Deborah thought swiftly. That was manageable, Elspeth could easily cover her absence. Although she was tempted to remain at Grosvenor Square instead to try and discover what her brother was up to, Gerard had never been one for generous gestures. But she did love Paris, was never averse to buying new clothes and the prospect was certainly tempting. Anyway, it would be churlish to refuse. She forced a warm smile. 'I'd be delighted to, Julia.' That wasn't completely true because the prospect of them being sole companions for several days wasn't exactly appealing. But even she could accept that a semblance of rapport between them would make life more agreeable. Julia rose and clapped her hands, a habit that Deborah always found childish. 'Excellent, I shall go and tell Gerard so that we can decide on a date and he can make the necessary arrangements.'

As the door closed behind her, Deborah felt somewhat perplexed. She still felt that she was being manipulated, although she had no idea why. She sighed. This trip could so easily turn into a disaster. It was not that she harboured resentment towards Gerard's wife, it was the natural order of things that one day another woman would become mistress of her childhood home, both here and in the country. She just wished that her brother could have chosen someone with an outlook nearer to her own. But would such a woman have wanted to marry a cold fish like Gerard with a prematurely receding hairline? Of course, one could never underestimate the appeal of a title.

Gerard was in his study. As Julia came in with her news, he rose from his desk to kiss her on the cheek. 'Well done, darling. But do you mind if we discuss it this evening as I have an urgent matter to attend to. Perhaps if you could let Fulton know that I don't wish to be disturbed. Although I shall take tea as usual.'

'But of course.'

After Julia had left, Gerard removed a cream vellum notepad from a drawer and thoughtfully unscrewed the top of his fountain pen. Ever since the letter had arrived from Annie Jones, his mind had wrestled with the problem of that dratted child. Even now he wasn't sure the name that had risen to the surface of his mind was the right one. But he had to make a decision and immediately. He also had to be prepared in case the man he approached refused to become involved. So he needed to list other likelihoods.

He put pen to paper and wrote his first choice, *Freddie Seymour*, followed after some hesitation by *Ivor Manfield* and *Charlie Andrews*. All young men who were known for their addiction to gambling. In Gerard's not inconsiderable experience, gamblers were always in need of extra funds, especially younger sons dependent upon their allowances. The question was whether one of them would be willing to undertake a task, which, while not illegal, did require both subterfuge and secrecy. And this time, Gerard was going to make sure that there was no possibility of future blackmail. He tapped the desk with his fingers. A private detective, that was what he needed. And one who could commence investigations into the three men immediately. There was a name lurking at the back of his mind and he frowned as he searched for it. Who was it who had used such a person? Then it came to him. That chap at the club whose wife had cuckolded him – the one who had bored him rigid over a couple of brandies. The name he'd mentioned had been so unusual that Gerard could actually recall it. Blaise Bonham, that was it, the alliteration had helped. He reached into a drawer and retrieving Kelly's Directory, paused as a parlourmaid brought in a tray with tea and shortbread biscuits. After pouring the tea she left the room and he couldn't help admiring her trim figure, feeling a twinge of regret that his days of dalliance would now have to be in the past. Not that he'd been in the habit of seducing the maids, for heaven's sake – not a whiff of scandal must ever sully his family's name. But whilst society might not look askance at a young man sowing his wild oats, it was a different matter altogether now that he was a married man, with every hope of soon siring a male heir.

Gerard bit into a shortbread and, refreshed by the Earl Grey tea, opened the directory and ran his forefinger down the entries beneath the heading Private Investigators. He soon found the name he was looking for and minutes later was picking up the telephone receiver and leaning back in the leather chair. His call was answered on the third ring. A good omen, because he needed a speedy response and swift action, and in order to obtain it he was prepared to be more than generous.

* * *

Gerard had arranged to meet Blaise Bonham at a public house in Fulham where he went into a warm, smoky fug of stale tobacco smoke and a hubbub of male conversation. The saloon bar was crowded but he managed to find a small table in one corner and taking a seat began to watch the door. He had arrived early for their appointment wishing to first appraise the private investigator. And within minutes a man entered, glancing around the room before his attention was caught by Gerard. Balding, wearing a checked jacket, with a yellow waistcoat over his protuberant stomach, he looked more like a bookmaker than a detective. But when he approached, Gerard noted that his brown eyes were both keen and intelligent.

'Mr Preston?'

Gerard rose and shook his hand. 'Indeed, and you must be Mr Bonham.'

'That I am.' He took an opposite seat.

Gerard smiled, and downed the last of his drink. 'First, let me get you a drink.'

'I wouldn't say no. I'm fond of a good malt.'

'Of course.' Gerard went to the bar aware that he too would be under scrutiny as Bonham would probably suspect that he had given a false name. His choice of apparel hadn't been easy, his usual wardrobe consisting of the finest bespoke tailoring. But he had taken a guess that a Londoner of Blaise's class would be less familiar with country clothes, and so Gerard was wearing a well-worn tweed suit he kept more for comfort than style. Let the man make of it what he would, the most important thing was that he didn't make the connection between Mr James Preston and the Earl of Anscombe.

Returning with a generous glass of whisky for each of them, Gerard wasted no time in furnishing Bonham with more details of his requirement.

'The fact is, old chap, that I find myself in a fearful predicament. It's urgent that I find a fellow in whom I can confide personal details in complete confidence. I shall need him to act on my behalf in rather a delicate financial matter, and as you know, there is always the possibility of blackmail in such cases.'

Bonham looked at him with speculation. 'You mentioned three gentlemen on the telephone. I take it that you want me to look into each of their characters.'

Gerard nodded. 'Background, the way they conduct their lives, whether they pay their debts, their reputation, that sort of thing.'

'And you said on the telephone that you need me to act urgently.' He frowned. 'It would need my putting aside cases I'm currently working on.'

'Might I enquire your terms?'

'I charge a registration fee of three pounds and then one pound per day plus expenses. I must warn you that as your case involves three investigations, the latter could prove to be substantial.'

Gerard frowned. 'You provide a breakdown of such?'

'Of course, and receipts when appropriate.'

'And you feel that this is a commission you would undertake?'

Bonham nodded, but his gaze was shrewd. 'There would be inconvenience, of course. I am not in the habit of delaying current investigations.'

'I will pay an extra pound on your initial fee and a bonus on completion to my satisfaction.'

There was a short pause. Gerard watched thoughtful expressions flit across Bonham's face.

'A bonus?'

'Shall we say a further pound?'

'Make it two and we'll shake hands on it.'

Gerard nodded, concealing his distaste as the man spat on his palm. Then he reached inside his jacket pocket and passed over a list written on thin plain paper. Prising the information from the porter at his club had taken an extremely generous tip; this unwelcome endeavour was already proving to be a costly business.

'These are the names and addresses of the three men.' Gerard removed several folded banknotes from his pocket – his wallet was monogrammed – and counted out the required amount. 'I rely on you to remember, Bonham, that speed is a vital factor in this matter.'

'You can leave it with me, Mr Preston.' He stood up and inserted the money into a leather purse. 'I don't have any means of contacting you, so might I suggest that you telephone me? Shall we say in a week's time? I would hope to have some news for you by then.'

Gerard nodded and watched Bonham leave, giving a genial smile to those he passed. A man who people would find it easy to talk to, yes, but it was to be hoped that he wore less conspicuous clothes when conducting his undercover business.

Chapter Four

It was almost a week later that the trip to Paris took place. Deborah sat behind the chauffeur and looked out of the window in silence, as beneath a slight drizzle the Daimler made its way to Victoria Station. There was no doubt that a general strike was looming and yet newspaper articles, at least the ones delivered to Grosvenor Square, expressed little sympathy with the strikers' cause. As for members of her own class, they were ostriches, the lot of them.

Once they reached Victoria, the chauffeur unloaded their luggage, and the two maids picked up their carpet bags and began to make their way into the railway station. Meanwhile the chauffeur gave the rest of their luggage to the waiting porter. 'Would you take care of the Countess and Her Ladyship?'

Deborah saw the perspiring man's face light up, no doubt at the chance of a decent tip. Julia gave not a backward glance as the chauffeur turned to leave, but Deborah, who had known Brown for many years, gave him a warm smile.

'Safe journey, my lady,' he said.

Julia was already sweeping through the crowded concourse, calling over her shoulder, 'I shall need to find something to read before we board.'

Deborah followed her into the noisy station to the WH Smith news stall and, while her sister-in-law browsed through magazines, picked up the *Daily Telegraph* and noticed an unfamiliar title, the *Workers' Weekly*. Maybe she would be able to learn more about the reasons why during the past months she'd become aware of a change in London's atmosphere. There was tension in the air, even well-dressed passers-by seemed subdued. On Sundays she couldn't help noticing small clusters of working-class men on their way to Speakers' Corner near Marble Arch, their pinched faces portraying their desperation. After a swift glance at her preoccupied companion, she bought both papers, folding the former over the latter. It was bound to arouse questions and she had no desire for Julia's disapproval to be related to Gerard. The train was already in the station and Deborah glanced to where their maids were waiting outside a first-class carriage.

'I won't be a moment,' she murmured to Julia and hurrying along the platform gave the offending newspaper to Ellen. 'Can you hide that for me?'

With a startled glance, she bent to put it inside her carpet bag.

Deborah returned to the stall to see Julia turning away with her purchases and frowning. 'What were you doing?'

'I bought Ellen a newspaper.'

'Then I only hope she can read. Wasn't she once a scullery maid?'

Deborah tightened her lips. 'That was a long time ago.'

'Well, come along, Deborah, we had better board.'

As they arrived at the carriage the porter stood outside to assist them, their expensive luggage already stowed. On seeing their mistresses safely settled, the two maids hurried away to their own third-class carriage. With Julia showing no inclination, Deborah handed the man a generous tip. Momentarily his gaze met her own with gratitude. 'Thanks very much, me lady.'

'I never tip,' Julia said languidly, as she made herself comfortable in the otherwise empty carriage. 'After all, these people are only doing the job they're paid to do.'

'But are they paid enough?' Deborah settled herself into the seat opposite.

Julia stared at her. 'Goodness, Deborah, I hope you're not going to talk boring politics all the way.'

Deborah suppressed a sigh of exasperation, thankful that they were soon on their way and, being familiar with the line down to Dover, she took little interest in the passing scenery, instead immersing herself in her newspaper. Mercifully, she was rarely interrupted by Julia, except when she leant over, wishing to display an illustration of a rather daring evening dress, glamorous fur tippet, or what she described as 'a darling hat'. And Deborah could understand the attraction of such light-hearted pleasures, but she couldn't help being in a more serious mood, having begun to read the latest reports about the threat of a general strike. One could almost taste the atmosphere of unrest in the capital.

She would often take a cab to the agency, but on the days when Brown drove her to Bloomsbury, he would take her to respectable addresses within a mile or less, and from those she would walk, the fresh air clearing her mind to embrace her secret identity. She recalled the strained expressions, lowered eyes and hunched shoulders of many she passed. There was an underlying current of worry everywhere, even growing anger. Deborah could remember the Great Unrest in 1912, with talk of ugly scenes, even violence, and her father saying that Britain had come close to a revolution. He'd also expressed sympathy with the plight of the coal miners, while her tutor, Mr Channing, had read articles from the leading newspapers to her, stressing that she should become aware of what an unfair and unjust society she lived in. 'Never forget that you are privileged, and when you are older, open a window into your soul for the plight of those who have not been so fortunate.'

Young though she had been, his words had never left her.

By early evening they were settled into the luxurious Hotel Regina Paris, opposite the Tuileries Garden, where befitting their rank Deborah and Julia were allocated spacious rooms on the first floor, while the two maids shared a cramped bedroom in the attics. At least, Ellen told Deborah, there was a proper bathroom along the corridor. She also confided that Colette, Julia's new French maid, found her mistress excessively demanding.

'You see, Ellen, how lucky you are to only have me to look after? I remember my mama often brought maids to tears.'

'I was scared stiff of your mother, begging your pardon, my lady. Not that she even knew I existed.'

Deborah smiled. 'Oh yes she did, Ellen. It was she who agreed that you should be trained to be my personal maid.'

Ellen's expression was one of such gratification that Deborah couldn't help laughing. She was feeling in a good mood, the crossing had been calm, their rail journey uneventful and the hotel had provided a late supper.

'Oh, Ellen?' she said as, after unpacking for her, the maid prepared to leave. 'Don't forget to let me have that newspaper I gave to you at Victoria.'

'Of course, my lady. I'll fetch it now.'

The following morning, after a breakfast of pain au chocolat, warm croissants, butter and apricot jam, Deborah sipped at her coffee with appreciation. Why was it that only the French could make coffee like this? Later, as despite it being March the weather wasn't unduly cold, they decided to take a stroll along the Rue de la Paix, where in the familiar odours, sounds and atmosphere of Paris, Deborah began to relax.

Julia too was in good spirits, even excited. 'I do so love choosing new clothes, don't you?'

Deborah smiled, the younger woman's enthusiasm was infectious. 'I have to admit that I do.'

They browsed a little at prestigious shop windows but were soon entering the richly carpeted salon of a famous fashion house, with glittering chandeliers and offers of champagne. As a procession of beautiful girls modelled elegant designs, Deborah leant forward as one particular dress caught her interest. Designed for evening wear, a vibrant emerald green, its crystal-encrusted silk shimmered with every move of the mannequin. Was the long neckline too revealing, the skirt too short? Deborah didn't care, she just knew that she had to have it. She caught the eye of the costumier and gave a smiling nod.

Julia gasped and protested. 'But I love it too, Deborah. You couldn't be so mean.'

Deborah resigned herself for capitulation. But the chic and astute Frenchwoman clicked her fingers and whispered to an assistant. Minutes later, a model with Julia's fair colouring began to walk towards them. Wearing a backless chemise dress, in a heavenly shade of azure, its bodice extravagantly beaded, the pleated skirt floated with every step.

'Your Ladyship, may I suggest that this new creation might be a better choice for you?'

Julia's face glowed and she clapped her hands while Deborah breathed a sigh of relief. And as this was only their first full day in Paris, she felt a small sense of satisfaction that Gerard was going to find his suggested trip an expensive one. And she was truly enjoying herself, revelling in a light-hearted sense of freedom.

The remainder of their stay involved several similar scenes, and Deborah began to feel a grudging admiration for the way that her sister-in-law dismissed a collection that wasn't to her taste with a gracious acknowledgement, simply sweeping out of a salon. And her attention to detail as they shopped was astonishing. Only a certain accessory, a particular pair of gloves, the perfect length of a feather boa would meet with her approval. Deborah herself was delighted with a shop selling a wide selection of exquisite belts, and a fragile companionship began to build between them.

'We must pay a visit to the Louvre while we're here,' Deborah said one morning.

Julia pulled a face. 'Must we? I find art galleries rather boring.'

'Maybe you had the wrong companion. Or you were shown the wrong paintings. Don't tell me that the *Mona Lisa* with her enigmatic smile doesn't intrigue you.'

'Maybe the first time I saw it, but I'm not into culture in the way that you are, Deborah.'

'Then how about a visit to the Folies Bergère?' Deborah burst out laughing at Julia's scandalised expression.

'Julia, I was joking! But seriously, Paris has so much to offer.'

'I know – clothes, clothes, and more clothes.'

'Now you are joking.'

'Perhaps a little,' she said, then added gaily, 'I suppose you're right, Deborah. I shall accompany you to whichever art gallery you choose, but in return you must agree to visit that wonderful hat shop we passed yesterday.'

'It will be a pleasure.' Deborah had to admit that the trip had not been a disaster after all, and although there had been a few difficult times, that must have been true also for Julia.

But her favourite time was in the evenings, when weather permitting, they would take a stroll by the Seine, their maids following closely behind in case ruffians were lurking under the bridges. Warmly clad in a wrap-over tweed coat and Hermes silk scarf, Deborah would walk beside Julia, cosy in her furs, finding that her sister-in-law was far too entranced by passers-by and their clothes to want to talk much, leaving Deborah to become immersed in her own thoughts.

Paris really was the 'city of love', she thought on their last evening. They strolled beneath the bridges watching the barges passing beneath them, with the Eiffel Tower and Notre Dame Cathedral outlined against the night sky. With the lights along the river the scene was a perfect one for romance, and her heart would feel a pang on seeing young couples, hand in hand, sometimes stopping to become entwined. Beneath a lamp she saw one young woman lift her face for her lover's kiss, her expression of such happiness that Deborah felt an unutterable sadness. She too had felt that joy. Could a woman ever find a love like that again? The familiar murmur crept into her mind: '*You look so seductive with your hair loose, so beautiful.*' That couldn't happen now, my darling, she thought, not in 1926. I look so different with my hair short and cut in the new fashionable bob, I'm not sure you'd like it. How could fate be so bitterly cruel, dashing all of her hopes, changing her future, while together with hundreds of thousands of other men, her young beau had lost his life. The poignancy of being here, in France, in the very country where he had been killed, thinking of him, still loving him, made her eyes shimmer with tears. She blinked them away and took a ragged breath. Damn that blasted war.

It was then that Julia, having paused to exchange a few words with a fashionable woman walking a French bulldog, caught up with her and said, 'You look awfully fierce.'

Deborah managed to smile. 'I'm just tired, that's all. I think it's time we returned to the hotel, don't you agree?'

And I wonder, she thought later, just what that brother of mine has been up to while we have been away. Whatever it was, it was something shady, she had no doubt of it.

Chapter Five

The day after Julia and Deborah departed for Paris, Gerard, notebook and fountain pen to hand, made the long-awaited call to Blaise Bonham. Tension was rising within him and it was a relief when the telephone was swiftly answered.

'Ah, Mr Preston, I have news for you.'

'Satisfactory, I hope.'

'I have every confidence, sir. Might I suggest that we meet so that I can give you my written report? Would this evening at the same venue be convenient? Shall we say eight o'clock?'

'I shall see you then.'

Gerard replaced the receiver. It had been tempting to continue the conversation and to make notes, but it would be far better to wait for a written report. He unlocked a drawer and taking out the cheap envelope, looked again at the misspelt letter. Annie Jones would have received his brief reply by return of post.

The matter will be swiftly attended to. Change nothing until then. You will be paid for your trouble.

Terse, yes, but deliberately so because he was determined to sever all contact with both the woman and the area in which she lived.

At ten minutes to eight, Gerard went through the swing doors into the stuffy atmosphere of the public house, relieved to see that the same small table in a dim corner was unoccupied. He went to claim it rather than first buying a drink, and it wasn't long before Bonham came to join him. Gone were his flamboyant clothes, this time he was wearing a grey double-breasted suit. 'Good evening, Mr Preston.'

Gerard nodded. 'Whisky?'

'That would be most kind.'

Gerard went to the crowded bar. He loathed having to queue among the cluster of working-class men waiting to be served, his nostrils offended by the sourness of stale clothes and perspiration. Worse still, the burly man in front of him had a carbuncle on the back of his neck. Gerard's sensibilities were so offended that when his turn came to order, he almost forgot to disguise his clipped upper-class vowels.

Carrying the glasses back to the table, he sipped his malt whisky. 'You have your report?'

Bonham put a sealed white envelope on the table.

Gerard narrowed his eyes. 'But you have ascertained that I would be able to trust at least one of these men?'

'In my professional opinion, yes, but of course nothing is guaranteed in this life.'

Gerard looked down at the envelope. There was a strong temptation to read its contents, but secrecy was vital and he wouldn't take the risk of reading it in a public place. Better to accept that Bonham had conducted his enquiries in a satisfactory manner, and to pay the man.

'And your account?'

Bonham retrieved a brown envelope from his pocket. 'My expenses were, as I warned you, sir, substantial. You will understand that I had to carry out my investigations not only in London, but elsewhere.'

This envelope Gerard did open. Minutes passed while he scanned the sheet of paper and the receipts attached. Then he gave a decisive nod. 'That all seems satisfactory, Mr Bonham.' He took an envelope from inside his coat and put it on the table. 'This is what we agreed.' Then he took notes from his breast pocket and, shielding his actions by counting out several beneath the table, folded them and passed them over. 'That will cover your expenses.'

The private investigator, his shoulders hunched, opened the envelope, glanced at its contents and inserted it into his jacket pocket. With a swift glance over his shoulder, he put the loose money into his wallet before handing Gerard a business card. 'Nice dark corner here, can't be too careful flashing cash about.' He raised his glass. 'To the success of your venture.'

'Thanks.' Gerard drained his glass, rose and began to thread his way through the crowded bar and out into the welcome fresh air. How people could bear to spend hours in such noise and close proximity to unwashed bodies, was beyond his understanding. He could only thank the Lord for his own quiet and civilised club, where a fellow could have a drink, good food, and intelligent conversation. Gerard had to walk a little way before hailing a cab and climbing in he called, 'Grosvenor Square'.

The man who had silently followed him melted back into the shadows, having discovered the information he wanted. Not for a second had Blaise Bonham believed that his client had given his true name. And now that he knew where to look, it wouldn't be impossible to discover Mr Preston's true identity. Not that he had any devious plan in mind, but in his line of business, such details could be extremely useful.

It was not until the following morning that, after breakfasting on kidneys, bacon and scrambled eggs, Gerard strode across the hall to his study, giving orders not to be disturbed. Last night he had scanned Bonham's report, but was keen to give it more detailed attention. Seating himself behind his desk, he removed a small key from his wallet and unlocking the top left-hand drawer withdrew the brown envelope. There was one single sheet of foolscap paper, and three headings. After reading it through again, he underlined the salient points.

Freddie Seymour, aged twenty-four.
Third son of a wealthy family, of good appearance and
well mannered. Doesn't cheat or renege on his debts,
although rumour has it that his father is refusing to pay
his latest gambling bill. Doesn't drink to excess so not
likely to have a loose tongue. It would seem that his
sexuality is suspect in some quarters, although with no
real evidence. If this doesn't make him abhorrent to you,
it could indicate that he is capable of discretion.

Ivor Manfield, aged twenty-three.
Only son of a good, if impoverished family. Has been
accused of cheating at cards, and doesn't pay his tailor. A
boastful young man and I doubt that he would be reliable.

Charlie Andrews, aged twenty-seven.
A womaniser, with a liking for parlourmaids, on whom
he has sired more than one bastard. He is currently
engaged to a young woman with prospects, but has a
mistress on the side. I would question putting your faith
in this young man.

Gerard raised his head with a warm glow of satisfaction.
Bonham had done an excellent job. It had been Freddie
Seymour who had been his preferred choice, although Gerard
had never been privy to rumours about his secret lifestyle.
Bonham's revelation would provide the perfect antidote to
any future threat of blackmail.

That same evening Gerard went to his club in St James's Street. His nerves were on edge as first he dined, then prowled the various rooms, both on the ground floor and upstairs, seeking the young man he needed. Anxious to begin negotiations he was becoming more and more frustrated, until at last Freddie Seymour appeared in the doorway of the drawing room. Tall, fair-haired and with striking good looks, he was obviously searching for someone without success and it was with a morose expression that he slumped into the nearest leather armchair.

Gerard rose and walked over. 'Mind if I join you, Seymour?'

He glanced up with an expression of surprise. 'Not at all.'

'Let me get you a drink.' Gerard raised a hand, and as a white-jacketed attendant came over, ordered Freddie his choice of brandy. 'How are you, Seymour? I think we've only spoken in passing so far.'

Freddie nodded. 'That's true, I know who you are, of course, but our paths haven't actually crossed.'

Gerard laughed. 'I've seen you in the gaming rooms, but I haven't been frequenting them lately. At least, not so often since I became a married man.'

'Maybe I should have followed your example, sir.'

'Married?'

'Lord, no. Not gambled that much. The occupation of gentlemen, they say, but it can be damned expensive.'

Gerard smiled. 'I think we have all discovered that.'

Their conversation paused as the attendant brought Freddie's glass, and he took an immediate sip.

'Were you expecting to meet someone? I saw you glance around.'

'I had hoped to,' Freddie admitted. 'But to no avail.'

'In that case, I wonder if you would be agreeable to taking a nightcap with me at my house in Grosvenor Square. To be honest, Seymour, there is something I would like to discuss with you, and here at the club isn't appropriate.'

Freddie looked puzzled. 'Of course. I'd be honoured to.'

Gerard smiled. 'I can assure you that all will become clear. And I would also add that our discussion might be to your advantage.'

Freddie took a more generous sip of his brandy. 'You intrigue me even further.'

'Then I await your convenience.' He waited until the other man finished his drink.

Once at Grosvenor Square, and after Gerard had dismissed the chauffeur, the butler came forward to take their hats and capes. 'I shall only be using my study, Fulton. You and the rest of the staff can retire for the night. I myself will secure the front door after this gentleman leaves. Tell my valet not to wait up for me.'

Gerard, now confident that there would be no possibility of their conversation being overheard, indicated a leather chair by the cheerful fire, and went to the sideboard. 'Let's have that nightcap. Whisky? Or would you prefer brandy?'

'I think I'll stick to brandy, thanks.'

Gerard took his own seat opposite. 'You must be wondering what is behind all this.'

'I confess that I am.'

'I may confide in you, in complete confidence?'

'But of course.'

'The problem is, Seymour, that a delicate situation has unexpectedly arisen. In order to resolve it, I shall need the assistance of someone whose reputation is beyond doubt. I feel that man could be yourself. But let me explain.'

Against the comforting warmth of the fire, Gerard outlined his plan, while all the time tension was rising within him. It was vital that this matter was settled because who knew what sort of woman this Annie Jones was. Suppose she had a suspicious husband who resented an extra mouth to feed? Not only that, but made it his business to make unwelcome enquiries? The possibility of discovery was becoming more of a threat every day.

After Gerard finished speaking, Freddie frowned. 'Do I understand correctly that you want no contact with the child, not even in the future?'

'That is true. Neither do I think it necessary for you to have any personal contact. I wish all arrangements to be conducted on an impersonal level – from a distance, as it were. It would be your responsibility to find a woman willing to take the child in. However, it would be wise to avoid these particular counties.' Gerard gave him a list of ones that both Deborah and himself were likely to visit.

He offered Freddie a cigar, before taking one himself. 'If you were to agree, you would not find me ungenerous. I could begin by arranging an immediate bank draft to settle any outstanding gambling debts.' Gerard saw a sudden flicker of interest in Freddie's eyes. 'And an annual commission for handling an arrangement I foresee applying for several years.'

Freddie leant forward. 'As I understand it, all I would need to do, once the child was moved and settled, is to open a separate bank account into which your bank would pay a monthly amount. Then anonymously to arrange for that amount to be forwarded on?'

'That is correct. And I would need you to act instantly.'

A silence fell between them and Gerard forced himself to remain patient. So much depended upon the next few minutes.

Freddie was now frowning. 'Who was taking care of the problem before?'

'Let's just say that there was a personal arrangement, which because of bereavement can no longer continue.'

Gerard clipped his cigar as Freddie lapsed into thought and agonising seconds ticked by.

Then Freddie's gaze met his. 'I'll do it.'

Relief flooding through him, Gerard said, 'Excellent.' He steepled his fingers. 'First of all, you will need the address of a woman called Annie Jones, and I can't emphasise enough the need for speed in removing the child from her care. As soon as possible, let me have the name of your bank and the number of the new account, and I will transfer money for any initial expenses.'

Freddie nodded. 'I won't let you down, sir.'

And, Gerard thought, whatever the amount of his gambling debts, it will be worth every penny if it removes the risk of future blackmail. I'm sure this young man wouldn't want his proclivities to become known to his family, or indeed to become public. It was all very satisfactory, very satisfactory indeed.

Chapter Six

With Julia's maid Colette having flounced out to remain in Paris with her family, it meant that on their return journey, Ellen was forced to travel alone. And when travelling from Dover to London, Deborah decided to go further down the train and check on her. But after finding the right third-class carriage, she was amused to see the fresh-faced girl deep in conversation with a young man. I needn't have worried at all, Deborah thought with a wry smile. She's enjoying her journey a great deal more than I am.

It was soon after she began the return to her own seat that she saw a tall man reading through pages of notes. He turned to go into a compartment, and tried to close the door properly, but it must have stuck because through the gap she could hear raised voices. About to walk past, curious she glanced inside to see three men smoking cigarettes and involved in hot debate.

'Evan, it was a good speech in Dover, but if a man can't feed his family, what else can he do? I'm not afeared of hard work, I've worked all me life, but it should be for a fair day's wage. But do the owners care? Not them, they sit on their fat backsides, take the profits and look down on the rest of us.'

Deborah paused and moving a few yards away stood as though gazing out of the corridor window. She wanted to hear more.

'Aye,' another man answered. 'And where would this country be without our labour, that's what I want to know? Mind you, it's the toffs that get my craw. They've never even had dirt under their fingernails, the pampered bastards. And they have the gall to call me "my man".' He spat the words out.

Despite the noise of the train, she could hear another voice, this time one of reasoned argument. 'Look, lads, I know how you feel, it's how we all feel, but for this strike to be successful we've got to direct our anger. We know we're in the right, but we're up against the establishment who have always had things their own way. And it won't be any different this time unless we're properly organised.' That was probably the man with the notes, Deborah thought. And could she detect a hint of a lilt? Welsh?

The first man again. 'But we've got no power. That bloody lot at the top have made sure of that over centuries. Deprived of education, deprived of a decent standard of living, while their women wear fancy furs costing more than would feed a family for months. I tell you, it's not a strike that's needed in this country, it's a bloody revolution.'

'That's dangerous talk, and you know it.' It was the previous speaker again. 'We have a fully justified case, which is what I wanted to get over at Dover. I've just read through my speech again, and I've a few extra points I want to make on Tuesday night in Battersea. The town hall holds a fair number of people. The only trouble is that I'll be preaching to the converted, when what's needed is for right-thinking politicians to come and hear our views.'

'Aye, and pigs might fly. But we'll be there to hear you, Evan, eight o'clock sharp.'

Deborah walked slowly on, deep in thought. It hadn't been until their second evening in Paris that she'd begun to read the the *Workers' Weekly*, her swift glance at the news-stand missing the fact that it was the official newspaper of the Communist Party of Great Britain. She could just imagine Gerard's outraged reaction to her having anything to do with such radical journalism. But the knowledge didn't prevent her finding much to read that was both shocking and deeply disturbing, the articles describing the depths of poverty and hardship suffered by men and their families, even if the breadwinner was in full-time employment. As for the coal miners, she couldn't imagine what it must be like to work underground in such appalling conditions, with the daily risk of being maimed or killed. It was a disgrace that there was such a sharp division between her own land-owning class, and the rest of the hard-working population.

'You've been away for ages,' Julia said crossly, when Deborah rejoined her.

'I told you, I wanted to check on Ellen.'

'Honestly, you do fuss over that girl.'

'She is a young woman travelling alone. Naturally, I feel some responsibility towards her.' Deborah hesitated. 'Julia, what are your feelings about the possibility of a general strike? It's beginning to seem unavoidable.'

'Oh, I don't bother my head about such things. After all, I don't suppose it will affect us very much.' She laughed. 'In fact, Charlotte Ellsworth tells me that her eldest son and several of his friends think it's going to be rather a lark. They're already talking of driving the omnibuses and trams.'

'I doubt it will be a lark for the workers,' Deborah said sharply. 'Don't you realise, Julia, that there are children starving out there?'

Julia did have the grace to look a little ashamed, but simply flicked over another page of her magazine. 'Mama used to say that the poor are always with us, always have been, always will be. It's just a fact of life.'

And told you, no doubt, Deborah thought, not to trouble your pretty little head about it. She looked out of the window, trying to control her rising temper. She really must learn to accept Julia for what she was. A perfectly normal young woman, one who could be amusing and pleasant if life was to her taste, but petulant if not. And that was by no means unusual in someone who had been spoilt all of her life. But Julia had made a determined effort to be agreeable during the past week, and Deborah respected her for that.

And once back at Grosvenor Square, Deborah knew that it would be even more futile trying to discuss the working men's grievances with Gerard, who would be scathing of her sympathetic views. And thinking of her brother, she began to wonder what they would find on their arrival in London. Had he really been plotting something? Or was she being a cynic?

They drew into Victoria Station, and as they left the train and followed behind a porter through the crowded concourse, Deborah looked over her shoulder for Ellen, only to see her walking beside the young man she'd been talking to on the train. Seconds later, a little breathless, she caught them up.

'Do come along,' Julia complained. 'I can see the chauffeur waiting.'

Amid the bustle of their arrival, with Fulton directing footmen to take their luggage upstairs, Julia asked, 'Is His Lordship at home?'

'I most certainly am.' Gerard emerged from his study and coming to greet her, kissed her cheek. 'Welcome back, darling.'

She smiled up at him. 'I have lots to show you. We enjoyed our trip, didn't we, Deborah?'

'Yes, we did and thank you, Gerard.' She looked at him

and smiled. 'I'm sure that you and Julia have a lot to talk about so I shall retire now. I wish you both goodnight.'

He gave her a swift nod. 'Fulton, refreshment for Lady Deborah in her rooms, and for Her Ladyship in the drawing room. I'll have whisky.'

Deborah watched the couple walk along the hall, Gerard's arm lingering around his wife's waist. Julia did seem to bring out the best in him. Deborah had never witnessed him display anything but the utmost courtesy towards her. Even affection. Could it be that he genuinely loved her? If so, then she could only hope that his cold feelings might soften, even warm towards herself. Feeling suddenly weary after the journey, she began to climb the broad staircase, looking forward to her scented bath.

On Deborah's return to the agency the following morning, Elspeth was longing to hear all about Paris, especially details of the latest fashions, then afterwards she brought Deborah up to date with business details.

It was soon after Elspeth returned to the outer office that Deborah heard a male voice almost shout, 'No offence, missus, but I want to talk to the organ-grinder, not the monkey.'

Deborah swiftly rose and went to the door. 'Is there a problem?'

The man looked to be about forty, thick-necked and broad-shouldered, with thinning mousy hair and a pockmarked drawn face. Her usual male clients, most of them looking for a domestic or clerical position, were always neatly and conventionally dressed in a suit and tie.

This man looked as if he worked on the docks.

'Me name's Dennis Pearson. I'd like a word, in private, like.' He jerked his head towards her office.

Deborah didn't move. 'I think you've come to the wrong agency.'

'It says on the sign outside *Staff Agency*.' His tone was one of truculence, and Deborah noted his weather-beaten features. Hardly the appearance of someone who worked indoors. 'I can't think of a single post on our books that would be right for you. I'm afraid we don't handle outdoor work.'

His eyes narrowed. 'What makes you think I want outdoor work?'

'Because, Mr Pearson, part of my job is to sum up people. And someone as strong and independent as you would appear, would be unlikely to be looking for a position as a footman.' She held his gaze.

'Sorry if I was rude,' he muttered, 'but I'm desperate, yer see. There's no jobs anywhere and I'm sick of being fobbed off by people.'

Deborah softened. 'We could let you have the names and addresses of agencies where you might have more success, if that's of any help.'

He nodded.

Elspeth got up from her desk and handed him a list of names. Deborah saw his hand shake slightly as he took it from her. 'Thank you, miss.'

They both watched him go, and then Elspeth said, 'I feel quite sorry for him.'

'So do I. How do these people cope, with no money coming in? I'd guess he's been going without food.'

Elspeth nodded. 'I remember when there were bad times in the parish, people used to do that, or at least exist on bread and water. Their main fear was of being evicted if the rent wasn't paid. It's an unjust world, isn't it?'

Later, sitting at her office desk and drinking a welcome cup of tea, Deborah sat in thought for a while, remembering the men and their discussion on the train. They had mentioned a date next week and opening her personal diary she made a note of it. Was there any good reason why she shouldn't go to the town hall in Battersea and hear this Evan speak? It shouldn't be impossible, surely?

Chapter Seven

Friday night found Deborah accompanying Gerard and Julia to a cocktail party at the Savoy, where in an elegant room buzzing with conversation and laughter, she took a canapé from an offered tray, and began to move around the room.

'Lady Deborah?' She turned to see a tall man smiling. 'Theodore Field, we met recently when I came to dine at Grosvenor Square.'

'Yes, of course,' she smiled. 'You're a Tory MP.'

'Guilty as charged. But then, I seem to recall that you take an interest in politics.'

'I'm afraid it's the fault of an excellent tutor I had. Not that it makes me into a bluestocking.'

He laughed. 'Heaven forbid.'

'But I do hope that you were in favour of our being granted the vote?'

'I most definitely was, and I think the restrictions need to be reviewed. It is ridiculous that someone such as yourself cannot vote until you reach the age of 30.'

Hadn't she previously thought him a pompous prig? Deborah swiftly revised her opinion. 'Agreed'. She sipped her drink.

He raised an eyebrow in query.

'A Gin Rickey, and yours?'

'I'm a simple sort, merely a champagne cocktail.'

She hesitated. 'Do you ever think that there are thousands of people in the country who will never be able to enjoy this sort of life?' She waved a hand at the crowded room.

He glanced around. 'That's true, but I doubt that many here will have your social conscience, Lady Deborah.'

'And yourself?'

He smiled. 'Shall we say that it would be an interesting subject to discuss?'

'Field. It's good to see you here.' To her dismay, Gerard had joined them. 'I wouldn't mind having a word, old chap.'

She was furious. This was just typical of her brother, to interrupt a private conversation, to dismiss her presence as of no consequence. Her eyes met Theodore's for one brief moment, then with reluctance she moved away to mingle.

The room was crowded, there were many acquaintances to greet, and it wasn't until later that she saw him threading his way through the throng towards her. Seeing that he was trying to catch her attention, Deborah excused herself from her companions.

'I'm afraid I must leave,' he murmured. 'I regret that we didn't have a chance to finish our conversation. Would you care to continue it over dinner one evening?'

She had no hesitation. 'I'd be delighted to.'

'Would tomorrow evening be too soon?'

'Not at all,' she said. 'I happen to be free.'

'Then I shall call for you at about eight.'

Deborah watched him leave. He was a confident devil, she thought, but that only added to his magnetism. It was strange that the undoubtedly handsome MP had hardly registered with her that first evening, then she remembered that he'd annoyed her with a facile remark and she'd moved to talk to others before leaving for another engagement. She smiled to herself, enjoying what was, for her, a rare physical attraction. Or was that because of the number of cocktails she'd enjoyed?

Deborah had been longing to wear the emerald green silk dress she'd chosen in Paris, and dining with Theodore Field would seem to be the ideal occasion. But shortly before he was due to arrive, the main topic of conversation in her bedroom was of the young man Ellen had met on the train.

'You blush every time I mention him,' Deborah teased.

Ellen's colour rose even higher. 'I do like him.'

'And?'

'He's written me a note asking if I'd like to go to a music hall.'

'And would you?'

'Yes, but it's on Tuesday and it's not my half-day.'

'Well, I think you deserve an extra one. After all, once Colette left, you had extra duties with having to look after Julia as well.' Deborah felt laughter rising in her, as she saw Ellen give a slight grimace.

'She *is* hard work, Lady Deborah.' But her face lit up. 'Are you sure you won't need me?'

'I'm certain I won't.' And she wasn't being completely unselfish. It meant that alone in her room she would have complete freedom to dress down for her planned visit to Battersea.

Deborah gave a last glance in her mirror, liking the way the silk material outlined her slim yet curvy body. She had never had the ideal 'flapper' boyish figure, but although she didn't 'bandage' her firm breasts as fashion dictated, a softly boned corset worked miracles elsewhere.

'You look beautiful, Lady Deborah. But I do miss your hair being long. I used to love dressing it in different styles.'

'I have a tinge of regret myself. But we have to move with the times, don't we?'

Smiling, she left and going down the staircase and across the hall, Deborah joined Gerard and Julia in the drawing room. Her brother glanced up and raised his eyebrows.

'The dress looks lovely on you,' Julia said.

'Thank you. I'm dining with Mr Field.'

Gerard gave her a sharp glance. 'The devil you are.'

It was at that moment that the butler announced, 'Mr Theodore Field,' and as he came in, Deborah's gaze flew to him and her pulse began to race. Thank goodness it hadn't been too many cocktails.

Gerard moved forward. 'Good evening, Field, this is an unexpected pleasure.'

He nodded, turning to greet first Julia and then Deborah, to whom he gave a warm smile.

'May I get you an aperitif, sir?' Fulton hovered.

He asked for a dry sherry, and said, 'Lady Deborah and I discovered a shared passion for politics.'

Gerard snorted. 'Then good luck to you, old man. My sister has rather unconventional views.'

Fortunately they moved on to less contentious subjects and soon finishing his drink, Theodore said, 'I've booked a table at the Café Royal, so perhaps . . . ?'

And within a few minutes, a sable wrap around her shoulders, they were seated in the front of the Bentley parked outside. Theodore smiled at her. 'No chauffeur, I'm afraid, so I hope you'll feel safe with me.'

I feel anything but, she thought, but not with regard to you driving. Intensely conscious of his close proximity, with a sideways glance she felt pleased that he was clean-shaven. She had always felt that moustaches and beards aged a man. Deborah felt an excitement rising within her, looking forward to the evening in a way that was becoming rare. Her position in society meant that invitations to dine, to attend parties, or soirées were so frequent that she often attended out of social duty rather than any expectation of enjoyment. She had always preferred a one-to-one conversation over lunch or dinner but such invitations, plentiful during the years following the end of the war and when she was younger, came less often now.

'Penny for them?' Theodore murmured as he expertly overtook another motor car. She smiled, noticing how close-fitting his grey gloves were. A strong hand, she thought, she liked that in a man. 'I was thinking how glad I am that we're going to the Café Royal.'

'I read that it's described as the epicentre of fashionable London.' He began to laugh. 'But I think the Nash terrace with its colonnades has much to do with it.'

They drove along Regent Street and when the car drew to a halt, a commissionaire came to open the passenger door and to take the car keys.

Theodore turned to her. 'Would you like another aperitif before we go to the restaurant?'

Did she really want to sit in a crowded bar? She'd much rather learn more about this intriguing man. Deborah shook her head. 'If you agree, I'd prefer to go straight in.'

And despite the short notice, they were shown to a prime table and the next few minutes were spent discussing the menu and ordering. Then they both relaxed and smiled at each other across the table.

'Tell me, Lady Deborah . . .'

'Just Deborah, please.'

'And my friends call me Theo. I was going to ask about

that tutor of yours, the one you say encouraged you to have an interest in politics. He must have been quite an unusual man.'

'I owe him so much. I don't think my father ever realised what a gem he had found.' She smiled. 'Nor did he ever discover it, not really. I was very circumspect in what I revealed about many of our discussions. My greatest fear in those young years was that Mr Channing would be replaced by a narrow-minded governess, who would think me capable only of needlework and watercolours.'

When he laughed in disbelief, she said, 'Such outdated views about women still exist.'

'I suppose you're right. I remember that a maiden aunt was so horrified at emancipation that her hair turned grey.'

Keen as she was to discuss politics, Deborah was even more interested in Theo himself. 'Would you believe that apart from knowing you're an MP, I know absolutely nothing about you?'

He smiled. 'Tell me what you'd like to know. I'm not married, but I expect you already know that. Neither am I a libertine.'

She began to laugh. 'Libertine! Now that is an old-fashioned word.'

'I suppose it is, but you know what I mean.' Theo told her that after Eton and coming down from Oxford, he worked in the City until war was declared. 'Along with many of my contemporaries, naturally I enlisted at once.' There came a shadow over his eyes. 'None of us had any idea, or could ever have imagined the horror, the carnage that lay ahead. I was lucky, wounded only once and then not seriously. I pray to God that there's never another one. It changed our country forever. I still carry a sense of guilt that I lived through it, when so many failed to return.'

Deborah waited as he paused. 'Afterwards, I decided to enter politics. I could see there was much that needed to be done, and so I became an MP. And you, Deborah? I do know that sadly you lost your fiancé in the war.'

She nodded. 'And within a few weeks, my parents to Spanish flu. I can't deny that was a very dark time for me.'

He stretched over to cover her hand with his own. 'It must have been awful for you, I'm so sorry.'

'I know that I only went through the same as thousands of others. But such losses can affect your whole life. That is if you let them.' She looked down at their hands, liking the feel of his skin against hers, until he removed his own as the waiter arrived with their first course.

'So,' Theo said, 'you made a comment at the cocktail party that implied that you are interested in the conditions of the working man. I must suppose that will include the forthcoming threat of a general strike? Or is it that you wish to know the government's plans?' He began to laugh. 'Perhaps you are a sort of peacetime Mata Hari.'

Deborah had to struggle with her own laughter. 'I hardly think so.'

'Neither do I. But is there something, other than what you have read in the press, that has sparked your interest?'

Deborah described the scene she had overheard on the

train returning from Dover. 'I want to understand why there is such desperation. In fact,' she paused, 'I've decided to go to Battersea next Tuesday to hear this man Evan speak.'

He stared at her. 'You can't possibly be serious.'

'Why not?'

'Because these meetings can sometimes get out of hand, even violent if tempers flare. And if I recall, that hall will hold hundreds. Heavens, Deborah, as a woman you will not only be conspicuous, but you are a member of the aristocracy. And there is a lot of anger out there.'

'And how are they to know that, the latter I mean?'

He shrugged. 'With your looks and manner, not to mention clothes, you couldn't be anything else.'

She took a sip of her Chablis. But there is something you don't know about me, Deborah thought. Wasn't she 'something else' whenever she went to the agency?

'I'm sure I can deal with that.' She met his concerned gaze. 'I have made my mind up, Theo.'

A full minute passed in silence. Then in a tone that brooked no argument he said, 'In that case, I had better come with you.'

Chapter Eight

On Tuesday, Deborah's mind was so full of feverish excitement that at the agency she was finding it difficult to concentrate. And although she was keen to hear the talk at Battersea, uppermost in her thoughts was the prospect of seeing Theo again. Even now she could remember the touch of his hand, brief though it was, and during the rest of that evening he'd been most attentive. Yet when he had driven her back to Grosvenor Square, he had not even offered a chaste kiss on her cheek. But the connection between them was so tangible that Deborah was certain he found her attractive. She had seen it in his expression in those distinctive grey eyes . . .

'Miss Claremont?' The door opened and Elspeth's voice broke into her thoughts, her formality revealing that there was a client in the outer office. 'Are you available to interview?'

'Yes, of course.'

Elspeth ushered in a young girl of perhaps seventeen. Her pale face was pinched, her thin shoulders hunched beneath a brown woollen shawl.

Deborah rose and indicated the chair before her desk. 'Please do sit down.' Elspeth, with a doubtful expression, handed over a completed application form and then left.

Deborah's swift glance at the form caused her spirits to sink. Making her tone gentle she said, 'So, Miss Wilkes, you are looking for a position as either kitchen maid or scullery maid.'

The girl nodded.

'Do you mind if I call you Edna?'

She shook her head.

Deborah looked at the form again. The personal history was a familiar one. Dismissed without a reference and for the same tragic reason she heard so often. At least this girl had been open about her shame, instead of Deborah having to prise the truth from her. 'Edna, I take it that despite your difficulties, you are able to take another position?'

She nodded.

'But the baby? Do you have someone to care for it?'

'It was stillborn.' Her voice was flat, devoid of emotion.

At first Deborah remained silent. Then in a quiet voice said, 'Oh, my dear, I'm terribly sorry.'

She gave a shrug. 'It was for the best. I wouldn't 'ave bin doing it any favours bringing it into the world, not a bastard,

77

especially as it was a girl.' She stated the fact in a monotone, but not before Deborah had seen a flash of pain in her eyes.

'Will the father not help you?'

'He was a soldier, and once he'd had his fun, he was off. Forced me, he did, but I expect they all say that.'

'I'm not here to judge anyone, Edna. Just to try and give them a second chance, if that is what they need.'

'Well, I need one, miss. I can't live on fresh air much longer.'

Deborah could sense the hopelessness that enveloped the girl and getting up went to the door and whispered to Elspeth, 'Tea and biscuits?'

Returning, she sat again behind her desk.

'I come here, miss, rather than try a factory, cos at least I'll 'ave a roof over me head in service.'

Deborah had heard this statement so many times, and could appreciate its truth.

Respectable lodgings or rented rooms were difficult to find, although there were plenty of suspect ones, where a girl on her own would often be taken advantage of, or begin on the degrading slope to prostitution.

'You have no parents or family?'

She shook her head. 'Da was killed at the Somme, and Ma went with consumption. There ain't nobody else, at least not what I know of.'

'You haven't had much luck in life, have you, Edna. May I ask why you chose to apply to this particular agency?'

'It were Sarah Boot who told me about you. She used to rent a room in the basement of where I'm lodging. Yer got her a position somewhere outside London.'

'I remember her,' Deborah said, recalling the lively young woman she had liked so much. But this girl bore no comparison. Edna looked as though she'd had little fresh air or proper food for months, and given her circumstances that was probably the case. But her lacklustre demeanour would not augur well in an interview, even for such a lowly post. Deborah looked down at the few lines on the form. Few households would take on a girl who had 'got into trouble', it being considered that such an action could weaken the moral fibre of the rest of the staff.

It was a relief when Elspeth came in with a tray, which she put on the desk. 'I'm sure you will both be ready for some refreshment.'

Edna's eyes lit up and she made an involuntary movement towards the plate of biscuits, then withdrew her hand.

Deborah put a cup of steaming tea in front of her and offered her the plate. 'Please take two or three, I'm going to, I feel quite hungry this morning.'

As Deborah bit into one of her own biscuits, she saw Edna's hand tremble as she took one for herself, and almost moan with bliss as she crammed it into her mouth, swiftly followed by another, and another. 'Please finish them off,' Deborah urged. 'It's all part of the service.' She bent to take a file out of a drawer and opened it, trying to avoid embarrassing the girl, only for Edna to begin to cry.

'I'm sorry, miss.' She wiped her tears away with a frayed but clean hanky. 'Yer must think me stupid.'

'Of course I don't. Haven't you been through a most trying time?' Deborah thought sadly of the stillborn child. 'And I don't expect you found it easy to come here. I am going to try and help you, Edna. But I shall need some time to think about the best way. Could you possibly return next Thursday afternoon, say at three o'clock?'

She hesitated, 'Yes, miss.'

'You do promise to come?'

She nodded, getting to her feet and Deborah watched her trudge out of the door. It was going to take all of her own and Elspeth's ingenuity to place this one.

At six-thirty that same evening, Deborah was sitting and gazing at a hat. It was one she had planned to wear, one that she sometimes wore to the agency, but she now realised that it was far too stylish. As she never actually wore it when in her office, that had never been a problem. But tonight, at Battersea Town Hall, she needed to be careful. Having interviewed many over the years, Deborah knew exactly the sort of hat a respectable working woman would be wearing. A cloche, yes, but not she thought in frustration, one extravagantly trimmed with velvet ribbon. Fortunately, the hat she was considering – probably going to ruin if she made a mess of it – wasn't one of her favourites. With determination Deborah took a tiny pair of nail scissors and began to snip away.

At seven o'clock when she knew that Gerard and Julia would be dressing for dinner, Deborah opened her bedroom door and stepped out on to the landing to look down the sweeping staircase. The hall was deserted. Within minutes, a plain outdoor coat concealing her clothes, and wearing the successfully altered hat, she was opening the front door and walking along the pavement to where she could see Theo's Bentley already parked and waiting. Her only regret was that she wasn't wearing gloves. Even the lower-class women – she hated that description but could think of no other – wore gloves. But cotton ones, or knitted ones, not fine kid gloves. And Deborah had no others. She knew that Ellen was out and could have gone to her room and borrowed a pair of hers. But the risk of being caught not only on the servants' landing but invading her maid's privacy was one not to be contemplated.

Theo got out of the driving seat as she approached and his gaze sweeping over her said, 'Splendid!'

'Are you referring to me or my clothes?'

He laughed, and going round to the passenger door ushered her in. It was only then that Deborah noticed her silk stockings and cursed that she hadn't bought some rayon ones. But surely once seated in the hall, such a detail wouldn't be noticeable. It was much easier for men, of course. Theo simply wore a rather boring brown suit with an equally uninspiring knitted tie. He also sported a brown cap. Had he borrowed them from his valet? But there was no mistaking his confident air, how the silvering dark hair at his temples made him look distinguished, and when he turned to smile at her, those penetrating grey eyes.

'So,' he said, raising one eyebrow. 'Let the adventure begin.'

* * *

81

Once in Battersea, Theo slowed down and began to glance around for a suitable place to draw up. 'I think this car would be rather conspicuous, not to mention the risk of it being damaged if feelings run high, so I hope you won't mind a short walk.' Deborah could understand his logic but smiling to herself suspected that the gleaming limousine, which seemed quite new, held a special place in his heart.

Yet even though Theo had parked some distance away, there was already a steady trickle of people on the pavements, the number increasing as they neared the Victorian town hall, its facade larger and more impressive than Deborah had expected. A crowd was pouring through its open doors and she looked around to see if there were any other women, vastly relieved when she spotted one, her shoulders covered by a shawl, her red hair partly hidden by a plain hat. After they had joined the others to queue, eventually they went in where Theo guided her into the Grand Hall, set out with rows of chairs, which were rapidly filling. He ushered her into a row towards the back, settling on two seats near the aisle, murmuring, 'We'll be able to leave first. People will be pushing and shoving to get out. I'm not taking the risk of you getting hurt.'

'Thank you, Theo. I'm so glad you came with me.'

He smiled at her. 'It gave me an excuse to see you again so soon. But make no mistake, Deborah, I am interested in hearing what these people have to say. It's just that meeting you gave me the impetus to come.'

As they waited, she began to watch everyone as they came

in, surprised to hear so many different accents. Cockney, she'd expected, but gradually as the hall filled, she could detect northern accents, Welsh, Scots and Irish. Their faces fascinated her, although she was appalled at the abject poverty etched on some of them. Many of the men looked gaunt, others tired, yet there was still a general air of enthusiasm, expectation. Deborah tried to make herself small in her seat, difficult considering her height, and scanned the audience to see another two women, sitting near the front, their heads together as they whispered. She calculated there must be at least three hundred men packing the hall, some now having to stand down the sides and at the back. But although she was sure they would be here, it was impossible to spot the other men from the train, the ones who had been with Evan.

Turning towards her, Theo nodded at the platform. 'Battersea has always been known for its radical politics. Years ago, Christabel and Emmeline Pankhurst spoke here. I don't suppose you came?'

Deborah shook her head. At that time, the only contribution she was able to make to Women's Suffrage had been a monetary one. She should have come, would have come, if fate hadn't intervened. She looked at the four empty chairs behind a podium thinking that as it was almost eight o'clock, the speakers would soon be announced.

And then they were filing in, with Evan immediately recognisable. He was a striking figure, not only because of his tall stature and broad shoulders, but because he carried an air of authority, due no doubt to his experience as a speaker on behalf of the union. There was a stirring in the audience, and the atmosphere changed as everyone quietened down.

The first speaker was introduced as a Labour MP, but his voice was low, his words dull, and the following two speakers were equally uninspiring, if earnest and sincere. But any muttering was silenced as Evan approached the podium, and a cheer went up. He was compelling, his voice clear and commanding as he drove home the salient points of the workers' aims. Deborah was profoundly moved by the way he described the plight of the miners, then how in 1912 they brought about a strike, which at least forced the government to rush through a bill granting their sought-after minimum wage. But, and here his voice thundered, 'As you all know, not all districts adopted this, and many miners lost out. Have things improved for them since then?'

There came a roar from the audience, '*No!*'

Evan nodded. 'The owners are still cutting wages and extending hours while not investing in the mines. Men are still having to use pickaxes despite it now being 1926.' He paused. 'How many men in this hall earn enough to feed and clothe their families, while their employers live on the fat of the land? Yet appalling conditions still exist in some industries, with no thought given to the safety of employees. There is widespread failure to properly compensate anyone injured at work, maimed or even killed. And their families, through no fault of their own, can often end up in the workhouse where a mother is separated from her children. Is this the sort of country so many of its young people fought and died for? One of injustice – even cruelty?'

Deborah could see many heads being shaken and Evan continued in this vein, giving grim figures to extend his points, causing her to feel not only outraged but ashamed. Then he paused for a moment. 'Now I am not a Communist, but I am a member of the Labour Party, and of the Trades Union Congress, as are most of you. Brothers, we need to stick together, to persuade this government that changes not only *need* to be made, they *must* be made. We are no longer going to ask for a decent living wage, we are going to *demand* it.'

The audience erupted in approval of his words, and men turned to clap each other on the back, some throwing their caps in the air. Deborah felt exhilarated, carried away by the sheer justice of the workers' aims, and turned to share her feelings with Theo. But his expression was taut.

As they had waited for the speakers to arrive on the platform, Theo had observed closely the audience in the hall. There was no mistaking the strain on the men's faces, nor their determination. Working men, but ones who found it either impossible to find jobs, or didn't earn enough to have a decent standard of living. Those facts, he was, as an MP, familiar with. But it wasn't until Evan Morgan, the man Deborah had come to hear, began to speak, that Theo saw the real picture, the travesty behind the country's social justice system. And as he listened to the stirring speech, within him began to burn a sense of not only frustration but impotence.

Unlike anyone else in the hall, he was in uneasy possession of inside knowledge. Privileged knowledge of the government's current hard-thinking policies on the threat of disruption. The bitter fact was that apart from expressing his views on the floor of the House, he was in no position to influence or change them. And it had been like rubbing salt into a wound, to listen to the explosive sincerity in the hall.

When the meeting began to draw to a close, he realised Deborah would be in danger of being jostled and touched her arm. 'Shall we go? There will be a rush to leave soon.'

From the seats he had chosen it was easy for them to slip out, at which point he said, 'Your Evan Morgan is a man of burning conviction and an impressive speaker.'

'You're glad you came?'

He nodded. 'Although originally it was mainly to protect you.'

They made their way out of the building, and holding her hand he began to stride along the road to the side street where he had parked the Bentley.

Deborah said, 'Slow down, do, Theo, I'm becoming breathless.'

'Sorry.' He turned to her. 'How did you feel about it, the meeting, I mean?'

'Evan, as you said, was marvellous. But what really moved me was to be in the middle of all those men. One could actually feel their desperation.'

Theo looked at Deborah's eyes, which were ablaze

with conviction. 'I'm so glad I met you, Lady Deborah Claremont. You are one amazing young woman.'

She smiled at him, but spoke little as he drove them back to Grosvenor Square. Deborah, he thought with appreciation, was the only woman he'd ever met who had the rare quality of not always wanting to fill a comfortable silence.

Chapter Nine

Deborah turned to smile at Theo when he escorted her safely to her front door. 'Goodnight.'

'Goodnight, Deborah, I'll be in touch.' He leant over and kissed her lightly on the cheek before turning away to go swiftly down the steps to the Bentley parked outside.

She was still smiling when she went into the house, only to her utter dismay to come face to face with Gerard, who happened to be crossing the hall.

He frowned at her, his expression one of displeasure. 'Surely your income allows you to dress in a more suitable manner. Where on earth have you been?'

'I have been to a fancy-dress party, held by a member of one of my charities,' she replied tartly. 'Nobody you would be likely to know.' Subterfuge where Gerard was concerned was always a wise precaution.

'Thank God for that. I'm appalled. You look like a pauper.'

Deborah thought of young Edna Wilkes, whose only warmth was a thin brown shawl. How little her brother knew about ordinary people, never mind those in real poverty. She bid him a curt goodnight and continued up to her room, relieved that she wouldn't find Ellen waiting for her. Deborah needed to be alone, able to go over all the events of the evening. Her mind was still full of Evan's evocative words and the harrowing images they had provoked. She felt a hot wave of shame sweep over her. She wasn't blind, she had naturally been aware of her privileged life, known that others weren't so lucky. But the people in that hall? Never had she been in close contact en masse with what Gerard had been known to refer to as 'the great unwashed'. And yet those workers listening to Evan had been clean and respectable, struggling to lead a decent life. How dare people like Gerard and his idle cronies, secure in their inherited wealth and trust funds, dismiss and patronise them. She knew more of the real world than they did.

But later, before she went to sleep her thoughts turned to Theo. Meeting him had brought back so many memories, that feeling of attraction, the warmth of a man's hand, the longing to marry and enjoy again the passion of lovemaking. Since she had lost her fiancé, she had never been short of suitors, but Deborah knew the difference between fondness or affection and the heady sensation of being in love. She had waited so long, could it be that at last her life would change?

The following morning at the agency was a busy one, and it wasn't until they paused for coffee that Deborah and Elspeth were able to discuss the problem of Edna Wilkes.

'We can't possibly send her to our usual contacts,' Deborah said decisively.

'I agree,' Elspeth was frowning. 'She's very depressed and it shows. Not that she hasn't cause to be. But we wouldn't be doing her any favours sending her for an interview when she's almost certain to be rejected. We both know just how scathing some of these housekeepers are, not to mention the butlers. Even the mistress of the house gets involved sometimes.' She gave a heavy sigh. 'We could always tell her we don't have anything suitable.'

Deborah nodded. 'Everything you say is true. But do we want to turn her away?' She didn't speak for a moment, then said, 'Did I ever tell you what gave me the incentive to open the agency in the first place?'

'No, you didn't.' Elspeth looked at her with curiosity. 'I've often wondered.'

'When I was a child, we had a maid called Susie, at least she was Susie to me, although it was the custom then, as you know, for a servant to be referred to by their surname. Hers was Denton. A pretty girl, she used to make a fuss of me, you know, teasing me into laughter, ruffling my hair and I grew very fond of her.' Deborah gave a sad smile. 'I remember she had lots of freckles, which she said were angels' kisses. And then when I was about twelve, she just wasn't there any more.'

Deborah told Elspeth that her questions had been met with tight lips and frowns, the housekeeper muttering that Susie had been a 'wicked girl' and dismissed. Appealing to her mother, it was only then that Deborah discovered it was possible to have a baby without being married.

'But she's an orphan, where will she go?' Deborah's protests had been fierce. 'Will she get married?'

Her mother, every inch the cool aristocrat, had been terse. 'Apparently, the man responsible was not only married, he abused our hospitality. He certainly will never be welcome in this house again. Your father is furious.'

'But Mama, what will happen to her?'

'That doesn't concern us. It is quite usual in such circumstances for the girl to be dismissed, and without a reference. It is a harsh rule, but necessary as such a scandal reflects on the whole household. One must never condone lax behaviour among the staff, it can lead to debauchery.'

Deborah had taken her questions to Mr Channing, who told her to look up debauchery in her dictionary. Not much wiser, except thinking that it couldn't possibly apply to Susie, Deborah had then asked how important a reference was.

'Essential, as it will proclaim a girl to be of good character.'

He looked sadly at her over his half-moon spectacles. 'I'm sorry, Deborah, but I'm afraid Susie will never recover her reputation. And she'll find it difficult, almost impossible to find respectable employment.'

Deborah had been deeply troubled. If Susie couldn't find work, what would happen to the baby? 'I pleaded with my mother that she should be given another chance with us,' she told Elspeth, 'but it was hopeless.'

'Did you ever find out what happened to her?'

'Not for a long time, the servants wouldn't answer my questions, I think they'd been forbidden to do so.'

Deborah's mind went back to that never to be forgotten day, a year later. In the hope that Cook was in a good mood, and might give her a glass of lemonade and a rock cake warm from the oven, Deborah, hot and sticky from a game of tennis, had gone down to the kitchen. As she drew nearer, she suddenly heard Susie's name mentioned, and paused within listening distance.

Cook was talking to a new kitchen maid. 'The baby was stillborn, but better than being born a bastard, that's what I say. As for Susie,' Cook lowered her voice and Deborah crept closer. 'Now, not a word to anyone mind, especially them upstairs. I'm only telling you all this as a warning to behave yerself. Well, a few months after the birth, we found out the police dragged her body from the Thames.'

The kitchen maid's shock was audible. 'Yer mean she drowned herself?'

'I'm afraid so.'

Deborah froze, her heart began hammering in her chest, her mind filled with the dreadful image of Susie, weeping as she stood on the riverbank. Choking with tears, she turned and stumbled up the backstairs, wanting to reach her bedroom to throw herself on the bed. That lovely, lively girl! But to her dismay on crossing the hall she collided with Gerard. Distraught, Deborah blurted out what she'd just heard.

'I can't believe it, poor Susie.'

'Who's Susie?'

'She was one of our maids.'

He shrugged. 'Oh, a servant, you're getting upset about a servant?' Gerard appeared more intrigued than shocked. 'I'm sure I've read that a body becomes bloated when it's in the water for ages, I wonder why?'

Appalled by his lack of concern, she flashed, 'Why don't you look it up!' Then sobbing, she had fled past him.

As Deborah related all this, Elspeth looked sadly at her. 'God bless the poor lass. I suppose the man who ruined her got off scot-free.'

'Don't they always? It affected me greatly, Elspeth. It would have only needed a little generosity of spirit, less judgement and condemnation. And so, when I reached twenty-one and came into part of my inheritance, I decided to open a staff agency that was willing, in deserving cases, to actually give someone a second chance.'

'It was a risk, though, especially in the beginning,' Elspeth mused. 'We had to build up our reputation first. Still, we've not been let down so far. But,' and her expression was troubled, 'it would only take one or two for the agency not to be trusted. And this wouldn't be the first time that we've not taken someone on – for that very reason.'

Deborah knew she was right. But there had been something about Edna, apart from her evocative history, that made her determined to do all in her power to help the despairing girl.

When in the late afternoon she left the agency, it was to find that London was becoming enveloped in smog, and so her cab took longer than usual to reach Grosvenor Square. A gloved hand over her nose and mouth she hurried up the steps, looking forward to the welcoming light and warmth of her home.

'It's going to be a pea-souper, Fulton,' she told him as he opened the door.

'I'm afraid so, Lady Deborah. You'll be glad to be back safely.'

She smiled at him. 'Thank you. I'd appreciate some tea.'

She went up the wide staircase, looking forward to relaxing before changing for dinner, and going into her bedroom was met by a relieved Ellen. 'At last, my lady.' She helped Deborah out of her coat. 'There's a nice fire in the sitting room.'

Deborah gave her a puzzled glance, sensing a note of excitement in her voice. Then on opening the door to the adjoining room she considered her 'sanctuary', saw displayed on a side table, an extravagant display of hothouse flowers. Slowly, she went to remove the envelope resting amongst the blooms, hoping and then smiling as she saw the small white card with just one word, 'Theo'.

Chapter Ten

The following morning Deborah decided to pay a visit to a Catholic church. Not for any religious reason, her weekly attendance at her local Anglican church was merely duty undertaken to set an example to the servants.

It had been a particular circumstance that three years previously had brought her to the doors of St Malachy's. Not quite sure what to expect, she had been intrigued to see that the interior wasn't substantially different to that of her regular place of worship. A similar high altar with vases of flowers and before it rows of oak pews. But here prominently displayed was a rather beautiful statue of Mary, and another large statue of Jesus Christ with a bleeding heart, and before them both a stand of flickering candles.

The church had felt peaceful with a faint lingering incense in the air, and on meeting the priest, Deborah knew that she had found a kindred spirit.

She had been trying to help an applicant at the agency, a young man whose position as a footman had been compromised by an unnatural approach from a male servant. His revulsion had resulted in a false allegation of theft made against him, and despite his protests of innocence, he was instantly dismissed. Even now Deborah could remember how his face had turned crimson as he described his situation. She had been doubtful, it being her rule that any suspicion of dishonesty meant a negative decision, but he had pleaded with her, saying that his parish priest would vouch for him. And ever since then she had forged a useful relationship, if not with the church, then with Father Keegan.

His rotund figure was bustling around the pews as Deborah entered and he came forward to greet her with a smile. 'Miss Claremont! How are you? Come to see me about another of your lame ducks?'

She held out her hand to shake his. 'I'm very well, thank you, Father Keegan. As I hope you are. And the answer is yes, I have.'

He nodded. 'Come along to the presbytery and tell me all about it.'

She followed him to his home behind the church and into his bookish study, which always had a masculine aroma of tobacco smoke and malt whisky.

Deborah explained about Edna. 'I don't see how I can help her, not in her present state of mind. And it is that state of mind that concerns me. She needs hope, Father Keegan, and compassion. And I think her need is urgent.'

He frowned. 'And you judge her to be more sinned against than sinner?' His gaze fixed on her, and she knew that much depended on her reply.

Deborah gave a brisk nod. 'Yes, I do.'

'And a kitchen maid, you say?' The priest was thoughtful. 'Now I do know of a small household where a little extra help would be useful. And they're good people. I suppose I could have a word . . .'

'Would you? Although she's not of your faith, I'm afraid.'

He raised his eyebrows.

'Methodist,' she said, trying to keep her face straight. This was a dance they often shared.

'That's hardly her fault. Sure and doesn't the Lord love a lost sheep? And isn't it a Catholic family she'll be going to? I'll call round this evening and telephone you tomorrow morning.'

'Thank you.'

The priest went on to ask about Sarah Boot.

'I'm sorry, I meant to let you know. She's happily settled in Wiltshire.' Deborah smiled. 'She was a most likeable girl. It was Sarah who advised Edna to approach the agency.' She rose saying, 'I mustn't take up more of your valuable time, and I really am grateful to you.'

They walked back through the church where he shook her hand. 'I'll be in touch.'

As Deborah reached the door to leave, she put a generous offering into the poor box situated on the wall just inside the door. A last reminder to people to contribute, she thought, but couldn't help hoping that Father Keegan would empty it that very day. Surely its accessibility was a temptation for those with no conscience? Or was it that the kindly priest put his faith not only in God but also in his parishioners. Walking away from the church, a fierce gust of wind made her put up a hand to grab her hat, only to find it torn from her head to skeeter across the road.

'Hang on, I'll get it.' A tall man with pamphlets in his hand darted to rescue it from being crushed by an oncoming motor car. Coming back, he handed it to her with a smile.

But Deborah's shock on recognising him was such that she could only take the hat from him in silence. His expression impassive, he made to move away and she said swiftly, 'I'm sorry, seeing you took me by surprise. Thank you.'

He stared at her. 'I don't think . . .'

Deborah shook her head. 'No, we've never met. It's just that after hearing your talk last Tuesday, it seems such a coincidence.'

'You were at the Battersea meeting?' He looked incredulous.

She nodded. 'Yes, I was. And you put your case in such a vivid way that your words are still lingering in my mind.' Deborah saw interest flicker in his eyes, followed by a puzzled frown.

'I'm sorry,' he said, moving aside to let another man pass

by, 'but I can't help feeling curious that a young lady such as yourself would be interested in workers' rights.'

Deborah knew that however plain her choice of clothes, her voice would always reveal her true class. 'I can read the newspapers,' she said quietly. 'And despite being a woman, I do have a certain amount of intelligence. Of course I am aware of what is happening in my country.'

Evan's strong features tensed. 'I'm sorry, I meant no offence, Miss . . .'

'Claremont,' Deborah said. She smiled at him. 'And I'm sorry too, there was no offence taken.'

His answering smile lightened his countenance. 'I'm Evan Morgan, although you already know that.'

She shook his outstretched large hand, feeling its rough hardness. This man was no footman or clerk. 'I must thank you again for rescuing my hat.'

'It was a pleasure.' He touched the peak of his cap and giving her a brisk nod, continued on his way.

Deborah turned and watched his broad-shouldered figure stride along the pavement. Although on the Claremont estate in Berkshire there were gardeners and farm workers, she had never encountered anyone with such a combination of muscular strength, intelligence and good looks. It was true that she was becoming daily more interested in the present industrial dispute. Whether a general strike was wise, she didn't know, but if the establishment were unwilling to negotiate fairly, what other solution did the men have?

* * *

True to his word, Father Keegan telephoned the agency the following week, and Deborah felt a surge of relief as he told her that the family he had in mind were not only willing but eager to meet Edna.

'You did warn them that she is very downcast?'

'I did indeed. And took the liberty of confiding her history, in confidence you understand. Sure, there's no need for the girl herself to know that. Now this is the address, and she's to go along tomorrow at about eleven o'clock. I thought of taking her meself, but her own minister might think I'm trying to steal his parishioners.'

Deborah laughed, then said, 'Thank you, I do appreciate it.'

'God bless you, Miss Claremont. You're a good woman.'

That same afternoon, when Elspeth ushered Edna into her office, Deborah noticed that the young woman had made little effort. Her hair was still lank, her eyes pools of unhappiness. Almost immediately, Elspeth carried in a prepared tray and the girl needed little encouragement to cram three bourbon biscuits into her mouth.

Deborah poured the tea. 'Two lumps of sugar?' She noticed that the girl's hand shook as she took the cup and saucer from her.

'I won't keep you a moment,' Deborah murmured, and began to browse through a file to give Edna a little time. Then she looked up. 'I have news for you. There is a vacancy for a kitchen maid not too far from here. And it would be a live-in position too.'

'Do they know I've no reference?' Her voice was dull, but Deborah could see a tiny flicker of hope in her eyes.

'They know. You'll go for an interview? Don't worry, Edna. It's not a large household and they are kind people. I think it will be just what you need.' Deborah wrote the details on a sheet of paper.

'I'm ever so grateful, Miss Claremont.' She rose and took the address before hesitating. 'Do you think they'll like me?'

'I'm sure they will.'

'I shall need to wash my hair.' She put up a hand to touch it.

Deborah smiled at her with some relief. For the girl even to think that was a step in the right direction.

After Edna had left, Elspeth came in to the office. She looked at Deborah and said quietly, 'I shall pray for that lassie tonight. And please God, we've saved her from doing something stupid.'

But Deborah was thinking of the young girl's stillborn child. Such tragedies were by no means unusual but she had never been able to understand why a supposedly merciful God could be so cruel. After all, what was the point of allowing a conception if there was to be no live birth?

That evening, together with Gerard and Julia, Deborah went to an engagement party held at the Savoy Hotel. The two young people involved were the Honourable Cedric

Fairbanks and a young woman whose family were not quite 'top drawer', according to Gerard. He had mentioned the fact with disdain, which of course rankled with Deborah, who on being introduced to Barbara, Cedric's fiancée, decided that he was a very fortunate young man.

The occasion was well planned with a comfortable number of guests invited, most of whom Deborah was familiar with, making her realise yet again what a limited social circle she moved in. And although she was glad of the chance to catch up with Frances Bentwood and Claudia Faversham, it struck her afresh that they were, like herself, titled. We all live in a hothouse, she mused. How more stimulating the conversation would be if people like Evan Morgan were among the guests.

Claudia was, as usual, in full flow. 'Now, who do we think is the most eligible bachelor here, or most attractive?'

'Behave yourself,' Frances, a languid brunette, said. 'Don't forget that I'm a married woman.'

Claudia tossed her blonde head. 'One can always window-shop, darling.'

Deborah laughed. 'You truly are a merry widow, aren't you?'

'I was faithful to Archie when he was alive, but as he was so inconsiderate as to fall off his horse, I'm making the most of my freedom.' She was glancing around the room. 'Ah, there's Crispin. Now he's a man I would like to see more of! See you both later.'

Frances raised her eyebrows but a smile lingered around

her lips. 'She is incorrigible – I'm afraid Claude considers her far too fast to be a suitable friend.'

'Which opinion you totally ignore,' Deborah teased.

'Well, we three have been friends a long time, and one has to accept – how can I put it? – certain foibles?'

Deborah nodded. 'I agree, but I think she misses Archie more than she'll admit.' She gave a sigh, 'I suppose we should mingle.'

'Yes, but it's supper I'm looking forward to . . . I have developed a craving for sweet things.' Frances gave a wide smile. 'Number three is on its way, but we haven't yet told our parents, so keep it to yourself.'

'My congratulations, and of course I will.'

There was quite a throng, and it wasn't until after being introduced to various relatives of Barbara's, that Deborah saw Theo. He looked to be his usual urbane self, standing before one of the long windows, glass in hand and looking around the room. At that very moment his glance came to rest on Deborah and he began to move in her direction.

She tilted her head slightly to acknowledge that she had seen him but remained where she was, continuing her conversation with an elderly woman who had come from Berkshire to celebrate the happy occasion. 'My niece is a lovely girl,' she was confiding.

Acutely aware of Theo threading his way towards her, Deborah said, 'Let us hope they will be very happy together.'

Theo drew nearer and with a smile at Deborah's companion murmured, 'Please excuse us,' before lightly taking Deborah's elbow and guiding her to an empty space at the edge of the room. 'I'm so glad I've seen you.'

She smiled up at him. 'Thank you for the lovely flowers.'

Her gaze met his own, and what she saw in his eyes made Deborah's heart skip a beat. A longing came over her to spend more time with him, to understand him. And yes, to feel his closeness, the touch of his skin.

'When can I see you again? The theatre perhaps?'

'Actually,' she murmured, 'there's a play at the Lyric Theatre that I've been intending to see.'

He smiled. 'I know the one and I haven't seen it either. Shall I look into a convenient date? I wish I could stay longer, but I've another commitment.'

'That would be lovely.'

'Discussing politics again?' Deborah turned as Gerard and Julia joined them. 'Sorry to disturb, old chap. As supper is about to be served, I've come to collect my sister.'

Theo smiled at them. 'But of course. May I say that you look especially lovely in that charming gown, Countess?'

Julia's eyes lit up with pleasure. 'Thank you. It's one of Gerard's favourites.'

Deborah watched her brother's eyes soften as he looked at his young wife. She had always doubted whether he was in love with his bride before their marriage, suspecting that he was more interested in securing an heir. And that may have been true, she thought, but there was no denying his growing fondness for Julia. Gerard had always been cold and remote even as a boy. If Julia could make him a happier person, bring warmth and affection into his life, then Deborah continued to be glad to see it.

Chapter Eleven

The following morning in the front room of his aunt's terraced house in Greenwich, Evan Morgan was distributing piles of pamphlets between a group of out-of-work men. 'We're damn lucky to have a printer so sympathetic to the cause,' he said. 'He's made an excellent job of these.'

One of the men said, 'Aye, Bob's a good lad,' a comment that brought murmurs of agreement.

'So what's the next plan, Evan?' A dark-haired man who wore a permanent worried expression added, 'I can do today, but I'll 'ave to go down the docks termorrer, just in case I get taken on.'

'Of course, and that applies to all of you. Jobs have to come first, they're like gold at the moment, as we all know to our cost.' Evan's tone was bitter. Having months before completed his term of service with the Royal Monmouthshire Royal Engineers, and proud of the technical skills he now possessed, to his dismay he'd been unable to find a job where he could use them. Forced to accept temporary unskilled work, he was appalled at the working conditions and lack of regard for safety, and made the mistake of speaking out. Economics, the boss had explained, was the reason for his dismissal, but Evan had seen the steel in his eyes and he knew the real reason was fear. The owners were afraid of anyone disturbing the smooth tempo of their lives. It was of no concern that wages were at starvation level, all that mattered was a rosy balance sheet. A troublemaker, that was how they would see any man prepared to stand up for his rights. And if he gained support from others in his fight for justice, then he became a dangerous threat.

'Did we finish Bloomsbury?' The man spoke quietly, as was his habit, but Evan had never met a more committed supporter of their cause. The sole provider in a family weakened by ill health, Joe was desperate for the planned general strike to succeed, but his idealism made him vulnerable. 'We just need a living wage,' he would plead, thrusting a pamphlet to anyone who would take it. 'You just don't know, don't realise.'

'Don't want to know, more like,' his fellow workers would mutter, but Joe hung on to his belief that most people were honest, decent. Surely they would see that the strikers' demands were justified?

Evan answered the question. 'Bloomsbury?' He shook his head. 'Not quite, but we'll leave that until later in the week, then I'll do it. We'll start on Putney.'

'With so many other groups leafleting, we should just about reach everyone,' Joe said, his face alight with optimism.

Evan glanced round at the small and loyal group. Gaunt faces yes, but despite the desperation in their eyes, there was also a steely determination and a growing belief that the whole country was behind them.

At least his aunt would provide these men with a bowl of hearty soup before they left. He owed much to Bronwen, who had helped to raise the motherless Evan after his father died in a pit accident. It was only after Evan had left the local pit and enlisted in the army that she began to look to her own life. He had been thrilled for her when serving in a local haberdashery, she had met and then married George Clarke, an English salesman. Only Evan knew what a wrench it had been for her to move from her beloved Wales to England's capital city. But she had been happy there, and when recently widowed chose to remain in her comfortable home. Bronwen had been a suffragette and, as a fierce supporter of any struggle for justice, was only too pleased to offer Evan and his friends a base to meet and plan the next stages of their campaign.

'Let's hope so.' But Evan was wondering whether when he went back to Bloomsbury he might be lucky enough to chase another hat, one that belonged to a certain Miss Claremont. The brief encounter had been a rare lighter moment in these past driven few weeks. And despite knowing she would never be interested in a man like himself, that didn't prevent her clear, direct gaze and interest in his cause lingering in his mind. Nor her poise and lovely face.

A few days later in the drawing room in Grosvenor Square, Gerard, standing before the large mahogany fireplace alit with a blazing fire, was thoughtfully regarding his sister. Deborah was standing a little distance away from him, sipping her dry sherry as she chatted to Julia. Was it his imagination or was Deborah's expression more animated than he had seen for some time? Certainly, he had to admit that she looked well tonight in an ivory fringed dress and long ebony beads. The fashionable bob suited her, but there was always an underlying bitterness within him. Their mother, the then Countess of Anscombe, had been obsessed with her daughter from the day she was born. All of her attention focused on this usurper, and as his father, although kindly, had been a distant man, Gerard's hitherto cosy world became a lonely and bewildering place. He had watched the gurgling, happy baby grow into a pretty toddler, and then he was sent away to boarding school, a place he had hated with a vengeance. When terms ended he would come home with such eagerness, only to feel like an interloper. Was it any wonder, he thought, that he still harboured such brooding resentment?

'You'll be having supper after the theatre,' Julia was saying.

'Yes, I'm really keen to see this play, and so is Theodore.'

Gerard stiffened and then moved to join them. 'You are going out again with Field?'

'Yes, I am.' Deborah's smile was challenging.

'He's very charming,' Julia said. 'It would make an ideal match, don't you think so, Gerard?'

Deborah laughed. 'It's a little early to think along those lines, Julia.'

'Definitely,' Gerard snapped, then turned to the door as the butler announced, 'Mr Theodore Field.'

There followed fifteen minutes of polite conversation, mainly between Theo and Gerard, while Deborah said little, bearing the social necessity with some impatience.

At last they were walking towards Theo's car, where on opening the passenger door, he murmured, 'You look absolutely stunning.'

She flashed a smile over her shoulder. 'Thank you.' During their short journey he once again regaled her with a couple of witty snippets of conversation he had heard that day in Parliament. But she did notice that he was careful not to reveal their source, which pleased her. She had little time for gossipmongers, having no desire for her opinions or casual remarks to be the basis of general entertainment. And unexpectedly an image of Evan Morgan came into her mind. She doubted that he would be a man to indulge in tittle-tattle. Reflectively, Deborah turned to study Theo's profile as he drove. The two men, so different in background and education, were equally good-looking in their own way, although Theo's practised charm would not sit easily with anyone less privileged. Did it come with their mother's milk, or merely growing up surrounded by a veneer of civilised behaviour? An image of her brother came into her mind. He too, in the right environment could display an easy charm . . .

'A penny for them, you're miles away.' Theo turned to smile at her.

'Sorry, I confess I was. Just random thoughts, you know how it is. Or rather, not so random as one was about you.' Her gaze met his in a teasing manner.

He didn't answer as he parked the car, then came round to open the passenger door. 'I shall only forgive you if your thought was a flattering one.'

Deborah swung her long legs out and took his proffered hand. 'You can rely on it.'

'Then that bodes for an enjoyable evening.'

Unfortunately, the play, as they discussed later, didn't endear itself to either of them.

'I'm sorry I inflicted it on you,' Theo said.

'Yes, it was a bit heavy going. It's surprising, isn't it,' Deborah said, 'how people differ in their opinions? At least we felt the same, and yet the reviews were quite good.'

'It's the same with books, what one person enjoys another will find boring.' Theo was studying the wine list.

'I'm glad we came here,' Deborah said, looking around the small restaurant with interest. 'It's an awful confession, but I do get fed up with eating at the same venues all the time. You know, the Savoy, etcetera.'

'I agree. Sometimes I just want to dine in anonymity. Not that I'm vain enough to think that I'm instantly recognisable, but it is refreshing to avoid the myriad of acquaintances one seems to collect.'

'Yes, I know what you mean.' She became silent for a few moments. 'It's awful, though, isn't it? I feel ashamed. I mean, to complain about such a thing when we know, and I more so since Battersea, that many families literally go to bed hungry.'

'Indeed. You saw then how angry the situation makes me. And listening to Evan Morgan describe the plight of the unemployed, his plea for justice . . .' He paused. 'I can only say that knowing what I do—' Theo suddenly stopped. 'I can't say any more, not even to you.'

She stared at him, while a waiter brought their first course of smoked salmon and halibut terrine with cucumber relish. Then she said, 'I understand.'

And so the evening continued, with an ever increasing undercurrent of intensity making Deborah's nerve ends acutely aware of Theo's physical presence. At times she would meet his gaze to find an expression in his eyes that could only be interpreted in one way. This man wanted her. And her own feelings? Deborah was almost shocked at the realisation that she was beginning to fall in love. At one time she had to turn her head away, struggling to believe that at last it had happened again. Or seemed to be happening. Step back, she told herself, it is early days yet, but one look into Theo's eyes and she was undone.

Then, as they lingered over coffee and petits fours, Theo put out his hand palm up on the white damask tablecloth, expectation in his eyes. Deborah placed hers on top of it and his fingers closed around her own, warm and strong. His voice was soft, and every word left her breathless. 'I want to tell you, Deborah, that I haven't felt like this about a woman for a very long time.'

'I'm glad.' She spoke quietly, her gaze never leaving his own.

'Do you like to dance?'

'I love to.'

'Then we must dance together, and very soon.'

Later, when Theo drew up in Grosvenor Square, this time he leant over and kissed her lightly on the lips. 'I shall see you safely to the door, and then dream of holding you in my arms on the dance floor.'

'Don't leave it too long,' she murmured – she was longing to be held in his arms.

He kissed the tip of her nose. 'Lady Deborah, you are a forward minx.'

'I'm a little old for that description.' She began to laugh, but he reached over and placed a finger over her mouth, before replacing it with his own lips. His second kiss was searching, leaving her shaken. It was too dim in the car to see the expression in Theo's eyes, but she sensed his breathing deepen as he drew away. Seconds later they were walking hand in hand to Deborah's front door, and their fingers clung before parting.

Ellen was sewing in the sitting room as Deborah went into her bedroom, and coming to meet her, said, 'You look as if you've had a nice time, my lady.'

'Yes, Ellen, I have.' Deborah could hardly stop smiling. After all these empty years, was there really going to be love in her life again? Could she at last now put the past behind her? And finding herself unable to sleep, with the coal fire flickering in the grate and the downy pillows soft against her face, at last Deborah opened her heart to allow the sweet yet painful memories of her first and only love to flood into her mind.

Chapter Twelve

Anscombe Hall, Berkshire, March 1918

'Papa, I do feel a little uneasy about holding such a big party this weekend. The news from the front continues to be disastrous, and so many patients in the East Wing are suffering from dreadful injuries. Is it quite the right thing to do?'

'It's normality men need when they have leave, Deborah.' Her father answered her query with a frown. 'To have a chance to push aside the horrors of war. Surely you wouldn't begrudge our brave young officers that?'

She shook her head. 'Of course not.'

'I don't think anyone could accuse us of not fulfilling our patriotic duty.' He gazed at her. 'Don't forget that Gerard is serving his King and country. The fact that his leave coincides with his birthday is a cause for celebration, a thanksgiving too, that he hasn't been taken from us.'

'Yes, you are right, of course you are, Papa. I hadn't given the matter enough thought!' Feeling a little ashamed, she quietly left his study and walked along to the morning room to await the arrival of Abigail. Her best friend's home had also been adapted as a temporary hospital and both girls dutifully rolled bandages, and knitted comforters, socks and fingerless gloves designed to help 'our boys in the trenches'. When the war first began in 1914, neither had any inkling of the gruesome conditions, the rats and stinking mud those trenches held, nor of the carnage and destruction taking place across the English Channel. But gradually rumours began to circulate, and it became impossible not to pore over newspaper reports, to be shocked and appalled at the long lists of dead and wounded. At Anscombe, as soon as the first patients began to arrive, Deborah had realised that there was a role for her and now she spent most of her time in Berkshire. At first shielded from the more serious cases, as she became older she was allowed to read to and also write letters for maimed and disfigured patients. The experience had humbled her, making her understand it was not only on the battlefield that courage was needed.

And so on Friday afternoon, the guests began to arrive, with the majority being young officers. A few were pale and quiet, an odd one or two gave her a flirtatious glance, and then she turned to be introduced to a tall, dark-haired

Frenchman, whose smile lit up his expressive brown eyes.

'Lieutenant Philippe Lapierre at your service, Lady Deborah.' His hand took her outstretched one.

'I'm so pleased you could come.' Her voice was almost breathless.

He gazed at her for one long moment. 'I am too.'

His image remained with her as she greeted the rest of their guests, and that evening Deborah dressed with especial care, wearing an azure-blue dress, which not only revealed her bare shoulders, but exactly matched the colour of her eyes. It was with excited confidence that she went downstairs for drinks in the drawing room where her gaze immediately sought out the Frenchman, who turned as she entered. She saw him excuse himself from the couple he was talking to and begin to walk towards her, but at that moment her mother took her elbow, wishing to introduce her to a couple who had bought a neighbouring estate. As the man was the hunting and shooting type she despised, and his wife's conversation revealed her to be an odious snob, the interruption was especially galling. And later, the fates still seemed to be against them, because during dinner they were seated a little distance away, though each would glance across the table at times to meet the other's eyes for a few exhilarating seconds.

'My word, you've fallen head over heels,' Abigail teased, as they left the men to their port and brandy. 'You're wearing your heart on your sleeve, Debs. Where's that calm and composed expression I know so well?'

'Is it that obvious?' Deborah felt mortified.

'Don't worry, our French lieutenant is equally smitten. I've been watching the pair of you.'

'Really?' A thrill ran through her. 'Abby – what do you think?'

She laughed. 'That it's a pity he saw you first.'

When the gentlemen joined the ladies in the drawing room, Deborah saw his gaze search for her, and her breath quickened when he made his way to her side.

'Lady Deborah.' He gave a rueful smile. 'I wait for hours for a chance to speak to you, and now I cannot think what to say.'

Loving the way he pronounced her name, she gazed up at him. 'Deborah, please, Lieutenant.'

'And I am Philippe.'

Normally adept in social situations she found herself floundering, then said, 'Perhaps you could begin by telling me how you arrived here?'

'I am, as you say, acquainted with Jeremy Ashmore, who I believe you know.'

She nodded. 'I noticed that you came with him.'

'We were friends before the war, and met again at the front. Our leaves happened to coincide and,' he shrugged, 'I am unable to go back to my home because the area around Lille is occupied by the Germans.' His lips tightened. Deborah's heart went out to him. She couldn't imagine how she would feel if that happened here. Philippe then smiled. 'And so, Jeremy kindly invited me to his. Your brother came to visit and—'

119

At that very moment Gerard interrupted them. 'I see you've met my young sister, Lapierre. Deborah, you had better go and rescue Abigail, she seems submerged with young officers.'

Deborah moved away in resentment, and to her dismay there never came another chance to speak alone with Philippe that evening. However, after breakfast the following morning she saw him approach her mother, and felt her heart leap when a few seconds later she was beckoned to join them.

'Deborah, Lieutenant Lapierre would like to walk around the estate and is interested in its history. Gerard is busy, so I thought perhaps . . .'

'Of course,' she murmured, her pulse racing with excitement. Her mother added, 'Together with Abigail, of course.'

Philippe glanced sideways at her as they walked out of the room and whispered, 'Do you need a chaperone in the gardens of your own home?'

She whispered back, 'Leave it to me. I'll just fetch my hat and coat.' On seeing Abigail climbing the wide staircase, Deborah hurried to catch at her sleeve. 'Abby, you're supposed to chaperone me on a walk with Philippe.'

'What?'

'Exactly. Do me a favour and stay out of sight. If I'm asked, I'll say you had a headache.'

The other girl grinned. 'I'm jealous to death, you lucky devil.'

Collecting her outdoor clothes, Deborah hurried downstairs to find Philippe waiting in the hall. 'Let's go, before Mama sees us.'

'And your friend?'

'She has a headache.'

He laughed and was still laughing as, with the butler standing aside, they walked through the front door and began to stroll down the long tree-lined drive.

'We're lucky with the weather,' Deborah said, looking up at the clear blue sky. 'It poured down last night.'

'I'm glad we have some luck, I was beginning to think there was a conspiracy to keep us apart.' He looked down at her, 'I like the hat!'

Fascinated by his accent, she smiled. 'It was the first one I saw that would stay on if it was windy.' She knew, however, that the green small-brimmed hat suited her. 'Mama said that you were interested in the history of the estate?'

His mouth curved with amusement. 'That was just an excuse. I was desperate to spend some time alone with you.'

'So we can talk about something more interesting than my family's glorious past?'

'Well, if you put it like that . . .'

She laughed, loving the way she felt so at ease with him. 'You do speak English very well. Tell me about yourself.'

'The English is because of an excellent education.' He frowned. 'Is there another path we can walk along, one not quite so public?'

Her heart missed a beat. 'How do I know I can trust you?'

He leant towards her. 'Because I am a gentleman.'

She smiled up at him. 'In that case, we'll turn left after that large oak tree ahead, and walk down to the lake.'

And they did. Within minutes he had taken her gloved hand and as they walked through the woods, avoiding the odd wet puddle, he answered her question. 'You wanted to know about me? Well, I am twenty-two, clever, and pursued by all the young ladies.'

'Are you? Terribly clever, I mean?'

He roared with laughter. 'Oh yes, I have the brilliant mind.' He shook his head. '*Non*, I was trying to impress you.' He squeezed her hand. 'But I do have excellent taste in beautiful young women.'

'Oh, you're a flirt, then.' She pulled a face.

He stopped and turned to her, 'I am joking with you, Deborah. I'm not like that at all. I think I shall be grateful to Gerard for this invitation for the rest of my life.' His voice was husky, and what she saw in his eyes caused her own to lower in confusion.

They continued to walk as he told her that he was the only child of a widowed mother, how he longed to travel, to see the Vatican and the catacombs in Rome, to visit America. 'There is a wide and wonderful world waiting out there, *ma chérie*, and once this futile and destructive war is over, I hope to experience it.'

'You will, I'm sure of it.' Instinctively she moved closer to him, and turning to her, he said, 'Deborah?' Slowly and tentatively his lips came down to meet her own willing ones, and such a delicious warmth spread through her that she wanted their kiss to go on for ever.

Philippe gently released her and still holding hands

they carried on walking beneath what would, in summer, become a shady canopy of trees. And yet the damp smell of the foliage, which remained from when it had rained in the night, seemed to her to be more evocative than the most expensive perfume. But how could she let Philippe kiss her so soon? He was almost a stranger! Yet stung by disbelief that she could behave in such a way, Deborah knew that she would kiss him again in an instant.

Philippe was the first to speak. 'Deborah, may I ask you something?'

'Of course.'

'You won't laugh at me?'

'I promise.'

'Do you believe in love at first sight? I know you are young but . . .'

She caught her breath. 'Yes, I do. I felt it from the first moment I saw you.' She swallowed. 'Not that I know anything about love and romance.'

'So there has been no one else?'

She shook her head. 'I'm only eighteen, and with the war there's hardly been a chance.'

She saw a shadow in his eyes. 'And fighting in France, the same goes for me.'

'Of course, it could just be infatuation,' Deborah murmured doubtfully. 'I'm sure that's what other people would call it.'

Philippe nodded. 'And it could be, I suppose.' He smiled and swung her round to face him. 'But it's going to be wonderful finding out.' Again his mouth came down to claim hers, but this kiss was different, it was more confident and his arms drew her tight against him. She moulded her body against his and returned his kiss with a passion that rose so swiftly, it left her trembling. 'You make me feel . . .'

'I hope it's the same as you make me feel.' His voice was strained. 'Deborah, you know what it is like back at the house, I cannot get near you, not properly. Now that we have found each other, we must try to find a way of spending time alone together.'

Deborah, thrilling at the words 'found each other', only knew that being with Philippe, here in the woods where she had played as a child, she felt more alive than she had ever done in her life. When they reached the picturesque lake with its beds of rushes, she stood gazing across the still water.

'How long is your leave?' Her voice was almost a whisper, she dreaded hearing the answer.

His voice was quiet. 'I have one week left.'

Only one week? 'Don't let's even think about you going back,' she told him, sudden fear sweeping over her. 'Who knows, the war could end this very weekend!'

Philippe's bleak expression as he looked down at her was one that Deborah never forgot.

Chapter Thirteen

'Did you sleep well, my lady?' Ellen put Deborah's tray on her bedside table and went to draw back the curtains.

Deborah sat up to let her maid plump her pillows against the brass bedstead and stifled a yawn. 'I did indeed, Ellen, although not before I spent some time thinking about the past.'

'I hope they were happy memories.'

Deborah felt a twist in her heart. Yes, they had been happy memories, because fortunately sleep had soon overcome her. She nodded in answer to Ellen's question.

'I know it's your half-day. Are you planning to meet John again?' The young man who had travelled in the same compartment as Ellen on the journey back from Paris was proving to be a suitor.

Ellen blushed. 'Yes, we're going to a music hall again.'

'Really? You have found him the perfect gentleman, then?' Deborah laughed. 'I've lost count of the number of suitors you've given marching orders to.'

'Yes, well I've learnt my lesson. I didn't give him a chance to be anything else.' She glanced sideways at her mistress. 'I'm sure Mr Field is. I caught sight of him when he last came. He's ever so good-looking.'

Deborah smiled. 'He is, rather. Well, I hope your music hall will be more entertaining than the play we went to see. Neither of us enjoyed it.'

'But you looked radiant when you came home.'

A smile curved Deborah's lips and she took a sip of her chocolate. 'Thank you, Ellen. It would seem that life is becoming more interesting for both of us.'

The morning at the agency was quietly productive, and the afternoon began well with another young woman leaving the office with a better future before her.

'It's satisfying, isn't it?' Deborah said to Elspeth, 'knowing that we've made a difference to someone's life.'

Elspeth managed to nod before sneezing into her swiftly produced handkerchief, and admitted that she thought she was running a temperature. Brooking no argument, Deborah insisted that she must go home immediately. 'I can finish off here.'

'I should be over it by next Tuesday, unless it develops into the flu.'

'Let's hope not.' Deborah's exclamation was heartfelt. Influenza could still lead to complications.

Deborah went to her purse. 'Make sure you take a cab. Don't worry, I'll take it from petty cash later. And take good care of yourself.'

It was later than usual by the time Deborah locked the office and went downstairs to make her way back to Grosvenor Square. It was her habit to walk along the street to the far end and, on turning into the main road, hail a cab. She was deep in thought. There had been an applicant during the morning that neither she nor Elspeth had been sure about. Yet the woman had supplied a good reference, and to refuse to help someone because of a personal reaction was surely—

A rough sweaty hand covered her mouth. An arm seized her waist and as her attacker dragged her away from the pavement and into a narrow alleyway, Deborah's panic-stricken scream was stifled. Struggling and kicking against a burly, unshaven man, he shoved her head against a wall, groping to lift her skirt. Lashing out with her foot she managed to hit his shin, only for him to slap her hard across the face. 'Bitch!' His sour breath stank of onions. He bunched up her skirt and cold night air met the skin above her silk stockings. And then to her horror came the sickening sensation of his filthy fingers probing her bare thigh. Suffused with fury she twisted and fought but was helpless against his heavy body. Despairing, uncontrollable tears began to trickle down her face, as terrified she saw him begin to fumble with his thick leather belt . . .

* * *

It had been a long day, but Evan was feeling uplifted by people's reactions as he handed them a pamphlet regarding workers' conditions. There had been some, of course, who had brushed aside his offering with scorn, but he had expected such a response. Evan had long been an accurate judge of a person's social standing. A man revealed much by his tailoring and handmade shoes, a woman by her stylish hat and jewellery. And just a few clipped patronising words were enough to rile him. What did the wealthy, the upper classes, know of the realities of life, of the hardship caused to a man when he was denied the right to earn a living wage?

Turning into the last street on his list, he hesitated, looking forward to a hot meal when he got home. Should he bother? There were only a few pamphlets left, and there were unlikely to be many sympathisers here. But not one to give up on a task, he thought that at least he could use letter boxes. It wasn't a good idea to accost someone when the light was beginning to fade. The men would then be able to tick off Bloomsbury as another area covered.

It was when he was nearing the end that he heard the sounds coming from an alley ahead. He quickened his stride, cursing what he saw, and within seconds had the assailant by the scruff of the neck and hauled him away from his unwilling victim. 'What the hell do you think you're doing?'

The man grinned showing blackened teeth. 'Lay off! Yer can go next, if yer want.'

Evan looked in disgust at the attacker's loosened trousers, praying that he'd been in time. Still securing the assailant, he turned to the young woman, who was panting, her head lowered. 'I'm sorry, miss. But he won't bother you again, I'll make sure of it.'

Slowly she raised her head, and he was gazing in stark shock at the tear-stained face that had been haunting his thoughts. Good God, Miss Claremont! Furious, Evan's fist made contact with the man's face so hard that blood spurted from his nose.

He staggered. 'I said yer could go next!'

'Shut your filthy mouth. In fact, I'll shut it for you!' Before the thug could regain his balance, Evan hit him again, splitting his lip, before kneeing him in the groin, causing him to howl and double over.

'Evan? Evan! He didn't . . .'

He turned to her. 'You mean . . . ?'

Her voice was shaking. 'You came just in time.'

Relief swept through him. 'I'll keep him here – can you try and find a constable?'

She shook her head again, her eyes dark with alarm. 'No, please . . . I don't want that.'

'But you can't . . .' He stared at her in bewilderment.

'Please, Evan.' She was pleading with him. He couldn't understand her reaction. The brute belonged behind bars.

Not about to let the assailant escape scot-free, Evan bent and grabbed him by the throat. 'Name? And don't make one up, either.' He increased the pressure, squeezing the man's throat until his eyes bulged.

He spluttered, 'Joe.'

'And the rest!' Evan shook him.

'Fallon. Joe Fallon.'

'You're lucky this time. But remember this, Fallon. I've got a mate in the constabulary, and if you come anywhere near this young lady again, I'll report you for the pervert you are. Understand?'

He could only signal with terrified eyes, his face purple.

Releasing his grip, Evan watched him draw noisy strangled breaths and mop at his bleeding face with his sleeve. 'And if I hear of any other woman being assaulted round here, you'd better have an alibi.' Evan gave him a heavy shove. 'Now clear off, scum!'

Clutching at his trousers, the man lurched away.

Deborah was hurriedly straightening her clothes, her face scarlet with mortification. 'Thank you.' Her voice shook.

'You've had a dreadful shock, Miss Claremont.' Picking up her bag and handing it to her, Evan looked at her with concern. 'I passed a tea shop not far away.'

She nodded, tearful, her legs trembling as she took his arm, and a few minutes later they were sitting in light and warmth, a waitress in white cap and apron coming forward to take their order. 'We close in half an hour.' She cast a curious glance at Deborah who realised her cloche hat was crooked. She pulled it into place.

Evan said, 'We only need a cup of tea.'

Once the waitress had gone, Deborah looked down at Evan's reddened knuckles. 'Whatever would I have done? I shall be eternally grateful to you, Mr Morgan. I can't bear to think . . .' A shudder ran through her.

'Neither can I,' he said quietly. 'And, it was Evan earlier.' He smiled at her.

Having always thought of him as Evan, her previous use of his first name had been instinctive. How stupid to remain formal after what had just happened. She managed to smile back. 'And you must call me Deborah.'

They were silent for a few moments. She realised that he was looking closely at her face. 'What's the matter?'

His voice was abrupt. 'He hit you, didn't he?'

She nodded, fighting weak tears. 'After I kicked him.' She put a hand to her face. 'Does it show?'

'It's beginning to.' He tightened his lips. 'Had you ever seen the brute before? And if you don't mind my asking, why ever didn't you want him arrested?'

The waitress was bringing their tea, and Deborah waited until she'd gone before answering. 'No, to the first question. And the second? I have my reasons, Evan.' She was unable to explain that the constabulary would want to know her address, and once her true identity was revealed, their enquiries could lead to her connection with the staff agency. She wasn't prepared to take that risk. Deborah was only hoping that Evan's rough treatment and his threats would prevent her assailant from attacking anyone else. She felt colour rise in her cheeks. 'I'm sorry but I can't explain, it's too personal.' She studied his expression, anxious that he hadn't taken offence.

He stared at her for a moment and then picked up the

teapot. 'I'll pour, your hands aren't quite steady yet – not surprising after such an ordeal. And take plenty of sugar, that's what my Aunt Bronwen would advise.'

Deborah obeyed, grateful for the hot sweet liquid. 'Aunt Bronwen?'

'She brought me up. I never knew my mother, she died when I was born, and Da died in a pit accident a few years later.'

'I'm so sorry, Evan, that is really hard.' Trying to push her dreadful ordeal out of her mind, she said. 'We're both orphans, then, because I lost both of my parents in the Spanish flu outbreak. Although I was luckier than you, at least I had my mother and father for eighteen years.'

They continued to drink their tea, and she guessed that after what happened he too was grateful for it.

'Would you like another cup?' he asked.

'No, thank you. I'm beginning to feel a little better now. Tell me, how did you happen to be in the area? And thank goodness you were.'

'Part of our campaign for workers' rights is to try and leaflet as many areas as we can. I was finishing off Bloomsbury,' he explained. 'I've just remembered that I threw the rest to the ground when I saw what was happening.'

The waitress came and pointedly placed the bill before Evan, who dug in his pocket for a coin. He drained his cup. 'She'll be wanting to close, and I'm sure you will be wanting to get home, so . . .'

She nodded, and they both rose to leave. The tea shop

doorbell tinkled as they went out, the air feeling chilly after the inside warmth. Still feeling shaken and seeing in the distance a cab approaching, Deborah turned and said, 'I'm hoping the driver is looking for a fare. The sooner I get home, the better. I shall be always in your debt, Evan.'

'No decent man could have walked by. I didn't even realise it was you.' He paused. 'I'm glad we've met again, Deborah.'

'So am I, although I could have wished it to be in different circumstances.'

'I have to agree.' He smiled at her. 'Are you often in this area?'

She hesitated, on the edge of exhaustion. 'I work at the Bloomsbury Staff Agency.'

He gave a thoughtful nod and hailed the cab. 'I'd better go back and collect up those pamphlets, they're paid for out of union funds.'

'Goodbye, Evan, and again my eternal thanks.'

Smiling, he touched the peak of his cap and she watched him begin to retrace his steps.

'Where to?' Muffled in a grey scarf, the driver leant out of the window.

Never before had Deborah been so glad to say 'Grosvenor Square'.

Thankful that it was Ellen's official half-day, Deborah let herself into the house relieved to find the hall deserted. Swiftly she went up the broad staircase to reach the refuge of her own rooms. And it was only as she closed the door behind her, that at last the long-threatened tears came. Tearing off all her clothes and leaving them in a heap on the floor she hurried to the bathroom, turned on the taps, seized a glass jar and tipped rose-scented salts into the water before looking in the mirror. Evan had been right. Her cheek was reddening and hurt when she touched it. So even if she'd felt up to it, there was no way she was going down to dinner to face probing questions. Hardly waiting before the bath was full before climbing in, she began to scrub furiously at her inner thighs with a flannel. The very thought of that disgusting man touching her bare skin made her feel sick. And the odour from his hand against her mouth . . . she inhaled the perfume of the salts, leant to turn off the taps and sank down to soak. And when fifteen minutes later she stepped out to dry herself with a large fluffy towel, her thoughts were of her rescuer, because even though she fought against admitting it, the truth was that she was disturbingly attracted to him.

Clad in a pink velvet dressing gown and swansdown slippers, Deborah muttered, 'What I need is a stiff drink.' Hoping a maid had attended to the fire, she went to find the brandy she kept in a corner cupboard in her sitting room, only to be greeted by a display of hothouse flowers. Guessing who they were from, Deborah's lips relaxed into a smile even before reading the card. *Shall we dance the night away tomorrow?* Beneath the message was a telephone number. Theo had indeed not left it too long.

Whereas I, she thought with anger and dismay, will probably have to make him wait. She would have to see if her face was marked in the morning. She had already decided not to tell anyone, even Ellen, about what had happened. Although reason told her that it hadn't been her fault, it didn't prevent her from feeling ashamed. And however could she explain not fetching the constabulary, especially as that man was a danger to other women?

Chapter Fourteen

The following morning in the breakfast room, Gerard helped himself to a generous serving of kedgeree from the sideboard and returned to the table to frown at Deborah's vacant place. 'You say that she had a tray in her room last night?'

Julia, enjoying her scrambled eggs, nodded.

'It's most unlike my sister to miss her breakfast.' He settled himself in his chair. 'She must be unwell.'

Julia smiled at him. 'I must say it's rather cosy, having breakfast on our own.'

About to lift a fork of kedgeree, Gerard met Julia's coquettish gaze and smiled at the sight of her fresh complexion, her soft blue eyes. His young wife spared no effort to please him, and she was most indulgent in the bedroom. The only problem was that as yet there was no sign of a pregnancy. They had been married almost a year now. Surely enough time for the prospect of an heir. 'Yes, it is.' After finishing his breakfast he began to unfold his newspaper.

'Of course, if Deborah were to marry, it would be like this every morning,' Julia murmured. 'Not that I mind her presence, of course.'

Gerard was scanning the headlines in *The Times*. He glanced sharply at her. 'There isn't any sign of her marrying, surely?'

'Well, according to Maria, more flowers arrived yesterday.'

'How is your new maid settling in? I hope she's not a gossip.' Gerard had an acute dislike of what he called tittle-tattle among the servants.

'I'm afraid she does seem to be, although that can be useful at times. To know what is going on downstairs, I mean.'

'It's downstairs talking about what is going on upstairs that bothers me. Keep an eye on her, Julia.'

'Of course, darling.' She took a sip of her Earl Grey tea. 'I expect the flowers were from Theodore Field.'

'You're not intimating that he is serious?'

'He could be. It might be early days, but a woman can sense these things. Gerard, I have often wondered why Deborah remains single. I mean, I know she grieved after losing her young Frenchman, but since then surely she's had opportunities?'

'Of course. The sister of the Earl of Anscombe would always attract suitors.'

'Darling, she is also very attractive. Wasn't there anyone she was interested in?'

'Not when it came to the question of marriage.' Gerard's tone had a note of finality and he immersed himself once more in his paper.

But later, in his study he became thoughtful. Field not only sat in the House of Commons but was viewed as someone who could eventually hold office. A member of the Cabinet could only add prestige to the family. But surely Julia was reading far too much into what would probably be a short-lived dalliance. With regard to actual marriage . . . that was a far different matter. A proposal, if indeed it came, would resurrect a source of conflict between them. When another peer of the realm had appealed to him, Gerard, keen to have another title in the family, had tried to persuade his sister to accept the aristocrat. Deborah had listened to his advice, disagreed with his opinion, then turned down the proposal. Her intransigence on the subject had left him infuriated. If Field did indeed propose marriage . . . the same situation could possibly arise again. And then Gerard gave a shrug. He was taking Julia's fanciful idea far too seriously.

He began to search in a drawer for a communication from his agent at Anscombe Hall, recalling that it had mentioned a matter that needed his urgent attention. On taking out the file, Gerard saw the cheap envelope from the woman called Annie Jones, reminding him of how real the risk of a scandal had been. A revelation that if it became widely known would undoubtedly besmirch his family's good name. He scanned the few lines again with a frown. All these years later, would he ever be free from that bastard? He could only thank God that the threat of discovery had been avoided, even if the matter had cost him dearly and would continue to do so. But Gerard found it reassuring that in Freddie Seymour he had found the ideal fellow conspirator, a man who had much to lose if he reneged in any way on their bargain. Gerard, replacing the thin sheet of paper in its envelope, tucked it further down inside the drawer. His priority now was to ascertain whether he could avoid replacing the leaking roof on a tenant's cottage. Yet more expense.

Deborah had hardly slept, unable to forget her attacker's rough touch, his foul breath, knowing that she had only just escaped rape. He could even have slit her throat. And fear was building within her. Evan wouldn't be there the next time. If this could happen once, why not again? Was she exposing herself to danger every time she walked the streets of London? She tossed and turned, plagued with doubts as to whether she should tell Ellen, even Elspeth, what had happened. The attack had devastated her, and Deborah was beginning to long for the comfort of another woman's sympathy, her reassurance. But wouldn't that be selfish? Wouldn't it take away their confidence, their self-reliance? As working women, they needed to feel independent, not vulnerable because of their sex. She couldn't take that sense of freedom away from them.

And so she had made a determined vow of silence, and was now sitting up in bed, a lacy bedjacket around her shoulders, a hand mirror by her side, and a despondent heart. She had awoken with the hope that the red mark on her face would have faded. But to her dismay her reflection showed a swelling over her cheekbone and the beginnings of a large bruise. And so she was forced to fabricate a lie.

'That clumsy oaf should be reported.' Ellen was furious about the carelessness of the delivery man at the agency. 'Fancy carrying a huge box and not looking where you're going.'

'We just collided,' Deborah explained, unable to meet her maid's eyes. 'It was an accident, not anyone's fault, really.'

'I'll fetch you some witch hazel.'

'To tell the truth, I'm not feeling very well, either. I hope I'm not starting a cold.'

'You'd best stay where you are, my lady. And you've not had a bite of breakfast. Are you sure you don't want me to ask Cook for a nice boiled egg and soldiers?'

Deborah managed a smile. 'You make it sound like the nursery. I don't really feel like anything to eat. Perhaps another hot chocolate? And please don't mention my poor face to anyone else. Promise me, Ellen.'

She gave a vigorous nod. 'You can count on me.'

After she'd gone, Deborah thought about Theo and his lovely flowers. Now she wouldn't be able to see him that evening, dance with him, even though she was longing to. Not only did she look a fright, she simply didn't feel up to it. All she wanted to do was to pull the bedclothes over her head and shelter beneath them. She was ashamed to be in such a pathetic state. And suppose Evan had been a few seconds later and witnessed her actually being raped. Deborah's face flooded with heat at the thought of such a humiliating and sickening scene. She couldn't help wondering whether she would have suffered the assault had she been unmistakably an aristocrat. Would her expensive clothes have protected her, made him hesitate? Were working women, even respectably dressed ones as she had been, often subjected to such appalling ordeals? Did they report it to the constabulary, were they believed? The questions whirled in her mind until she realised that she was filling herself with panic. Taking a deep, ragged breath, she straightened her shoulders. She had too much pride to allow a thug like Joe Fallon to turn her into a nervous wreck.

As soon as Ellen returned, Deborah gave her instructions for Julia's new maid. 'Please could you ask that the Countess telephone Mr Field. His number is on the card that came with the flowers. A message to say that I am suffering a cold and will be in touch once I've recovered.' She paused. 'Actually, I may well have caught one from Elspeth.'

'I hope not. But you do look rather flushed. Would you like some aspirin?'

'Thank you, Ellen. Perhaps I will.'

Deborah didn't develop the imagined cold, but still remained in her rooms for the next few days, waiting until the bruise had faded enough to be disguised by cosmetics. At her request, a somewhat bemused Ellen smuggled in the latest issue of the *Workers' Weekly*, and Deborah pored over the articles, fascinated to read Evan mentioned as one of their most fluent speakers. But that didn't mean she neglected to read both the *Daily Telegraph* and *The Times*.

She also used her enforced leisure time to catch up on correspondence, and was delighted to receive an almost immediate reply to her letter from Abigail.

Debs, my friend,

As always, lovely to hear from you. In Scotland, we are so looking forward to the spring. It has seemed such a long and bitterly cold winter. And here, too, much of the talk is of the threatened general strike. You and I are of like minds about this, and I'm proud of you, actually going to one of the union meetings. If I had been in London, I would have come with you. But I'm afraid there are heated arguments in the family about the issue, especially with regard to my father-in-law, who being both a landowner and someone with shares in industry, has polar views from my own. Angus, of course, during the war, came to know many soldiers from working-class backgrounds, and that's given him a more balanced view. So at least there are no marital spats on the subject.

I like the sound of this Theo, and do hope that he might be the one to change your single status! Who would have thought when we were young that I would now have twins, while you are still fancy-free. But perhaps no longer? You see how well I know you, I can read between the lines.

The remainder of the letter detailed the children's progress, and a proposed date when she and Angus planned to bring them to visit their grandparents in Berkshire.

Deborah set the letter aside with a wry smile. What would Abigail have written had she known that her friend had only just escaped the 'fate worse than death'. However, her nerves were becoming calmer. What she needed now was to continue trying to erase the ugly images in her mind. Wasn't she safe now, comfortable in her own home?

And perhaps her first step should be to go downstairs for luncheon today. After that, she was determined to resume her normal routine. But she had made one crucial decision. Taking care not to reveal this address, surely it must be possible to arrange for a regular cab to take her to and from the agency itself. Deborah wanted never to walk by that repulsive alley ever again.

Chapter Fifteen

When at last Deborah saw Theo again, he entered the drawing room bringing with him not only a sense of normality, but in a way, a breath of fresh air. She hadn't once left the house since what she thought of as the 'ugly incident'. Neither had she attended a recent dinner party given by Gerard and Julia, pleading fatigue after her cold. In reality, Deborah hadn't been ready to face people, especially the inane chatter that usually characterised such gatherings.

But tonight would change everything. Surely being with Theo in an atmosphere of frivolity and music would restore her confidence? She gave him a warm, welcoming smile.

Gerard said, 'Good evening, Field. I must say that you're a devil for punishment.'

Theo laughed. 'I'm hoping that Deborah likes jazz, as I promised to take her dancing.'

'Are you sure that's a good idea?' Gerard frowned. 'After all, she has been unwell.'

'But you must admit that I've made a full recovery,' Deborah said swiftly. 'And yes, Theo, I love jazz.'

'So do I,' Julia said. 'But unfortunately, Gerard hates it, don't you darling?'

'It's not English. In fact I consider it quite uncivilised.'

'Ah well, we all have our different tastes.' Theo took a dry sherry from the tray Fulton offered and smiled at the urbane butler. 'Thank you, you have an excellent memory.' He turned to Deborah. 'Might I suggest that you wrap up warmly when we leave, a frost is forecast.'

'Yes, please be careful, Deborah,' Julia said.

Deborah smiled at them. 'Thank you for your concern, but there's no need to worry as I shall wrap up.'

'And I shall bring her home at a respectable time.' Theo glanced at Gerard. 'You seem very thoughtful. Surely you don't disapprove of Deborah enjoying jazz?'

'My sister tends to disregard my advice, I'm afraid.'

Deborah ignored him, growing impatient to leave.

'I wish,' she murmured to Theo as they left the house, 'that we didn't have to go through that social charade every time you come to collect me.'

'I could always ring the bell and stand on the doorstep!' He took her hand, swinging it as they walked to his car. 'I've missed you, Lady Deborah.'

She smiled up at him. 'And I have missed you, Mr Field.'

On arriving at the Savoy Hotel, after Deborah had checked in her fur coat, they dined in the Grill, and then strolled to the ballroom and into the swing of the 'St Louis Blues'. Shown to a table a little distance from the band, Deborah flashed Theo a grateful smile. 'This is perfect, an excellent choice.'

'Well, I did consider somewhere with light music.' He smiled at her. 'But I thought a jazz band would get your circulation going after your cold.'

She laughed. 'I didn't know you were a medical man. Oh look, there's Penelope Carstairs. Do you know her, she's the one in blue and silver?'

He glanced towards the dance floor. 'I've not had that privilege. She's a good dancer, though.'

'You haven't seen me!'

'Then there's no time like the present. I think the band is just finishing this number. Are you game for the next?'

To Deborah's joy, the musicians struck up her favourite Charleston, and as Theo led her on to the dance floor, her spirits were already rising. Smiling at him as they began to kick their legs, Deborah, her skirt flaring, felt exhilarated by the fast beat and the heightened atmosphere. Theo was a revelation, lithe in his movements, his steps matching her own, and they were laughing by the time the dance ended, and made their way back to almost collapse at the table.

'Wonderful, even if I am out of breath,' Theo said.

Their champagne had arrived and a waiter moved forward to fill their glasses.

'So, how did I compare with Penelope?'

He smiled. 'No contest!'

'You're no mean performer yourself.'

'I expect you thought all MPs were solemn and boring?'

She laughed. 'Just a little, but you're different, Theo.'

'And on what do you base your judgement?'

'I've met several in my time. But none that were willing to discuss politics, at least not with a woman.'

'You know my views on that matter.'

She sipped her champagne and said quietly, 'Yes I do, and appreciate them.'

He gazed at her. 'That dress suits you, I rather like you in red.'

She looked down at the silk dress with its dropped pleated skirt. 'I'm not sure whether I should have worn these long crystal beads with it, I look like a present left over from Christmas.'

He laughed. 'I'm not falling for that one. It would make me sound like someone in a Victorian melodrama.'

Mystified, she stared at him.

He leant forward and twirled an imaginary moustache. 'I would love to have you in my Christmas stocking, my dear.'

Deborah began to giggle helplessly. 'I didn't mean . . .'

'I know you didn't. But you really do look fetching.'

'Now you make me sound like a chorus girl.' She raised her eyebrows. 'What is it about MPs and chorus girls?'

Theo chuckled. 'Time, I think, for us to dance?'

Again they took to the floor, this time to 'Bye, Bye, Blackbird', and after taking Deborah back to their table, Theo excused himself and went over to speak to the bandleader.

'I just wanted to congratulate him,' he said on his return. 'They play well. I was lucky enough to see the Southern Syncopated Orchestra when they brought the jazz scene to London. Although I'm afraid black musicians didn't always receive a warm welcome.'

Deborah frowned. 'I seem to remember there was some sort of tragedy.'

He nodded. 'There was a collision between ships when the band was touring and several of the players were lost at sea.'

'But jazz lives on,' Deborah said.

Theo refilled her glass before gazing at her. 'And so does life. This is probably neither the time nor place to ask, but why during all these years, have you never married, Deborah? Your hand must have been sought many times.'

She hesitated. 'There has never been quite the right person, not since Philippe. And you? Is there a specific reason why you are still a bachelor?'

A shadow passed over his face. 'I too suffered a tragedy when I was younger. I was very much in love, engaged to be married and thought my future was safely planned.' He looked across at her. 'I think you and Marina would have liked each other. She often expressed concern about the lack of social justice in this country.'

Deborah said quietly, 'What happened?'

'She was passionate about riding and a fine horsewoman.' He paused a moment before continuing. 'But something must have happened to spook the stallion she was riding. She was found thrown with a broken neck.'

Deborah could see the pain in his eyes. 'I'm so terribly sorry.'

His smile was bleak. 'Her parents were devastated, as I was.'

After a short silence, Deborah gently probed, 'And afterwards?'

'Afterwards? Well, I wasn't interested for a while, and then the war came along.' He shrugged. 'And since then, I have refused to marry for the sake of my career, as people tend to put it. It's no use the voters preferring a man with a wife, if that wife isn't the right one.'

'That makes perfect sense.' Deborah was leaning forward to hear better, as the band struck up again. 'I'm afraid we've chosen a noisy spot to have this conversation.'

'But that is how the best discussions arise, spontaneously, don't you think?'

She smiled. 'I think you're right.'

He rose from his chair and held out his hand. 'Time to dance again, I think. But maybe after this, the next will be a slow one. Can you guess what I'm thinking?'

Deborah smiled up at him. 'That you are longing to hold me in your arms?'

He laughed. 'You are delightful, do you know that?'

The following number was indeed a dreamy blues one, when Theo drew her close, his arm firm around her waist. They began to waltz cheek to cheek and she nestled against him, loving the feeling of warmth, security, and the unmistakable physical attraction between them. It gave her the reassurance she needed. This was her life, her real world. And what had recently happened had no part in it.

Meanwhile, in the small house in Greenwich, Evan was having an argument. 'I'm not sponging off you, and that's an end to it.'

'And who says you're doing such a thing?'

'Aunt Bronwen, I've told you. I still have a few pounds in the Post Office. I can pay you board even if you won't take any rent.'

'Of course I won't take any rent. Didn't my George leave me the house? And if I choose to have my nephew living with me, that's my business. As for your food, don't you chop wood to light the fire, bring in the coal to keep it going? Not to mention the decorating you've done. Nor are you too proud to help me with the dishes. Leave it, boyo, having your company is worth far more to me than money.'

She was facing up to him like a bantam hen, Evan thought, looking at her indignant face. She may have grey hair but age hadn't dimmed her determined nature. He capitulated. 'Well, all right. But only until I get another job.'

She nodded, triumphant. 'You concentrate on getting all these other chaps a decent wage. You're doing God's work, Evan Morgan, and I'm proud of you.'

150

'If your God was a just one, there'd be no need for a general strike.'

'Don't blaspheme! Isn't it shame enough that you no longer go to Chapel? And haven't we got God to thank for you not being sent to that hellhole that was the trenches?'

'I was just too young. If it had lasted another year . . .' And where was this God of yours during all that terrible slaughter, Evan thought? But he knew better than to continue the debate. His Aunt Bronwen was devoted to her Chapel attendances, and Evan had come to believe that Karl Marx had been right. It was true that religion was the opium of the people. It was certainly the case that those struggling with poverty and hardship found comfort in faith in a higher being. But, for Evan, there was too much injustice in the world for him to be able to sustain such a belief.

He smiled at her. 'Come on, Aunt Bron, just because I want to support the union, there's no reason why I shouldn't work for a living. In fact,' he hesitated, wondering whether to mention it, then decided to be truthful. 'When I was leafleting in Bloomsbury, I noticed a staff agency. I doubt there will be any jobs for engineers, but I thought I'd give it a try.' Evan hated being unemployed, it was an affront to his masculinity, a waste of all the skill and knowledge he'd acquired.

But Bronwen was scathing. 'They'll probably offer you a job as a servant. How would you feel about that – waiting on your so-called betters?'

'It didn't say domestic staff agency. I write a good hand,

can handle men, have an analytical brain. They might be able to offer me something.'

He didn't mention that there was a certain young lady who worked there. One that he was keen to see again. Deborah had been much on Evan's mind since he'd rescued her. Had she been badly affected by it? Even now he had an inward shudder when he thought of how far the thug had been planning to go. And for Evan to be offered the chance to despoil her further as if she was a piece of meat! The man needed to be locked up. He was still puzzled why Deborah had become agitated when prosecution was mentioned, begging Evan not to report the crime.

He glanced at Bronwen, who was counting the stitches on her knitting needles. Maybe she could explain a woman's mind. But then he rejected the idea. Once she knew that there was a single young lady involved, he wouldn't get a moment of peace. Evan was well aware of her wish for him to marry, to provide her with a great-niece or -nephew. Once he was gainfully employed. Although it was obvious that Deborah came from a different class, higher than his own. Had her family fallen on hard times? Was that why she was employed at this agency, because of a need to supplement their income? Whatever the reason, he had to admit that he found her very attractive. But whether she would be interested in a man like himself was open to question.

Chapter Sixteen

At the Savoy, Deborah was protesting that she felt not the slightest bit tired, but Theo was adamant. 'I promised Gerard to bring you home at a reasonable hour.'

She knew he was being sensible, but that didn't prevent her feeling resentful that once more, even if only in a subtle way, her brother was controlling her life. When she returned from the cloakroom with her coat, Theo was standing near the door, and yet again she realised what a striking man he was, so stylish in his dark overcoat with a white silk scarf casually around his neck. She imagined he would be an imposing figure when he stood to speak in the House of Commons. He was smoking, a habit she herself had so far managed to avoid, although she knew that many women felt that a long cigarette-holder added to their air of sophistication.

Theo turned, saw her and smiled, then minutes later they were in his Bentley and driving back to Grosvenor Square where he parked a few yards away from the house.

He switched off the engine and for a moment there was silence, then with one accord they turned to each other and she was in his arms, his mouth seeking hers, their kisses deepening and his lips moved to the warm hollow of her throat. With a groan he drew away. 'This is hardly ideal, a parked car in public.'

'I know.'

Theo opened the door and came round to help her out of the passenger seat. 'We must try to find a way of spending time alone together.'

Deborah felt her throat close with emotion. Within seconds she was turning her key in the front door, and she could only lift her hand in a goodnight gesture as he returned to the car and drove away. With a mind in turmoil she slowly climbed the stairs to her bedroom. Those words, those evocative words . . .

1918

'*We must try to find a way of spending time alone together.*' Philippe had repeated the words again as they walked back to join the rest of the weekend house party.

'I'll think of something, leave it to me,' she said, giving his hand a squeeze before releasing it as they turned away from the wood into the main drive. 'We must be circumspect from now on, and not raise any suspicions.' As they went into the house, she said, 'So, Lieutenant Lapierre, I hope you found our talk interesting.'

'I am always pleased to learn more of your country's history.' He turned to her with a slight bow. 'Now, Lady Deborah, if you would excuse me, I have a letter to write.'

'Of course.' She turned to go upstairs seeking Abigail, when Gerard came into the hall.

'Did I see you come in with Lapierre?'

'You did. Mama asked me to tell him about the history of the estate.'

'And you wandered off with him on your own?'

'Abigail was coming, but she's suffering with a dreadful headache.' She looked coolly at him. 'Honestly, Gerard, I was in the company of a brave soldier, one fighting alongside our own forces, not someone likely to assault me.'

'I don't doubt his honour,' he snapped. 'It's just that I think your behaviour doesn't always fit your station in life. More decorum is needed, Deborah, I have told you that before.'

'And I, Gerard, have told you that this is not the Victorian age.' She watched him stalk off and then ran upstairs to find her friend.

Abigail was looking through her wardrobe.

'How's your headache?'

The other girl laughed. 'Miraculously disappeared.' She went to sit on the green-velvet ottoman beneath her window. 'Come on, then, tell me all about it. Every little detail, mind.'

Deborah took off her hat and gave her hair a shake. Then

155

going to sit on a bedside chair, felt her colour rise. 'He's wonderful, Abby. I think I'm in love. No,' she corrected herself, 'I know I am, head over heels, in fact.'

'It's a bit quick, Debs.' Abigail frowned. 'A pash, yes, but love's a big word.'

'I know, but Philippe feels the same. It was love at first sight, for both of us.'

'I must admit that you look absolutely radiant. I'm jealous to death.' She hesitated. 'Are you absolutely sure? I mean, you hardly know each other.'

Deborah bit her lip. 'We just need more time together. I was wondering, do you think you could help?'

'How do you mean?'

'He'll be leaving tomorrow morning, along with the other guests, even though he's got another week's leave. But I can just imagine Mama's face if I ask her if he can stay on, especially if I tell her what I've just told you. If she did agree, which I doubt, she'd make sure we were never alone together. And it isn't infatuation, Abby, it really isn't. Philippe makes me feel so alive, and . . .'

'Deborah Claremont, you've let him kiss you!'

'Abby, if it wasn't for the war, we would have been debutantes. I'm sure we'd have allowed likely suitors at least a kiss.'

Abigail began to laugh. 'I know I would have done, if only to experiment.'

'There you are, then. Anyway, I couldn't help myself. But you can see our problem.'

There was a short silence, then Abigail's expression changed to one of concern. 'Have you thought about this, Debs? Who knows how long this war will last? Aren't you lining yourself up for heartbreak if . . .'

'If Philippe is killed, you mean?'

'If not that, we've both seen first-hand how terrible the injuries can be.'

Deborah stared at her. 'Are you saying that if you fell head over heels in love with an officer, and he with you, that you'd reject him, send him back to the trenches without even a hope?'

Abigail looked embarrassed. 'I don't know, Debs.'

'That's because you've never felt like this, at least not yet. You'll understand when it happens to you. I can't describe it, I only know that I want to spend every minute with him. But how to manage it?' Deborah paused. 'That's why I'm appealing to you, Abby. You couldn't invite me to come to Tedlington Manor for this coming week? Say you think I've been looking pale or something and need a change of scenery?'

'And . . . ?'

'Well, your estate adjoins Jeremy's, where Philippe is staying. Your parents wouldn't think it odd if they came over to visit. Perhaps on a pretext of cheering up some of your wounded soldiers.'

'I can't imagine that Jeremy would find that an attractive prospect. He's on leave to get away from the front, not to be reminded of it.'

Deborah felt ashamed. 'I know, and you're right of course. I'm being selfish.'

'I'm not unsympathetic, Debs, honestly. I'll telephone Mama this afternoon. You ask yours if you can have a break from your hospital duties. I'm sure between us we'll be able to come up with some ideas.' Then her face lit up. 'I know, neither of us are brilliant at languages – I could point out that we could take advantage of French conversation. Papa would approve of that.'

'And we could also meet them elsewhere as well.' Deborah's mind was racing ahead. 'I'm sure Philippe will ride. And maybe you and I could go on an outing.' Then her spirits fell. 'But how about Jeremy, we can't just assume that he'll fall in with our plan.'

'You leave Jeremy to me.' Abigail grinned. 'I know we've always thought him boring, and he's not blessed with good looks, poor boy, but haven't you noticed how he becomes tongue-tied every time he's near me? He'll jump at the chance.'

The plan had worked out so well that Deborah was amazed that it had been so easy.

And she hadn't been completely untruthful to her parents: Abigail's mother had indeed invited her for a week-long visit. Besides, she tried to justify her action, what was the point of Philippe being several miles away from her, wasting time they could have spent together? Deborah determined to confine the possibility of his being killed or maimed to a small, hidden place in her heart, but it wasn't easy. Surely

God couldn't be so cruel? Not when she and Philippe had only just found each other.

Abigail's home was set in spacious grounds, surrounded by woodland, and with several tenant farms. Although large, the house itself didn't have the gracious design of Anscombe Hall, but her parents, quiet, sober people, little given to large-scale entertaining, had always made Deborah welcome even as a child, and she was enormously fond of them. Their warm smiles greeted her just before luncheon on Monday. Apart from outwitting Gerard, she wasn't used to deceit so couldn't help feeling uncomfortable, but reassured herself that it wasn't as if she and Philippe were planning to do anything wrong. Just spend blissful moments with each other. Anyway, everything was different when there was a war on.

'I cannot bear the thought of leaving you tomorrow.' Philippe's arms held Deborah more tightly. They were curled up on a couch in the summer house. It was cold in there after the winter, and she suspected slightly damp but was too wary of arousing suspicion to light the small oil heater. At least, she thought, when he comes to England again, the weather will be warm, with blue skies and sunshine. And she was convinced that by then her parents, knowing that letters were being exchanged, would make Philippe welcome at Anscombe Hall. And there would be no need for this endless deception, even though her mother wouldn't be as lax as Abigail's, who seemed to believe in leaving 'the young people' to their own devices. Deborah, grateful for his complicity, had developed a new respect for bookish Jeremy, who had been a staunch support, while even Abby admitted that he had hidden depths. And the week had been a wonderful one. She and Philippe had been able to spend hours together, walking, talking, sharing their hopes and dreams. And, of course, finding nooks and crannies where, unseen and undisturbed, they could spend time in each other's arms.

'I shall write to you often,' she promised.

'And I too, as often as I am able.'

She gazed up at him. 'Do you remember how you said it would be fun finding out whether it was merely infatuation we felt for each other?'

He laughed. 'I do.'

'And? Has it been fun?' She began to tickle him.

'*Mais non*, stop it!' He looked down at her, suddenly serious, and lifted her chin.

'Deborah, I cannot wait for us to be married. You want that too?'

She smiled up at him. 'You know I do.'

'Then when I next come to England, we shall get engaged?'

She nodded. 'I shall persuade my parents, while you are away.'

Philippe lowered his lips to her hand and kissed it. 'And I shall request this from your papa.' He gazed into her eyes. 'Do you know how much I want to lie with you, *mon ange*? Really know?'

'I know how much I want you to, but . . .'

160

He placed a finger over her lips. 'I too, feel the "but". And I would never do anything to harm you.' He glanced at his watch. 'I think we must return to the house.'

'One last kiss before we join the others?' She rose from the couch.

He stood up to join her, taking her into his arms. 'Let us say *au revoir*, not goodbye,' he whispered, and a few minutes later they left the summer house and began to walk decorously back for afternoon tea.

It sounds so normal, so English, Deborah thought. And yet she could hardly bear the thought that tomorrow, on their reluctant return to France, not only Philippe, but Jeremy and Gerard would be facing war and bloodshed. And after helping to nurse injured soldiers she had a clear image in her mind of the unspeakable horrors of the trenches.

Deborah stared ahead and spoke quietly. 'You come back to me, do you hear?'

Chapter Seventeen

Deborah awoke the following morning, with a feeling of unutterable sadness. It was why she tried to lock away the memories, the joy that had been so swiftly followed by grief. She had never sought to replace Philippe in her heart, that would be impossible. Yet she had never been able to accept, like so many women of her generation who had lost men they loved, that her future would be one without hope.

With determination, she dismissed her nostalgic mood and submitted to Ellen's ministrations. 'And how are things with you and John?' she asked as Ellen fastened a single strand of pearls around her neck.

'Very well, my lady.' Ellen grinned. 'We've got to the kissing stage.'

Deborah began to laugh, trying to imagine her mother's expression if her own maid had made such a statement. 'That's exciting then, isn't it?'

Ellen gave a vigorous nod. 'Though I'm going to ask him to shave off his moustache.'

'That is a huge demand, Ellen.' Deborah's tone was teasing.

'Maybe, but who likes a prickly kiss?'

'A large number of the female population, it would seem; unless they have no choice. You'll be treading on sensitive ground, you know.'

Ellen tossed her head. 'Maybe, but at least I can try.'

Deborah got up from her dressing stool and, from Ellen's proffered selection, chose a crisp white blouse. 'The navy skirt, I think, Ellen.'

'It's cold, my lady. I think you should wear a warm camisole.'

'Then I will. The heating in the office can be erratic at times.'

She smiled to herself when after breakfast she left the house, warmly wrapped up in a plain navy wool coat and red cashmere scarf. And as it was so cold, she was glad that her cab, now on regular order, was waiting for her round the corner. Deborah found no difficulty in being punctual in her habits, and always left home within five minutes of her planned time.

On the journey, she gazed out of the window at the now familiar sight of small groups of men, even at this early hour, either huddled against walls, or standing around a lamp post. One didn't have to try hard to imagine their conversation. We are hurtling towards a massive strike, she thought, and the government doesn't seem to care. It was obvious the working men had right on their side, so where was the English sense of fair play? Evan would say it was buried beneath employers' greed.

Deborah was still in a reflective mood when, an hour later, Elspeth appeared at her office door, her cheeks flushed. 'I have Mrs Tideswell, the housekeeper from Foxhole Villa on the telephone. She insists on speaking to you.'

Deborah gave a heavy sigh. 'Oh dear, that means trouble. You'd better put her through.'

Several minutes later, she slammed down the receiver and went into the outer office. 'That woman is an absolute bitch! I'm sorry, Elspeth, but she really is. There was nothing wrong with the young woman we sent there. Amy Vernon – do you remember her?'

'Wasn't she a dark-haired girl with freckles?'

'That's right. Well, according to Mrs Tideswell, Amy is impertinent. She's going to have to dismiss her. And is now demanding a better replacement.'

Elspeth frowned. 'Hasn't this happened before – with this particular housekeeper?'

'It most certainly has. And her tone on the telephone was most unpleasant.' Deborah bit her lip. 'I'm inclined to refuse to send anyone else, but I suspect that she's the sort of person who would delight in doing us harm.'

'What about Doris Laverton? She's due to come back tomorrow morning. We had her down for the Hammersmith position.'

Deborah considered. 'She's older, certainly. Maybe Mrs Tideswell resents the young, pretty ones? Doris seemed sensible too. Yes, Elspeth, a good idea.'

'And the Hammersmith position? I know they said it wasn't urgent, but . . .'

'I fully expect Amy to come back to us. She could be just the answer.'

Deborah, returning to her own office, tried to calm down. Not a good start to the day, and she really shouldn't let people ruffle her like that.

Evan, after making his way to Bloomsbury, had been unable to pass the alley in the street leading to the agency without the memory surfacing of that awful day when he'd witnessed Deborah being assaulted. But now, after glancing at the words on the shining brass plate by the front door, he began with some trepidation to climb the steps to the first floor. It wasn't the fact that he was applying for a job that caused his misgivings, but whether Deborah would regard his coming to her place of work as an intrusion. And so it was with relief tinged with disappointment when he found himself greeted by a brown-haired, middle-aged woman.

'Good morning,' Evan said, 'I wondered whether you have any vacancies for someone like myself? I am an engineer by profession, but am willing to consider other positions.'

The woman's smile was a warm one. 'Shall we get you registered first, and then your form will help me to check our files.' She handed him a clipboard, passed over a fountain pen, and indicated a small table with a chair before it.

'Thank you.' Glancing around he noticed another door. Perhaps Deborah could be in there? He sat at the desk, and began to answer the questions on the two pages. Some were straightforward, others required more thought and during the next ten minutes the silence was disturbed only by the ticking of a round mahogany clock on the wall, until the telephone rang.

'Bloomsbury Staff Agency.' A short silence. 'One moment please, I'll transfer you to Miss Claremont.'

Evan tensed. So, Deborah *was* here. Adrenalin rushed through him at the thought of seeing her again, and as soon as the form was completed, he took it over.

'Thank you, Mr Morgan, please sit down.'

Evan studied her expression as she read through his answers.

She looked up. 'We will certainly do our best to find you a post, you have much to offer. But as you know, the employment situation is extremely difficult at the moment. And I have to confess, that the majority of our clients look for domestic work.'

'As I said, I'm willing to consider anything.'

She smiled at him. 'My name is Mrs Reid, I'm Miss Claremont's assistant. She is on the telephone at the moment, and afterwards I'll take in your application form.'

Evan stared at her. He had never expected Deborah to be in a senior position here. It was even more puzzling when the older Mrs Reid seemed so capable. He frowned.

Did that mean that Deborah could have helped him

before in finding employment? And if so, why hadn't she told him? Could it mean that knowing of his union affiliation, she'd thought he would be a risk to the agency? After all, such a business would need to protect its reputation. And Evan knew only too well that employers, especially during the crucial unrest in the country, regarded men such as himself with suspicion. When he thought back, he realised that Deborah had revealed little about herself and her life. Whereas she was aware of many aspects of his own.

There was a click, and Mrs Reid said, 'Ah, Miss Claremont is now free. I won't keep you too long.' She picked up his form and gave a light tap on the door of the other office before going in.

Deborah finished the note she was writing and glanced up at Elspeth.

'We have a most unusual prospective client,' Elspeth said. 'And if only I was twenty years younger . . . !'

'I've never heard you say that before,' Deborah began to laugh as she took the application form, and then seeing the name at the top, her hand stilled. Slowly, she placed it on her desk and swiftly scanned the first few lines. It was the same Evan Morgan. He was actually here? In the outer office? Quietly, she said, 'This is someone I know. Could you leave it with me for a few minutes?' Deborah sensed, rather than saw, Elspeth's curious look, then as the door closed, tried to calm her breathing. She had been impulsive, telling him where she worked. And selfish not to have told him before. After all, what harm was there in Evan knowing that she ran an employment agency? Why had she been keen to be secretive, it wasn't as though she was revealing her true identity and class? She knew that she would never see him again once he discovered that she was an aristocrat, a member of the establishment he so despised. But she could at least try to help him find employment. She buried her head in her hands. How could it happen that two so different men seemed to have claimed a place in her heart? Not that Evan had even intimated that he had feelings for her, but Deborah knew, oh yes, she knew. And what was she going to do about it? Nothing but heartbreak lay ahead if either of them pursued that attraction, and yet . . .

With a sigh, she applied herself to her profession and steadily read through the application form.

She pressed the intercom. 'Could you show Mr Morgan in, please.'

There was a moment's silence, and the electric charge between them was tangible even as Evan stood inside the door.

Deborah rose. 'Evan, this is a surprise, a welcome one. Please, do come and take a seat.' She watched as he eased his tall frame into the chair before her desk.

'It was a surprise to me, too. That you held such a responsible post. With being so young, I mean.'

She smiled, although her heart was doing leaps. 'I'm a hidden genius, didn't you know?'

He smiled back, 'Maybe, but even so . . .'

Deborah was floundering, and then admitted, 'Actually, the agency belongs to me.'

He stared at her. 'You mean . . .' An expression of discomfiture crossed his face.

'I had no idea that—'

'I was fortunate enough to receive a legacy, and when the agency, already well established, came on to the market, it seemed like a good investment.' All of which was true. She added in a quiet voice, 'You are wondering why, knowing your circumstances, I didn't offer to help you?'

He shrugged. 'I suppose I am.'

'I don't know, Evan, and that's the truth. I wasn't thinking properly, and I apologise. However,' she looked down at the form again, 'you have a lot of experience, even more than I imagined.' She began to relax, and smiled across at him. 'This is the point where I'm supposed to probe, to find out more about you as a person. It has taken years to build our reputation, so I have to be very careful who I recommend for a particular job.'

He remained silent for a few seconds. 'What do you want to know?'

She shook her head. 'I don't need to ask you anything. We'd be honoured to have you as one of our clients. It's just that . . .' Deborah studied the form again. 'You don't really fit in with our normal applicants, and there is nothing to suit you on our books at the moment.' She paused. 'But what I do have is contacts. And nothing would please me more than to return the favour I owe you.'

'You don't owe me anything, Deborah.' He met and held her gaze.

'We both know differently. Every time I think . . .' Her voice faltered.

'Don't. Think about it, I mean.'

'I do try not to.' She straightened her shoulders. 'Now, tell me, how are things? Are you still giving talks on behalf of the union?'

He nodded. 'Yes, I am. And the mood out there is hardening, I can't see any chance of a general strike not going ahead. Feelings are running high all over the country, there will be no turning back now, unless the government show some sign of meeting our demands. We have over two hundred unions behind us.'

'And all in support of the million locked-out miners, refusing to accept a cut in wages for working longer hours.' Deborah slowly shook her head. 'Honestly, I despair of justice at times. But won't all of these workers be risking their own livelihoods?'

Evan nodded. 'Millions of them, but our only strength is solidarity, and the hope that a general stoppage will cause the public to put pressure on the government.' His expression became grim. 'Too many of these MPs have no idea of what life is like for ordinary people.'

Thinking of Theo, Deborah said quickly, 'I'm sure that can't apply to everyone in the House.'

'You think not? Well, perhaps you're right. I only know how it looks to the rest of us.'

Then Evan smiled. 'I'm sorry to get on my hobbyhorse, Deborah. Or should I call you Miss Claremont, as we're discussing my employment?'

She laughed. 'It will always be Deborah to you.' Their gaze met and held, and feeling her colour begin to rise, she glanced away. 'Although I'd be grateful if you could publicly refer to me as Miss Claremont.'

'Of course.'

She put aside his application form. 'I promise to do my best with this, Evan, but if you could give me, say . . . a couple of weeks?'

He nodded. 'I'll call in and see if there's any news. But I think you will have rather a challenge on your hands.' Evan rose to leave, pausing at the door to look back. 'It was good to see you again.'

'It was good to see you, too.' For several minutes after the door closed Deborah remained motionless. She had never imagined that Evan would come to the agency. And yet, why not? It was a perfectly logical step. Thoughtful, she opened a drawer and taking out a new Manila file, printed his name on the front. Before inserting his application form she scanned it again, thinking how ludicrous it was that a man of Evan's calibre and experience should be unable to find work. There really was something wrong with the way this country was governed.

And yet Deborah knew that as Lady Deborah Claremont, she possibly had it in her power to help him. After all, wasn't she on friendly terms with some of the most influential people in the country? But was she willing to take a risk that might be detrimental to her work here at the agency? If her true identity were to be discovered, and Gerard made aware, it would be disastrous. Was she willing to risk that for the sake of one man?

Chapter Eighteen

Several days later during breakfast, Gerard was scanning the headlines in his newspaper and became thoughtful. It did seem that the threatened strike was likely to go ahead, paralysing not only commerce, but every service that affected the general public. He had followed the progress of the workers' claims, he even had a reluctant inkling that they had some right on their side, but that didn't shake his conviction that to give in to what was little better than blackmail would create a dangerous precedent. The government should never allow itself to be held to ransom by the working class, most of whom were an uneducated rabble. He decided that it was time he had a word with Fulton, to ascertain whether any members of the household staff were allowing themselves to be influenced by the current political unrest. That, he would not tolerate.

He glanced across at Deborah, who was spreading honey on her toast. His sister had always held unconventional views, inculcated he considered by her tutor. Channing had been not only an academic, but a political free-thinker, hardly a suitable choice to influence a young girl during her formative years. Where, he wondered, did her sympathies now lie? It was unthinkable that she should support the working classes. Perhaps a discussion with Theodore Field might be illuminating.

He smiled at his wife. 'Julia, my dear, don't you think it is time that Mr Field was invited to dine with us?'

She had been desultorily sipping her coffee, but brightened immediately. 'You are right, of course, darling.' She cast an arch glance at Deborah. 'I'm sure your sister would welcome it.'

No, I wouldn't, Deborah thought. She felt a flicker of suspicion, wondering whether Gerard had an ulterior motive for his suggestion, but then dismissed it. After all, the invitation was one of normal courtesy. She gave her brother a sweet smile. 'Yes, of course I would.'

'We'll discuss the other guests later, Julia.' Gerard stood, and folding his newspaper left to go to his study, his refuge from what he considered to be the empty chatter of women.

Julia put down her coffee cup. 'Do tell, Deborah, how things are with the handsome Theodore. You have been seeing quite a bit of each other.'

Deborah looked at her. 'It really is very early days. We just enjoy each other's company.'

'Well, I shall be observing you both when he dines with us. I flatter myself that I've quite an eye for a budding romance.'

'That must make life interesting for you,' Deborah said, but was careful to keep her inner sarcasm from her tone. Since Paris, she had managed to accept Julia as she was, superficial but well-meaning, her saving grace being that she made Gerard happy. And a content Gerard made life easier for everyone.

Julia gave her tinkling laugh. 'I just love matchmaking.'

'Then I shall have to call you Emma Woodhouse.' At Julia's frown of bewilderment, Deborah gave an inward sigh. 'She's a character in Jane Austen's novel, *Emma*.'

'And she liked matchmaking?'

Deborah nodded. 'I have a copy if you would like to borrow it.'

Julia shook her head. 'I'm afraid I'm not much for reading. I must go, I have an early appointment at the milliners.'

'You choose some charming hats.'

'Thank you. I think that the Countess of Anscombe should always look chic, don't you?'

Deborah smiled. 'Yes, I do. I hope you have a pleasant morning.' She too began to leave so that the servants could clear the breakfast table. She smiled her thanks to the butler.

'Excuse me, Lady Deborah.'

She turned. 'Yes, Fulton.'

175

'It's just that the chauffeur is wondering whether he has done something to offend you, as lately, his services on several mornings a week seem not to be needed.'

Deborah was furious with herself. It was understandable that Brown would feel perplexed. After all, for the past five years he had driven her on most of those days, to either Bloomsbury, or suitable destinations, such as shops, within easy walking distance to the office. And the system had worked, she had never had to counter any curious questions about her 'charity committees'.

'Please reassure Brown that he has done no such thing. It has simply been a whim of mine to take a short walk on those mornings. I thought that after my bout of influenza the fresh air would be beneficial. And afterwards I simply take a cab.'

'I quite understand, Lady Deborah.'

Giving him a warm smile, she left the room and went swiftly upstairs, her breathing rapid. She must remember that her daily life, her routine, was always open to observation downstairs, and arousing curiosity was never a good idea. The incident made her question yet again whether she would be wise to involve her aristocratic connections to help Evan.

It was when she was later eating her turbot during luncheon, that the phrase 'fish on Fridays' came into her mind, followed by an image of Father Keegan.

'A penny for them?' Julia said.

'Oh, sorry, I was miles away.'

'That, Deborah, was only too apparent.' Gerard's voice

was one of irritation. 'Is it too much to ask that when you give us the pleasure of your company at mealtimes, you partake in the conversation?'

Julia gave her tinkly laugh. 'I see someone got out of bed the wrong side this morning. You are a little grumpy, darling.'

But Gerard would not be mollified. It was true, he was feeling out of sorts and not only because of all this damned unrest in the country. Freddie Seymour hadn't been seen at the club recently, and Gerard was now hesitant to enquire openly about him. Was the young man still keeping his promise? Any risk of that child's existence being revealed was negated only by Gerard's instructions being carried out to the letter. The occasional slight nod from Freddie had been reassuring. Heaven forbid that something had happened to him.

Even though it was still April, the sun felt warm on Deborah's face as she started on her way to visit St Malachy's Church. Everywhere she could see signs of spring, the clusters of daffodils were glorious, buds of blossom and leaves were appearing on the trees, and just to see the blue sky made her spirits rise. But it was too far to walk all the way, and eventually she hailed a cab. She found the priest outside, talking to someone she assumed was a parishioner, and seeing his acknowledgement, pushed open the heavy doors to the church and went into its now familiar atmosphere of tranquillity. Deborah walked down the side aisle towards an altar devoted to Mary, the Mother of God, and slipped a coin into a slot on the candle stand. Taking three slim candles, she lit two in memory of her parents, and after closing her eyes for a few minutes, the other in memory of her beloved Philippe. Sometimes, she felt moved to do this, rather liking the idea of thoughts and prayers for loved ones flickering up to heaven. Not that she was sure that such a place existed. But if it did . . .

She heard the church door open and turned to see Father Keegan approach. He glanced at the stand of candles and gave her a warm smile. 'We have a prayer that we say to Our Lady, Miss Claremont. *To thee do we send up our sighs, mourning and weeping in this vale of tears.* And to be sure, lighting a candle for a loved one can be a great comfort.'

'Good morning, Father.' Deborah smiled warmly at him.

'Would you care for a cup of tea, now – I was just about to ask my housekeeper for one?'

'Thank you, that would be most kind. You have probably guessed that I come requesting help.'

'And if possible, I will be happy to give it.' They began to make their way out of the churchyard. 'The placement of the young girl Edna has been a huge success.'

'That's wonderful news. As you know, I was worried about her state of mind.'

'Aye, and rightly so, but she is even coming to Mass on Sundays with the rest of the family. And already has more colour in her cheeks.'

Deborah glanced at him. Would this kindly man be able to help this time? It was one thing to suggest a position for a kitchen maid, but another to find a situation for a man with Evan's experience and qualifications. An engineer? And not only that, but a man who could be described as a union firebrand?

Once they were sitting in Father Keegan's familiar study, the housekeeper came in, and with a smile for Deborah, put down two cups and saucers with a plate displaying two digestive biscuits, before bustling out. He grinned. 'The woman has me on a diet, so she does. I'm only allowed one.'

'You can have mine,' Deborah offered.

'Now, wouldn't that be cheating?'

She laughed and found herself enjoying their companionship, then Father Keegan reached out to take up a pipe and began to fill it. He paused. 'Now where are the manners my dear mother taught me? Would it be acceptable with you, Miss Claremont, if I was to have a smoke?'

She smiled. 'But of course it would.'

He finished the ritual of lighting his pipe. 'And now, how can I help?'

Slowly, she explained about Evan.

The priest frowned. 'He sounds rather different from your usual clientele.'

She nodded. Should she mention that she had met Evan before? 'He once did me a great service.'

Father Keegan regarded her as he drew on his pipe. 'And I take it that you'd like to repay him. You've explained his attributes, which are most impressive. But what sort of man is he?'

Her reply was instant. 'He's tall, presentable, intelligent. And I would say that he has integrity.' Deborah hesitated. 'However, he is also a man of strong political opinions, especially in regard to the threatened general strike.'

'Active?'

'I have to confess that he is.'

The priest closed his eyes as he became deep in thought, leaving Deborah to glance once more around the cosy study. She looked at the hundreds of books, many of which had shabby covers but were undoubtedly well loved, comparing the shelves with the library in Grosvenor Square, which was rarely used.

'Does this young man play chess?'

The sudden question startled her. 'I'm afraid I have no idea.'

'If you can, Miss Claremont, try and find out. Will you be seeing him again soon?'

'In about another week, I think.'

'Good, that will give me the time I need. I'm not promising anything, mind.'

'Thank you.'

After a tap on the door, the housekeeper came in. 'Just to remind you, Father, that you have a meeting with Sister Mary Winifred in ten minutes.'

Deborah rose and held out her hand. 'I do appreciate your giving me your valuable time.'

The priest smiled. 'I'll be in touch, Miss Claremont.'

She left and before going to hail a cab, went to the church to make her accustomed generous donation to the poor box as always, unsure whether Father Keegan was aware of her gesture. Deborah suspected that he most likely was, and was appreciative of his silence. Effusive gratitude would be embarrassing for both of them.

Chapter Nineteen

Deborah entered her sitting room a few days later to be met with the glorious scent of cut flowers, and smiled in anticipation as she went to read the accompanying card. They just had to be from Theo. She was right. '*I've missed you. Shall we have supper and dance again on Friday?*'

He had been busy due to late sittings in the House, and she had missed him too. Going to her writing table, she wrote a swift acceptance and went into the bedroom where Ellen was folding silk stockings and placing them in a drawer. 'Could you arrange for this to be posted, please?'

'Of course, I'll take it down to the hall now.' She put aside her sewing, and standing up gave a knowing smile. 'It was a lovely bouquet.'

'Thank you for arranging them.'

'I enjoy it,' Ellen said. 'We never had any flowers in our house, not from what I remember. Ours was a terraced house, what they call two-up two-down. We only had a backyard, and no way could we afford to buy them.'

'No garden? I'm sorry, I didn't realise.'

Ellen smiled. 'How could you, my lady?' Deborah watched her leave before returning to read in the sitting room. She had often been driven along roads lined with small terraced houses, but had never wondered what they were like at the back. It showed a shameful lack of curiosity. Yet to grow up and live in surroundings without the colour and fragrance of flowers . . . how much she took such luxuries for granted.

Ellen wasn't long before she returned, when it was to hover in the doorway. 'My lady, I hope you don't mind my asking . . .' She hesitated.

Deborah laid aside her book. 'Yes, Ellen?'

The words came out in a rush. 'It's about that newspaper I've been getting for you, the *Workers' Weekly*.'

'You haven't mentioned it to anyone?' Deborah's query was swift.

Ellen shook her head. 'No, of course not. It's just that you seem interested in these things, so I wondered what your opinion was, about this strike, I mean?'

'I think it's a pity that in order to get the justice they deserve, these men are forced to take such an action.'

'But do you think it's right?'

Deborah gazed at her. 'What alternative do they have?'

'It's going to cause a lot of bother for everyone,' Ellen said slowly. 'I mean, what if the omnibuses don't run, and the trains? And then there's John – he's talking about joining it in support of the miners. Suppose he loses his job?'

'Remind me, Ellen, what exactly does he do?'

'He works for a printing firm.'

'And are the other employees also going to join the strike?'

Ellen nodded. 'That's what he says.'

'Well, the company couldn't very well sack everyone.'

'No, but John worries that management might make examples. Doesn't mean that he's not determined to join in, though.'

'Then, just between ourselves, I admire him for it. He sounds like a young man of principle.'

'Yes, he is.' She paused. 'He's also a Roman Catholic.'

'Oh, I see. Does that bother you?'

'Not me, but it would the rest of my family. We've always been Church of England.'

Deborah tried to reassure her. 'I'm sure if it got to the stage when you both wanted to marry, something could be sorted out.'

'You don't know my dad,' she muttered darkly.

Problems, problems, Deborah thought as Ellen returned to her sewing. But wasn't that always the case? She didn't imagine that anyone went through life free of them. It was Shakespeare who said 'the course of true love never did run smooth'. How true that is. Instinctively Deborah glanced across at the vase full of Theo's beautiful flowers. Was it only several weeks ago that they had met? And then there was Evan Morgan, a man from a far different walk of life who only had to enter a room for her to be drawn to him. And the truth of it still bewildered her. She gazed down at her mother's sparkling sapphire ring, one Deborah always wore, unless she was at the agency. Whatever would the Countess of Anscombe have thought of her daughter's unsuitable thoughts? And she didn't dare to think of Gerard's reaction. He would probably have her locked up in an asylum.

Deborah could still remember her fury and outrage during the reading of her father's will. The silver-haired lawyer, with his half-moon spectacles had droned on and on, her own mind frozen at the implication of the words, *I wish my son Gerard, the future Earl of Anscombe, to be the guardian of my daughter Lady Deborah Claremont until she reaches the age of thirty years. To handle her financial affairs and approve her choice of husband should she wish to marry.* Deborah had no doubt that her father's intention had been an honourable one, in order to secure her future. A man of old-fashioned values, he would have felt the need for his daughter to be protected against fortune-hunters. The fact that she had been born in a different era, capable of handling her own inheritance, wouldn't have occurred to him. And he had always had a blind spot where Gerard was concerned. But thirty? She had been horrified. Her brother might be generous with her allowance, and Deborah did have a separate bequest from her mother, but Gerard seemed to feel he had the right to monitor her personal life. And she knew without doubt that, as a die-hard aristocrat, he would never understand or approve even a friendship with a man like Evan.

When Theo took her dancing again, it was to the Ritz Hotel, where the dreamy music in the Palm Court was absolute bliss. As Deborah glided past the orchestra in Theo's arms, her cheek nestling against his, she felt a surge of affection for him. And not only because she found him so attractive. It was more than that. During the whole evening there had been a warmth between them, a growing closeness. Their conversation, devoid at Theo's request of any mention of politics, had instead been relaxed and often humorous, underlined with a mutual delight in being together again.

When the music finished and hand in hand they began to leave the dance floor, she glanced up at him and smiled.

'Happy?' he murmured.

Deborah nodded.

'So am I. These past few hours have been just what I needed.' He pulled out her chair and when she was comfortably seated, took his own adjacent one.

A waiter came to pour them more champagne.

'It's been a tough week?' She gently touched his hand.

'It's been a tough few months.' He took a sip of his drink and said, 'I know I asked for no politics, but I have wondered a few times whether you ever heard that young man, Evan Morgan, speak again.'

She shook her head. 'I took notice of your warning that it might not be wise to go alone.'

A silence fell between them, Deborah feeling uncomfortable that she wasn't telling Theo the whole truth. That she had seen and spoken to Evan several times since then. Was she brave enough to reveal the ugly scene in the alley? That Evan had by chance been able to come to her rescue? But that would involve explanations and, as yet, she wasn't ready to confide in Theo about the agency in Bloomsbury, or what she sometimes thought of as 'her other life'.

Theo was lighting a cigarette. 'I have to admit that I have enormous sympathy with his cause.'

'I'm glad, Theo,' Deborah said, 'because that's how I feel. But does that mean you have spoken out against the government's intransigence?'

'In the House you mean? Oh yes, Deborah, I've spoken out, several times, along with various other MPs, but it hasn't achieved anything.' His lips tightened, 'If only I was in the Cabinet . . .'

'You're tipped to be in the future.'

Theo nodded. 'I know, but it will be too late to help these poor fellows. What haunts me is that we have been preparing for this strike for months. The poor bastards haven't got a chance, they'll be outwitted in every way.' He leant over and placed his hand over hers. 'You mustn't breathe a word of this.'

She was staring at him, appalled.

'It's important, Deborah.'

'Yes, of course I'll respect your confidence.' But her mind was in chaos. All those millions of people struggling for the right to be paid a decent wage. The government had already orchestrated their failure. It was heartbreaking. 'But I think it's dreadful, Theo. How can you belong to such a party?'

He shrugged. 'I've always been a Tory, as was my father. Don't be misled, Deborah, the party has many attributes. But if one wants to change things, to influence some of their outdated policies, the only way to achieve it is from within.' His frown deepened. 'But in this instance they are so very wrong. It's inbred in them, I'm afraid, to support the mine owners rather than the miners themselves, they always have done.'

'Even if they victimise the workers?'

'It would seem so.' His lips tightening, he stared moodily into the distance.

Deborah began to sip her champagne, looking at the dance floor, at the many fashionably dressed couples moving gracefully to the music; such a joyful and romantic scene. She felt troubled herself by their conversation, but realising that Theo was in need of distraction, she rose and held out her hand. 'Enough of serious matters, I think. I want to dance with you again.'

He glanced up and smiled. 'Even though it's another slow number?'

'Absolutely.' Deborah waited while he stubbed out his cigarette and joined her, then melted into his arms to the gentle strains of 'I'll See You in My Dreams'. Theo held her close against him and as she felt his lips touch her hair, Deborah's smile was soft. She had always felt that Theo was a man not only of integrity but with a social conscience similar to her own. And tonight he had confirmed it . . . could it really be there was a happy future for her after all?

Chapter Twenty

In Greenwich, on hearing the noise of the letter box, Bronwen went to find on the doormat a typewritten envelope addressed to Evan. Picking it up, she took it into the kitchen where he was shaking salt and pepper over toast spread with beef dripping. 'This just came for you. It doesn't look as though it's from the union, though.'

Evan waited until he had finished eating and took a swallow of strong tea, before opening the envelope and scanning the few lines.

Dear Mr Morgan,
Miss Claremont wishes to know whether you play the game of chess, and she would be most grateful for an early reply.

Yours faithfully,
Mrs E. Reid

Evan read it again, aware that Bronwen was pretending not to be interested.

'It's from that staff agency I told you about.' He passed the letter to her.

Her voice squeaked. 'Chess? In heaven's name what has that got to do with you getting a job?'

He shrugged his shoulders.

'Well, do you? Play chess, I mean?'

Evan leant back in his chair, linked his hands, and stretched his arms above his head. 'As a matter of fact, I do. I played in the army.'

'I'd have got you a chess set if I'd known. I've never seen the point of games like cards and such, spending time with nothing to show at the end of it. I'd rather get on with me knitting.'

Evan laughed. 'Now don't you go spending your money, Aunt Bronwen. Who would I play with, anyway?'

She looked sharply at him. 'I hope you don't think that because a man is unemployed he hasn't got a brain.'

'I'd never think that,' Evan said quietly. 'I'm one myself, aren't I? But chess isn't a game to play when you're undernourished, tired and cold.'

'That, I can well imagine.' Bronwen was frowning. 'I do think it's a funny thing to ask.'

'I agree. But I don't mind what sort of job it is, as long

191

as I can earn some money. My savings are whittling down at an alarming rate.'

'I've told you, we could manage without you paying your board.'

'And then you'd be in the same boat, with your savings going down.' Evan shook his head. 'I shan't let it come to that.'

Bronwen picked up the letter and read it again. 'This Miss Claremont? What's she like?'

'Very professional.'

'That's not what I meant, and you know it.'

Evan's lips twitched. 'All right, Aunt Bronwen, you win. I think you could describe her as a young lady.'

'How young?'

'Mid twenties, I should think.'

'Then if she's a "young lady", like you say, why does she have to go out to work?'

Evan threw back his head and roared with laughter. 'You don't give up, do you? If you must know, she came into a legacy and used it to buy the agency as a going concern.'

Bronwen regarded him. 'Did she now? And when did she tell you all that? If I didn't believe gambling to be the work of the Devil, I'd lay a bet this wasn't the first time you'd met.' She pulled a chair away from the kitchen table and sitting opposite Evan, poured herself a cup of tea. 'Go on, boyo, tell me all about it.'

With some reluctance, Evan told her about the wind-blown hat. 'She recognised me from one of the Battersea meetings.'

'Well, if she attends union meetings, that must mean something.'

'Such as?'

'She's on our side, supports the miners' cause.'

'I think she has sympathy for it.'

Bronwen was frowning. 'I went once to hear you speak, and there were hardly any other women.'

'I bet you saw one with red hair. She's been several times.'

'I sat behind one. Why? Do you know her?'

He shook his head. 'Not personally, but I gather she comes so that she can report back to a relative.'

'Don't think you can distract me. This Miss Claremont, you must have seen her again, after you'd rescued her hat, I mean.'

He nodded, but had no intention of revealing the incident in the alley. That was Deborah's business. 'It was when I was leafleting in Bloomsbury. We went to a nearby cafe for a cup of tea.' Evan saw the alert expression in his aunt's eyes. 'Now don't go reading things into it. She's just helping me to get a job.'

'In that case, you'd better write straight back.' Bronwen went into the front room and took a writing pad out of the sideboard. 'You've got your own fountain pen, and I can post it when I go to the butcher's.'

Evan grinned. At times, his aunt treated him as if he was still ten years old, but he didn't resent it, not one bit. Without her love and care, he would have been sent to an orphanage, and he'd heard enough about those places to know what a lucky escape he'd had. But he agreed with her. What possible relevance could it be whether he played chess or not?

'And the man says he's reasonably proficient?' The priest's Irish accent was even more pronounced over the telephone.

'His exact words, Father. Of course, he was in the army for several years, I would imagine chess was a popular pastime.'

With his promise that he would get back in touch that same day, Deborah replaced the receiver. She felt intrigued, but was brought back to reality by Elspeth's tap on the door as she ushered in a client. Ronald Wiseman, in his thirties, was looking for a clerical job, preferably as a bookkeeper, and Deborah, at their last meeting, had found him not only difficult to like, but actually repellent.

Greeting him, she indicated the chair before her desk and forced a smile.

'Do you have anything for me?' His tone was cold, almost arrogant.

Deborah nodded, still unsure whether, despite good qualifications and glowing references, she was doing the right thing in placing him. Then she reminded herself that she was in business and the office in question was in urgent need of help with their accounts. 'Yes, Mr Wiseman, I have. Messrs Avon & Carruthers in Clapham have a vacancy.' She outlined the salary and hours, trying to avoid his basilisk stare. 'Would you be interested?'

He inclined his head. 'Not my preferred location, but in the present climate, one cannot be too choosy.'

'That is true. You will need to ask for a Mr Robertson, who will interview you at eleven o'clock tomorrow morning.' She picked up a white foolscap envelope and passed it across to him. 'This contains all the details you need.'

He took it from her without comment and put it inside his overcoat pocket. 'Then I wish you good day.' Seconds later he had gone.

'Not a word of thanks,' Deborah exclaimed as she took his file into the outer office.

Elspeth pulled a face. 'He gave me the creeps.'

'Me too,' Deborah said. 'Who else is due to come in?'

'A far different prospect. That jolly woman who's wanting a position as a cook.'

'Meg Daniels?' Deborah smiled. 'She's like a breath of fresh air. I'd employ her myself if I could. Isn't she going to be at the same establishment as Sarah Boot?'

'If she's willing to go to Wiltshire. Would you like your coffee now?'

'That would be lovely.' Looking down at the appointment book and seeing Evan's name brought to Deborah's mind the increasingly alarming newspaper headlines. The threatened strike was gaining even more momentum, and unless the government intervened, could only be a matter of days away. If Father Keegan did find employment for Evan, would he be able to take it? Wouldn't the union need him to help organise picket lines?

And a general strike would involve massive organisation. Knowing the strength of his feelings against injustice, she doubted that Evan would put his own interests first. And that seemed doubly unfair. Both for himself and the priest who was trying to help him.

But Deborah had another, even more pressing concern. When she did see Evan, if she felt again that undeniable attraction, would her feelings lead her to warn him of the government's subterfuge? Yet to do so would make her a traitor as far as Theo was concerned. He'd confided in her, trusted her. But wasn't there a wider issue? A higher principle? One where millions of working people, exploited and lowly paid, were fighting for the justice they deserved.

She took a chocolate biscuit from the tray that Elspeth brought in and, in frustration, bit so fiercely into it that half of it crumbled and fell on the floor. 'Sorry.'

'You don't have to tell me if you don't want to, but it's obvious something is troubling you.' Elspeth bent to pick up the broken biscuit.

Sorely tempted to ask her advice, Deborah was deterred by the fact that she would have to expose her mixed-up feelings towards Evan, not to mention the moral issue of betraying Theo's confidence, a man with whom she was in love. How could someone else solve her dilemma if she found it difficult herself? With a wry smile, she shook her head. 'Thank you, Elspeth, normally I would, but I'm afraid this is something only I can sort out.'

And as she travelled back to Grosvenor Square, and saw out of the cab window a news-stand's stark headline NOT A MINUTE ON THE DAY, NOT A PENNY OFF THE PAY and beneath it STRIKE IMMINENT, she realised that time was running out. Somehow, she was going to have to make a decision.

Chapter Twenty-One

Although he'd promised to wait a couple of weeks before returning to the agency, Evan decided to go a day earlier. Everywhere the atmosphere was heavy with nervous anticipation about the proposed strike and, if it was announced, his support would be sorely needed. Although he dared to hope that Deborah's efforts had been successful, he knew that a man with his skills and experience would not be easy to place. He knew, too, that he was fooling himself. He just couldn't wait to see her again.

When he arrived, he went up the stairs and after knocking on the agency's door opened it to see Deborah's assistant on her hands and knees searching under her desk. He waited a moment then murmured, 'Good morning.'

She raised her head, only to bang it on the underside of the desk, and Evan bent swiftly to help her up. 'Sorry, I didn't mean to startle you. Are you all right?'

With a grimace, she rubbed her scalp. 'Don't worry, no harm done.'

'What were you looking for? Can I help?'

'My fountain pen.'

'Let me have a look.' He knelt and peering into the dark space, spotted the three gold bands on the cap of the Conway Stewart pen, his long arm reaching it with ease.

Getting up, he handed it to her and with a relieved smile she settled back into her chair.

'Thank you, Mr Morgan.'

Impressed that she had remembered his name, he smiled at her. 'I was hoping to see Miss Claremont.'

'Actually, she's in, which is rather unusual for a Monday. The possibility of the strike, you know. She did mention that you were due to come in this week.'

Deborah, becoming ever more aware that Evan could suddenly appear at the agency, had been forcing herself to come to a final, if reluctant decision. Her loyalty must lie with Theo, who had given her his trust. It had not been easy, she had struggled with her social conscience for hours. And then after listening to the latest BBC news bulletins, she realised that to betray Theo's confidence would be futile, any intervention that Evan could make would simply be too late. The country was already mobilised to draw industry to a close.

And so, when Elspeth came in and said in a stage whisper, 'He's here,' Deborah's hand stilled, sensing exactly who she meant. 'Who is?' She managed to keep her tone even.

'Mr Evan Morgan.' Elspeth placed a small pile of post on the desk. 'Shall I tell him to come through?'

'Yes, of course.'

Seconds later, Evan was inside her office, and smilingly she gestured to the chair before her. 'Good morning, Evan, I'm glad you decided to come a little early. This must be a busy time for you.'

'Good morning, Deborah, and yes, it is.' His voice was strong, confident.

She wavered, her stomach tied in knots. What was it Theo had said? That they hadn't a chance? But what good would it do to tell him except to load her with guilt for betraying a man she was falling in love with. And yet, when she gazed across at Evan, her pulse was even now racing. 'I do hope so, Evan, I really do.'

Deborah looked down, trying to breathe more evenly. 'Actually, I have some good news for you. It depends, really, on whether you are willing to consider work far different from anything you've done before.'

'If you're afraid of offending my pride, I'm beyond that, Deborah,' he said. 'Pride doesn't pay the bills. But I do confess to being a little mystified why you wanted to know if I play chess.'

She laughed. 'I thought you might be.' With an effort, acutely aware of his physical presence with only her desk between them, she managed to keep both her manner and tone professional as she outlined the suggestion that had come from Father Keegan. Evan leant forward. 'So this ex-army officer is looking for what, exactly?'

'The best way I can explain it is a sort of combination of factotum and companion. He was badly injured in 1916 and is confined to a wheelchair. Since then, the Colonel and his batman have been a team, but unfortunately the latter developed chronic bronchitis, which has left him too weakened to continue.'

'I see.' Evan hesitated, 'I take it that personal services would be needed?'

Deborah nodded. 'He would want help with the usual duties of a valet, such as dressing, shaving etcetera, but apparently nothing more intimate. His bathroom has been adapted for him with facilities he can manage.' She smiled at him. 'Interestingly, it would seem that your engineering background provoked interest, and then came the request to find out whether you play chess.' Deborah detailed the location, hours and salary.

Evan's reply was slow and considered, and she guessed that he was not a man given to impulsive decisions. 'I've never considered being a servant but . . .'

'Oh no . . .' Her reaction was instant. 'This is not a servant's position, not in the usual sense. You would not live in, and would have status in the household.'

'Certainly the salary and hours are more than fair,' Evan said.

'And the location would seem to be convenient.'

'Absolutely.' His brow was furrowed. 'However, let's suppose that I was offered the position? If the Colonel is looking for someone to start immediately, that I could do. But what about the strike? I can't renege on the promises I made. And we don't know how long it will last.'

Deborah nodded. 'Yes, I can see that could present problems. However, I didn't conceal that you were politically active and it doesn't appear to have been an obstacle so far.'

'Well, "nothing ventured, nothing gained", as they say.'

'Shall I ask Mrs Reid to telephone for an interview for you?'

He nodded. 'Today, if possible.'

Deborah pressed the button on the intercom and made the request.

There was a short silence between them, then she said with a smile, 'And how is your Aunt Bronwen?'

He smiled back. 'She's fine, getting all fired up as the strike approaches.'

'Oh yes, I remember now, she was a suffragette, wasn't she?'

'A fearsome one, I would imagine.'

Deborah laughed.

'And you, Deborah, how is life with you?'

An image of Theo came into her mind and their lovely evening together at the Ritz and the Palm Court ballroom. 'It's rather enjoyable at the moment.' She looked across at the tall, broad-shouldered man a few feet away from her. What would he think if he knew her real identity, that she was titled? Why on earth had she told him that she worked at an

202

agency? Without that, their paths might never have crossed again, and her life would be far less complicated.

Elspeth popped her head around the door. 'Would three o'clock this afternoon be suitable?'

Evan twisted round. 'Perfect, thank you.'

'I'll write down the name and address,' Deborah said. 'I was looking at your file earlier.' She removed it from a small pile on her desk, opened it and made a note of the information. 'I shall keep my fingers crossed, Evan. Not only that you will be successful, but that the position will be one you'll enjoy.' She smiled. 'I suppose much will depend on how well you and the Colonel get on.'

He gave a slight grimace. 'The only officers I've met have been—' he bit back the word he would normally use, but from Deborah's expression guessed that she knew what he meant.

'Then let's hope he's different.' The Colonel's recent conversation with her during their brief telephone call may have been brisk but he'd been courteous, and she had great faith in Father Keegan's judgement.

She saw hesitation in Evan's eyes, a reluctance to leave, and knew that she too wanted to prolong his presence. For one long tense moment their gaze met and held, then picking up the small pile of post, Deborah smiled up at him, 'Good luck, Evan. I hope it all goes well.'

He nodded, getting up to leave. 'My thanks for the chance, Deborah.'

She heard the outer door close and, in an effort to tear

her thoughts away from him, went in to talk to Elspeth. 'I've been thinking, how will you manage to get here if the strike does go ahead?'

Elspeth frowned. 'I've been thinking about that. It seems likely, if rumours are correct, that volunteers will come forward, at least to drive the trams and omnibuses – university students and the like.'

'I wonder whether they understand what the issues are really about,' Deborah said, 'especially with government warnings that it would be tantamount to a revolution, which isn't the union's intention at all.'

Elspeth said, 'I think some people in the government are scared it will develop into a violent revolution like the Russian one.'

'That's ridiculous,' Deborah protested. 'This is England. That would never happen here.'

'Maybe not,' Elspeth said, her tone wry. 'But there's no doubt we're a divided country.'

'I'm afraid that's very true. It makes me feel ashamed.'

'You couldn't help being born with a silver spoon, Deborah. But sadly, neither could those born without any spoon at all.' She shook her head. 'If you could have witnessed the pitiful scenes I did in our parish . . . but I've described those before.'

'Yes, I'm afraid you have.' Deborah paused, reflecting, then glanced at her watch. 'Time for our lunch break, I think. What do we have today?'

Part of Elspeth's duties was to prepare and bring sandwiches for them both, which served to prevent curiosity were Deborah to request such a thing in Grosvenor Square. 'Egg and cress,' she announced, putting the Closed sign on the door. 'I'll just go and make the tea.'

Deborah went back to sit behind her desk for a few moments, knowing that she needed to sort out her thoughts and her feelings. She had been so determined to follow her head and not her heart where Evan was concerned, a hard-fought-for resolution that had seemed eminently sensible. And then as soon as he appeared at her office door . . . her body had responded in a way that even now brought colour to her cheeks. Was she ever going to be able to forget this man? And if not, then what sort of future lay ahead for herself and Theo?

Chapter Twenty-Two

As he made his way out of Bloomsbury, Evan's emotions were mixed. Excitement yes, at the thought that all these months of unemployment might be coming to an end, but also a slight bewilderment at what he sensed was an alteration in Deborah's attitude towards him. It hadn't been that she had been cool, rather the reverse, but that spark hadn't been ignited between them. It had hovered, he was sure of that, but it was almost as though there was a wariness in her, a slight distancing of herself. And he found it disconcerting. Could it be that she felt disappointed he hadn't suggested they meet outside the agency? But how could he begin to court any young lady while he was without a job and income, and certainly not someone like Deborah, who worked hard to make a success of her life. Of course, her good fortune in being left a legacy had made that possible, something that the majority of people could only dream of. He headed towards a Lyons Corner House for something to eat. It was lucky that with the prospect of seeing Deborah again, he had taken care with his clothes. A sports jacket and grey flannels, his best shirt and tie were exactly what he would have chosen to wear for a job interview.

The substantial double-fronted house was at the end of a tree-lined drive in an exclusive residential road. Blackheath was an area that Evan was reasonably familiar with and had always struck him as a quiet backwater, now contrasting even more so with the city's prevailing atmosphere of tension. He walked up to the oak-panelled front door and hesitated. As a prospective member of staff, would he be expected to go to the rear of the house? And then, recalling Deborah's insistence that it wasn't a servant's position he was applying for, he shrugged and pressed the bell. Within seconds, the door was opened by a tall, thin man wearing a black jacket and striped trousers.

'Good afternoon.' Evan made his tone brisk. 'My name is Evan Morgan and I have an appointment for an interview at three o'clock.'

The butler inclined his head. 'Yes, of course, Mr Morgan.' Evan entered into a spacious hall and the butler led the way along the soft pile of an Axminster runner on the polished oak floor, to a wide door on the left of the hall. Opening it, he announced, 'Mr Morgan, Colonel.'

'Thank you, Weston.' The voice was deep, the tone not unfamiliar to anyone who had served under an army officer. When he'd first joined up, it had caused resentment in Evan. Eventually he had come to accept that it was inherent in men who were educated at English public schools, and unintelligent to judge a man's character simply by the way he spoke. One could apply that prejudice to regional accents as well, which made no sense at all.

Evan stepped forward, conscious of the door being closed behind him.

The Colonel, stockily built, with a ruddy complexion and thinning sandy hair, swung his wheelchair into a position where he could see Evan clearly.

'Thank you for coming, Mr Morgan. Please, come and sit opposite me.' He indicated a brown leather armchair and held out his hand. 'Sorry, I can't get up.'

Evan shook it finding a surprisingly strong grip. 'Rotten luck, sir.'

'Wasn't it? I take it you didn't do active service?'

Now seated, Evan smiled at him. 'I'm afraid not, working down a Welsh pit I was in a reserved occupation.'

'Well, thank your lucky stars.' He paused. 'I suppose the agency told you what the position entails?'

'Yes, they have. To be honest, I've never done anything like this before. I was in the Royal Monmouthshire Royal Engineers until a few months ago. As you know, in the present climate work is difficult to find.' He shrugged.

'Sometimes I wish I'd signed on again, instead of leaving.'

The Colonel's gaze was steady. 'So it wasn't that you'd had enough of the army?'

'I think it was more curiosity to see what life was like outside the forces, sir.'

The man before him nodded. Evan noticed how alert his blue eyes were beneath his bushy eyebrows, and also that his beard was in need of a trim. Would that be part of his job?

'You are a single man?'

'Yes, sir.'

'Well, so far, Mr Morgan, I am beginning to feel that we should get on together quite well.' The Colonel smiled; it was a quirky sort of smile with a hint of humour. 'Do you feel inclined for a game of chess?'

Evan glanced over at a carved ivory chess set on a nearby small table, which was high enough to accommodate a wheelchair. 'Certainly, although I haven't played recently, I'm afraid.'

'Don't worry about that.' It was then that the door opened and a maid came in carrying a tea tray. 'Ah, Maisie,' the Colonel smiled at her, 'such excellent timing.'

Evan enjoyed the refreshment and was beginning to relax, having found the Colonel's manner towards the fresh-faced young girl reassuring. When the game of chess began, Evan discovered that the pieces, although larger than any he had previously used, handled well with perfect balance and soon he forgot any anxiety and became totally engrossed. His opponent proved a skilful player, and an hour later, triumphed with a call of 'checkmate', and leant back with a satisfied smile. 'A good game, Mr Morgan.'

'Thank you, sir. I enjoyed it.'

'So, do you have any questions of your own?'

Haltingly, Evan explained how involved he was in the strike movement. 'I wouldn't like to leave you in the lurch, if it does take place.'

The Colonel steepled his fingers. 'There seems little doubt of it. I can only tell you, Mr Morgan, that I have the utmost sympathy with your cause.'

Evan was trying to weigh up the character of the man. He was unlike any army officer he'd previously encountered. 'It's good to hear that, Colonel.'

'I think you and I would do very well together, and so I am willing to take that risk, if you feel the same. Would you be happy to take the position, shall we say on a month's trial?'

Evan had no hesitation. 'I would, sir.'

'Can you begin tomorrow?'

'Of course, unless . . .'

'Well, if necessary, I shall have to continue with the care a nursing agency can provide.' He snorted. 'Nursing is not what I require, I don't care to be treated like a patient, if you take my meaning.'

Evan smiled. 'Yes, I do.'

'Then I shall telephone that nice-sounding Miss Claremont and give her the good news.' He held out his hand, 'Until eight o'clock tomorrow morning, unless . . .' He turned, wheeled the chair to his desk and opening a drawer, withdrew a card. 'In case you need to get in touch.'

Evan shook his hand and the Colonel pressed a bell behind his desk. Within seconds the butler reappeared. 'Mr Morgan will be joining us, Weston, hopefully from tomorrow. Perhaps you can introduce him to the rest of the staff.'

It was only later, as he was making his way home to Greenwich that Evan realised that no mention had been made of his engineering skills. Yet it would seem from what Deborah had described, that this quality had been a major one in securing him an interview. It would be interesting to discover why, he thought, as he paused on the pavement to cross a busy road.

The Colonel's telephone call came just as the agency was closing. Elspeth had already left and Deborah replaced the receiver with a feeling of euphoria. This meant that she had been able to repay Evan in some way for rescuing her, preventing that violent thug from subjecting her to the ultimate degradation. Rape happened, she knew it did, but how could a woman ever completely recover from such a thing? She often woke in the night trembling and clammy with fear after reliving the nightmare. She had been so close to disaster, including catching some awful disease.

But today had been a good day, so she wouldn't dwell on what might have happened, but on what was happening now. Tomorrow morning she would telephone Father Keegan with the good news about Evan, and thank him for his help. She checked from the window that her cab was already waiting, locked the office and went downstairs. The evening promised to be a peaceful one as Gerard and Julia were dining out. A tray, I think, she mused on the journey home, and afterwards a brandy, and begin to read my new novel.

When she arrived at Grosvenor Square her plan was thwarted, but in a wonderful way, by a note from Theo.

My darling, it would seem that my presence will shortly be much needed in the House and I'm already missing you. May I call for you at around 8 p.m.?

We could dine and dance in our own private world and thus save my sanity. Please telephone and say yes. With my love, Theo xx

Deborah hadn't the slightest hesitation.

Chapter Twenty-Three

Deborah felt as if they were in another world as held in Theo's arms that evening they danced the hours away. There was no talk of politics or strikes, just the sheer pleasure of being together. At least that's how it appeared to her and she had no doubt of Theo's happiness, it was openly in his eyes and his smile. He gazed down at her. 'Did you mind my calling you "my darling" on the note I sent?'

'I rather liked it.'

'And are you?' he murmured softly.

She drew back slightly and smiled up at him.

'I hope so, Theo, I really do.'

When hand in hand they left the dance floor and returned to their table, Theo said, 'I think another glass of champagne is called for.' Once the waiter had refilled their glasses, Theo, reaching over to take her hand raised it to his lips. 'Deborah, my lovely Deborah, when all this business is over, the coming strike I mean, would you care to come down one weekend to my home in the country?'

Her heart began to race. 'I'd love to.'

'How else are we ever going to be alone together, really alone? Other than being in a parked car?'

She nodded, while her lips curved in a teasing smile. 'Long walks in the country, for instance?'

'That too, if you so wish.' Then his expression became serious. 'I would also like my father to meet you. He's not in the best of health, so I'm hoping we can go sooner rather than later.'

'It could be months, Theo, before a settlement is reached.'

His lips tightened. 'I very much doubt it.'

An image of Evan with his eyes alight with hope for justice came into her mind, but Deborah pushed it away. Tonight was hers and Theo's, she didn't want any troubling thoughts. When the music of the last waltz began, he drew her once more into his arms to slowly circle the floor as the crooner's velvety voice began, '*I'll be loving you, always . . .*'

The following Tuesday morning, 4th May, the first full day of the strike began. The TUC announced its long-awaited action at one minute before midnight, and already breakfast at Grosvenor Square was fraught with tension.

Gerard could hardly contain his fury. 'Printers!' he

exploded. 'Never mind stoppages by railwaymen, transport staff, dockers and iron and steel workers,' he was ticking them off on his fingers. 'What about my daily newspaper?'

Deborah's tone was ironic. 'I'm sure that millions of people will have to make worse sacrifices, Gerard.'

He ignored her. 'It's a disgrace, an absolute disgrace.'

She persisted. 'They're coming out in solidarity to redress injustice.'

Julia, always one to retreat from any confrontation, was casting nervous glances between them.

'I might have known you would side with the masses, Deborah,' he snapped. 'Not that you know anything about the subject.'

'And you do?'

'I know my duty, and it grieves me you don't know yours. You're a traitor to your class, Deborah, I've long suspected it. But I'll allow no one in this house, and that includes you, to give support of any kind to the perpetrators of this attack on democracy. Because make no mistake, that's what it is.'

'I was given to understand,' Deborah retorted, 'that democracy was supposed to be government by the people, for the people. I fail to see how it has served the starving miners.'

'It's a complicated issue,' Gerard said.

'And I, as a mere woman, am incapable of understanding what's involved?'

'I was against women being given the vote, as you very well know, and I've since had no cause to change my mind.'

'It was granted only to a relatively small number of us,'

she pointed out. 'All women over twenty-one should have the right, and the sooner the better.'

'Then I can only despair of England's future.'

Julia was reassuring. 'But darling, surely most women will vote the same way as their husbands?'

Gerard didn't reply, he was drumming his fingers on the table, deep in thought.

'I don't think either of you should leave the house today. We will have to see how this situation develops.'

'At least we can agree on something, Gerard.' Deborah, having finished her coffee, dabbed at her mouth with her napkin. 'That would appear to be eminently sensible. Now, if you would excuse me.'

Her step up the staircase was swift, her mind dismissing Gerard's narrow and outdated opinions, instead racing with worried excitement. She had to believe that Theo was mistaken, that the strike would prove to be successful. She was also bitterly regretting that she was unable to offer her public support because if she and Theo were to have a future together, which she was fervently hoping, then she needed to consider his political career.

Waiting for her was Ellen, looking pale and anxious. 'I heard downstairs, my lady. This means that my John will be one of the strikers. Do you think he'll be arrested?'

'I can't think why he should be.'

'They might want to make an example. I don't trust this government.'

And that, Deborah realised, was part of the problem. One

would have thought that after all the suffering the Great War had inflicted on the country, people would be pulling together. But that would never happen until every citizen was treated fairly. Why couldn't politicians see that? And then she thought of those she knew socially, their closed minds and self-interest obvious. Yet Theo is different, she thought, and there must surely be others in the House of Commons? She mentally dismissed the House of Lords, having always considered that privileged birth rarely denoted an understanding of ordinary people. Gerard was a prime example. As for her brother's political commitment, he rarely voted in the second chamber, and his attendance could only be described as spasmodic.

Deborah phoned Elspeth and closed the agency. It was not a decision she had taken lightly, but allowing the agency to function would be to defy the strike action, and the whole intention was to bring industry to a halt. Otherwise, how else could the workers make their case? Deborah did have another strategy, which had been in place for some time in case the strike went ahead. She might not be able to give her physical support, but she could give meaningful financial help. All those workers, in support of the miners, were going to suffer even more hardship. There would still be families to feed, bills to pay. She had a considerable inheritance, not only from her mother but also from her maternal grandmother. In trust, yes, but had only been so until she reached the age of twenty-one. It was money from her father's estate that was controlled by Gerard until she reached the age of thirty.

Always one to donate generously to deserving charities, Deborah decided to make immediate enquiries as to whether a strike fund had been set up.

Without the agency to go to, the rest of the day found her restless and with the threat of a headache, so after luncheon she decided to try and take a nap. The previous night her sleep had been a disturbed one, as she'd indulged herself by dreamily going over Theo's every word, the desire she had seen in his eyes, and those increasingly passionate kisses before he'd bid her goodnight. And his invitation to Wiltshire could hold an undercurrent of meaning. Deborah had attended enough weekend parties in the Home Counties to know that many a guest would creep along luxuriously carpeted corridors to another conveniently situated bedroom. It was something she herself had never taken advantage of, despite several oblique – some even blatant – invitations.

But now, everything had changed. If Theo did come to her room, in the same way that she had, all those years ago, gone to Philippe's . . .

And at the thought of the young man she had loved, even adored, Deborah couldn't help her mind drifting back to that final leave when her parents, now aware of the affection between them, had offered Philippe hospitality at Anscombe Hall.

Chapter Twenty-Four

1918

Philippe's leave was agonisingly short, and the couple spent every available minute together. Reunited after months of separation, the attraction and love between them deepened with every day.

Deborah tried hard to keep the hours light, filled with joy and happiness in an effort to diminish the nightmarish images she knew must fill Philippe's mind. She had been shocked to see how pale he looked when he arrived. Thinner too, with eyes that seemed haunted, only lighting up when Deborah flew towards him and regardless of her parents watching, drew him to her, placing her warm cheek against his chilly one, whispering, 'Welcome, my darling.'

Philippe had smiled down at her, then punctiliously polite, greeted and thanked the Earl and Countess for their invitation. 'It means much to me, to be able to spend my leave at Anscombe Hall.'

It had seemed interminable having to share Philippe on that first day, and Deborah would willingly have skipped dinner that night, but was only too conscious that her wonderful Frenchman needed, as Cook would say, 'feeding up'. His delight in seeing her again was glaringly obvious, as were their covert glances at each other across the table. Deborah couldn't take her eyes off him, thinking despite his pallor, how handsome he looked in his uniform.

She was grateful to her father when he said, 'I'm sure on this first evening, Lieutenant Lapierre, you will hardly wish to discuss the situation in France, so I propose we all take our coffee together in the drawing room.'

The Countess looked sympathetically at their guest. 'You must need sleep after your journey. I'm sure we will all understand if you retire early.'

'Yes, but Mama, maybe Philippe would like some fresh air beforehand? Perhaps a short walk.' Deborah saw her parents exchange a glance.

Then her father nodded. 'That sounds sensible.'

Later, as hand in hand they strolled in the grounds, Deborah laughed. 'The last thing we want to be is sensible.'

Philippe smiled. 'But let us wait until we cannot be seen.' He gazed down at her. 'I would like us to visit the lake in the wood again, I have thought of it often.'

She nodded. 'But we'd better walk faster, or we'll be away too long.'

She managed to keep up with his long strides, while his hand held hers ever more tightly as they hurried through the wood until they came to the grassy verge of the lake, when each turned to the other with one accord. Philippe drew her to him with urgency, holding her so tight that she could hardly breathe. 'I can't believe I am at last with you,' he said, and their lips clung together, the kiss deep and sweet. Eventually he relaxed his hold. 'I have dreamt of this. I never want to let you go, *mon ange*.'

Deborah reached up a hand and stroked his face. 'I've missed you so much. God bless you for coming safely back to me.'

His mouth curved in a wry smile. 'I made a special prayer to the Virgin Mary,' he murmured, his lips again seeking hers while her own parted and for long moments there was no war, no parents waiting, nobody else in the world except themselves.

Tears filled her eyes, of happiness mixed with sadness. Their separation had seemed endless, but her joy on seeing Philippe again was shadowed by thoughts of what he must have gone through. 'I love you so much,' she whispered.

But seeing the exhaustion in his eyes, she took his hand and began to lead the way back to the house. 'Soft pillows and a cosy bed are what you need. Most of all undisturbed sleep.'

'I wish that you could be with me.' He turned to smile at her.

'So do I,' she said with a laugh. 'But I hardly think your sleep would be undisturbed if I was.'

He raised her hand to his lips and kissed it. 'I shall be more your Philippe tomorrow, I promise.'

And he was true to his word. At Deborah's instruction, no maid disturbed him and Philippe slept until midday. Downstairs, on alert for his bell, a maid took up a tray of coffee with scrambled eggs, and when he joined Deborah in the morning room, she was relieved to see that he was looking more relaxed.

He bent to kiss her, and she drew him down beside her on the sofa.

'We must try to be circumspect,' she whispered. 'Mama has only gone out for a moment.'

He gave a grin. 'This word "circumspect"? It means I cannot kiss you?'

She smiled up at him. 'Well, just a little one, then.'

His lips met hers for a brief sweet moment. 'That is, how do you say, a butterfly kiss.'

She was laughing when her mother came into the room. 'Lieutenant Lapierre,' she said. 'I trust you were comfortable and had a restorative sleep?'

He rose. 'I did, Your Ladyship, and I am most grateful to you. But to oblige me, please no military title, it is Philippe.'

She smiled. 'Of course.' She turned to Deborah. 'Have you any plans to entertain our guest this afternoon?'

'I have, Mama,' Deborah said. 'If Philippe should wish it, I thought we could ride?'

The Countess frowned. 'I would have thought that more a morning activity.'

'Yes, but that wasn't possible. And the weather might not be suitable tomorrow.'

'That is true. It is a pity that Gerard is not due any leave, he will be sorry to have missed you, Philippe.' She looked at them both. 'I am sure you have lots to discuss, so I will see you at luncheon.'

As soon as the door closed, Philippe rejoined Deborah on the sofa and sought her hand.

She hesitated. 'It is, of course, possible that Papa might come in, so . . .'

He gave her a swift kiss. 'We discuss?'

She nodded. 'Tell me more about your childhood.' And as Philippe described the chateau, the woods surrounding it, his bedroom filled with boyhood treasures, she felt she could see the small, sometimes lonely boy spending time with the motherly cook in the kitchen, loving being with his dog, his horse. '*Mon chien*, my dog, was Beau, and my horse, Gaston. I hope to find Gaston waiting for me when . . .' He paused, adding in a bitter tone, 'But one never knows what the Boche are capable of.'

She squeezed his hand in sympathy. 'And your mother? You say that she spent much time in Paris.'

'When my father was alive, yes, but not afterwards. Living together at the chateau, we became very close.' His lips twisted, 'For it to be impossible to see her is hard.'

They sat for a few moments in silence, then Philippe

turned to her. 'It was terrible news about Jeremy.'

She nodded, becoming silent for a moment, thinking of the solemn young man who had played such a crucial part in bringing her and Philippe together.

Then, in an effort to lighten their mood, she suggested that she played the piano. 'I'm only showing off, but I've got some super new sheet music.' And they were cheerful tunes, she thought, absolutely nothing to remind him of the war.

But it seemed impossible for the subject to be avoided, as later Philippe mentioned that he felt it his duty to visit Jeremy's parents. 'He was,' he told Deborah's father, 'not only a brave officer, he was my friend. I would wish to bring them some comfort.'

'An admirable sentiment,' the Earl said. 'If tomorrow morning would be convenient for you, I shall arrange for the chauffeur to drive you over there.'

'I shall come too, Philippe,' Deborah said.

Her father shook his head. 'That, my dear, would be inappropriate in the circumstances.'

Deborah felt slightly resentful. Not about the visit to Jeremy's parents; she could understand that, but those precious hours with Philippe would be lost to her. 'Could I be dropped off to see Abigail?' she asked. 'It would give her a chance to say hello to Philippe.'

'We would have entertained, including Abigail,' her mother reproached, 'but you insisted that Philippe would need a quiet few days.'

'Deborah was correct, Your Ladyship. It is wonderful for

me to be here, able to walk in your peaceful grounds and woods. I require nothing else.' He smiled at her, the smile that Deborah doubted anyone could resist, and she saw her mother's eyes soften.

The days and hours of Philippe's leave seemed to melt away, and far too soon the prospect of him returning to France, to the front, hung over the young couple like a black cloud. Deborah did her best to distract him, trying to guide their conversation away from the inevitable, but both were becoming more subdued.

'To be with you, *ma chérie*, I cannot say how wonderful it has been.' He was holding her in his arms, secluded as they were in their special place by the lake. There was a gentle breeze rustling the leaves of the tree where they stood, with occasional birdsong the only sound to intrude on their private world. 'We have talked of our future together, my Deborah, but,' he smiled down at her, 'I have not made the formal proposal.'

With one knee resting on the grass, he gazed up into her eyes.

'Lady Deborah Claremont, may I, Lieutenant Philippe Lapierre, have the honour of making you my wife?'

Deborah, her heart beating wildly with excitement and love, knew that she would never forget this moment. 'My darling, I would be so very proud and happy.' Her eyes filled with tears, not only of happiness but desperate hope. She reached out and drew him to his feet, her hands going

225

up to cup his face. 'I love you, Philippe Lapierre, don't you ever forget it.'

'And you, *chérie*, are the light of my life. But now I have to ask your papa's permission?'

She nodded. 'He likes you, I can tell.' She laughed with sheer joy. 'But not as much as I do . . .'

Later, Philippe emerged from her father's study with a wide smile. 'He has given us his blessing.'

'Did he say anything else?'

'That we were very young. But in these difficult times, such things do not seem so important.'

'I must tell Mama,' Deborah flew upstairs to her mother's room, to be greeted by a knowing smile and hug.

'I have never seen such love, such devotion,' the Countess said. She raised one eyebrow. 'Please God, we will have a wedding soon.'

'Philippe is going to write to his mother. It would be unthinkable for her not to be able to attend. Do you think the Germans would allow her to come?'

Her mother shrugged, her lips tightening. 'Who can foretell what that nation will do?'

There was champagne that night, and with the staff informed of the news, congratulations to the young couple when Deborah took Philippe downstairs to meet them.

But much later, her euphoria dimmed when unable to sleep, Deborah's mind filled with an image of Philippe in his room at the other end of the corridor, resigned and filled with dread, knowing that he was returning to France to face certain danger. She couldn't bear to think of what dark thoughts he must have, so slipping on her ivory silk dressing gown, Deborah silently opened her door.

Philippe's unlocked room was lit by moonlight when she went in, and as she came closer, he turned on his pillow to face her, wordlessly pulling back the coverlet, and slipping beneath the cool linen sheets she snuggled into his embrace. They lay together in silence, her head resting on his chest for what seemed to Deborah an eternity. She longed to comfort him, to love him, her body aroused by feeling his warmth close to her skin. When at last he moved, she raised her head to willingly meet his lips and as his hand moved down to her breasts she pushed down the narrow straps of her silk nightdress to free them. Deborah had no inhibitions, this man was her love and he needed her. They needed each other. Their lovemaking was full of sweetness, then passion, and afterwards, as they lay against the pillows, Philippe lifted one hand to gently stroke her forehead. 'You look so seductive with your hair loose, so beautiful.'

'Maybe I am wanton.' But her lips were curving in a smile.

He leant over and kissed her. '*Non, chérie*, you are my angel.' He hesitated, and then removed his gold signet ring. 'I was going to give you this tomorrow morning.' He took her left hand and slid it on to her third finger. 'You see, that is the crest of my family. Will you wear it for me, until I buy you a diamond, yes?'

Philippe's ring, still warm, was too large for her, and she placed it on the small bedside table. 'I shall wear it on a chain around my neck to keep it safe.' Then turning back to him she said softly, 'Are you tired?'

'Are you?'

She shook her head.

'So, I think we shall not be doing much sleeping?'

She smiled up at him. 'I was hoping you would say that.'

It was early in the morning as daylight began to creep into the room that Deborah slipped from beneath the sheets and, picking up Philippe's ring, silently made her way back to her own room. Further sleep was impossible. Instead, she dwelt with a lovely warm feeling on all that had passed between them.

At breakfast the following morning, she hardly dared to look at Philippe, afraid her colour would rise, or her face reveal what had happened. And later, when they had to say farewell, she thought her heart would splinter as she saw Philippe's love for her shining out of his eyes.

But it was only when her father, who had contacts in the War Office, called her into his study and told her the news, that Deborah truly discovered the physical pain of heartbreak.

Because within twenty-four hours of his return to the front line, Lieutenant Philippe Lapierre was listed as killed in action.

Chapter Twenty-Five

Deborah remained for a while immersed in the poignant memories. Just a few more months, and the war would have been over. She was struggling to suppress tears. Dwelling on that last weekend with Philippe had brought to the fore the terrible time that had followed. Shattered by grief for his tragic loss, within weeks she'd suffered the deaths of her beloved parents, and during the following traumatic months had thought that she would never be able to smile or laugh again. She had worn Philippe's ring on a slim chain beneath her clothes for years following his death, not wanting to have it altered. Hadn't the circle of warm gold lain next to his skin? She couldn't bear the thought of a stranger handling it.

With a sigh she rose and going over to her desk, took out a small leather box. Opening it she gazed down at the signet ring surrounded by black velvet, her finger tracing its engraved crest.

'Was I wrong not to send it to his mother?' She spoke the words aloud. It had always lain on her conscience. But the ring had been all that she had of him, and Philippe had wanted her to have it. At one time Deborah had wondered whether to go to France to find his childhood home and share her sorrow with the mother to whom he had been so close. But time had passed, and she eventually decided that her visit would only reopen old wounds for them both.

Now, Deborah was aware that this was a final farewell. She would always keep love in her heart for Philippe, but life was at last moving on, bringing with it the chance of marriage and, please God, children. Slowly she closed the lid, replacing the box in the drawer. Her lost love would have wanted her to be happy.

The following three days of the strike seemed interminable to everyone. Gerard was dismissive about Deborah's determination not to leave Grosvenor Square.

'Let these ruffians affect your way of life?' he snapped. 'It's betraying your heritage.' He glared at his sister. It was typical of her to take such an individualistic view of the situation. The upper classes needed to show their solidarity, their superiority, or the whole social structure could tumble. And then where would she be? A title would be of little value. Even worse, one had to remember what happened to the Russian aristocrats in 1917. 'Not that I would wish you to venture out alone. Although I expect Theodore Field will have far more important things on his mind than squiring you around London.' His tone was one of sarcasm.

'Do I take it, Gerard, that you have some objection to my seeing Theo?'

'It is my opinion that you are spending far too much time together.'

Always placatory, Julia said, 'So I don't need to cancel my luncheon engagement tomorrow? I'm sure that Brown will look after me.'

Gerard shook his head. 'My view doesn't apply in your case, I'm afraid. The strikers could do anything, surround the car or even attempt to push it over. I can't risk you being hurt.'

'My safety doesn't seem to enter into it,' Deborah said with some resentment. 'But you're talking nonsense, Gerard. These are workers fighting for their just rights, not a crowd of thugs.'

'And have you ever met one, a striker, I mean?' Gerard didn't give her a chance to reply. 'No, I thought not, so you are not in a position to pass judgement either.'

'My maid told me that her brother is involved,' Julia said. 'Apparently he's a bus driver. She thinks the strike is justified too.'

'That girl is a chatterbox and a gossip. I've noticed it before. In your position, Julia, she is not a suitable person. I wish you to dismiss her.'

231

His face a mask of displeasure, Gerard rose to retire to his study for a cigarette. His tolerance of female company was limited. And Julia should not be listening to the views of servants. His mood worsened even more when he reflected there was still no sign of a future heir. When this sorry business of the strike was over, he would arrange for his young wife to seek medical advice. A peer of the realm needed an heir and a spare, and the sooner Julia became pregnant, the happier he would be.

And then there was the situation regarding Freddie Seymour and the maintenance of the child. By giving a generous tip to a porter at the club, Gerard had ascertained that the young man had not only been absent from the premises, the porter had heard a rumour that he was out of the capital due to illness. In which case, Gerard considered, a note to himself might have been a courtesy. One could only assume that the monthly allowance he paid to Freddie was being forwarded. What if Seymour's illness was fatal? The thought of his lawyers or family trying to unravel the financial arrangement Freddie had with Gerard, was not one to countenance.

Gerard was well aware that Deborah regarded his pride in the family name as an obsession and, thinking of his sister, he began to wonder whether this dalliance with Theodore Field was likely to lead to a proposal. The man might be a prominent public figure, but there still wasn't a title.

The following day, to Gerard's satisfaction, a government newspaper, the *British Gazette*, edited by Winston Churchill

MP, was published. He was not so impressed when, in response, the TUC produced its own newspaper, the *British Worker*. And while he immediately bought the former, Gerard had no intention of reading what he thought of as a 'working-class rag'.

On the fourth day of the strike, Ellen burst into Deborah's sitting room. 'Oh, my lady, you'll never believe it. I never thought to see the day!'

Deborah turned from her writing desk in alarm. She could see fear in her maid's eyes. 'Good heavens, whatever has happened.'

'There's armoured cars in Oxford Street with machine guns.'

Deborah drew a swift breath, appalled. 'The government would never use them, not against their own people.'

'A man, an old soldier he was, told me they were primed and ready. What if they shoot my John!'

Deborah took hold of her maid's trembling hands. 'Ellen, calm down. They're just trying to frighten the strikers, that's all. Look, you go down and ask Cook for a nice cup of tea. And take your time.'

Alone again, she began to pace the room. She had read in Gerard's copy of the *British Gazette* that the government had prepared for the strike over a period of nine months, using the 1920 Emergency Powers Act to set up the Organisation for Maintenance of Supplies. Volunteers were already being used to run trains and buses. But to bring in troops? She had never imagined that could happen, not in England in peacetime. Had Theo known about all this? He must have done, and

233

the knowledge would have lain heavily on him. How must it feel to sit in the House listening to laws being passed that are against your own principles? And yet what Theo had said was true, the only way he could influence things, improve social conditions, was to be inside the seat of power.

As day followed day, with even London's taxi drivers joining the strike, the last straw for Gerard seemed to be the postponement of Dame Nellie Melba's farewell concert at the Royal Albert Hall.

'I've a good mind to leave and go down to Anscombe Hall. What do you say, my sweet?'

Julia was biting her lip, and Deborah guessed that there was little in the country to attract her. Her sister-in-law was a city girl, loving the shops, the parties, the art galleries. Although Julia was honest enough to admit she knew little about art, she did enjoy looking at the historical fashions portrayed.

'Wouldn't that mean retreating?' Deborah queried, tongue in cheek. 'According to the government, the strike is a constitutional attack on them. Isn't that tantamount to a war? I hardly think our ancestors would feel proud of you leaving the field of battle.' She'd actually much prefer Gerard and his moods to be absent, but could never resist riling him.

Her brother stared at her. 'And what useful purpose do I serve by staying? You might share your undoubted wisdom with us.'

Deborah regarded him. 'You did say that not allowing the strike to affect our normal way of life was vital. Yet if you decamp, wouldn't that mean they had won? At least with regard to the Claremont family, or more specifically, the Earl of Anscombe.' Her tone had been calm, measured, but beneath her eyelids she saw Gerard flinch.

'You have an unfortunate tongue, Deborah. But this time you may have a point. Julia, you have no objection to remaining in London?'

Her relief obvious, Julia smiled at him. 'Not at all, although it is getting a bit of a bore not being able to go out.'

'Don't worry, my sweet, it will soon be over.'

'I hope so,' Deborah said sharply. 'Apparently, the outpatients department of Great Ormond Street Hospital has had to be closed. When sick children are going to be affected, don't you think the government should come to a settlement?'

'I'm sure they will, and soon. But, my dear sister, I doubt it will be to your satisfaction.'

An image of Evan flashed into her mind – of his zeal, his enthusiasm, the set of his jaw when he talked of the plight of the miners; the tyranny of the pit owners. Was it really going to be the case that after the meetings, the growing hope, the sacrifice of millions of people joining the strike, it would all be in vain? Suddenly she couldn't stand the sight of her brother's complacent expression and excusing herself escaped from the drawing room to the solitude of her rooms.

Ellen had managed to obtain a copy of the *British Worker*, and for the next hour Deborah studied the latest news.

On reading that a cheque for £5,000 had been received in support of the strike from the All Russian Central Council of Trade Unions, dismay swept over her. Although her anxiety subsided on learning of the TUC's refusal to accept it. That would be a step too far, in her opinion, and she wondered whether Evan would agree with her.

But she had no way of knowing his views. And it was a strange realisation to think that she may never see him again, unless he found some pretext to come to the agency. For Deborah, the prospect gave rise to mixed feelings. Becoming so sure of her love for Theo, she neither wanted nor needed any confusion. And yet she *was* confused by the way she felt drawn to Evan. It wasn't only physical attraction. She genuinely liked him. She enjoyed talking to him, listening to him, watching his face light up, the enthusiasm in his eyes as he talked of his passion for justice. Could she and Evan ever be just friends? Would that be possible?

Chapter Twenty-Six

The following morning, Ellen brought in Deborah's hot chocolate and opened the curtains to let early sunshine flood in. 'I can't believe what they're saying downstairs, Lady Deborah. That even the churches are against the strike now!'

Deborah settled herself against her pillows and took a welcome sip of the creamy liquid. 'I'm afraid that's true, Ellen. I was surprised also. Apparently, Cardinal Bourne declares it to be against the duty we owe to authority and to God. And Catholics have been told to uphold and assist the government.' She wondered how Father Keegan felt about reading that pronouncement from his pulpit. From the few conversations between them, she had gained a distinct impression that his sympathies lay elsewhere. 'What else are they saying downstairs?'

Ellen was opening a drawer to take out fresh underclothes. 'Well, Cook never stops complaining about shortages in the foodstuff she needs. She's having to alter the day's menus. I think she's lucky to get what she does, begging your pardon, my lady. Most people will have to go without.'

'I'm sure that's true. And I hear that two of the footmen have volunteered to help with civil defence.'

Ellen nodded. 'Off like a shot they were, once His Lordship gave his permission.'

Deborah put down her now empty cup. 'I would have thought the servants would be on the side of the workers.'

'Most are. But James and Henry think it'll stand them in good stead in the future, with His Lordship, I mean.'

'Oh, I see.' Deborah gave a wry smile. It would seem that in all walks of life principles gave way to self-interest.

She was planning that morning to reply to Abigail's latest letter from Scotland, in which she promised that as soon as the strike was over, she and her husband Angus would be coming south.

Our plan is to divide our time between staying with his parents and mine. But of course, we shall come up to London so you and I can meet either there or if you visit Anscombe Hall. Maybe even both. You'll be amazed how the twins have grown. I still miss you terribly, Debs. There is truth in the saying that old friends stay the closest. I'm dying to hear all the gossip so do save it up. And don't think you have a hope in heaven of my not meeting Theo!

    Much love

    Abby xx

Deborah smiled. Abigail was right, there was a special closeness between friends who had known each other since childhood. Deborah was friendly with several young women within her social circle, but in truth they were more well-liked acquaintances. She couldn't ever imagine confiding in them the way that she could Abby. And, she thought, as later she began to reply on her headed writing paper, it might even be that if she told Abby of her confused feelings about Evan, she might help Deborah to see the situation more clearly. There was one thing for certain, she could trust her plain-speaking friend to give her an honest opinion.

Luncheon found Gerard in one of his black moods, ever more frequent these past few days. And this time, it was fury that trade unions had advised strikers to wear their service medals in order to show their patriotism and previous military service.

'Parading in military formation! It's an affront, that's what I call it.'

'An affront to whom?' Deborah asked.

'To their regiments. I doubt they were expected to be displayed as revolutionary badges.'

'Oh for heaven's sake, Gerard, you do talk tosh at times.'

Silence fell. 'Deborah, you may be my sister, but that doesn't give you the right of impertinence.'

'I'm sorry, but you infuriate me. Where is this revolution you keep mentioning? Have there been lives lost? Blood on the streets? Aristocrats beheaded?'

'We are,' her brother said with ice in his tone, 'endeavouring to enjoy luncheon, and I would thank you not to use such emotive language in front of Julia.'

Immediately repentant, Deborah knew that she had overstepped the mark and swiftly apologised to her now wide-eyed sister-in-law. Did she and Gerard never have rows, she wondered? And for one dizzy moment imagined Julia flinging cruel, angry words across the floor of their room. But only for a moment, because Deborah suspected that her brother's obvious fondness for his young wife owed much to the fact that she was compliant with his every wish.

The rest of the meal passed in a cool atmosphere, and afterwards Gerard was quick to excuse himself saying that he needed to attend to paperwork.

'Deborah?' Julia said, as she sipped her tea. 'Why do you enjoy provoking him so much?'

'Our views differ so widely, that I just cannot resist challenging him. We have always been the same, ever since childhood.'

'I suppose, as an only child, I find that difficult to understand.' Julia hesitated and waited until there was no maid present. 'May I be frank with you? I do consider us friends now, after Paris.'

Deborah smiled at her. 'So do I.'

'It's just that . . . well, I know you're the soul of discretion . . .'

'What you say to me will go no further, I promise you.' Deborah was now curious. She couldn't remember such a direct approach from her sister-in-law.

Julia's inward breath was audible. 'I am beginning to wonder if there is something wrong with me.'

'You mean with your health? Oh, Julia, I am sorry. Can I help in any way?'

Julia shook her head. 'Only by allowing me to confide in you.'

'But of course.'

Slowly, Julia began, 'Gerard and I have been married almost a year now, and you must know that he is desperate for a son and heir.'

'Oh, I see. You're becoming anxious that so far there's no sign of that happening?'

Julia nodded.

'I was worried for a moment, I thought you might have a serious illness. Julia, it's still quite early days. Some couples have to wait a long time; it can vary enormously.'

'But that's usually because the woman is older than me. I'm young and according to a medical book I looked at, I should be at my most fertile.' Julia's cheeks became pink.

Deborah thought for a moment. She could sympathise

with Julia, because knowing Gerard, she could imagine that he wouldn't react at all well to his expectations being thwarted.

She gave an encouraging smile to her sister-in-law. 'It could be that a change of scene might prove beneficial. I don't mean Anscombe Hall, but Italy maybe, or romantic Venice.'

Julia brightened. 'A sort of second honeymoon. That's an excellent idea, Deborah, thank you. Of course, we'll have to wait until life returns to normal.'

'You mean the strike? Yes, of course. Mr Baldwin's radio broadcasts are appealing to everyone to trust him, so perhaps even as we speak, efforts are being made to achieve a satisfactory solution.'

'You are so clever, Deborah. I can never understand politics myself.' Julia smiled. 'Perhaps it's as well you can, considering your friendship with a certain member of parliament.'

Deborah laughed. 'You mean Theo? And yes, I have to admit that it does help.'

There was a short silence as Julia hesitated. 'And do I hear wedding bells in the distance?'

Deborah gave a non-committal smile. 'A little early to think of that.'

'But you're not against it, marriage I mean? I met someone the other day who considered it female servitude. I thought it most odd.'

'I think it can be, in certain circumstances. Julia, you must have led a very sheltered life if you don't know that. I'm not against marriage per se, not at all. But the lives of some wives, especially where there is poverty, can be akin to being a domestic slave, and often one who suffers physical abuse.'

'Surely the law wouldn't allow it, I mean a woman being beaten?' Julia's expression was one of horror.

'I'm afraid the constabulary won't interfere between husband and wife, at least not at the moment.'

'Then that should change, it does seem rather unfair.'

That's putting it mildly, Deborah thought. But after Julia had left the room, she began to muse. Was a change in the law something she might persuade Theo to campaign for? And if she were married to him and in the future he became a Cabinet minister, it might mean a chance, albeit behind the scenes, to help to redress other injustices. And then she had to smile. Heavens above, she was running ahead of herself. Theo had never even hinted at a proposal. Or was he waiting to see if such an alliance would have the approval of his father?

Later, thoughts of the current situation regarding the strike returned, and she studied the latest edition of the *British Worker* with its advice to its readers to 'Stand firm. Be loyal to instructions and trust your leaders.'

I can only hope the unions are worthy of that trust, was the phrase that leapt into Deborah's mind.

Chapter Twenty-Seven

Evan had always trusted their leaders. He was also proud of the orderly conduct throughout of the striking workers, and the fact that the country remained staunch in their support for the strike, now in its eighth day. But rumours were that the TUC had been holding secret talks with the mine owners. There had been talk before that the union bosses weren't really behind the strike; that given the surge of intent they had wished only to control it.

'It's going to fail, fall apart,' he told Bronwen, returning after a strike meeting.

'You know my opinion of mine owners. As far as I'm concerned, the TUC might as well sup with the Devil.' She gave him a worried glance. 'You look done in, lad. I managed to get a bit of scrag end, so there's a tasty stew in the oven.'

'Thanks, Aunt Bron, I could do with it!' Evan sat at the table. 'But what if the strike is called off without any concessions? After all their hardship and loyalty, will people have to go back to work having achieved nothing at all?'

'The miners won't go back,' Bronwen retorted, dishing up his food. 'They'll battle on.'

'Aye, and starve while they're doing it.' Evan picked up a spoon and moved the stew around on his plate to cool it. 'What will it all have been for?'

'Mr Baldwin promised in one of his broadcasts that he would ensure a square deal.'

'Maybe, but who for? I'm afraid I don't have a lot of faith in our prime minister. There are too many vested interests in the House of Commons. The rich look after their own, they always have. Mark my words, those blasted mine owners won't budge an inch.'

Bronwen remained quiet as Evan polished off his meal, then said, 'At least you've got a job to go to.'

'Maybe, but I had such high hopes, we all did.'

'You could be wrong, you know.'

'We'll have to wait and see, won't we?'

But they didn't have to wait long, because on the 12th of May, the TUC unilaterally called off the strike. With no guarantees of fair treatment for the miners, the bewildered strikers began to drift back to work. There was only one exception, the men they had supported for nine long days. The miners, desperate for justice, had decided to struggle on alone.

* * *

Early the following day, Evan set out for Blackheath. The morning was cool, the air fresh, and his long legs easily covered the not inconsiderable distance to the peaceful tree-lined avenue where the Colonel lived. But keen though he was to make a success of this chance Deborah had given him, his mind and heart were still heavy since the body blow of the TUC's announcement. Thousands would feel gutted by what had happened. As he walked past imposing residences with their manicured lawns and flower borders, Evan contrasted the comfortable lives of their inhabitants with those of the miners, toiling below ground, emerging into daylight exhausted, with blackened faces and lungs full of dust. Did these wealthy people give even a thought as to how the coal for their cosy winter fires had been hewed from the ground? What long hours were worked for starvation wages? And now these brave men had been betrayed.

However, as he walked up the drive to the Colonel's house, Evan knew he had to subdue his anger in order to present the right attitude. He approached the front door, which on a single ring of the bell was opened by the butler, who smiled and stood aside. 'Good morning, Mr Morgan, if you would care to come downstairs and change.'

Taken aback, Evan looked down at his second-best suit.

Weston smiled. 'I should explain that the Colonel prefers a member of staff such as yourself to dress appropriately. Black trousers with a striped waistcoat? Provided at his expense, of course.'

Evan, blessing the fact that he was wearing black shoes,

followed the butler to the backstairs and down into the kitchen. He hadn't expected this, but at least it would wear out someone else's clothes rather than his own. The two men passed through the kitchen where a couple of maids sent Evan a welcoming smile, and Weston showed him into a small room next to the butler's pantry. 'The wardrobe in the corner is for your exclusive use and the key is in the lock. I hope I've estimated your size correctly.' He glanced at his watch. 'You should just about have time for a cup of tea.'

Satisfied with the fit of the clothes, fifteen minutes later Evan had just drained his cup, when one of the bells on a nearby wall jangled. Below was the name, Colonel Driscoll Bedroom.

'I'll show you to it as it's your first morning,' Weston said. 'The Colonel usually has his refreshment at eleven o'clock, when one of the maids will bring it up. I suggest you join us down here for your own.'

The butler led the way past the room with the chess table where Evan had been interviewed, and to a wide door at the end of the hall. 'This used to be the late mistress's sitting room until the Colonel was injured in the war, and then adapted as his personal quarters.'

So his employer had been widowed, Evan thought, as Weston opened the door and announced him. The Colonel, already fully dressed but red-faced with exasperation, greeted Evan with obvious relief.

'That will be all, thank you,' he told the buxom nurse by his side.

'Are you sure there is nothing more I can do for you, Colonel?' She looked conspiratorially at Evan. 'I'm afraid we're in rather a bad mood this morning.'

The Colonel barked, 'I wish you a good day.'

She gave an angelic smile and Evan opened the door for her to leave.

'Dratted woman, I cannot abide the patronising attitude of some of these people.'

Evan laughed. 'I promise I won't refer to you as "we".'

'You'd be out on your ear, if you did.' He wheeled his chair to a door at the side of the room. 'You may as well have a look at the facilities.'

Evan stood in the entrance to a well-equipped bathroom, complete with a hoist over the spacious white-enamelled bath and support bars on the wall around the lavatory.

'I can see to myself for that,' he nodded at the WC, 'but will need your help with my morning bath and also with dressing.' The Colonel turned his wheelchair, and in the bedroom showed Evan an enormous mahogany wardrobe with a central full-length mirror. 'It might be a good idea to familiarise yourself.'

Evan opened the double doors to see more clothes than he would have imagined one man could possibly need. A tie rack was on the inside of one door, and a number of narrow shelves held a supply of shirts and fine knitwear. There was a row of shoes on racks on the floor, while two drawers at the base of the wardrobe contained underwear and socks.

'It's very well organised, sir.'

'I like things to be shipshape, even though I wasn't in the navy.'

Evan was tempted to ask his army regiment but thought better of it, reminding himself that he was merely an employee. Maybe when he got to know the other man better. 'How can I be of service at the moment, sir?'

'You can wheel me into my sitting room, where I'm hoping Weston will have brought in the morning post. Assistance helps my shoulder muscles.'

'Of course.' Finding it a little awkward to manoeuvre at first, Evan managed the short distance fairly smoothly, going ahead to open the door and once inside noticed a silver salver on the desk containing several envelopes. He positioned the wheelchair in what he thought to be a practical position, and stood back.

'Thanks.' The tone was brusque but the Colonel turned and smiled. 'I shall be occupied for at least half an hour. Perhaps you could sort out whatever mischief that nurse has been up to with my laundry. You will find a bag somewhere in there to put it in, then just pull the bell cord and a maid will collect it.'

Evan nodded and quietly left the room to return to the other one. The task was swiftly completed, and he couldn't help thinking that if his occupation so far came under the heading of 'work', then he had hitherto been sorely exploited. And he still had no idea in what capacity his engineering skills might be used.

At a loose end for several minutes, he went to gaze out

of the full-length windows in the centre of which was a door leading to the well-kept garden. Twin lawns and deep herbaceous borders were lined by tall privet hedges. Beyond he could see an extensive vegetable section. A large greenhouse was to the side, where he imagined a gardener would be nurturing flowering plants for the summer. There was also a small summer house. Evan's experience of gardening was limited to Bronwen's small London patch, but in his youth in Wales he had worked as a delivery boy for a local grocer, his ride on his bicycle sometimes taking him to the back doors of large houses. Their gardens, tranquil in their beauty, had always entranced him.

Glancing at his watch, he realised it was almost time to return to his duties, and he was curious to discover exactly what they might be. It lifted his spirits to be told that the Colonel valued fresh air and enjoyed surveying what was happening in the gardens. Evan, relishing the thought of regular exercise, was glad he had kept himself fit, because not only was the wheelchair solidly built, its occupant was no lightweight. 'Do you normally have a rug over your knees, sir?'

'I do. You'll find it in the ottoman in my bedroom.'

Not a word about the strike being called off, Evan thought, which rather surprised him, based on their previous conversation. However, he was not to wait too long for the subject to be raised.

It was during the afternoon that the visitor arrived. She was not ushered in by the butler, instead the door was flung open and the room immediately energised.

Evan, having brought back the Colonel from his postprandial nap in his bedroom, was at the side of the room ringing for a maid to bring a tea tray. The young woman who came in didn't even glance at him.

'And what do you think of it, my dear uncle? Words absolutely fail me. After all the months of planning, agonising and organising . . . need I go on?'

'You are, of course, talking about the debacle of the strike?'

'You bet I am.'

'Now mind your manners, my dear. You haven't even noticed my new assistant, Mr Evan Morgan. This young lady is my niece, Mrs Geraldine Parry.'

She swung round and Evan saw her hesitate a moment and then her eyes widen.

'I'm sorry, Mr Morgan, I just feel so full of anger about it. And you must be even more so.'

Evan was taken aback by her comment. And it was true, anger was indeed blazing from her green eyes.

'I have heard you speak several times,' she explained.

There was something vaguely familiar about her and then his mind cleared. Of course, the red-haired girl who regularly came to the public meetings. It was said that she reported back to a relative. Could that be the Colonel? He gathered himself. 'It's good to meet you, Mrs Parry. Actually, I do recall seeing you in the audience.' He turned to his employer. 'The majority of the people tended to be men so . . .'

The Colonel chuckled. 'Her hair, I suppose.'

'I did wear a hat!'

'Even so, it will always betray you. She'd never make a criminal, would she, Evan?'

He wasn't sure whether he was more surprised by the Colonel's familiar manner or the fact that he'd used Evan's first name. 'That's not for me to say, sir.' He hesitated, 'As you have a guest, I shall give you some privacy. Is there anything you need?'

He shook his head. 'Nothing at the moment, and if I do, my niece will look after me. Ah,' he brightened as a maid came in with a tray of tea. 'Thank you, Maisie, and I see you have brought an extra cup for Mrs Parry.'

'Hello, Maisie, are you well?'

The maid smiled. 'Yes, thank you, madam.'

Evan began to follow the girl out of the room, and before he closed the door heard the visitor say, 'I do hope I get a chance to talk to him. Personally, I think the cause of the collapse was a lack of cohesion and organisation between the striking unions.'

'She's lovely,' Maisie confided as they walked along the hall. 'Ever so attentive to him, she is. Cheers him up no end.'

And extremely intelligent as well, Evan thought. He'd liked her forthright manner, and as a fleeting image of Deborah came to him, he realised that the two young women would probably have much in common. He frowned, as ushering Maisie before him, they went down the backstair. Now that he was working, there would be no chance to go to the agency and hear what Deborah thought about what had happened. Yet Evan was fighting his urge to write and suggest they meet. Her attraction for him was undoubtedly strong, but there was no denying they came from different backgrounds. He knew what Bronwen would advise. He could almost hear her saying 'Don't stir up a hornet's nest'. But didn't all of life hold out challenges?

Chapter Twenty-Eight

Following the end of the strike, the first few days back at the agency proved to be the busiest Deborah could recall. While some employers were understanding about employees withdrawing their labour, many others sought to punish such recalcitrants by dismissing them.

One such victim had touched both the hearts of Elspeth and herself. A hard-working man of good character, Danny Wilson had five children with a wife in poor health. And yet she had encouraged him to join the strike, believing implicitly as he had, that justice would prevail, that the ill-treated miners would achieve the shorter working hours and increased pay they deserved.

'I've never bin out of work,' he told Deborah. 'I'll turn my hand to anything. I can't believe the gaffer sacked me. I were only off nine days.'

She looked at him, a burly man whose nose must have been broken at some time, and his steady gaze impressed her. 'A foreman, you say?'

'Yeah, miss, in the building trade, but I tell you I'll try anything. Can't afford not to have a wage comin' in, and that's a fact. I come 'ere because a mate got a job through you. Mind you, that was a servant so . . .'

Deborah thought for a moment. Normally, she would explain that the agency didn't handle his sort of employment, but she did have contacts with a couple of building firms, in fact a client had only recently gone to work at one as an assistant clerk. It might be worth a telephone call. But it would be futile to send the man for an interview if the prospective employer viewed the strike action in the same way as his last. And if that intolerance was established, the names of either one or both firms would be added to a list that Elspeth was currently compiling.

'I shall make some telephone enquiries, Mr Wilson. I can't promise anything, I'm afraid. But if you could return tomorrow, say around three o'clock?'

'I'll be 'ere, and thank you, miss.'

Deborah watched him leave and then glancing at her watch realised it was lunchtime. She was hungry too; it had been non-stop all morning.

It was after she and Elspeth had eaten their ham sandwiches that the topic of Deborah's planned visit to

Theo's home was raised, and within seconds she was gazing at her assistant in horror.

'There's no mistake, Deborah, I knew as soon as you said the name.' Elspeth rose and went to fetch the relevant file. 'Felchurch Manor is where two of our clients are working.'

Deborah's mind was in chaos. 'I can't believe it didn't register with me! But that was the first time Theo's ever mentioned it, normally he just refers to Wiltshire.'

Elspeth was running her finger down a column. 'Here it is. Sarah Boot – if you remember you took a liking to her.'

'I do remember,' Deborah said, her breathing ever more rapid. 'She was a parlourmaid who took a lower position.'

'That's right. The other is Meg Daniels, who went as cook. A jolly sort of woman. Both placements were earlier this year.'

Deborah nodded. She was fighting panic, wondering what on earth she was going to do. She had always feared this situation would arise, that as a guest in some large household, she would come face to face with one of her clients. And for it to be Theo's home was nothing less than a catastrophe.

'I doubt Mrs Daniels would see you,' Elspeth said.

'That is true. But Sarah, being a housemaid, is a different matter.'

'I'm afraid so. Although less likely your paths would cross than if she were a parlourmaid.'

'It's still a risk. And she could have been promoted.'

'Deborah, it's not very likely, not after such a short time.'

But Deborah wasn't feeling logical. Because there was no way she could avoid going to meet Theo's father either this time or in the future. Nor did she wish to. She bitterly regretted that she hadn't been truthful and told Theo about the agency. She had toyed with the idea of doing so once at Theo's home, but now her hand was being forced. It was unthinkable that Theo would discover it through household gossip.

'I'm sure Sarah Boot would recognise me,' she said.

'You would have to ask her to respect your privacy.'

'Maybe, but what if Theo happened to be with me at the time?'

'I see what you mean. You're in a quandary, Deborah, and I sympathise, I really do.' Deborah's mind was in turmoil. She was going to have to tell Theo beforehand, and she wasn't at all sure how he would react to the revelation. Deborah thought of their many long and frank discussions, how open he had been about his own personal life and the tragic loss of his fiancée. Yes, she had briefly talked of Philippe, but only after Theo had first mentioned him, it being general knowledge that she had been engaged to someone who was killed in the war. But how stupid she'd been not to explain then about the agency. The problem was that being secretive had become second nature to her. Otherwise she would have been considered a curiosity in her elitist social circle. A member of the aristocracy working? A staff agency? *Quelle horreur*! She could well imagine the trite comments. *One would have to mix with the lower orders, for heaven's sake.* And if she was honest, it had always given her a tiny frisson to know that part of her life was conducted in secret. Or had it been that she enjoyed a sense of superiority to her wealthy and idle friends.

It didn't matter now, because despite all her efforts, the truth had to come out. Not that she was afraid that Theo would tittle-tattle, he wasn't that sort of man. But he would be hurt, rightly so, that she had kept it from him. And confused as to why.

She could, of course, postpone the dreaded moment; after all, her weekend visit was planned for the end of the month. But avoidance would only bring with it endless worry and heart-searching, after which she would still have to face the problem. Later in the week Theo was taking her out to dinner, she would tell him then.

They dined in the same small restaurant she had liked before. Deborah's anxious gaze watched every nuance of Theo's expression, as he listened to her halting explanation of the double life she had lived for so many years. But his face remained impassive and Deborah became increasingly afraid that she may have lost his trust forever.

Slowly she finished speaking, her eyes questioning his, her hand grasping the stem of her wine glass in an effort to control her trembling fingers. When the silence between them stretched, her frantic brain began to seek an escape. Should she simply leave? Walk out before despairing tears betrayed her? Theo wasn't going to forgive her, and she couldn't blame him. He must think her duplicitous at the very least.

Then to her astonishment Theo not only smiled, he began to chuckle. 'It's unbelievable! Lady Deborah Claremont, the sister of the Earl of Anscombe, going out to work for all the world like an ordinary woman.'

'You don't mind?' She stared at him in bewilderment.

'I think it's marvellous.' He stretched out a hand and it was an overwhelming relief to gain strength from his firm, warm grasp. 'Deborah, my beautiful Deborah, I've always respected your intelligence, your social conscience. But to know that you actually put the latter into practice? Why on earth would I mind?'

'Gerard would be horrified if he knew.'

'Darling, I am not Gerard. I hope I have a more liberal view of life.' Then he frowned.

'But I do wonder why you have waited until now to tell me?'

Deborah bit her lip, unsure whether to reveal the true reason. Then encouraged by Theo's reaction, she decided to be honest. 'I'd hesitated to do so in the early days, and then I wanted to find the right time.' She gave his hand a squeeze. 'I'd actually decided to talk to you about it at Felchurch Manor. Perhaps when we were walking in the rose gardens you've mentioned.' She hesitated, 'But I've rather had my hand forced.' At his questioning look with some embarrassment she told him of the two clients who had now joined the household staff.

'And you only just made the connection?'

'Theo, you had never mentioned Felchurch Manor by name, you just referred to Wiltshire.'

'I usually do,' he said reflectively. He smiled at her. 'It's going to be rather intriguing, don't you think, waiting to see if this Sarah Boot recognises you.'

'More than that,' she said. 'I'm going to have to hope she'll be discreet.' She was feeling almost euphoric at Theo's reaction to her news, but that didn't mean she was complacent. After all, it would be a juicy bit of gossip for Sarah to regale to the other servants, especially Meg Daniels, the cook. And it was going to be very awkward to explain to the girl why that shouldn't happen.

'A monetary incentive?'

Deborah shook her head. 'I'd rather not. I don't think she's that sort of girl at all. And couldn't such a thing be the first step to blackmail?'

He gave a rueful smile. 'Perhaps you should be the politician.'

She laughed. 'And don't think I haven't thought of it!'

His expression became serious. 'Tell me, has the ending of the strike had much effect on your agency?'

Deborah told him of the increasing number of applications, and of the recent one from Danny Wilson. 'An honest, hard-working man, with an invalid wife and five children. Fortunately, I've placed him, and it is instances like that, Theo, which give me such satisfaction. But what comes over from people is bewilderment. Mine too, if it comes to that. Nine million people withdraw their labour in support of their fellow man, which says much about the nobility of the working classes. And the government give not an inch?' Her voice rose with indignation. 'So where does that leave the miners?'

'Exactly as they were before, poorly paid and overworked.' Theo's tone was bitter. 'I hate injustice, Deborah, and nor do I enjoy being frustrated in my efforts to ameliorate it. The problem is that so many MPs hold entrenched views. The opinion was that to allow people to defy their government, for it to concede to their demands, would create a dangerous precedent. And always there hung in the air the threat, imagined or otherwise, of it turning into a workers' revolution, one involving violence.' He gave a shrug. 'I am not sure myself how the mine owners won round the TUC, but I suspect they both shared a fear that if the strike went on too long, the country's economy would suffer.'

Deborah gazed at him. 'Do you think the miners are right to hold out?'

'Desperate times call for desperate measures, and what choice do they have? But if you are asking me whether their struggle will be successful, then I doubt it very much.' He glanced at his watch. 'As I warned you, I have a committee meeting in the House first thing tomorrow.'

She nodded, and then reached over the table to take his hand in hers. 'Theo, thank you so much for understanding.'

He smiled. 'I hope, Deborah, that I'll be able to show understanding about anything that's important to you.'

After a moment's silence, she said, 'You're a wonderful man, do you know that?'

'And you, my darling, are rapidly becoming the light of my life.'

Although as Theo drove her back to Grosvenor Square, there was still uncertainty in her mind. Theo would never reveal her secret, aware of the scandal it would cause in their social circle. But would Sarah Boot be able to understand that?

Chapter Twenty-Nine

The following week Deborah received another letter from her friend, Abigail. It was short, but one she read with increasing pleasure.

Dear Debs,
We have been forced to change our plans. We are still coming down, in fact setting out tomorrow, but as both of Angus's parents are suffering from influenza, we have decided to visit the London house first. I shall telephone you once we're rested from the journey. I can't wait to hear all your news,
Much love,
Abby xx

As Deborah had expected, within forty-eight hours of the family's rest period after the long journey, Abigail, minus Angus, but plus two excited little girls, was making herself at home at Grosvenor Square. In Deborah's sitting room, the twins flung themselves at Deborah for a hug, while she laughed saying, 'Good heavens, you're getting so tall!'

'I'm the tallest,' Morag declared.

'No, you're not, I am.' Fiona gave her sister a push.

'Now then, girls, I've told you that there's scarcely anything between you.' Abigail smiled at her friend. 'Total horrors, aren't they? Thank heaven they have a nanny.'

Deborah laughed. 'You know you adore them. And they're the image of you.'

'They've certainly got my blonde hair.'

'But Papa's eyes.' The twins spoke together, causing Deborah to laugh yet again.

'Well, I think you're both enchanting. And I love your sailor dresses.'

The two little girls preened themselves, then looked at her expectantly.

Deborah deliberately made them wait a few seconds, then whispered, 'Try looking behind the chair your mama is sitting on.'

With one accord they dashed to see, and a squeal went up as their present was found. 'Look,' Morag went to show Abigail. 'A skipping rope.'

'And you've got different colour handles, red and blue,' Abigail said. 'Clever Aunt Deborah!'

'Can we play with them now?' Again both spoke together.

'Later, when we go out,' Deborah promised. 'But for now, if you go with Ellen to see Cook, I think she may, just may, have a treat for you.'

'And only if you're good,' Abigail called after them.

The two young women began to relax, with Deborah saying, 'Abby, they're delightful.'

'Thanks, Debs.'

'So, how are you? Still living in married bliss?'

Abby laughed. 'I suppose you could call it that. If you're asking if I'm happy, then my answer is yes. Not that Angus can't be difficult at times, but tell me a man who isn't. And I don't suppose I'm perfect. But he was the right choice, which is a miracle when you think how young I was, and we hadn't known each other for very long.'

'Everything was different then, though, because of the war. People had to snatch happiness wherever they could.'

'It was such a pity that you couldn't be at our wedding. Still, I suppose you couldn't help being stricken with pneumonia when you were miles away, visiting your Aunt Blanche.'

'At least I saw her again, before she died.' Deborah turned away, indicating a display of pink roses on her desk. 'These came this morning from Theo.'

'They're lovely. I can't wait to meet him. Is he "the one", Debs?' She laughed. 'I can see by the way your face lights up, that he could be.'

'He hasn't proposed yet. But I am going down to Wiltshire to meet his father at the end of the month.'

'And if he pops the question there?'

Deborah smiled. 'What do you think?' And then she couldn't help frowning as she thought of Evan.

'What is it?'

'As perceptive as ever! Now you're going to think I'm mad, but . . .'

'Why?'

Deborah told her how, when coming back from Paris, she had seen Evan on the train, then heard him speak at Battersea. She paused. Could she, should she tell her best friend about the ugly scene in the alley? Deborah knew that several weeks ago her distress would have made it impossible for her to do so. Suddenly the temptation was overwhelming. 'He also rescued me from being raped.'

'What!' Abigail stared at her in horror. She listened as Deborah recounted what had happened.

'Good grief, Debs, what a terrible thing to happen.'

'You're the only person I've ever told about it. So you won't . . .'

'Of course not. I can understand your not wanting people to know. So what happened with this Evan, afterwards I mean?'

'He took me to a tea shop, and we talked for a bit, and since then he's become a client at the agency.' Deborah paused. How could she explain something when she was mystified by it herself? 'There's something between us, Abby, and I'm sure he feels it too. Yet when I'm with Theo, I'm so sure that I love him. But what is tormenting me is how can I then feel attracted to someone else?'

'Easily,' Abigail said promptly. 'People do it all the time. You know yourself of marriages where either the husband or wife, or both in some cases, cast longing looks at other people. They don't necessarily do anything about it.'

'Yes, but that's usually after years together, when familiarity can become boring. Not in the early stages of love, surely?'

'You say that he's working class?'

Deborah nodded.

'You don't think it's just that "you fancy a bit of rough", as they say.'

'Abigail!'

She tossed her head. 'Well, it has been known. In fact, just between you and me, there was a ghillie on our estate a couple of years ago. And honestly, Debs, I found myself thinking about him at the most odd times.'

'Did you have conversations with him?'

She shook her head. 'No, nothing like that. I kept well away. But it was his physique! Angus, as you know, has quite a slight build, and one couldn't help wondering . . .'

Deborah exploded into laughter. 'You're making it up, just to make me feel better.'

'I'm not! Anyway, he only stayed with us a matter of months. I was rather glad to see him go, to be honest.'

There was a noise at the door as the twins burst in, with Ellen following. 'Cook made us little iced buns with our names on them, Mama.'

'Oh yes, and how many did you have?'

'All of them, two each!'

Deborah got up and went to look out of the window. 'It's a lovely day out there. Would you like to go to Hyde Park?'

'Yess . . .' They rushed to pick up their skipping ropes.

'Ellen, would you mind taking them to wash their hands first?' Abigail said.

'Not at all, my lady.'

In Greenwich, Bronwen was slicing a large crusty loaf. 'I'll make us cheese and pickle sandwiches,' she called through to Evan, who was relaxing in an armchair in the front room.

'Can you pack some celery as well?'

'Yes, if you pull one up and wash it.'

Evan grinned, knowing it was his aunt's least favourite job, understandable as an old nailbrush was needed to scrub off the outside soil, not to mention parting the stalks to be rinsed. The small patch of earth behind the house was invaluable in supplying them with some, if not all, of their vegetables. He knew Bronwen would have loved to grow flowers, but had to content herself with a cheap bunch off a market stall marked down at the end of the day.

He was relishing having a whole Saturday off. The Colonel's batman, who left his service because of illness, had returned for just the weekend to help the Colonel to bathe, shave and wear his full dress uniform in readiness for his regiment's annual reunion.

As he passed through the scullery on his way out to the tiny garden, Bronwen was boiling a kettle to make a flask of tea. 'We'll take a Thermos as well.'

'And some fruit cake?'

She nodded. 'We don't have a picnic that often, so I intend to make the most of it.'

Half an hour later, they were ready to set off, with Evan carrying a small wicker picnic basket, which had been a retirement present to Bronwen's late husband.

'It's not too heavy, now?'

'If you're not careful, I'll carry you as well!' He smiled down at her, feeling in a good mood. He always liked being out in the fresh air. Hyde Park would attract many others on such a sunny day but that was fine with Evan, it always lifted his spirits to see people enjoying themselves. And he owed Aunt Bronwen this day out, although he planned to spend the evening in convivial male company. Evan had never been a heavy drinker, but enjoyed a couple of beers as much as the next man. And the fact that he also had Sunday off, meant that tomorrow he could help out at a local soup kitchen. Bronwen usually did her best to help too, her sharp humour often raising a smile on the most downcast faces.

At first they just strolled around, with sunlight flickering through the leaves on the trees, families enjoying the sunshine, nannies wheeling perambulators, and excited dogs barking. Evan took a kick at a ball that was rolling away from a small boy, and Bronwen laughed at him. 'Let's go and see the horses in Rotten Row, and then find a good picnic spot. I shall need a bench to sit on, though. Gone are the days when I could sit on the grass. Well, I could sit on it, it's getting up would be the problem.'

He'd always liked horses, although when he lived in Wales, he'd hated to think of the poor pit ponies, confined underground in the mines. Not to eat fresh grass, or breathe in clean crisp air, it went against nature. But the horses they were seeing here were well fed and groomed, although he suspected that Bronwen was just as interested in the fashionable people riding them.

It was when he was admiring a glossy black stallion, expertly controlled by its male rider, that the two little girls with sailor collars skipped towards him. They were obviously having a race and smilingly he moved out of their way. Only then did he see the two young women who were accompanying them . . .

Abigail must have heard Deborah's sharp intake of breath because she swiftly took her friend's arm. 'Debs?'

'It's Evan Morgan . . .' She began to slow down and releasing her arm, a curious Abigail followed suit.

When they came face to face, Deborah felt her face flush a little as she saw the warmth in Evan's eyes. 'This is unexpected, Evan.'

He smiled, 'Yes, it is. How are you, Deborah?'

'I'm very well, thank you.'

He turned to the slightly built woman by his side. 'This is Miss Claremont, Aunt Bronwen. If you remember, I mentioned her to you. Deborah – this is my aunt, Mrs Clarke.'

Bronwen held out her cotton-gloved hand to be shaken. 'How do you do, Miss Claremont? It's nice to put a face to the name.'

Deborah smiled and introduced Abigail, ignoring her raised eyebrows when her correct title wasn't used.

Bronwen said, 'I imagine, Mrs Munro, that those two little imps who were skipping, belong to you?'

'Heavens, yes, I must see where they've gone.' She began to hurry ahead.

'How is the job progressing?' Deborah asked Evan.

'It's working out well, although I've yet to discover why the Colonel needs my engineering expertise.'

'I have no idea either, but I'm sure all will be revealed eventually.'

Evan smiled at her, and the momentary silence was broken by Bronwen. 'It's certainly a lovely day.'

'That's what we thought,' Deborah said. 'It seemed a pity to keep the children indoors.'

Young voices reached them as the children returned, shepherded by their mother.

Bronwen smiled down at them. 'And how old are you two?' she asked the identical twins.

'Six and a half,' they chorused.

'I'm Morag . . .'

'And I'm Fiona.'

'What lovely names. Now let me guess, were you born in Scotland?'

They both nodded, giggling.

'And I was born in Wales.' She turned to Evan. 'Well, we mustn't delay these good people any longer. You've already carried that picnic basket too long.'

'A picnic!' Morag began to jump up and down. 'Can we join them, Mama, can we, please?'

'Of course we can't,' Fiona told her. 'Cook told us she was making a special luncheon for us. *And* we're to eat in the dining room.' The last few words were pronounced with self-importance.

Deborah laughed. 'That's true, and we ought to return.' But her gaze was on Evan, and he held it for one long moment, before she said, 'It was lovely to meet you, Mrs Clarke, and to see you, Evan. Enjoy the rest of your day.'

It took another fifteen minutes of seeking a suitable spot to have their picnic before Bronwen declared herself satisfied with an empty bench under a tree with spreading branches. 'Shady and quiet,' she said, and as they sat with the wicker basket between them began to unpack their food. The bread was crusty and fresh, the cheddar cheese had a sharp tang, the celery was crisp, and Bronwen's home-made fruit cake delicious. Evan, who had expected comments from his aunt about the people she had just met, was surprised that she was so quiet. Instead, there was only the sound of birds chirping in the branches above, and the sound of a bat and ball nearby to disturb their peace. It was only when Bronwen had poured their tea from the flask that the atmosphere changed.

She handed Evan his drink, then squaring her shoulders said, 'You and I, boyo, have some serious talking to do.'

Chapter Thirty

Evan remained silent until he had finished his drink, then turned to his aunt. 'That sounds a bit ominous.'

Bronwen gazed at him, anxiety in her eyes. 'You could say that.' She hesitated.

'What's wrong, Aunt Bron?'

She took a deep breath. 'It's this Miss Claremont . . . Didn't you tell me that she ran the staff agency, the one you applied to for a job?'

'Yes, she does.'

'And that you first met her when her hat blew off?'

He nodded.

'What sort of hat was it? Like the one she was wearing today?'

Evan frowned, remembering how lovely Deborah had looked in a blue velvet cloche. 'Not really, it was just a hat, I suppose. I think it had a small brim.'

'Not the sort of hat that a lady of quality would wear?'

He laughed. 'I don't know any ladies of quality.'

'You've got eyes in your head, you know what I mean.'

Slowly he shook his head. 'No, I suppose not.'

'So when you met her, what did you think was her background?'

'A step up from mine, that was for sure.'

Bronwen persisted. 'And if today had been the first time you'd seen her?'

An image came into Evan's mind, not only one of a stylishly dressed Deborah but also her fashionable friend and the sailor dresses of the children. Slowly he said, 'I'm beginning to see what you mean.'

Bronwen hesitated. 'Miss Claremont is a very attractive young woman. I can understand why you're smitten. There's no use denying it, any fool could see you were attracted to each other.'

'I'm sorry, but I rather think my personal life is my own business.'

'And, ordinarily, I'd agree with you. But I can't stand by and see you get hurt.'

'And what makes you so sure that I will be? Lots of people marry out of their class. Not that I know Deborah well enough even to think that far ahead, but . . .'

Bronwen was shaking her head. 'Yes, I know, but it's

usually within reason. And sometimes, just sometimes, it can work out. But with your Miss Claremont, it would be an entirely different kettle of fish. Evan, I worked in a posh haberdashery shop for years and used to handle all sorts of fabrics. I could tell you the price of cloth just by looking at it.' She paused, 'I also know haute couture when I see it.'

'Aunt Bronwen, what exactly are you getting at?'

She put a hand on his arm. 'My love, that group were members of the aristocracy, and if not quite that, something very near.'

He stared at her in shocked disbelief. 'You're wrong, you've got to be. Deborah came to one of my talks in Battersea, and her views are the same as ours, she deplores social injustice.'

'And all credit to her. But just think, Evan . . . her manners, her posture, her air of confidence. That only comes with one thing, birth and wealth. I'm sorry, my love, but you're from different worlds, far different.'

Evan felt the beginnings of anger, as he tried to make sense of what Bronwen was saying. He said slowly, 'Then tell me, why does she work for a living? It wouldn't make any sense.'

'I don't know the answer to that. But I'd bet a pound to a penny that I'm right.'

He gazed at her, seeing only loving concern in her eyes. But Deborah couldn't be a member of the aristocracy. He could never have anything in common with those sort of people.

'I'm sorry, Evan.'

He could see that his aunt was feeling distressed after expressing her opinion and he placed his strong hand over her worn one. He knew, too, that she only had his best interests at heart, but his feelings were in a state of chaos.

'I'm going to have to do some thinking, aren't I? But I still find it difficult to believe what you've said.'

She gave a quiet smile. 'You do that. And to be honest, I'm about ready to go home for an afternoon nap, if that's all right with you. It's been lovely, but I get tired more easily these days.'

And I, Evan thought, need to spend some time on my own. I'll go over everything in my mind, every minute I've spent with Deborah. And if there *is* some mystery about her, I'm damned well going to solve it.

At first, when they returned to Grosvenor Square, the two friends' time alone was limited by the almost constant presence of the children. But as soon as they were alone, Abby's advice was forthright.

'He's madly attractive,' she said. 'And you're right, there is something between you, I could sense it even in that short time. But Deborah, what the hell are you playing at?'

'How do you mean?'

'Leading him on, it's cruel, and unlike you. You must know that it could only end in tears.'

'But I haven't . . .'

'Not physically, maybe, and thank God for that. But the longer you have any association with him, the more he's going to get hurt. And feel a fool into the bargain when he discovers the truth: that his Miss Claremont is actually Lady Deborah Claremont. He's the sort of man who resents our class, take my word for it.' She held up a hand when Deborah began to interrupt . . . 'No harm will be done if you cut him out of your life now, but do you want this Evan to know that you've been lying to him ever since you met?'

'I haven't lied, not as such. I was just being myself, at least the person who runs the agency.' Deborah added, 'I had no idea that personal feelings would become involved.'

'Maybe, but now it's within your power to stop them.'

Any further conversation on the subject was curtailed by the little girls returning with Ellen, and obviously tired. As a parting shot over her shoulder as they left, Abigail said, 'Think about what I've said, won't you?'

'Are these your friends?' Theo asked. It was three days later and they were in the American Bar at the Savoy. He was glancing beyond her.

Deborah turned to see the two people she liked best in the world. Abigail looking stunning in blue shot-silk, while Angus, whom Deborah hadn't seen for twelve months, looked healthy and relaxed. She rose to kiss his cheek. 'It's lovely to see you.'

'It's been far too long.' Angus smiled at her, and as always, she felt the warmth of his friendship. She turned and introduced them both to Theo. Abigail glanced at Deborah and raised one eyebrow, causing Deborah to stifle laughter. That had been their signal as young girls if they found a man attractive. She'd never had any doubt that Theo would meet with approval.

While they enjoyed their cocktails, Theo began to tell Angus and Abigail how much he was looking forward to Deborah's visit to his home in Wiltshire.

'Deborah mentioned that your father isn't well, Theo.' Abigail's tone was sympathetic.

'I'm afraid not. He found the winter particularly trying. Mainly because he wasn't able to ride as often as he would wish.' He smiled at her. 'But it isn't a serious illness, at least I hope not. He had a bad bout of bronchitis, which seems to have left him with a weak chest.'

'That happened to my father,' Angus said, 'although lately he's improved tremendously.'

'He puts it down to Scottish fresh air,' Abigail said. 'Perhaps your father might find the same? We always have a huge New Year gathering, and you'd both be welcome to join us.'

Angus smiled at her. 'Of course they would, darling. But if they're not used to Scotland, they'd probably freeze and catch pneumonia! But there's always the Glorious Twelfth. Do you shoot, Theo?'

Deborah knew that Theo, like herself, was opposed to blood sports, and glanced at him. But she needn't have worried, he was the consummate politician.

'That's most kind of you, Angus. But no, actually neither of us do. I'm afraid our family have never been so inclined.'

Angus laughed. 'Well, an open invitation still stands, just avoid the bloody winter.'

After dining in the Grill, they planned to go along to the ballroom. Abigail collected her beaded evening bag. 'I'll just go and powder my nose.'

'I'll do the same,' Deborah said. They left the men at the table and threaded their way through the restaurant.

Minutes later, they were standing before the gleaming mirrors to touch up their appearance, and after another woman had left, leaving them alone, Abigail turned to her friend, her forehead creasing in a frown.

'Theo is perfect for you, I really like him, and I can tell that Angus does too. You would be absolutely mad to rock the boat! Added to which, he's the most attractive man I've seen for ages. If it wasn't for Angus, I'd be saying to you exactly what I said about Philippe.'

'Which was?'

'You know very well. That it was a pity he saw you first.'

Deborah laughed. 'You don't change, do you?'

'Well, if I don't talk some sense into you, who will? Seriously, Debs, I can so easily see you marrying him. And there's his political career too. You could become involved, use that brain of yours.'

Deborah closed her bag. 'It's the only time I've fallen in love; not since Philippe.'

'Exactly, and I'm thrilled for you. And it would be a chance for you to have children, I know you've always wanted them.'

The silence between them was broken by Abigail saying, 'So why risk throwing it all away? Theo isn't the sort of man who would stand being messed about, Debs.'

Startled, Deborah stared at her. Had she become too self-absorbed, too intent on trying to understand this strange attraction between herself and Evan? Theo was her future, she truly believed that, and she would be devastated if their love for each other didn't lead to an engagement and marriage.

Their conversation was interrupted by two young women coming into the Powder Room, their carefree voices echoing around the room. Abigail opened the door to leave, with Deborah following.

As they approached the table to see the two men turn and smile, Deborah touched her friend's arm. 'You don't need to worry,' she said quietly. 'I shall deal with it. I promise.'

Chapter Thirty-One

At home in Grosvenor Square, Gerard was feeling in an expansive mood. Not only had Freddie Seymour at last turned up at the club, but he'd agreed that in future to keep him more informed. They were relaxing over a drink together, with the only other member in the room gently snoring in a corner.

'Just between ourselves, old chap,' Gerard said, 'I had this hideous thought that your illness could have been fatal. Which led me to question what would happen about our arrangement in such a regrettable circumstance?'

'Yes, of course,' Freddie said slowly. 'You have no idea where the child is.'

'And that was at my request. But on reflection, could you

furnish me with the information? Perhaps in a sealed envelope?'

'Of course.'

'Will you instruct your solicitor? There are always ways that a gentleman can keep his personal finance confidential.' He smiled at the young man opposite. 'But let us hope that you will live to a ripe old age.'

Freddie laughed. 'I shall drink to that.'

And I, Gerard thought, can rest assured that I now have everything covered. Another reason for Gerard's present good humour was the prospect of spending time in Italy with his young wife, especially as when suggesting the trip, she'd described it as a second honeymoon. His fervent hope was that the romantic cities of Rome and Venice would work their magic and shortly after their return, Julia would have good news for him.

So when at breakfast Deborah raised the subject of a dinner party for Abigail and Angus, he was swift to agree. He genuinely liked Angus, and would welcome another chance to have a discussion with Theo.

'That sounds lovely,' Julia said. 'Who will be your guests?'

'I think you know Claudia Faversham and Frances Bentwood? They were Abby's bridesmaids and I know she likes to keep in touch.'

'Yes, I've met all of them. Didn't Claudia lose her husband some months ago?'

'She did. Not that she gives much indication of it. I'm afraid she's getting herself rather a doubtful reputation,' Gerard said drily.

Julia nodded, but didn't comment. 'That will make nine so far,' she said. 'Do you wish to keep it quite small at ten, Deborah? Although we would need another man.'

'I'd quite like to, but if you would prefer to include your own guests . . .' Deborah gave an inward smile. Her sister-in-law revelled in planning the perfect table.

'I'll give it some thought.' Julia said.

'And I, my sweet, shall retire to my study and ensure everything is in order before our Italian trip. A month is a long time to be away.'

As he left, Julia glanced across at Deborah with a happy smile. 'I'm so glad you suggested it.'

She smiled back. 'We'll keep our fingers crossed, then.'

In the event, the guest list for the party numbered fourteen and, not unexpectedly, Claudia flirted outrageously with the wealthy widower Julia had invited. She was obviously delighted with her matchmaking, although Deborah suspected that the man himself, a quiet bookish sort, wasn't quite so comfortable. But there was a relaxed atmosphere with laughter, everyone enjoying the food and wine. Afterwards, they left the men to enjoy their brandies and cigars, where in the drawing room, Theo immediately became the topic of conversation.

Claudia was the first to offer her opinion. Lighting a cigarette through her long cigarette-holder, she blew a perfect smoke ring, then said, 'Well, Deborah, it's taken you a long time, but he was worth waiting for.'

'He's awfully charming,' Frances said.

'I think there is rather more to Theo than just charm,' Deborah said with a smile.

'You'll be saying it's his brain and his politics that attract you next, darling,' Claudia drawled. 'Not his undeniable good looks.'

'Debs was always the one with a social conscience,' Abigail said. 'Personally, I think they're ideally suited.'

'And so do I,' Julia reached out for another bonbon from one of the silver dishes on the coffee table. 'I fully expect an engagement to be announced, and very soon.'

'Honestly,' Deborah protested. 'You're all running ahead. Remember we met less than three months ago.'

'More than enough time,' Claudia said. 'I'd have had him in bed by now.'

Julia gasped, while Abigail frowned. 'You, my dear friend, will be losing count,' she said. 'We've hardly been in London a fortnight and I've already heard your name being bandied about.'

Claudia shrugged. 'I don't care any more.'

Deborah said, 'Oh, Claudia, I know that people deal with grief in different ways, but all this won't bring Archie back, you know.'

'Maybe, but it helps me to forget.' Her lips tightened. 'Bloody horse!'

Abigail turned to Deborah. 'Didn't you tell me that Theo lost his fiancée in the same way?'

She nodded. 'I'm afraid so, she was out riding and was

285

thrown. But it was a long time ago. Before the war.'

'We'd have something in common, then,' Claudia said with bitterness. 'So when you tire of him . . .'

There was a moment's silence around the room.

'You're unbelievable, do you know that?' Frances said, but she wasn't smiling.

'Disgusting, that's what you meant to say.' Claudia's eyes suddenly filled with tears.

'I didn't!' Frances exclaimed.

'Yes, you did, and you were right. And bed-hopping doesn't even help. Archie would be furious with me.'

'Then why not stop?' Deborah, who was sitting next to her on a sofa, lightly touched her hand. 'Go down to the country for a while. Most people have short memories, they'll soon be talking about someone else.'

'Lead the life of a nun, you mean.'

I have for years, Deborah thought, but that was too personal to share, even with her friends.

Julia, who had remained in a shocked silence during the scene, said quietly, 'If the opposite isn't making you happy, what is the point? And you don't want to spoil your chances of getting married again.'

Claudia gazed at her. 'You think being respectable and having a husband is all a woman should aim for?'

Deborah tried to lighten the conversation. 'Well, unless we can hope to be the first female prime minister, why not?' She ignored the expressions of disbelief. 'It will happen one day!'

'In the meantime, to come back to our original statements, we shall watch and wait to see if Deborah lands the gorgeous Theo,' Abigail said.

'You make him sound like a fish!' Deborah put a hand to her mouth as the men came into the drawing room to join them.

'What's that about fish?' Angus asked, and not waiting for an answer, turned to Theo. 'That's another sport we can offer in Scotland. Salmon fishing.'

Even Julia couldn't keep her face straight.

During the evening, Gerard had been observing his sister and Theo. There was no doubt of the couple's feelings for each other. He glanced across at her as she stood with her suitor in a corner of the room, smiling up at him. They made an attractive pair, and it could be that a Member of Parliament might be the best she would be able to contrive. There was also the possibility that Theo's rise to power might be a swift one. Now, a Cabinet minister would be a welcome addition to the Claremont family. Even he himself, the Earl of Anscombe would find his standing enhanced if Theodore Field were to be elected prime minister.

Every time he thought of the scene in Hyde Park, Evan was unable to quell a simmering resentment that he may have been patronised, manipulated. And that was something he wouldn't stand for. Not by Deborah, not by anyone. Or could Bronwen be wrong? Yet there was one thing he had always found difficult to understand. That was even though distressed and shaken after being assaulted in the alley, Deborah had been horrified at his wanting to report it to the constabulary. Could Bronwen's suspicion about her status be the reason?

However, something happened a week later that proved a welcome distraction. One morning, as Evan was pushing the wheelchair around the garden, his employer said in a brisk tone, 'Do you see that ivy-covered archway over there?'

Evan had noticed it before, although the Colonel had never shown any interest in what lay on the other side. 'I do.'

'Wheel me through it, Evan. I want to show you something.'

Intrigued, he turned right and wheeled the chair through the arch, surprised to see a one-storey building. It looked to be fairly recently built, with double doors that were padlocked.

The Colonel searched his top pocket and produced a key. 'Can you wheel me in front of the doors?'

Evan did so, and waited while the Colonel unlocked them.

'Now reverse a little, Evan.'

His employer's use of his first name had served to make their relationship one of friendliness rather than formality, although the Colonel could revert on occasion to asperity. But Evan appreciated the gesture, just as he was beginning to understand and like the man he worked for.

When the chair was a little distance from the doors, the Colonel said, 'Go on, pull them open.'

Evan did, and then returning to the wheelchair guided it inside, only to stare in amazement. Before him, on a huge table, was the extensive layout of a partly built model railway.

'What do you think?'

His reaction was instantaneous. 'Bloody marvellous.' Evan felt a grin spread over his face. So this was why his engineering skills were required.

'It is, isn't it? The whole place was built especially for it, with an even temperature and dry atmosphere. My pride and joy, Evan. I can't do it on my own, so how do you feel about helping me design the rest of it?'

'It would be an honour, sir! When can we begin?'

The Colonel slapped the arm of his chair. 'That's the spirit. And the answer is this very afternoon. I'll give you a key. The only other one belongs to my niece, Mrs Parry. You know, for a young woman, she shows an amazing aptitude for all this.'

But Evan was hardly listening. He just couldn't believe his good fortune. To be able to earn his living by spending hours working on such a fascinating project? Already he was filled with enthusiasm.

His employer was leaning over the layout, picking up an engine and stroking its shiny exterior. 'I've got several books on the subject, so we can look up any technical details.'

The prospect exhilarated Evan, and as they left and he

padlocked the doors, he realised this opportunity would never have come his way if he hadn't met Deborah. He was fed up with all these doubts circling in his mind. It was time he got in touch with her and found out the truth.

Chapter Thirty-Two

With Abigail, Angus and the children having departed to Berkshire, Deborah found herself free to concentrate on the promise she'd made to her friend.

What had actually occurred between herself and Evan? Nothing – only a heightened emotional tension whenever they met, and in Deborah's case at least, a persistent memory, and confusion. She thought of Abby's accusation that she had led Evan on, but knew that wasn't true. However, she had been guilty of crossing a line, of allowing what Gerard would undoubtedly call an unsuitable friendship to develop. She could hardly have done anything else after the ugly experience in the alley. Not only that, but she'd loved talking to Evan, fascinated by his political zeal, his . . . she sought for the correct word and could only think of 'ordinariness'. And if it sounded snobbish, she didn't mean it in that context. More of a difference of culture and experience of life. But Deborah did have to face one fact. Evan was a proud man. He would fiercely resent the fact that she had misled him about her identity.

However, the decision she'd been wrestling with was taken out of her hands, because within a few days, when Elspeth brought in the morning's post, there was an envelope marked *Personal*. On opening it her glance fell to the signature. It was from Evan.

Dear Deborah,

It was good to see you in Hyde Park, looking so well. I hope this request doesn't feel odd, but I would like very much to meet you for tea. Maybe at the Lyon's Corner House most convenient for you?

If you are happy to do this, perhaps you could suggest a convenient date.

But rest assured that I shan't be offended if I fail to hear back from you.

With best wishes,

Evan Morgan

She stared down at it. A completely acceptable note, friendly and polite. And of course she would accept. But her feelings were descending into chaos. She knew that even if Abigail hadn't extracted Deborah's promise, she couldn't have continued to deceive Evan about her true identity. And she felt deeply apprehensive about revealing it. She knew his feelings towards the privileged classes, and he was a man of strong emotions, his fury with that brute in the alley had shown that.

But she would arrange to meet him as soon as possible, because her visit to Wiltshire was fast approaching. Deborah's hope was that when they were in the country, in a different environment from the social whirl of London, she and Theo would become even closer. She neither desired nor needed thoughts of Evan to be a distraction.

Rising from her desk she went into the outer office.

'Elspeth? Do you ever go to a Lyon's Corner House?'

'Yes, of course.'

'Which would you recommend?'

'Either Coventry Street or Tottenham Court Road. I find them both very good.' Elspeth raised her eyebrows in query.

Deborah merely smiled and went back to her office. Tottenham Court Road it would be. A little further away from Grosvenor Square, and so she would be less likely to encounter anyone she knew.

Evan saw the letter propped on the mantelpiece as soon as he arrived home from work. Bronwen bustled into the sitting room behind him, and glancing at the handwritten address in a clear, flowing hand, he guessed she was bursting with curiosity.

'Well, go on, boyo, open it.'

He raised his eyes to heaven. 'Is there no privacy in this house?' But he inserted his thumb under the flap of the envelope and ripped it open. As he'd thought, it was from Deborah, suggesting the Lyon's Corner House in Tottenham Court Road, on Saturday afternoon. Luckily, he wasn't working then. The short note ended in the same way as his own. *With best wishes*. Silently he handed it to his aunt.

Bronwen scanned the lines and compressed her lips. 'Are you going to have it out with her, then?'

'That's one way of putting it.'

She nodded. 'It's for the best.'

Evan was early and waited outside the tall building for Deborah to arrive. He wanted to study her appearance, to try and see her from Bronwen's perspective. But when she alighted from a cab just minutes before their appointment, Evan could see little of the elegant and fashionably dressed young lady they had seen in Hyde Park. Deborah was dressed plainly, in a grey costume and white blouse. Her hat was also grey, and untrimmed. Very similar, he realised, to the other times he'd seen her.

She smiled at him, and he stepped forward. 'How are you, Deborah?'

'I'm very well, thank you, Evan.'

'I just thought . . . well, I've lots to tell you, so shall we go in?' He stepped aside to hold open the door. Their conversation was desultory until he'd found what he considered a decent table in a quiet corner, and once seated, Deborah removed her gloves. Evan gave them a curious glance. Even he could see that they were superior to the type of glove Bronwen wore. But then, Deborah would have more money to spend on clothes, owning as she did a successful staff agency.

A waitress, neat and smart, wearing a starched cap with a big, red 'L' embroidered in the centre, came to take their order. Both chose scones, although Deborah asked for Earl Grey tea.

When the girl had left, Deborah said, 'It was lovely to meet your Aunt Bronwen.'

'It was a coincidence bumping into you like that.' Was it his imagination or did Deborah seem rather tense?

She smiled. 'You said you had lots to tell me? Is it about working for the Colonel? I was hoping all was going well.'

'It is.' With a mental image of the model railway, he described it to her. 'Of course, it's only partially completed, but the space, the potential. Building it is going to be a real joy.'

'Thus the interest in your engineering skills!'

'Exactly.'

'I'm so glad, Evan. It's just what you need, after the collapse of the strike. Something so absorbing.'

He nodded. 'That doesn't mean that my interest in politics has lessened, though. In fact, I feel even more driven to get involved.'

'Good. The country needs more men like you.'

His gaze met hers before she looked away. He frowned, thinking that there was something different about her. It was in her manner, her eyes.

The waitress brought their refreshments, Deborah thanked her and began to pour their tea, putting a slice of lemon in her own. As far as Evan was concerned, tea was just tea. Even the Colonel didn't drink anything fancy. He watched as she began to first slice her scone and then butter it for each mouthful, her movements delicate, neat. He cut his own clumsily, buttered it and began to spread strawberry jam and cream.

Deborah's throat was feeling so dry with nerves that although the scone was delicious, she had to struggle to eat it. Then, after taking a few sips of her tea, she replaced the cup in its saucer; it was no use, she couldn't delay any longer.

'I'm glad you got in touch,' she said quietly. 'It has given me the chance to talk to you about something. Evan, I haven't been entirely truthful with you.'

'About what, Deborah?' Was there an edge to his voice? Swiftly, she glanced up, but his eyes were steady.

'About my name.' She hesitated. 'I'm afraid my correct name is not *Miss* Deborah Claremont, but *Lady* Deborah Claremont.' She held her breath, then saw in his eyes not the surprise and bewilderment she'd expected, but a deep sadness.

'*Lady* Deborah Claremont?'

She nodded. 'My brother is the Earl of Anscombe.'

'Do I now need to address you as Your Ladyship?'

She flinched at his cutting tone. 'Of course not.'

Evan was staring at her, slowly shaking his head. 'So Aunt Bronwen was right. She suspected after meeting you that you were a member of the aristocracy.'

'I'm so sorry to have misled you, Evan.'

'So am I. No man likes to be taken for a fool.'

'I never wanted you to feel like that.'

'Was that why you were so against calling the constabulary that time? Because of your position in society?'

Miserably, she nodded. 'Can you imagine what it would have been like? It was bound to have been reported in the newspapers. I couldn't have borne the shame of it.'

'Yes, I can understand that. But you could have trusted *me* with the truth.'

'It wasn't that . . . it just never seemed relevant, somehow.' She looked at him, her eyes pleading. 'Evan, I couldn't help being born with a title.'

'No more than I can help being born without one. But that isn't the point, Deborah.'

She felt humiliated. He was going to hate her, to wish they had never met.

'So, in a way, you've been leading a double life.'

'I could never have run the agency using my real name. I wanted to give something back, Evan, to help people. And if I don't achieve anything else in my life, I know I've done that.'

Silence hung in the air before he said, 'Forgive me if I ask a personal question?'

'Of course.'

His voice was tense. 'Did I imagine it, or did you too feel the attraction between us? I need to know, Deborah.'

Deborah's breathing quickened as her gaze met his. She knew that she owed him the truth.

'Yes, I did,' she said quietly. 'I still do.'

Evan was silent for a moment. 'Is that why you're now telling me your real name? To prevent my taking things further?'

'Something like that, yes.' Deborah wondered whether he now disliked her as much as she disliked herself, at least at this precise moment.

Evan's voice was tight with anger. 'Do you know what I think, Deborah? That in other circumstances, you and I could have had something special.' His jaw tightened. 'But it all has to go to waste, just because of the class divide in this godforsaken country.'

Deborah knew she had to be honest with him. 'It's not only that.' She raised her eyes to his. 'All these years, ever since I lost my fiancé in the last year of the war, there has never been anyone else. And then,' she gave a wry smile, 'in a matter of weeks, I met first Theo, and then you.'

'Theo? Is he someone titled like yourself?' His voice was flat.

'Not titled, no. He's in the government, a Member of Parliament.'

'And you don't become one of those if you're born poor,' he said bitterly.

'But Theo does have a social conscience, Evan. In fact, he came with me to hear you speak in Battersea.'

'So you were going out with him even then.'

'We had just started spending time together. I'm going to his home in Wiltshire next weekend to meet his father.'

'That sounds as if it's serious.'

'I'm hoping so. But then how can I be so attracted to you?' She shook her head in despair. 'In reality, we hardly know each other. I just don't understand it.'

Evan said, 'There's a lot in life I don't understand.' He paused for a moment. 'But it would never have worked between us, Deborah. In your heart of hearts, you must know that.'

'You don't think we could have overcome it, despite the difference in our backgrounds? If I hadn't met Theo, I mean.' Despite her resolve, her voice was wistful.

Evan's voice was harsh. 'Not in my case, Deborah. All my life, ever since Da was killed in the mine, I've hated your class, their arrogance, their inherited wealth and land. I would never have fitted in with their way of life, and nor would I ever want to.'

With a catch in her voice she said, 'I would have liked us to remain friends, but I don't think that would work somehow.'

He was silent for a moment. 'I think it would be impossible.'

Deborah's eyes stung with tears. She wanted to put out her hand to touch, hold his, to feel for the first time his skin against hers. She didn't want this man to go out of her life, but there seemed to be no alternative. 'I suppose this is goodbye, then?'

Evan's gaze was searching her eyes, her face. Then his lips twisted. 'I could say unless I'm in need of another job, but even then . . .'

She nodded. 'I understand. But I'm still glad that we met. And good luck with your political ambitions, Evan.'

'Thanks, and I wish you all the best.' He hesitated, pain in his eyes. 'Be happy, Deborah.'

Averting her head to conceal her distress, she picked up her gloves, rose and walked away. Emotionally drained and emerging into the noise of the busy Tottenham Court Road, she stood for a moment and then sought to hail a cab. She had done the right thing, the only thing. It was of Theo she should be thinking now, the man she was in love with and hoping to marry.

Chapter Thirty-Three

The following Thursday had been a busy day at the agency, and after her return to Grosvenor Square, Deborah found it a welcome distraction to choose her wardrobe for the coming visit to Felchurch Manor.

'What about this for one of the evenings, my lady?' Ellen took out of the wardrobe the emerald silk dress Deborah had bought in Paris.

'Yes, definitely. But not the red one I wore at Christmas. I don't want to look fast!'

'You could never look that, Lady Deborah.' She held up an ivory dress with sequinned fringes. 'And this one? It goes well with your long ebony beads?'

Deborah nodded, as she did when Ellen suggested taking

some cashmere in case the weather turned cold. She was going to miss her in Wiltshire, but at Theo's suggestion had willingly agreed to manage with one of the resident maids.

'I want to have you to myself on the journey,' he said. 'It wouldn't be the same with someone else in the car.'

As for Ellen, her face had lit up at the prospect of time off to spend with John who had promised to take her to another music hall.

Punctually at ten o'clock on Friday morning, Theo arrived at Grosvenor Square. Wearing a tweed jacket, his expression was carefree as he opened the passenger door. Deborah turned to thank Fulton after he'd stacked her suitcase and hatbox into the boot of the Bentley, and sank onto the soft leather seat.

Once in the driving seat, Theo leant over and fleetingly touched his lips to hers. 'Did you bring your riding habit?'

'Of course. I never travel without it.'

He laughed, slowly drawing away. Deborah, watching him expertly handle the leather-covered steering wheel, wondered yet again whether she should learn to drive. She mentioned it.

'Why not?' Theo said. 'It's jolly useful not to have to depend on others.'

'Brown, our chauffeur, usually drives me, but if Gerard or Julia need him, then I take a cab.'

'Which works in London, but in the country being able to drive yourself would give you independence.'

'Then you aren't against it, women driving? After all, we are encroaching on male territory.'

Theo smiled. 'I wouldn't dare to admit it, even if I were. Which I'm not, as I'm sure you've guessed.'

'I was only teasing.' Deborah snuggled into her comfortable seat, watching the scenery as they began to travel further out of the capital. 'I'm looking forward to seeing Felchurch Manor and to meeting your father.'

Theo was indicating right and slowed down for a moment, glancing at her. 'And he is looking forward to meeting you. Apparently, his health has improved this last week or so. He's arranged a small dinner party for Saturday evening. Just a few close friends, at least that's what he said on the telephone.'

'Yours or his?'

'Probably both. But he didn't consult me, so I have no idea who.'

She laughed. 'So I may hear a few indiscreet comments about your youthful exploits.'

'Perish the thought.' Theo turned and lightly touched her hand. 'What I'm hoping for is lots of private time to spend with you. We've always been surrounded by people, and even when dining alone, it's been in public restaurants.'

'Yes,' she said softly. 'I feel that too.'

As the miles passed, their conversation lapsed, although Deborah did mention her concern about encountering Sarah Boot. 'I just hope she'll not prove to be a gossip.'

'She'll have me to deal with if she does.'

She smiled at him, then began gazing out of the window at unfamiliar scenes, picturesque villages, and the gradual changing of the landscape.

'I think you'll like Wiltshire,' Theo said. 'It's a beautiful county with its areas of chalk downland. But I'm sure your excellent tutor informed you of that.'

Deborah turned to him. 'He also mentioned Stonehenge, and Salisbury Cathedral.'

'Both of which I shall take you to see, but not this weekend. We can plan such outings for when you next come to Felchurch Manor. I thought perhaps a longer visit in August, after the Summer Adjournment?'

A feeling of warmth swept over her, surely that meant that he, too, was looking to the future.

He smiled at her. 'Or do you think we'll be bored with each other by the time Monday comes?'

'There is not, I think, the slightest chance of that,' she said. 'Of course, your father may not like me.'

'Not a chance of that either,' he replied promptly.

Their long journey was broken by a delicious luncheon in a black-and-white timbered small hotel, and the early part of the afternoon was a relaxing one, with Theo occasionally pointing out passing landmarks. They had just exchanged some affectionate repartee when Theo suddenly braked, causing Deborah to jolt forward, putting out her hand on the dashboard to steady herself. 'What's . . .'

But Theo was already pulling up the handbrake and scrambling out of the car. She hurried after him and with horror saw prostrate at the side of the road, half on the grass verge, a young black-and-white collie, its side bloodstained. As they approached, the dog began to whimper, its brown eyes pleading.

'Some bloody moron's knocked him down, and driven on!' His expression thunderous, Theo bent to look at the dog's injury, checking in vain to see if there was a collar. 'He's still bleeding.' Gently, he stroked the dog's head. 'It's all right, boy, it's all right.' He went to open the boot of the car and, removing a tartan rug, opened the back door, before returning to the grass verge. 'Deborah, can you give me a hand?'

'Of course,' Deborah was full of disbelief and compassion for the defenceless animal. How could any decent human being just leave him?

Theo was soothing and reassuring the dog, saying, 'Right, as I lift him, you put the rug underneath.'

The tricky manoeuvre was accomplished, and gathering him up Theo carried the dog to the car and laid him on the back seat. Then after seeing her into the passenger seat, he started the car.

'How far do we have to go?'

'Around five miles or so, I'll get our vet to look at him.' His tone was curt and glancing at his profile she could see a muscle twitching in his left cheek. 'I can't abide cruelty to animals.'

As they travelled, Deborah glanced over her shoulder to look at the dog, distressed to hear the occasional whimper. 'Poor thing, it's a good job we came along.'

* * *

Felchurch Manor was larger than Deborah had expected, its architecture graceful, with the house itself set in mature parkland. Theo smiled down at her as he drove up the long drive. 'It's been in the family for 200 years.'

'It's beautiful.' She meant it, there was something appealing about Theo's home, even from the outside.

Theo turned left before the house and slowly drove the car to the back and into a large, well-kept stable yard. As he drew to a halt, a middle-aged man with a weather-beaten face came forward, his face alight with surprise.

Theo got out of the car. 'Harry, look what I found at the side of the road. Just left there by whichever hooligan ran him over.' He opened the back door and indicated the injured dog on the back seat. 'I'd like the vet to see him.'

'Yes, sir.' He turned, calling over to a youth who was sweeping out a stall. 'Jimmy?'

The stable lad came over and with care they lifted the dog and blanket out.

'We'll put him in an empty stall, sir.'

After watching them leave, Theo guided Deborah back along the wide path that led to the front of the house. 'Ah, here's Langton.'

A tall man of military bearing, immaculate in black jacket and striped trousers, was coming to meet them, his gaze going with alarm to Theo's bloodstained clothes.

'Don't worry, it's from an injured dog.' Theo explained what had happened, and then introduced him to Deborah.

'Arthur will attend to your luggage, Your Ladyship.' The

butler turned to Theo. 'Would you like the car to be valeted, sir?'

'Thank you, an excellent idea.' Theo ushered Deborah through the oak front door and into a hall with a vaulted ceiling; a vase of crimson peonies rested on a gleaming circular table in the centre, while a golden retriever uncurled itself and rushed forward, its tail wagging furiously.

Theo bent to fondle her ears. 'Emma, come to say hello, have you?'

The butler hovered. 'Sir, might I suggest a change of clothing?'

'Before I see my father, you mean? Yes, of course.'

Theo turned as a buxom woman dressed in the inevitable black hurried forward, introducing her to Deborah as Mrs Beresford, the housekeeper.

'Welcome to Felchurch Manor, Your Ladyship. This is Cotton, who will be looking after you.' The trim young maid in frilled white cap and apron who was now by her side, gave a shy smile.

'Thank you so much.' Deborah turned to Theo, raising her eyebrows.

He glanced at his wristwatch. 'Shall we say at seven in the drawing room?'

After giving him a warm smile, Deborah followed the maid up a wide staircase and into a spacious room, with casement windows overlooking the lawns and herbaceous borders of a walled garden. The curtains and drapes were cream patterned with pink roses, and the double bed a four-poster.

'Would you care for some refreshment before I unpack, my lady?'

'I would love some. Earl Grey tea, please.'

Deborah freshened up in the adjacent bathroom and going to relax on a green velvet chair thought about the weekend ahead. For so long there had been within her a sense of something missing in her life, a need to experience again the depth of love and passion she had felt for Philippe. This evening, too, was important, when for the first time she would meet his father. Yet what could possibly go wrong?

And then seeing the young maid come in carrying a tray, Deborah remembered Sarah Boot.

Chapter Thirty-Four

For Theo, dinner that evening was accompanied by pleasure at seeing Deborah so relaxed in his home environment – her warm glances and smiles across the table made that plain. And it was patently obvious that his father was enjoying her company.

'You're very like him, you know,' she said, when Frederick Field briefly left the drawing room.

'Yes, people do remark upon it. It's good to see you both getting on so well.'

'I like him, how could I not?'

Her smile lit up his heart. He'd been so fortunate to have found her. He looked across to where she sat in a comfortable chintz armchair, smiling to himself as she popped a chocolate into her mouth. Such a delicious mouth! Theo, he told himself, you're becoming besotted.

'Are you tired after the journey?' he said softly.

'I am a little,' she admitted.

'And so am I. But we have the whole of tomorrow to look forward to. A ride in the morning, I thought.'

Deborah nodded. 'That sounds a wonderful idea.'

It was late on Saturday morning when Theo at last reined in his favourite black stallion. 'Can you see over there, where the wood begins? That's our boundary. We have forty acres.'

'I think the whole estate is delightful.' Deborah smiled at him. She had proved herself to be an excellent horsewoman and, despite the damp weather, the last two hours had been the most enjoyable he had spent for years. They wheeled round their horses, Deborah's chestnut responding easily to her guidance, while Theo controlled his more spirited mount and the horses walked on.

'You are very like your father,' Deborah said. 'Although it would appear that he's the more bookish of the two of you.'

'If you discount political tomes and biographies, yes,' Theo said. 'I've never been able to read fiction for pleasure, with the exception of Dickens, that is. It was a bone of contention between us during my formative years.'

'But you do seem to be close.'

'Yes, we are.' He smiled at her. 'You really impressed him, darling.'

'He actually said so?'

'Yes, he did.' He looked across at the intelligent young woman he had fallen in love with so soon after they'd met. He had wanted Deborah to see his home – possibly her own future home. A romantic at heart, Theo also wanted a marriage spent in both physical and emotional harmony. It had been a joy to discover that Deborah thought deeply about social justice, and took an interest in politics. He encountered so many young women who were spoilt and shallow in their thinking. Take her sister-in-law Julia, for instance. Charming yes, and decorative, but he doubted she and Gerard had an equal relationship with regard to thoughts and decisions.

'Penny for them?' Deborah asked, smiling at him.

'I was just thinking how wonderful it is to have you here with me.'

'It's lovely for me too. And it was good to see the dog looking better this morning. What will happen to him, once he's recovered?'

'Efforts will be made to trace his owner.' Theo frowned. 'But with the vet saying that he's not a pure breed, and the lack of a collar, Harry's wondering whether he'd strayed from Gypsies. Apparently, some were recently in the area.' He turned towards her with regret. 'Sorry, Deborah, I hate to bring this ride to a close, but it's time we were getting back.'

'Yes, I know you have an appointment. But how about I race you back to the house!'

* * *

Theo won easily with Deborah laughing as they cantered noisily into the stable yard, and after handing their horses over to a groom, they strolled over to the stall where the dog lay.

Deborah bent and patted his head, rewarded by an attempt to lick her hand.

'If no one claims him, I hope a good home can be found.'

Harry grinned. 'A young lad who comes with the laundress has already taken a liking to him. I doubt if she'd take him, though.'

'If it's a question of his keep,' Theo said, 'I'd cover that.'

'Well, sir, that's a right generous offer. I'll pass it on.'

Theo took Deborah's hand as they walked along the path to the front door of the house. 'Thank you, sweetheart, for a lovely morning. As you know, I have some constituency matters to catch up on, so I'll see you at luncheon?'

Deborah went lightly up the stairs. The morning's ride had given her quite an appetite and judging by dinner last night, Meg Daniels, as her references had claimed, was an excellent cook. She was smiling as she reached the wide landing – only for her heart to somersault as she came face to face with Sarah Boot!

Sarah's startled gasp proved there was no hope of not being recognised, and Deborah put a finger to her lips. 'Sshh.' She glanced around. 'Is there anywhere we can talk privately?'

Flustered, the young maid nodded and opened an adjacent door. The large bedroom was empty, and from the dusters and brush in her hands, it was obvious that she'd been cleaning it.

Deborah closed the door firmly behind them, feeling not a little nervous.

She smiled. 'Hello, Sarah, how are you?'

The girl's eyes were wary. 'I be well, Miss Claremont. But . . . what are you doing here? Has someone bin complaining about me?'

Deborah was swift to reassure her. 'No, no, nothing like that.' She hesitated. 'Sarah, can I trust you to keep whatever passes between us as completely confidential? That you won't tell another living soul?'

Her eyes widening, she nodded vigorously.

The two young women were standing opposite each other. Deborah almost suggested they sit on one of the two bedroom chairs, but knew that would make Sarah feel uncomfortable. 'I am here, Sarah, as Mr Theodore's guest for the weekend.'

Sarah's brow puckered. 'I thought he was bringing a Ladyship.'

'That's right. You see, *Lady* Deborah Claremont is my real name. I just use *Miss* Claremont at the agency. Confusing, isn't it? But I'm sure you can understand why.'

Sarah hesitated, 'I think so.'

'I know it sounds strange, but with the exception of

Mr Theodore, no one else knows about this, not even my friends. So, please can you keep it a secret?'

'Of course I will.'

Deborah could see bewilderment in the young girl's eyes and tried to explain. 'While being a member of the aristocracy brings privileges, I can't deny that it also brings a strict code of behaviour. Not even my brother is aware that I own and run a staff agency. If he was, he would immediately forbid it.'

'Oh, I see.'

'It's ridiculous, I know, but people like me aren't supposed to work for a living. I just wanted to help people.'

'You certainly helped me, miss . . . I mean, Your Ladyship.'

Deborah gave an inward sigh, seeing already a change in the young girl's manner. Whereas at the agency she had spoken openly, responding to Deborah's friendly approach, now there was deference. Blasted title, she thought. Sometimes I wish I didn't have one. 'So please don't breathe a word, not to Mrs Daniels, who also came from the agency, not to anyone.'

'I won't, I promise.'

'You are happy at Felchurch Manor?'

She beamed. 'Best position I've ever had.'

Deborah gave her a warm smile. 'I'm so pleased and I'm glad I've seen you again, Sarah.'

'Thank you, miss. I mean, Your Ladyship. I'd better get back now.' She opened the door and looking out, whispered, 'The coast's clear.'

Deborah touched her lightly on the shoulder as she passed, and then made her way to her own room. That was not only one obstacle dealt with, but it was good to see Sarah looking so well; it was astonishing what good food and security could accomplish.

Lunch was a light meal of consommé, poached salmon, new potatoes, and fresh garden peas, followed by a delicious lemon tart, and afterwards Deborah retired to her room for a rest. Later, the three of them played cards, whilst lamenting the now endless rain. The time was enjoyable, and she found herself liking Frederick Field, whose build and grey eyes were so like Theo's.

Theo felt a surge of both love and pride as Deborah entered the drawing room that evening. Nostalgia too, because the green silk dress was the one she had worn the first time he had taken her out to dinner. Tonight she looked even lovelier, her eyes full of happiness, and he exchanged glances with his father, recognising admiration in his eyes too.

Theo went to her and murmured, 'Darling, you look stunning. Come and meet my two closest friends.' The couple standing in the window smiled as they approached.

'Deborah, may I introduce Bertie and Jennifer Manston? This is Lady Deborah Claremont. Bertie and I grew up together, while Jennifer . . .'

'Has been married to Bertie for a lifetime, well in truth

eight years.' The flame-haired woman gave a teasing smile to her husband and a warm one to Deborah.

She took to them both immediately, liking Bertie's open pleasant face while Jennifer had several laughter lines around her eyes.

'I want to know what this reprobate is getting up to in London. Apart from ruling the rest of us,' Bertie said.

'Do you live in Wiltshire?' Deborah asked.

'Lord, yes. Wouldn't live anywhere else,' Bertie said. 'We have a place about fifteen miles away.'

Theo, glancing towards the door, gave a groan. 'Father didn't mention *she* was coming.'

Jennifer turned round. 'Glory, watch out, Theo.'

The voice that carried across the room was piercing. 'Theo, my absolute darling, so wonderful to see you.'

Theo controlled his intense dislike. Felicity Carruthers had been chasing him for years, her whole reason for living would seem to be to become Mrs Theodore Field. Or rather, he suspected, the wife of a possible future Cabinet minister. 'This is rather a surprise,' he said.

'Yes,' she trilled, completely ignoring the others. 'Mummy had a headache, so I tagged along with Daddy. After all, I couldn't miss a chance to see how you are.'

'I'm in excellent health, Felicity. Lady Deborah Claremont, may I introduce the Honourable Felicity Carruthers.'

Deborah held out her hand, which received a limp shake, before Felicity's attention returned to Theo. 'You're *so* naughty. I was in London only last week but couldn't manage to get hold of you.'

'Hello, Felicity – we're over here,' Bertie, with a wink at Deborah, gave a slight wave.

'Yes, I know,' she snapped. 'Don't be so impatient.'

'We've known each other for years, Deborah,' Bertie explained. 'She was just as obnoxious in pigtails.'

Theo saw Deborah's lips twitch.

'You look well, Felicity,' Jennifer said.

'You too. Not another sprog on the way, then?'

Theo swallowed hard. The very thought of her as a politician's wife! His despairing gaze met Deborah's and she moved closer to him, turning her head to whisper, 'I haven't a rival, then?'

'Heaven forbid.'

Felicity cut in. 'And what are you and . . .'

'Lady Deborah,' he supplied.

'Whispering about?'

Theo took Deborah's arm. 'Now that would be telling, my dear. But I really must introduce my guest to the others.'

They moved away, and he could sense Deborah trying to control her laughter.

'You haven't experienced being locked in a cupboard with her during a game of sardines. And I'm talking when she was seventeen!'

'It's a wonder you got out alive.'

'Now, if it had been you in there . . .'

317

'You would have wanted to stay forever!' She turned to look at him, and what he saw in her eyes sent his pulse racing. He may have thought deeply about the night ahead, but Theo couldn't help wondering what her reaction would be if he *did* visit her room . . .

Chapter Thirty-Five

Early morning sunshine flooded into the bedroom as the young maid drew back the curtains. 'It be a lovely day, my lady. I've brought Earl Grey tea, I hope that be right.'

'It's perfect, and very welcome,' Deborah reassured her, trying to recall her name.

Cotton, that was it. It always seemed so cold to address servants by their surname, although it was a widespread practice.

'Do you wish to go down for breakfast, Lady Deborah, or shall I ask Cook to prepare a tray?'

'Thank you, but I shall go down.' As Deborah sipped her tea, her thoughts went back to the previous night. She had half-expected or even hoped that once the house was quiet, Theo would have come to her room. Although even now she was unsure what her reaction would have been. It was ironic that she had so often repulsed gentle taps on her door on other weekends in the country, yet here, when she was so longing to be alone with him, her room had been sacrosanct.

As they left the table after breakfast, Theo murmured, 'The staff are expected to attend church, and I do too when I'm here.'

She smiled at him. 'It's the same at Anscombe. I wouldn't dream of not going to the Sunday service.'

Bells were ringing out from the centuries-old flint church at the edge of the village, as together with Theo's father they made their way down the central aisle to the family pew on the right-hand side. Deborah was aware of heads turning to look at her, as by her side Theo nodded and smiled at members of the congregation.

The sermon was mercifully short. The traditional hymns were sung with gusto, and with sunlight shining through the glorious stained-glass windows and the heady scent from flower arrangements, Deborah felt an unexpected sense of spiritual renewal. And when, on leaving the church, Theo introduced her to the elderly vicar, she murmured, 'A splendid service,' and was rewarded with a gentle smile.

There was only a short time spent in the house on their return, to enjoy coffee, and to check on the recovering dog. At last, with Deborah beside him in the Bentley and the windows wound down to enjoy the gentle breeze, Theo drove away.

'I'm going to take you on a short tour of my favourite places.' He reached out to take her hand.

'Are you sure you should be doing that while in charge of a vehicle?' she teased.

He laughed. 'I know these roads, darling. I just wanted to touch you, that's all.'

And as they drove through picturesque villages, and alongside small woods, their trees displaying early summer leaves in varying shades of green, neither spoke very much. The atmosphere between them was too fraught with sexual tension, and it took all of Theo's self-control not to draw over to the side of the road and take Deborah into his arms. But at least they would soon reach the secluded spot he'd chosen.

'Here we are,' he said, parking the car in a quiet lane. He opened the passenger door for Deborah, and, going to the boot took out a hamper and rug.

'Can I help?'

He shook his head, smiling, and after locking the car, balanced the rug on top of the wicker hamper. 'It's only a short walk. Just over the stile ahead and we'll be there.'

'A stile? It's ages since I climbed over one of those.'

Theo glanced down at Deborah's short pleated skirt. 'I'll look away, don't worry.'

She laughed, and with agility made her way over.

Theo reached to put down the hamper and rug on the other side before joining her. 'I found this spot by chance a few years ago. I've always intended that when I found that special someone, I'd bring her here.'

She lifted her face to his and gently kissed his lips. 'I rather like being called a "special someone".'

He smiled down at her. 'Come on, let me show you, you'll love it.'

Ahead was a cluster of trees, sunlight dancing among the leaves and before it a rippling stream. A majestic oak tree shaded the perfect picnic scene, with only the sound of water moving over the pebbles. She smiled up at him. 'It's perfect, Theo.'

'I'm glad.' He bent and kissed her, then kissed her again. 'Before I get too distracted,' he murmured, 'let's get organised. I was worried that the ground wouldn't be dry after yesterday's rain, but it seems fine.' He spread the rug on the grass and opened the hamper. 'We have two bottles of champers! If we drink both we'll be squiffy.'

'What a lovely thought.' Deborah smoothed down her skirt and sat on the rug, her back supported by the tree. 'But if you will insist on driving yourself . . .'

'I enjoy it,' he admitted. 'Besides, in that way we can travel just the two of us.' Taking out a bottle, he expertly popped the cork, the sudden sound causing several birds to emerge from the trees and flutter away.

Deborah laughed. 'Now we're truly alone.' She took the glass he offered and crossing her ankles gave what sounded like a blissful sigh.

Theo joined her on the rug. 'Let's see what else Cook has provided for us.' He uncovered the contents of the hamper. 'Slices of cold chicken and ham, smoked salmon, crusty rolls, salad, tomatoes, hard-boiled eggs, mayonnaise, even cheese and fruit cake.

'A veritable feast.' Deborah laughed. 'Aren't you glad I sent Mrs Daniels to you?' Her eyes were sparkling as she sipped her champagne and he thought how absolutely lovely she was. She turned and his heart softened to see the tenderness in her eyes. He shaded his eyes and looking up at the blue sky with the sun now blazing overhead, took off his blazer and tie.

'I shouldn't have left my hat in the car,' she said.

Theo rose to his feet. 'I can soon remedy that.'

Deborah watched him go, realising this was the first time she'd seen him dressed so informally. He looked younger and even more attractive.

Returning with the hat, he relaxed back on to the rug and looked at the hamper. 'What can I tempt you with?'

Deborah's gaze met his as Theo turned to her, and slowly his eyes crinkled at the corners with first amusement, then something else entirely, and leaning towards her their lips met, warm and soft. She breathed in the subtle scent of his cologne as he moved closer, enfolding her in his arms, kissing her again, more deeply this time and the next few minutes were lost in their delight of each other. He drew away, his intense gaze holding her own, his eyes darkening with desire, and then they were again in each other's arms, and his lips moved down to the hollow of her throat, and to the soft swell of her breasts. She could feel the heat of his breath through the silk of her blouse, and Deborah held his head against her, and kissed his hair before he drew away.

'If "music is the food of love", then we'll have to settle for food.' He was smiling at her, but she noticed a pulse beating in his temple. His gaze, too, was on her lips and she blew him a kiss.

'We have lots of time,' she said, putting on her hat. 'Shall I serve?'

He nodded, and reclined comfortably on the rug. Did Theo ever do anything clumsy? She smiled to herself, she didn't care if he did, she only knew that she loved this man. And she knew in her heart that he loved her, but that didn't mean she wasn't desperate to hear him say those magical three words.

Deborah would always remember this Sunday picnic, the way they had thrown caution to the wind and drank both bottles of champagne. How delicious the food had been, eaten to love and laughter, as each had at times attempted to feed the other, with Theo claiming random kisses. Until at last the atmosphere changed between them, and Theo took her shoulders, and gently lowered her on to the rug. Overhead, Deborah could see the sun glinting through the trees, only for it to be blocked by Theo as he began to undo the buttons of her silk blouse, pushing down thin straps to release her breasts. To feel him touching her bare skin, his lips adoring her, was heavenly. For so many years she had been starved of physical closeness to another human being. He raised his head to claim her lips in a kiss that seemed never to end.

Eventually, he drew back and said, 'I'm head over heels in love with you, Deborah.'

'I was rather hoping you were.' She smiled up at him. 'Because I love you, too, Theo, very much.'

He replaced her straps and fastened her blouse. 'This is going to be the most unselfish thing I can remember doing.' He kissed the tip of her nose. 'I want to take you this very minute, Lady Deborah Claremont. There is nobody to see us. But when we finally come together, as I hope and pray we will, it will not only be glorious, but in a soft bed with white linen or silk sheets, and the whole romantic night before us.' He smiled down at her. 'Are you decent yet?'

She looked down at her clothes and nodded.

'Good, because I have no intention of proposing to an improper woman!' In one lithe movement, Theo rose and knelt on one knee before her.

'I love you, my wonderful Deborah. I would consider it the greatest honour in the world, if you would agree to marry me.'

She smiled at him, overwhelmed with love. 'I'm longing to become your wife, Theo.'

Rising, he retrieved his blazer and felt in the inside pocket. 'I hope you will like this, darling, but I'll understand if you'd prefer something more modern. It belonged to my mother.' He opened to reveal a square-cut emerald ring surrounded by dazzling diamonds.

She caught her breath. 'It's beautiful, I love it.'

He slipped it on to the third finger of her left hand. 'And it fits perfectly.'

'It really is lovely.' She held out her hand to admire the way the sunlight caught the precious stones. Deborah hesitated, and said tentatively, 'Would you mind terribly if we kept our engagement to ourselves, perhaps for the next week?'

At his startled frown, she said swiftly, 'Only Gerard will be back from Italy by then. He's still my guardian, I'm afraid. So just until we have his seal of approval?'

She laughed at his affronted expression. 'He can't possibly refuse it.'

Theo kissed her. 'Nothing, Lady Deborah, is going to prevent my marrying you. But if that's what you want, then that is what we'll do.'

She replaced the ring in the box and with reluctance gave it back. 'You're a sweetheart, do you know that?'

'As long as I'm yours.'

Her gaze met his and she gave him a swift kiss. 'There's no doubt of that, my darling.'

Could any day be happier? But as they collected the debris of their wonderful picnic, she thought life is never all joy, is it? And only she knew there was a crucial obstacle to overcome, before she could feel really secure about their future. And she had waited too long already.

The burden of that knowledge preyed on her mind all evening, a time when she should have been feeling ecstatically happy. Theo could obviously sense something was wrong, and more than once she had to avoid his concerned glances.

Fortunately, his father didn't seem to notice anything amiss.

After their coffee, she excused herself to them both. 'I think I'll retire early, I have a slight headache.'

'Possibly a little too much sun,' Theo said, his eyes sympathetic.

She smiled at him. 'Possibly. Goodnight.'

Once in her bedroom, she politely submitted to the attentions of the young maid, Cotton, but dismissed her as soon as she could. Deborah opened the window and stood before it for several minutes listening to the country sounds of an owl's hoot and the occasional bark of a fox. Then with a deep sigh she closed it slightly and, walking over to the bed, slid beneath the cool sheets and lay with her head on the soft pillow. She couldn't put it off any longer, she had no alternative.

It was time to allow the painful memories to surface.

Chapter Thirty-Six

1918

For Deborah, the days and weeks following Philippe's death passed in a miserable daze. She would never see him smile again, his eyes alight with love, or feel his arms around her. The life they had planned would never happen. And when first her mother, then her father, succumbed to the terrible Spanish flu epidemic, she fell into a chasm of grief.

And so the cessation of her monthly bleeds was at first attributed by her maid to shock. 'It will probably right itself, madam.'

But it didn't, and with the affliction of morning sickness came the terrifying realisation. She was pregnant.

Waters, a thin sour-faced woman, who had previously attended Deborah's late mother, had a pride in the

Claremont name almost equal to that of Gerard. Her expression cold with disgust, she said curtly, 'I shall, of course, have to inform the earl.'

Deborah didn't answer, her shattered mind still coming to terms with her discovery. When the summons came to go to her brother's study, frightened and nervous she forced herself to go to the room that held so many memories of her late father. Her heart racing with apprehension, she had to struggle against a wave of nausea as she turned the brass doorknob and went in.

Seated behind his desk, Gerard's face was white with fury. 'Deborah, I have just been informed of a situation so shocking, so abhorrent, that I can scarcely believe it. Is what Waters has reported true? Are you pregnant?'

She raised her head and lifted her chin, refusing to be cowed. 'Yes, it is true.'

'And I assume the father, a man I took to be a gentleman, is Lapierre.'

'Yes, of course it is Philippe.'

'Who conveniently got himself killed before the truth came out,' he sneered.

Deborah struggled to control an urge to slap his face. 'That's a terrible thing to say. A cruel thing.'

'Yes, well it's a cruel thing the two of you have left me to cope with.' He leant forward. 'Let me make one thing clear. I don't care what happens to Lapierre's bastard. What I do care about is you besmirching the Claremont name. What our parents would have thought of their daughter, I can't imagine. Eighteen years old, with any chance of a decent marriage ruined. You are despicable, Deborah.'

She knew she should say she was sorry, but the words wouldn't come. It would mean confessing that she regretted the most wonderful night of her life. And she would never feel that.

'I can see there's not an ounce of shame in you. However, from now on you will do exactly what I say. The first thing is to find a doctor willing to perform a termination.'

Deborah stared at him in horror. 'I couldn't do that. It's murdering an unborn child; Philippe's child!'

Gerard's tone was cutting. 'So what do you have in mind? Parade your bastard for everyone to see?'

'I haven't thought that far. But you are not going to bully me into having an abortion.'

'You wouldn't be the first woman to do it. I could easily find out the name of a trustworthy doctor.'

'For the last time, my answer is no!'

Gerard drummed his fingers on the desk. 'Then you'll have to go away, and soon.'

He gazed at her, his lip curling with derision. 'You were always spoilt as a child, Deborah. I'm not surprised it's come home to roost. Just get out of my sight. And I don't need to tell you to keep this disgraceful situation to yourself.'

She was now fighting tears, struggling not to break down in front of him. 'But Waters knows.'

'You can leave Waters to me.'

* * *

She saw little of her brother after that. He breakfasted early and frequently dined at his club. But several weeks later, she was again summoned to his study.

Gerard's gaze swept over her in a way she found humiliating. Fortunately, her slim body was only slightly thickened, but Deborah knew it was time she left London.

'You will go to Wales,' he said abruptly.

'To Aunt Blanche?' She was shocked. Aunt Blanche was her godmother and a fearsome spinster. She would never understand about Philippe.

'Aunt Blanche has suffered a slight stroke.'

'I'm sorry to hear that.' She hesitated. 'You mean I am to go and stay with her?'

'Certainly not. Although her illness will be given out as the reason for your absence.' He stared coldly at her. 'I have rented, in the name of Mrs Deborah March, a decent-sized cottage in a village several miles away. You will wear a wedding ring, as a widow whose husband was killed in the war. Your laundry will be dealt with by a reliable woman from the village. You will not be seen by anyone, I repeat, anyone.'

She frowned. 'No other staff?'

He shook his head. 'Waters will attend to everything you need.'

Deborah had to admit in retrospect that her brother had been efficient. The stone-built detached cottage did have a certain rural charm, and was comfortably furnished. Apparently its owner, an army officer, was serving in India. Beginning to feel tired after the train journey, she explored the few rooms, pleased to see there was a rear garden, which would enable her to take fresh air and exercise.

'Is it to your liking?' Gerard asked, as she returned to the sitting room. 'Hardly suitable for Lady Deborah Claremont, but I think a war widow would be satisfied.'

'Yes, you've done very well. I'm grateful to you, Gerard.' Later, feeling desolate, she watched a cab arrive to take him to visit Aunt Blanche, where he would stay overnight before returning to London.

Gerard never again visited the cottage, although Deborah dutifully wrote a fortnightly short letter whose envelope bore the Wales postmark. He didn't reply, although her mail was forwarded. A bulky envelope addressed to Waters would arrive regularly, which Deborah guessed contained money. But the other woman's attitude towards her was consistently one of ill-concealed contempt, which made her a cold and disapproving companion. Neither was she an imaginative cook, and the plain meals she prepared were unvarying in their monotony. Bored, and desperate for contact with her previous life, Deborah would occasionally exchange letters with Abby, who would praise her for staying in the wilds of Wales to look after her ailing aunt. Deborah hated lying to her close friend, hated the whole charade, but knew it was necessary.

As for the birth itself, she had broached the subject with Gerard before he left.

'What about when . . . you know . . .'

'You are confined? You are young and healthy, and as Waters informs me that she helped with her mother's confinements, that should be sufficient.'

Deborah was shocked. 'Not even a midwife?'

'Of course, if there are complications, and considered necessary. I am not a monster, Deborah. Just someone trying to protect our family name. The fewer people who see you, the better. Waters will, of course, attend church on Sunday mornings, and inform the vicar that you have been prescribed complete rest, and don't wish to be disturbed.'

Fortunately, her pregnancy caused her few problems. It was the boredom, being deprived of intelligent conversation, or laughter. Books were an essential distraction, and she spent hours knitting exquisite matinee jackets and a delicate shawl, with every stitch holding the love she would be unable to give her child.

Deborah had been painfully forced to accept that there was no possibility of keeping her baby. A suitable adoption would be arranged, otherwise scandal would not only taint the Claremont name, but Philippe's child would always bear the stigma of being a bastard. The decision almost broke her heart.

It was on an evening at the end of April when Deborah felt the trickle of water down her thighs. Her heart pounding, she reached for the handbell by her side, and as soon as Waters was framed in the doorway she assessed the situation. 'So, your waters have broken. Any pains?'

Deborah shook her head, but then a painful contraction caused her to double over.

And almost as soon as she was in the prepared bed in the spare room, there came another, and then another. She was frightened, having expected a slow start to her labour. Surely that was more normal? But when Waters returned, there were no expressions of reassurance or even encouragement. Nor any respect for the difference in their status. Heavy rain began to lash at the window, while the grim-faced woman thrust a piece of rolled-up rag at Deborah. 'Bite on that when a contraction comes, go with it, don't try and fight it. And hold on to the bed rail.'

Her gaze fixed on the other woman, Deborah obeyed every barked-out instruction. She had never imagined there could be such pain. Once she screamed out in agony.

'My mother once took seventeen hours,' Waters scoffed. 'But we working classes are made of stronger stuff.' She lifted Deborah's nightdress and lowering her head peered underneath.

Deborah gritted her teeth at the humiliation. She hated this woman. And as another contraction threatened to rip her apart, struggled not to make a sound. Stronger stuff? The Claremont family was renowned for its courage.

Although Waters told her everything was progressing normally, all Deborah could think was that her own poor mother must have suffered like this.

The struggle seemed endless, and when at last, totally exhausted, Deborah gave birth, she heard the emotive sound she would never forget. The plaintive first cry of her baby. Lifting her head, she could see Waters cutting the cord. 'Is it a . . .'

'A boy, a fine boy.' The now smiling maid wrapped the baby in a towel, wiped his face, and her plain features softened by tenderness, gave the small bundle into Deborah's outstretched arms.

Gazing down in wonder at the crumpled little face she held him nestled against her, his black hair – so like Philippe's. Her eyes filled with tears. This little mite would never know who his real parents were . . .

As she placed a glass on the bedside table, Waters said, 'Let me have him now while you drink this. It will help with the afterbirth.'

Deborah reluctantly handed back her son and watched the maid place him carefully in a blanket-lined drawer. Already her arms felt empty without him. Then obediently she drained the glass.

And that was the last time she ever saw her baby.

Chapter Thirty-Seven

On waking that morning, Theo felt happier than he'd been for years. And it was all due to his lovely Deborah. But at breakfast he was puzzled to see that Deborah was subdued, her face pale, her eyes shadowed. Yet earlier she'd said that her headache was better.

Then after they rose and left the room, she caught at his hand. 'Is there somewhere we can be undisturbed? I need to talk to you.'

Puzzled, Theo said, 'Yes, of course.'

His father had remained at the table immersed in his morning paper, and Theo went back. 'Might I ask if you intend to use your study in the near future?'

Frederick Field shook his head. 'No, not at all.'

Feeling bewildered, Theo guided her to the quiet room at the end of the hall. Despite the warm morning, a small fire had been lit in the fireplace, on either side of which was a burgundy leather winged chair. Deborah went to sit in the one on the right-hand side.

When she looked up at him, her eyes were full of appeal. 'Theo, please could you ensure the butler doesn't disturb us?'

'Darling, you're beginning to worry me. Are you sure you're not unwell?'

Silently, she shook her head.

Theo went to instruct Langton before walking back to the study, his every step apprehensive. Whatever Deborah wanted to talk to him about was obviously worrying her. Surely she hadn't changed her mind about marrying him? They were made for each other, their time together yesterday had proved that. He could have sworn she was as much in love with him as he was with her.

Deborah didn't think she had ever felt so nervous in her life. Her whole life, her future depended on how Theo was going to react. She looked down at her hands and saw they were trembling. And then he was opening the door and closing it behind him.

Silently he took the seat opposite her.

Deborah's voice was shaky. 'Theo, I'm sorry, but I have something to tell you. It's about myself and my life many years ago. I vowed then I would never reveal this to anyone. Only the man I wanted to marry, someone I would trust with my life.'

He frowned, leaning forward, his expression one of intense concern. 'Deborah, there's no need . . .'

She held up a hand. 'No, darling, please let me speak.' She gazed into the flickering flames of the fire, and into her memories of that fateful year, when she had met and fallen in love with Philippe.

'The night before he was due to return to France, I just could not bear to think of him lying alone, dreading what was ahead. And so I went along to his room, thinking to hold him close and reassure him. But we were so in love, that you can imagine what happened.' Her voice became even quieter. 'Within forty-eight hours he was killed. It's always been a comfort to me we had that night together, that he knew how much I loved him. I've never regretted it, not once.'

Then with a rapidly beating heart, she described how shocked and frightened she had been on later discovering she was pregnant. Her stomach churning, she glanced over at Theo, anxious about his reaction. He was gazing into the fire, his expression taut.

'Gerard arranged everything,' she said. 'No one else ever knew about it, not even Abby. I was sent away to Wales, and after long lonely months gave birth to a little boy. I was allowed to hold him only for a few precious minutes, before being given a glass of medicine to dull the after pains. I only realised it was a sleeping draught when I woke up hours later to find my baby gone, taken away to a wet nurse.'

With tears now stinging her eyes she forced herself to continue. 'But sadly he only lived a short time, after catching an infection.' And then her voice broke. 'I wasn't even allowed to go to my own son's funeral.'

Silence fell in the room, the only sound the grandfather clock in the hall striking the hours. Theo still hadn't spoken, and eventually Deborah said, 'And this is what I needed to tell you.'

Theo had listened with growing horror to the sad story being related to him. There was such pain in Deborah's voice, he could only imagine the courage it was taking. Many young women would have entered marriage hoping to keep their past a secret. His heart went out to her as he listened to the tragedy of her baby's death. When she became silent, he was stunned for several minutes, crucially aware that this could be a turning point in both their lives. Despite his compassion, his first reaction was one of anger that Deborah hadn't told him sooner. That she had kept hidden this important part of her life, even while they were falling in love. Yet he could understand her reticence to risk hitherto the slightest hint of scandal. And how could he judge or resent her expressing her love for Philippe on the eve of his departure for France? She had been so young, they had both been young. And he himself was hardly a saint. He was crazily in love with Deborah, knew in his soul that he would never find a love like this again.

He didn't know why he was hesitating! She must be in an agony of anxiety. Swiftly he rose and went to her, bending to lift her trembling hands to his lips. 'Oh, my poor darling. I am so very, very sorry. But please don't worry that it makes any difference to us. I love you, Deborah, I shall always love you.'

She whispered, 'And you still want to marry me?'

'Your honesty in telling me this has made me love you even more.'

'I was so scared, Theo. I couldn't bear the thought of losing you.'

'There is no chance of that, ever.' He drew her up and into his arms. Holding her close, Theo gently kissed the top of her head. 'I hate the thought of you going through such a terrible ordeal alone.'

Deborah looked up at him, and he could see tears brimming in her eyes.

'Darling, please don't cry.'

'I'm sorry,' she said, as she tried to blink away the tears. 'It's just the reaction.'

'Of course. I think you've been terribly brave.' He bent to kiss her lips, a tender, loving kiss. 'Do you think a brandy would help?'

She gave a weak smile. 'Yes, I think it might.'

Theo went to the small sideboard and, returning, handed the glass to her. Then, after Deborah had taken a couple of sips, said, 'Are you sure you feel well enough to return to town? We could easily stay another night.'

'Thank you, but I'm happy to leave as planned, Theo.' Her smile was a little shaky although he was relieved to see colour gradually return to her cheeks.

When a couple of hours later Deborah said goodbye to Frederick Field, his smile was warm, and Theo, knowing his father as he did, detected a knowing twinkle in his eyes as he said, 'I hope to see you again, very soon.'

But before leaving, they went to the stables to check on the young collie.

'He's going to be absolutely fine,' Harry said, then told them of the young lad's disappointment. 'He's not allowed to have a dog. Something to do with the cottage being small and the laundress couldn't risk the washing getting dirty.'

'I suppose that's understandable,' Deborah said. 'A pity, though, I can't imagine growing up without a dog.'

'A shame we can't keep him here, Harry,' Theo said. 'But you know my father's views.'

Harry grinned. 'Bitches only. But not to worry, Mr Theodore, I'll soon find him a good home.'

The atmosphere in the car wasn't completely relaxed. Deborah realised that would be impossible after the emotional turmoil of the morning. While Theo concentrated on driving, she continued to try and calm her thoughts and nerves. Because having at last allowed those traumatic memories of her pregnancy and childbirth to surface, to be spoken aloud for the first time, she couldn't seem to subdue them.

Waters had remained in Wales having been offered a position with Aunt Blanche. News that had filled Deborah with relief, as she'd been dreading having to request the maid's dismissal. She only knew that she wanted the woman out of her life.

And then she mentally gave herself a shake. It was time to put the past back where it belonged, in a hidden compartment in her mind. She glanced lovingly across at Theo who must have sensed it because turning, he gave her a warm, reassuring smile, briefly touching her hand.

It was then, for the first time all weekend, a fleeting image of Evan came into her mind. The memory of their meeting in Lyon's Corner House seemed almost distant now. So much had happened since and there was no room in her heart for anyone other than Theo, not any more. Apart from the wonderful hours spent in each other's arms at the picnic, he had been so compassionate and understanding earlier that morning. Many men would have had a far different reaction to her confession. And also on learning of her secret life at the agency. Deborah couldn't think of any other man she knew from her circle of acquaintances who would have been so intelligently accepting of her circumstances.

And thinking fleetingly again of Evan, Deborah was hoping that he would soon meet someone who would make him a wonderful wife. He deserved to be happy.

But now she couldn't help stifling a yawn, sleep having evaded her for much of the previous night.

'Why don't you have a nap, darling?'

Theo's voice was tender, and once again reassured that their future together was safe, Deborah snuggled into the leather seat, relaxed and closed her eyes.

Chapter Thirty-Eight

It was two weeks later, when Evan was studying a book on railway engines, that his Aunt Bronwen came into the sitting room to stand before him. And she remained there.

Frowning, he glanced up. He hated to be disturbed when he was reading. Then seeing the expression on her face, with resignation he put the book down.

'I think you should look at this.' She held out the *Tatler*.

'You know I despise those sorts of magazines.'

'I only ever see them in the hairdressers. I've been for a trim and they've let me borrow this one. Evan, lad, just humour me.'

He took the publication from her and turned to where she'd marked the place with one of her late husband's pipe cleaners. Bronwen believed everything had more than one use.

Evan's breath stilled. It was a photograph of Deborah, a happy smiling Deborah, her face shadowed by the large brim of her hat. Beside her stood a distinguished-looking man. Within seconds he'd read the caption. *Mr Theodore Field, MP, and his soon-to-be bride, Lady Deborah Claremont*. He studied the man's intelligent face, remembering Deborah telling him of his interest in social justice, and that he had even come to Battersea to hear Evan speak.

'I must say they look well suited.'

'Yes, Aunt Bronwen, they do.'

'So that's that, then.' She surveyed him for a moment, then gave a nod and held out her hand for the magazine. 'I'll take that back. Yer dinner'll be ready in half an hour. A nice steak and kidney pudding.'

'Sounds good.'

Evan's book lay unheeded as he grimly reflected on what he'd just seen. So, Deborah had gone ahead and made a *suitable marriage*, then chided himself for his sarcasm. There was no doubt it was a love match and he genuinely wished them happiness.

Evan had always been a man who accepted reality. Yes, following their parting at the Lyons Corner House he'd felt regret for what might have been, but a future for himself and Deborah could only ever be a fantasy, especially in this country. One day these social divisions would change, must change. In the meantime, he was determined to continue as an active union member, speaking out against injustice wherever he found it. In fact, he was due to speak on Friday, the main thrust of his speech being the continuing deplorable conditions of the miners. Their strike action and that of the rest of the country had been a travesty achieving precisely nothing.

His concentration having been interrupted, he put the book aside and began to muse on the following day when he was due to go to the Colonel's house in Blackheath. Evan still found it difficult to believe how much his life had improved since working there. Although it was a disgrace that the level of unemployment was so high in the country that someone like himself, an engineer, had to work as a servant. But at least being involved in the design and building of the model railway had given him back some self-respect. The Colonel was sparing no expense, and it was Evan's aim to make the layout one of supreme professionalism.

'We have a visitor early this evening, someone you may wish to meet,' the Colonel said as Evan wheeled him around the garden. He indicated to stop by a particularly colourful display of dahlias, leaning forward to touch the flowers for a moment. 'Father Keegan, a local Catholic priest. He's kind enough to give me a game of chess sometimes. Not that I'm of his religious persuasion, you understand.'

'Is he a good strategist?'

'Indeed he is.' The Colonel chuckled. 'Always helped along by a couple of whiskies. It was through Father Keegan that you came here.'

'Really? But I don't know any Catholic priests.'

'You'd be Chapel, I expect, coming from Wales.'

'Rather lukewarm, I'm afraid.'

'Well, that's neither here nor there. The good father seems to have some sort of connection with Miss Claremont at the staff agency.'

Evan frowned, Deborah had never mentioned a priest. But he supposed that in her line of work she would have many different contacts. I wonder, he thought, whether he is aware of her true identity? Not that Evan would ever betray her confidence, although he'd wondered more than once how she'd managed to lead two separate lives without it being discovered. Although she did wear spectacles and plain, serviceable clothes at the office. A world apart from the elaborate and fashionable outfit she wore that day in Hyde Park.

He leant forward to hear what the Colonel was saying. 'It's going to be a busy day. My niece is visiting this afternoon. I think she's becoming really involved in our project.'

'Mrs Parry is very well informed,' Evan said. He appreciated the way that the Colonel's niece treated him as an equal, and her company had enlivened more than one working afternoon. He also knew a little more about her now, thanks to the garrulous cook.

'She's the daughter of the Colonel's late brother,' she told him. 'Poor thing, she was only married a month before her husband was killed. That dratted war took the cream of our young men, it did.'

But Evan did wonder how and why the Colonel and his niece had become so sympathetic to the miners' plight. The surname Parry would indicate a Welsh background, but that would belong to her late husband. She had even attended union meetings before the strike – hadn't she heard Evan himself speak, and more than once? But the Colonel was a senior army officer, almost certainly public-school educated. Such people rarely considered the plight of the working classes. It would be interesting to find out. However, Evan, ever conscious of his paid position in the household, was still wary of asking outright personal questions.

The Catholic priest arrived half an hour before Evan was due to go off duty, and after greeting the Colonel, turned to Evan with a warm smile and appraising glance. 'Are you settling in, now, Mr Morgan?'

'Indeed I am, Father.'

'Although it was a job to raise a smile out of him on the day after the strike was called off,' the Colonel said.

Evan glanced sharply at him, relieved to see humour in his eyes. It was only banter, then, although Evan thought he'd disguised his true feelings well.

'My parishioners would have found the same problem with me, which is why, the Blessed Lord forgive me, I tried to avoid them. Sure, between the three of us, it didn't sit well with me having to preach one thing from the pulpit and believing the opposite.'

'My niece tells me that Evan here is a powerful speaker, Father, if you'd care to hear him. When are you next on the platform, Evan?'

Startled, he said, 'This coming Friday, sir.'

'You could accompany my niece, Geraldine, Father.' He began to chuckle. 'It will be incognito for the pair of you, she covering her red hair, and yourself covering the dog collar.'

Father Keegan laughed. 'You know, I might just do that. Let me have the details before you go, Evan. But why does she need to cover her hair?'

Evan, who was bringing both men their whiskies, listened intently. The red hair in question was a mass of unruly curls, and Geraldine was extremely attractive. His memory was sketchy as to the clothes she wore when attending meetings, but his overall impression was of dowdiness. Very different from the fashionable clothes she wore when she came to visit her uncle.

'Wanting to blend in, I think. She feels even the cut of her hair would proclaim her of a higher social class. She also wears a shawl rather than a coat. A young woman of strong opinions is my niece. Like her late father.'

Silently Evan put the glasses down and stood back, prepared to wheel the Colonel to the chess table at the appropriate time.

'Sure, I remember now,' Father Keegan said, taking an appreciative sip of his malt. 'Didn't he once write to *The Times*, castigating the government of the day for their lack of Christian charity in the way they dealt with the poor.'

The Colonel laughed. 'Yes, and there was his name beneath for everyone to see. My father was apoplectic. But then he was a die-hard Tory, whereas Hugo was nothing if not a rebel. At least he didn't join the Communist Party; I think he'd have been disinherited.' He shook his head. 'I, for one, never thought he'd join the established church. Would have made bishop if he hadn't died of that wretched heart attack.'

He turned to Evan. 'If you could settle me over there, I shall proceed to thrash my opponent. Evan's a considerable chess player, you know, Father.'

'Then I shall have to arrange the right time to play him. If that's all right with you, Evan?'

'I'd relish the chance. I've never played a priest before.'

'I warn you, the Almighty sometimes smiles on me.'

Evan laughed. He manoeuvred the Colonel into position and as Father Keegan sat opposite, left the two men to enjoy the evening.

He walked home briskly in the soft evening air, glad of the exercise and thinking of the coming Friday. He was a confident speaker, and Geraldine had already heard him several times. But would it be different now that he had spent so much time with her. Then he dismissed the thought. Why on earth should it?

Chapter Thirty-Nine

At the agency, Elspeth was delighted by the news of Deborah's engagement.

'You've told me so much about Theo,' she said, looking down at the photo of the happy couple together. 'I hadn't realised he was so handsome.'

'He is, isn't he? You would like him, Elspeth, you really would. He's such an honourable man. I'd trust him with my life.'

'And that sentiment proves that you've chosen the right man.' She hesitated. 'If you don't mind my saying so, I thought you seemed attracted to Evan Morgan. Mind you, right from the first moment he came in to the agency, I was myself, even at my age.'

Deborah was startled at first and then began to laugh. 'I suppose if you can own up, then so can I. I didn't realise it was so obvious.'

'Well, I know you so well.' Elspeth smiled at her. 'It's wonderful to see you looking – the only word is radiant.'

Deborah smiled at her. 'Thank you.' She paused, but decided not to raise the topic she guessed must be uppermost in Elspeth's mind. Deborah herself was trying to come to terms with the fact that once she was married her life would undoubtedly change. Not only might Theo be uncomfortable with her working, as an MP's wife she would have other commitments. The subject had been preying on her mind. Having been so used to being independent, to making her own decisions, she wasn't going to find it easy to defer to someone else. No, not defer, that was the wrong word. Hadn't Theo said more than once that he wanted an equal marriage? But Deborah had a suspicion that wouldn't include her running the agency, or being away from home three days a week.

Instead, she asked about the day's appointments.

'The diary is clear this morning,' Elspeth said. 'Although we still haven't anything to offer that young woman who only recently left the workhouse.'

'Millie Walker, you mean?'

Elspeth nodded. 'I feel so sorry for her. What a start in life to be abandoned at ten years old.'

'She was released into employment in the kitchen of a school, wasn't she?'

'Yes, and terribly bullied by the cook. You haven't yet met her, but I could sympathise with her unwillingness to remain there.'

'At least she had the good sense not to leave without finding another live-in position. Otherwise she'd be left homeless and probably end up back where she started.'

'Or something even worse,' Elspeth said darkly.

Deborah nodded. But an idea was coming into her mind. 'You formed a good opinion of her?'

'Most certainly.'

'Then I think maybe a visit to Father Keegan might help.'

Elspeth brightened. 'I'll keep my fingers crossed.'

Some of the gravestones in the churchyard were adorned with vases of flowers as Deborah walked past them, but there was no sign of the priest in the cool and dim interior of the old church. She had telephoned earlier, and guessing he would be enjoying his morning break, she made her way round to the presbytery.

The housekeeper promptly answered Deborah's ring and opened the door wide with a welcoming smile. 'Good morning, Miss Claremont. Himself is in his study and expecting you.'

Smiling her thanks, Deborah tapped on the door and went in. 'Good morning, Father.'

'Ah, good morning, and isn't it a day fit for the angels?'

She laughed. 'Yes, it is. How are you?'

'I'm well, and one only has to look at yourself to see

353

that you are too.' Pipe in hand, he raised his eyebrows in query.

She smiled her assent, and watched him tap the tobacco into the bowl and light it. What pleasure such a routine seemed to give men, and fleetingly she wondered what it would be like to do the same. But a woman smoking a pipe? Not exactly unheard of but certainly frowned on.

As the fragrant aroma of the smoke drifted towards her, the priest said, 'Actually I met your chess-playing protégé last night.'

'You mean Evan Morgan?'

'Indeed. And a fine young man he seems. In fact, I'm planning to hear him speak this very Friday.'

That was good to hear, Deborah thought. It was just like Evan not to allow the strike's defeat to throw him off course. 'And you've heard good reports from the Colonel?'

'Excellent. The man's planning and building an extensive model railway, you know. Not that I've been allowed to see it yet. Evan is proving a great collaborator, so I'm told.'

He relaxed back in his chair and folded his hands over his ample stomach. 'But I don't suppose you've come here to talk of past successes. Am I to take it you've another lost sheep?'

She smiled. 'You could describe her as that.' She told him of Millie's unfortunate start in life and her present predicament. 'Out of the frying pan in a way, I think, although perhaps more comfortable. Apparently the cook is a tartar, and considers anyone leaving a workhouse to be the dregs of the gutter.'

'A common opinion among the ignorant.'

'I'd love to find her a decent position. But I'm not finding it easy. People are often unwilling to give a workhouse girl a chance.'

'Scullery maid or kitchen maid?'

Deborah nodded.

'And of amiable nature?'

'I think she just deserves the chance to be, Father.'

He sighed. 'There are a lot of troubled souls in the world, Miss Claremont, and we can't help them all. But I'll do my best. My housekeeper may know of an opening somewhere. Give me a day or two and I'll be in touch.'

It seemed a shame not to enjoy the glorious weather for a while before returning to the agency, so Deborah decided to take a stroll through a nearby park. And seeing a secluded bench in the distance she walked towards it and settled down to think. It was opposite a small lake, at the moment mercifully devoid of noisy small boys sailing their boats. Or, she thought with Abby's twins coming to mind, little girls with their skipping ropes. Children were a subject she and Theo had already discussed, and they were both looking forward to having a family and soon.

Theo had at first been hesitant when the topic came up.

'Deborah, you are certain about this? I mean, after your earlier traumatic experience.'

That was another thing she liked about Theo. He hadn't hidden away her confession as though it were a shameful secret. And the fact that at last she'd been able to talk about what had happened, to confide in someone, she'd found a comforting, even healing, experience. Her love for Philippe had ended in tragedy and so had her love for their baby. Nothing could ever change that. But although their memory would always live in her mind, Deborah wasn't going to allow it to shadow her life with Theo.

'It will be totally different next time,' she told him. 'For one thing, I'll have proper medical care, and hopefully a strong and healthy baby.' She'd sometimes wondered whether her own fragile health after her bereavements, and the lonely and depressing months in Wales had contributed to weakening the baby she was carrying. Did a mother's mood affect the growing life in her womb? She could only console herself that it wasn't that unusual for a baby not to survive more than a few days of life. Some mothers, especially those in poverty, had to suffer the heartbreak of losing several children.

Deborah was forced to revisit that traumatic time almost as soon as Gerard gave permission for the engagement. When within half an hour of Theo leaving Grosvenor Square she was informed that her brother wished to see her in his study, she didn't fool herself that this would be anything other than a confrontation.

'My congratulations, Deborah,' was his greeting. His tone was reasonably warm but she knew that icy glint in his eyes and waited.

'I think you may have guessed that wasn't my only reason for wishing to see you. It gives me no pleasure to raise the subject of your unfortunate past again, but I need your reassurance that you have obeyed my wishes.'

She was under no illusion as to the strength of his feelings. Gerard had always maintained that no one, absolutely no one, should ever discover what had taken place during those bleak months in Wales. Whereas she had always been adamant that if, and when she married, her husband must be told the truth. She'd tried to convince her brother that it would be dishonest not to, and even if she didn't reveal it before her marriage, on becoming pregnant, any midwife or doctor would know that she'd previously had a child.

Gerard's reaction to that had simply been one word, 'Nonsense!'

Deborah again remained silent.

'Come along, Deborah! Can I take it that you haven't confided the unsavoury details to your intended?'

'I think that is between myself and Theo.'

He stared at her. 'But you haven't told him.'

'I didn't say that.'

His expression darkened with anger. 'So, you have.'

'I didn't say that, either.'

Gerard hit the desk with his fist. 'Deborah, you know

how I feel about protecting our family name. Skeletons should stay in the closet. If I find out . . .'

'But you won't, will you? Not without admitting knowledge of something you'd rather remain hidden.' She turned to leave, and as she opened the door said over her shoulder, 'And that, dear brother, is my last word on the matter.'

Chapter Forty

Gerard was suffused with anger. How dared his sister defy him? Not only that but leave him discomforted at not knowing the truth. *Had* she told Field? If she was going to continue with this intransigence he would never know, and that did not sit well with him, not at all. And if Field did know, how trustworthy was he? He had known politicians who after several whiskies or brandies were often less than discreet.

He drummed his fingers on the desk and forced himself to think rationally. Deborah may not have revealed her secret at all; it just gave her pleasure to rile him – as it always had! He doubted that Field would have gone ahead with the engagement if he was privy to the truth. If the man was fool enough to do so, he certainly wouldn't want his constituents or indeed anyone to know that his wife had borne an illegitimate child. No, he decided, there was nothing to worry about.

Julia received Deborah's news with delight.

'I always said you and Theo were made for each other. I'm thrilled, Deborah, I really am. We must celebrate with an engagement party.' Her face lit up at the thought of one to organise.

'I'm not sure we want an elaborate affair, Julia. A small party, maybe, but it's only going to be a short engagement. We plan to marry soon, perhaps in about three months?'

Julia clapped her hands. 'That's even more exciting. We could go to Paris to choose your wedding dress!'

Deborah laughed at the impulsive suggestion. 'What a good idea, let's do that.' She would have been quite happy with a London couturier, but wanted to provide a distraction for her sister-in-law. Apparently the trip to Italy, their second honeymoon, hadn't – as yet – achieved the hoped-for-outcome. And Julia's woebegone face, when thinking herself unobserved, had not gone unnoticed. Another visit to the French capital would prove a welcome distraction for her.

'Where do you plan to live?'

'We shall look for a place in London, as Theo will need to be within easy reach of the House. Hopefully, we will find a property that is in good order.'

'Even so you'll be able to consult interior decorators, and

choose your own furniture. I would have loved that.'

Deborah could well imagine the pleasure such a task would have given Julia, although Gerard had allowed her to express her own taste in her private sitting room. And she had to admit that she herself would enjoy the experience. She was also aware that she was fortunate to have the option. I doubt, she thought, that the wives of miners or even those of most of the working classes ever did.

'Julia, what would give me pleasure to celebrate my engagement is if you could authorise champagne in the Servants' Hall? Don't you agree that it would be a nice gesture?'

'Yes, of course, I'll attend to it straightaway.'

Deborah smiled at her. 'I have a feeling that our trip to Paris will be a resounding success. Although we'll have to stay long enough for the final fitting.'

'All the more time to shop,' Julia said promptly. 'I'll ask Gerard to be kind enough to make the necessary arrangements.'

'And your new maid? Is she likely to desert you over there?'

Julia. 'I doubt it, a Dublin girl, she's still thrilled to be here in London.'

Deborah watched her leave the room, thinking how delighted she would be when invited to be a matron of honour.

Theo's father had expressed warm approval when Theo had telephoned with the news.

'Well done! Deborah is a charming and intelligent young woman, I liked her very much. And I don't expect it's escaped

361

your notice that her status can only enhance your political career. Have you thought of a date for the wedding yet?'

'I hope in about three months.'

'Excellent, I don't believe in long engagements. They take the bloom off, if you know what I mean.'

Theo laughed. 'I think so.'

'Nevertheless, a party will be expected.'

'Please, Father, only a small one. And only invite Felicity if absolutely necessary.'

A chuckle came over the line. 'She's away on a cruise.'

Theo replaced the receiver with a feeling of satisfaction. All seemed to be going smoothly, although he was aware that Deborah would soon be swept up in wedding arrangements. He was fortunate there wasn't an overpowering mama to cope with; he'd seen many a man almost emasculated in the hectic period between a diamond ring and a gold one. Then he instantly regretted the sentiment as crass and insensitive. It would naturally be a sadness for Deborah not to have her mother present on her wedding day.

Theo, too, had been thinking of the question of where they would live, and had already registered with several upmarket property agents. He had no wish to begin their married life in his bachelor apartment. He and Deborah had discussed their preferences, and already there were five properties he'd arranged to view but didn't want to tire Deborah at this stage. Once he had a shortlist, it would be different.

To make the final choice together would be an experience he'd look forward to.

Going to collect his briefcase as he was due at the House for a crucial debate, he thought that soon he and Deborah must have a serious discussion about the staff agency. Theo had no intention of putting any pressure on her, he admired enormously her initiative and courage in what she'd achieved. But her life was bound to change after they were married. He thought of his father's comment. Yes, Deborah, beautiful and articulate with a keen interest in politics, would most certainly be a distinct asset to his career. But although Theo was aware that colleagues considered him ruthless with regard to his political ambitions, that didn't apply to his personal life or he would have married long ago.

Deborah was staring in astonishment at her maid. 'Oh, Ellen, congratulations, that's wonderful news!'

Ellen was blushing, but her smile was one of pure happiness. 'I know it's only a few months since we met. If you remember, it was on the train back from Paris. When John proposed you could have knocked me down with a feather! But we're right for each other, I'm sure of it.'

'Any young man who can make you look like that has my approval.' Impulsively, Deborah hugged her. 'I'm so pleased for you.'

Looking a bit sheepish, Ellen said, 'Down on one knee he went, in Hyde Park in broad daylight. Said he couldn't wait any longer or he'd lose his nerve.' She paused, 'Lady Deborah, I know we servants aren't supposed to wear jewellery,' shyly, Ellen undid the top button of her black dress and took out a thin chain with a ring threaded on it, 'but look . . .' Deborah saw a gold ring with three of the tiniest diamond chips she'd ever seen. Ellen's eyes were shining with pride. 'He must have saved up for ages to afford it.'

'It's beautiful, Ellen.'

'I know, my lady. Ain't it exciting? Both of us, I can't believe it.'

'You're not planning to get married just yet, are you?' Deborah felt a pang of panic. How could she possibly plan her wedding without her loyal friend? Because that was how she thought of Ellen. She was more than just a servant, she was her confidante.

Her maid shook her head. 'We'll have to wait until we can afford it. But John doesn't want to wait too long.' Her cheeks became even more pink.

Deborah laughed. 'Don't forget to invite me to the wedding.'

'Oh, my lady, whatever would people say?'

'I don't care what anyone else thinks, but perhaps I'd better just come to the church. I shall miss you, terribly.'

'I shall miss you, too, Lady Deborah, I shall cry when I leave, I know I will.'

'But you'll have lots to look forward to. Your own home, for instance.'

Ellen beamed. 'That'll be the icing on the cake. John says he's good at decorating and such and he's going to make it a little palace.'

Deborah smiled at her, having already decided that a generous cheque would be the best engagement present she

364

could give the young couple. 'Well, I think it's time I took myself off to the agency. And congratulations again, Ellen. But I would like to meet your John one day. How dare he steal you away!'

'That would be a real honour, my lady, thank you.'

Romance seemed to be in the air Deborah thought when, coming out of the front door, she noticed a young couple holding hands walking along the pavement.

'Good morning, Brown,' she said as she took her place on the back seat of the Daimler. On realising that her change of routine was causing comment, she now only used a cab service on leaving the agency.

Early that afternoon Father Keegan telephoned to say that his housekeeper knew of a local vacancy for a kitchen maid. 'She reports that the cook there is a comfortable sort of woman, so it might suit your Millie quite well.'

'Thank you, Father, that's really helpful.' Deborah made a note of the details. She sat back in her chair, thinking that her relationship with the priest would be one aspect of the agency she would really miss. And what of Elspeth, her right hand and good friend? Would it mean that their paths would no longer cross? Deborah, whose mind had taken second place to her emotions since Theo's proposal, was only now beginning to realise that making the decision to relinquish the secret life she'd built was going to be far from easy. She had enjoyed so much knowing that she was helping people less fortunate than herself.

She glanced down at the third finger on her left hand. It was bare, devoid of her glittering engagement ring. Neither was she wearing it on a chain around her neck as the outline of the large stones could be seen beneath a silk blouse. Deborah suddenly felt angry. She hated this necessity to hide her pride and joy in being Theo's fiancée. Why didn't she face the fact that in three months' time she would not only be married, but to a public figure. Within twelve months she could even have a child. Hadn't she learnt that life was all about compromises, sacrifices? Although, she thought with a touch of asperity, the latter did seem to apply mainly to women.

And Deborah's last thought as she heard someone enter the outer office, was that this was not a decision she could, or should, make alone. She needed to talk to Theo.

Chapter Forty-One

Abby sent a swift reply to Deborah's announcement.

Debs, at last, at last! And wasn't Theo worth waiting for? You, my dearest friend, are going to be ecstatically happy, I just know it. Congratulations from Angus who thoroughly approves of your choice. But the most excited inhabitants of this chilly great house are the twins. They are clamouring to be your bridesmaids, and have talked of nothing else since. Please say they can, because they'll be drowning in tears if not.

You say that the ring belonged to Theo's mother, but haven't described it. So, another letter as soon as you can, and most importantly some indication of the date, so Angus can write it in his diary.

> *Written in haste and happiness,*
> *CONGRATULATIONS,*
> *Love*
> *Abby xx*

Deborah put pen to paper immediately. She invited Fiona and Morag to act as her bridesmaids as they were her favourite little girls, and described her engagement ring.

> *There is one person I especially want to be my chief bridesmaid but because you're married, apparently you would have to be my chief matron of honour. You are far too young and attractive to fit that description! Would you mind? Will you do it?*
> *Love*
> *Debs xx*

When Theo telephoned to suggest they dined at the Savoy Grill that night, Deborah was glad to have a chance to talk to him. The agency dilemma was threatening to overshadow her thoughts of the coming wedding, which should be uppermost in her mind. She decided to wear an ivory silk dress with sequinned fringes, one that Theo had previously admired. But instead of ebony long beads, Deborah twinned it with pearls, wanting to see the overall effect. Drop pearl earrings completed the picture, but after Deborah suggested this combination might be ideal for her wedding dress, Ellen hesitated.

'It does suit your colouring, my lady, but . . .'

Deborah gazed at her. 'You thought I would wear white?'

Ellen nodded. 'If I didn't, people wouldn't half talk . . .'
She gasped and put a hand to her lips. 'I didn't mean . . .'

Feeling uncomfortable, Deborah merely said, but with a
reassuring smile, 'Our circles are very different, Ellen.'

At Grosvenor Square, after greeting Gerard and Julia, Theo
went over to Deborah and kissed her on the cheek. 'I'm
missing you already,' he murmured.

She smiled up at him. 'Me, too.'

'My warm congratulations, Theo,' Julia said, as he
accepted a dry sherry from the butler. 'Deborah and I have
been making all sorts of plans to celebrate.'

Deborah laughed. 'Don't worry, darling, only a smallish
party, although we are planning to go over to Paris to shop.'

'There you are, Field, one of the penalties of having a
wife,' Gerard said.

'This will be a special trip.' Julia's eyes were sparkling. 'To
visit the fashion houses and arrange for Deborah's wedding
dress. And I can hardly return from Paris without finding
something delightful for myself.'

Theo laughed, turning to Deborah. 'Speaking of parties,
my father seems to feel that an engagement party will be
expected in Wiltshire.'

She smiled. 'I'd better make sure I'm in the country, then.'

Theo took another sip of his sherry and turned to Gerard.
'Are you dining out this evening?'

'At the Hamiltons. You know them, of course?'

Theo nodded, thankful he wasn't joining them. This particular couple had a reputation for holding dinner parties where the guests were as tedious as themselves.

When they were comfortably seated in the Bentley, Theo said, 'Why Paris, darling? We have some excellent fashion houses here in England.'

'I made the suggestion on impulse, I'm afraid.' As they drove, she told him the reason: that she had wanted to lift Julia's spirits.

'Such an altruistic gesture is typical of you.' He turned to smile at her.

'Is there anyone in your family who I should invite to be a bridesmaid?'

'You mean nieces? No, I'm afraid not.'

'How about close friends?'

'Well, Bertie and Jennifer, who you met at Felchurch Manor, have children, but they're both boys.'

'How old are they?'

He shrugged. 'I'd imagine around seven and five.'

'Perfect,' she said with delight. 'They could be pageboys.'

He laughed. 'I can't imagine those two dressed up like little Lord Fauntleroy.'

'I think we can do better than that. Would you ask Jennifer for me?'

'Of course. It's a good feeling, isn't it, planning a day that will be the beginning of our life together?'

'It's wonderful.' Deborah held up her hand so that the square-cut emerald and surrounding diamonds glinted in the late sunlight streaming through the windscreen. 'I do love my ring.'

Later, their happy, light-hearted mood continued but once their coffee and liqueurs were served, Deborah at last mentioned the agency. She spoke hesitantly. 'I've been wondering, Theo, what to do about the agency. Once we're married, I mean.'

He leant back and held her gaze. 'I suppose you mean the question of whether marrying me will mean that you have to relinquish it?'

She nodded.

'And how does that prospect make you feel?'

'Sad. Yet I can see that perhaps it might be the right thing to do. Not only because you are a rising star in the government,' she held up a hand as he was about to demur, 'yes, you are, darling. It's common knowledge. But everything has now changed. My time will no longer be just mine, to spend how I wish.' She smiled at him. 'I shall have a husband.'

'I'd hate to think that falling in love with me had resulted in you losing your independence.'

Deborah put out a hand to cover his on the table. 'Theo, you are now my life, as our marriage will be. I've done my best to help people more unfortunate than myself, but nothing lasts forever.'

'I would never put pressure on you, you know that.' He frowned. 'I admit that I don't want to have to compete with a business; I'd like you to be able to join me whenever possible. But how about your assistant? Would she have the expertise to manage the agency for you?'

Deborah gazed thoughtfully at him. 'Elspeth has the experience to do so. However, I'm not sure whether she would want the responsibility.'

'Darling, you won't know unless you ask.'

Deborah said slowly, 'So, you are suggesting that I retain the agency. It *is* in the name of Miss Deborah Claremont. And you wouldn't mind?'

'I would imagine that you already hold private investments; this would just be an additional one. Why should I mind?'

'Theodore Field, I love you!'

And so it was that on her very next day at the agency, Deborah, after glancing in the diary to view the day's appointments, said to Elspeth, 'Are you free to have a chat?'

Elspeth nodded. 'Shall I make tea?'

Deborah shook her head. 'We might be disturbed later, and there's something I wish to discuss with you.'

Elspeth followed her into the inner sanctum, and with an apprehensive expression took the seat on the other side of Deborah's desk.

'I thought you might be worried about the future of the agency,' Deborah said. 'Once I marry Theo, I mean.'

Elspeth nodded. 'Yes, I confess that I am.'

'The subject has been much on my mind, too,' Deborah

admitted. 'Obviously, I won't be able to carry on as before.'

'Yes, I can understand that.'

'So I wondered how you would feel about sitting on this side of the desk – in other words, running the agency yourself?'

Elspeth gasped. 'In view of Theo's political position, I've been preparing myself to hear that you were going to sell it.'

Smiling, Deborah shook her head. 'Actually, it was his suggestion that you may like to manage it. As far as I'm concerned, it would simply be viewed as an investment. Even married women are allowed to have those, I believe.'

Elspeth was gazing thoughtfully at her.

'There would be a higher salary, and you would, of course, have to appoint an assistant. And I wouldn't interfere, Elspeth. Although it might be helpful to both of us to perhaps have the occasional lunch together.' Deborah smiled, 'I confess that I would hate us to lose touch.'

'I feel the same,' Elspeth said. 'I've been feeling quite sad about it.'

'You will think it over then?'

'I don't need to. My husband used to say that one should never shirk extra responsibility. Mind you, that was when he was trying to persuade a parishioner to help out.' She smiled. 'My answer is a definite "Yes", Deborah. And thank you for having such confidence in me.'

The telephone's loud ring in the outer office then summoned her, but Deborah noticed with pleasure that Elspeth's step was light, and knew the right decision had been made.

She sat for a moment, musing over some of the clients who during the past few years she had enabled to have a second chance. It was then that Evan came into her mind. Without the help from herself and Father Keegan, would he still be unemployed?

Chapter Forty-Two

It wasn't until two weeks later, that Evan met Father Keegan again. Once more the priest and the Colonel had arranged to have a chess evening together and Evan had already completed his employer's dressing routine. He thought it a sign of the mutual esteem between the Colonel and his visitor that the former was happy to relax in his burgundy silk pyjamas and dressing gown, a cravat neatly tied around his neck.

When he came into the sitting room, Father Keegan, having first greeted his host turned immediately to Evan. 'I can't tell you how much I enjoyed listening to you speak, Evan. You raised several points with which I entirely agree, and it was good to hear someone express them so vividly.' He turned to the Colonel. 'This young man's talents are being wasted. Although I don't mean to denigrate the valuable service he gives you.'

Evan was frowning. 'I'm grateful for the work, Father. It's a hostile environment out there as far as employment is concerned.'

'And that's a crying shame. But even so, when the good Lord's given you the gift of eloquence, Evan, and a deep social conscience, it's a pity you can't use that attribute more widely.'

The Colonel smiled. 'I can tell you were accompanied by my niece. If Geraldine was a man, she'd be described as having a fire in her belly as far as injustice is concerned.' He turned to Evan. 'She too, was full of praise for you, wasn't that so?'

'Yes, sir.' Evan smiled, thinking of Geraldine's rapt expression as she'd sat in the audience. Rather than being nervous because of her presence, he'd even smiled at her almost successful attempt to disguise her distinctive appearance. 'I shall be getting a swollen head.'

'Nonsense,' the priest said, 'you're not the type. And by the way, Colonel, when are you going to show me the "holy of holies". In other words, this railway layout you're so proud of.'

'So that is why you wanted to come earlier! But Evan is due to go home.'

'I could stay later, sir. I don't mind a bit. That's if you feel ready to reveal how far we've got?'

The Colonel shrugged. 'Then, why not. *Carpe diem* was always my motto.'

'I'll fetch the shawl for your shoulders, and a rug.'

Watching Evan walk out of the room, the Colonel commented, 'A fine military bearing too. Your thoughts are in line with mine, Father. That young man could have a future in politics, and in a wider field than trade union work.'

Bronwen found Evan in a thoughtful frame of mind the following day, and said impatiently, 'You know, boyo, I might just as well eat on my own for all the company you are. What's on your mind?'

He glanced up. 'Oh, sorry.'

'Well come on, then. Or is it something personal? As you know, I'm not one to pry.'

He stifled a grin. 'It's just something that Father Keegan said. You know, the Catholic priest who came to hear me speak?'

She nodded, then frowned. 'He's not trying to convert you, is he? That lot have a reputation for trying to increase their flock.'

He laughed. 'No, nothing like that.' He repeated the conversation.

Bronwen's shoulders stiffened with pride. 'And what else happened?'

'We all went out to look at the model railway.'

She sniffed. 'Honestly, grown men playing with trains.'

'It's much more than that, Aunt Bron. It will be a mechanical marvel after I've finished with it.'

'So you keep saying.' She began to collect their used plates. 'Pudding? It's syrup sponge.'

'Do I ever say no?'

She went out smiling, and Evan's thoughts drifted back to Geraldine. He'd never met a young woman like her, or even an older one for that matter. The extent of her interest in the workings of the model railway was surprising. An image came to him of how she bit her lower lip when concentrating, and he smiled. He was enjoying his job far more than he had anticipated, although he knew this was because of the personalities involved. If the Colonel had, for instance, been typical of his kind, or at least the officers Evan had encountered before, and if the staff had resented his senior status in the pecking order, then daily life would be very different.

In Paris, Deborah and Julia were feeling exultant. After visits to various fashion houses, Deborah found a couturier whose ideas appealed to her, and one afternoon on seeing the proposed sketch of a wedding dress, knew instinctively that the simple yet elegant style was perfect. She felt the quality of the ivory silk, admired the delicacy of the lace panels, and without hesitation gave a delighted smile to the designer, nodding her approval. Only then did she remember to give Julia a chance to express her own opinion. Which she did in true Julia style, by clapping her hands.

The couturier, thin, elegant, and dressed in black, smiled. 'I am glad you are both pleased. Lady Deborah, if you would be kind enough to follow me, I shall arrange for your measurements to be taken.'

It was then, when standing in a small corner room in her chiffon and lace chemise, that Deborah, who was fluent in French, heard the name.

'*The costume will be sent to Lille within a few days, Madame Lapierre. And as always, thank you for your custom.*'

Deborah froze. *Lapierre? Lille?* Hadn't Philippe told her that when his father was alive, his mother had spent much of her time in Paris? It was perfectly feasible that she would still visit the fashion houses. Could she really, after all these years, be within a few yards of her? Swiftly Deborah moved as if to go to the door, before remembering that she was in a state of undress. But even hearing the name had shaken her, and she heard the concerned voice of the seamstress. 'My lady, shall I fetch a glass of water? You look quite pale.'

'Thank you, that would be most kind.' She sat on a plush red-velvet chair in one corner and tried to pull herself together. Should she make enquiries at the fashion house? But she knew immediately that confidentiality was sacrosanct in such places. They would never reveal details of another client. Yet to hear that name spoken aloud after all these years had truly shaken her. Her hand trembling, she took a few grateful sips of water, then rose and allowed the seamstress to complete her task. But even as she got dressed again, her mind was racing. Could the woman really be Philippe's mother?

By the time she returned to the salon to join Julia, Deborah was full of impatience to return to the hotel. Only in silence and privacy was she going to be able to sort out her chaotic thoughts.

'I'm sorry, Julia, but I seem to be developing a headache. Would you mind awfully if I went back to the hotel?' She didn't like lying, but was convinced that if she didn't have some privacy, she really would develop one.

'Of course not. In fact, I'm quite happy to do the same. I feel a little tired myself.'

'Then I'll just confirm arrangements for the fitting.'

When she was alone at last, Deborah sat propped against pillows on her bed and tried to sort out her confused thoughts. Every instinct was telling her that the Madame Lapierre referred to at the fashion house could be Philippe's mother. Which would mean that she was not only alive but possibly still living in his childhood home.

And the realisation brought to her mind an image of Philippe's gold signet ring bearing the Lapierre family crest and lying in a blue leather box in a drawer in her dressing table. She thought of his widowed mother, living alone with a husband and son to mourn, and knew there was only one honourable action. But would Madame Lapierre understand why it was that Deborah had never contacted her, even to tell her of their engagement? That she'd been so traumatised not only by Philippe's death but also by those of her parents? And then there had been the shock of learning she was pregnant, and later, another bereavement to bear when the baby died. By then too much time had passed.

But now, Deborah thought, I am shortly to marry another man. So didn't that mean that in all justice she should return the signet ring to its rightful owner – Philippe's much-loved mother?

Chapter Forty-Three

Deborah had made her decision about Philippe's ring, planning once the wedding was over, she would make arrangements for it to be returned to Madame Lapierre. But now, with the fitting for her wedding dress completed, she was becoming impatient to return to London.

Julia too, having made 'several delightful purchases', announced herself ready to return home saying, 'After all, there is your engagement party this weekend.'

It was during the journey back when travelling on the London train and alone in the carriage, that Julia once again raised the subject of her inability to conceive. 'I had hoped for a sign while we were in Paris, but it didn't happen. Deborah, I'm becoming so nervous about it, I do think I should seek medical advice.'

'You could,' Deborah said, 'although I still think it too soon.'

'I'd just like to be reassured there is nothing wrong.'

Deborah looked at her with sympathy. 'Why do we women always feel responsible for everything? The problem, if there is one, could easily lie with Gerard.'

Julia looked horrified. 'He's too proud a man even to consider it.'

And that statement, thought Deborah, was putting it mildly.

Two days after her return to Grosvenor Square, Deborah went to visit Father Keegan. It would be unthinkable for her not to let him know what was happening at the agency. But even as she neared the church, she was still undecided whether or not to reveal her true identity. At the moment, only Elspeth, Theo and Evan were aware of it, and wouldn't it be wiser for it to remain so? And yet her conscience was troubling her. Suppose, for instance, the priest were to discover the fact for himself, mightn't he feel he'd been deceived? She liked him too much – had even become a little fond of him – to let that happen.

So, it was with her decision made that she sat opposite him in his study. She saw his glance immediately alight on her sparkling engagement ring and his face creased in a warm smile. 'I see my congratulations are in order, Miss Claremont. May I wish you every happiness.'

'Thank you, Father. Although I did have a special reason for wanting to see you.'

'Let me guess now. You'll be giving up the agency?'

'Not exactly, although I'll no longer take an active role. Mrs Reid, who you've often spoken to on the telephone, will be managing it.' Deborah smiled. 'I'm hoping you won't mind her getting in touch – even if she *is* the widow of a Presbyterian minister!'

'Not at all.' His eyes twinkled. 'It could lead to some interesting discussions! And your future husband, now, would he be anyone I know?'

'I doubt it unless you visit the House of Commons. Theodore Field, a Conservative MP. He once went to hear Evan Morgan speak, and was impressed. I think you'd like him.'

The priest studied her. 'I'm sure I would. I too have heard Evan speak and been impressed. In fact, the Colonel and I think that young man should go into politics.'

Deborah stared at him. 'I entirely agree with you.' She was trying to recall whether Theo had friends in the Labour Party. A man with Evan's background, even with such potential, would need an influential contact. Could this be another way she could help him?

Then Deborah hesitated. 'Father Keegan, I have something else to tell you, this time about myself. I'm afraid that my brother being the Earl of Anscombe means that my real name is not Miss, but Lady Deborah Claremont.'

His eyes widened, then he chuckled. 'God bless my soul. To think I've been taking tea with a member of the aristocracy.'

With some embarrassment, Deborah went on to explain her reasons for not using her title.

'I quite understand. And it will go no further. Life goes through various phases, and you have helped many people to have a second chance. You should always be proud of that.' He smiled at her. 'So, I suppose this is goodbye.'

She nodded. 'If there is ever anything I can help you with . . .'

'I'll remember.' He rose and shook her hand. 'Well, I'd better get on, I've a young couple coming to see me for pre-marriage guidance.'

Deborah laughed. 'I'd better go then, before you include me.'

But as she left, she looked over her shoulder at the kindly priest and with genuine regret said, 'Thank you again, Father. I shall miss our talks together.'

'And so will I. God bless you.'

At the Savoy, their London engagement party was a light-hearted affair, the small number of guests carefully chosen. Deborah was sad that Abby was unable to attend, but consoled herself that soon she would be seeing her friend at the wedding.

The following weekend they went to Wiltshire where, at Felchurch Manor, Theo's father greeted Deborah warmly, kissing her on the cheek. 'Welcome to the family, my dear. I'm delighted with the news.'

'The time is whizzing by,' she told her future father-in-law as he led the way into the house. 'I can't believe it's only seven weeks to the wedding.'

'Have you decided where to go for the honeymoon, yet?'

'Now then,' Theo said. 'Isn't that where I am supposed to surprise her?'

'Nonsense, your mother thought it a ridiculous notion, because the bride had no idea what to tell her maid to pack.'

Deborah laughed and turned to Theo. 'Maybe we should talk about it, darling.'

On the evening of the second engagement party, Theo took Deborah downstairs to formally introduce her to the staff. She'd known that this was inevitable, and worried that Meg Daniels, the cook, might recognise her from the agency. It was the housekeeper who explained her absence. 'She will be sorry to have missed you, Lady Deborah, but is indisposed with a heavy cold.' It might only be a postponement, Deborah thought, but a welcome one, while Sarah Boot played her part perfectly.

The party itself went with a swing, being held at a large country hotel with a lively band. Theo invited Bertie Manston to be his best man, and Deborah asked his wife, Jennifer, if she might like to take on the role of a matron of honour.

She looked surprised and then delighted. 'I'm flattered. I'd love to, and thank you.' Jennifer laughed. 'I'll be able to keep an eye on our two terrors. I still can't see them as angelic pageboys.'

'Don't worry,' Deborah said, smiling. 'I know two bossy little girls who will keep them in order.'

It was a lovely evening, with happy toasts as Deborah met more of Theo's friends. She couldn't help being aware of some envious glances: her fiancé was without doubt the most handsome man in the room.

Later, back at Felchurch Manor they went out into the garden, ostensibly to look at the stars but in reality to melt in the darkness into each other's arms.

'I'm beginning to count the days,' Theo murmured, his lips against her hair.

'I know.' She snuggled closer.

'If you only knew how tempted I am to come to your room.'

She laughed softly. 'And I sometimes lie in bed, hoping that you will.'

Theo drew her to him, bending to kiss her bare shoulders, his lips travelling down to the swell of her breasts. Their kisses became deeper, more passionate, then at last with reluctance, they drew apart. 'Darling, let's wait until we have the perfect moment.' He smiled down at her. 'When we are completely and utterly alone. No prying eyes, or whispering servants.'

'You are right, as always.'

'I wonder if you'll still be saying that when we have been married for a long time?'

Deborah laughed. 'It will be interesting finding out. I love you very much, you know.'

'And I adore you. Sweet dreams, my love.'

There were many congratulations and introductions at the local church on Sunday morning, and afterwards Deborah found it a relief to relax with coffee and the Sunday papers.

The morning room remained silent apart from the rustle of pages from Theo and his father.

Eventually, as it was a lovely day, she said, 'Darling, I think I'll take Emma for a walk before lunch. Did you want to come, or . . .'

Theo glanced up. 'Actually, if you don't mind, there are one or two articles I need to read.'

She smiled at him. 'Not at all.'

The golden retriever was in a lively mood and ran ahead as Deborah explored the gardens surrounding the house. She loved the way she felt so relaxed here, and amused herself by indulging in a fantasy vision of happy children playing beneath the large oak trees. Then realising that Emma was galloping towards the stables, Deborah began to hurry after her, although she doubted the retriever would bother the horses.

But even as she approached, she could see Emma furiously wagging her tail, as a young boy leant over to stroke her. One of the grooms came forward. 'Sorry, my lady. The lad's not supposed to come here on his own, only when the laundress is with him.'

The boy muttered, 'I'm not doing any harm!'

'No, but you'll get a tanning if you're not back in time for your dinner.'

With his back to her he scrambled up, beginning to hurry away. Then suddenly he glanced over his shoulder.

There was something familiar about him. Was it the way he held his head, the set of his shoulders? Impulsively, she called out, 'Just a minute . . .'

He turned, looking wary and came back to stand before her, at first hanging his head and then lifting it to gaze directly up. Deborah gasped. She couldn't tear her gaze from his face, those warm brown eyes . . .

She managed to control her voice, to keep it calm. 'Don't worry, you're not in any trouble. You like dogs, don't you?'

'Yes, miss.'

The groom was still lingering. 'My lady, to you. And take your cap off!'

Hurriedly he obeyed. Deborah caught her breath.

He was looking scared. 'I'd better go, my lady, or I'll be late.'

'Yes, of course.'

Deborah watched him go, then turned on trembling legs to walk back to the house.

What on earth had happened there?

As soon as they were by themselves, she told Theo about the startling resemblance. 'It was such a shock, I can't understand it. Don't you think it strange?'

He looked at her with concern. 'It's upset you, hasn't it?'

She nodded, still feeling shaken.

'There is such a thing as a double, the Germans have a name for it, a doppelgänger.'

'Yes, I know, but . . . do you know anything about him, Theo?'

He shook his head. 'I've never actually seen him.'

Deborah was thinking that there *was* someone who might know more. Weren't servants privy to most things in a household?

Unwilling to draw attention to her connection with the under-housemaid, she had to wait until she could find Sarah Boot going about her duties. It hadn't been easy either, to pretend that Deborah had come across her by accident, nor to bring up the subject of the boy in a light and casual manner. At first Sarah had been full of congratulations. But did reveal that the laundress had only recently joined the household.

'At first,' Sarah told her, 'we thought Robbie was hers 'til he called her Auntie. He's a nice lad and ever so polite.' She paused. 'Although he does look a bit sad sometimes.'

Deborah wanted to ask where they had lived before, but knew her continued interest would spark the maid's curiosity. Unfortunately the information had done nothing to erase the boy's intriguing image from her mind, rather the reverse.

On repeating the conversation to Theo, he said, 'I'm sure the resemblance is only a coincidence, darling. Try to put it out of your mind. Let's just concentrate on the wedding and getting the house ready. If it's still bothering you after that, I promise to help in any way I can.'

Chapter Forty-Four

Back in London, initially Deborah found it a struggle to put the image of the young boy out of her mind, still trying to convince herself that a simple coincidence was the logical explanation of the resemblance. And then the hectic build-up to the wedding took over everything.

A few days after her return she accompanied Theo to view three properties that he'd shortlisted. They were all spacious, attractive houses within easy distance of Westminster, but she fell in love with one in the heart of Belgravia, faced with beautiful Portland stone. With white pillars at the top of steps leading to the front door, it not only had an impressive frontage but was situated in an elegant crescent overlooking glorious gardens.

'I love the long casement windows,' she later told a smiling Theo. 'And it had such a peaceful ambience. Did you feel it?'

'I was too busy looking at you. Have you any idea how lovely you are when you're thrilled with something? Your whole face lights up. But yes, it was my choice too. Are you absolutely certain, because if not, we can carry on searching.'

She shook her head. 'I love it, Theo. I'm sure we'll be very happy there.'

'Then I'll contact the agents first thing in the morning.' And within twenty-four hours he telephoned Deborah to say that the house was not only secured, but had the added advantage of immediate possession.

Hearing that, Deborah began to busy herself with arranging her future household. Ellen, of course, would accompany her as lady's maid, and Theo planned to bring his own manservant. Deborah, on Elspeth's recommendation, interviewed suitable applicants for the positions of housekeeper, cook, footmen and parlourmaids at Grosvenor Square. However, the ideal butler was proving more elusive. But after attending the funeral of one of his parliamentary colleagues, Theo invited his butler, a dignified man with a warm smile to apply, and that was another problem solved.

And so the weeks flew by, until at last the much-anticipated day arrived. The wedding itself took place at St Margaret's Church between Westminster Abbey and the Houses of

Parliament. It was where Deborah's parents had been married.

On the actual morning, there was much excitement in Grosvenor Square. Abby's twins, Fiona and Morag, immediately took charge of the pageboys, who rebelled at being told what to do 'by girls'. Eventually, their nannies managed to calm them all down by threatening to fetch their mothers. The four visiting matrons of honour were dressed by their maids in adjacent bedrooms, while Julia preferred to remain in her own.

Deborah, in her own apartment, stood quietly as Ellen brushed her hair until it shone, then slipped the cool silk of the wedding dress over her bare shoulders. She fastened a gleaming pearl choker around Deborah's neck and clipped on the matching drop earrings. And lastly the late countess's lace veil, which was held in place by its diamond tiara, fell into long soft folds.

'My lady, you look absolutely beautiful.' Ellen's eyes were misting over. 'I'm not going to cry, I'm really not.'

Deborah gave her a tremulous smile, then let her own gaze wander over her reflection. It was actually happening. Was she nervous? Was there a bride anywhere who wouldn't be? But her overwhelming feeling was one of joy. Because in a few hours from now, she would no longer be Lady Deborah Claremont, but Lady Deborah Field. And she wanted that more than anything in the world.

And so she arrived at the church to the stirring notes of the 'Trumpet Voluntary'. The fashionable congregation stood, but as the bridal procession moved slowly down the aisle, Deborah's eyes sought only the man she loved.

Three weeks later, in the Italian Lakes, or more precisely beside Lake Garda, the honeymooning couple were lying entwined in their sumptuous four-poster bed. 'You, my darling,' Theo murmured, 'are the most beautiful woman in the world.'

Deborah turned to him, 'And you,' she said softly, 'are the most loved.'

He smiled at her. 'Now those words could lead to our first marital row. Because you can't possibly love me as much as I love you.'

She kissed her finger and placed it over his lips. 'I think you are going to have to convince me.'

'What again?'

'Yes, please.'

'Lady Deborah Field, I have said it before, you are a minx.'

She held out her arms, loving the feel of his bare skin against her own. 'Don't worry,' she murmured, 'We won't be disturbed, I haven't yet ordered breakfast.'

When much later the breakfast trolley was wheeled out to the sunny balcony, Theo, who had enjoyed his croissants and coffee, watched Deborah bite into a ripe peach with amused indulgence. He thought how lucky he was. Deborah had delighted him on their honeymoon, not only with her passionate response to their more intimate moments, but by her positive attitude to everything. With her privileged background, she could easily have become blasé, but there was no hint of that. And her happiness was contagious. He had been able to banish from his mind all thoughts of Parliament, in fact of any problems at all. Instead they had lost themselves in each other, enjoying boat trips to other lakeside towns, taking picturesque drives, merely strolling around Riva del Garda itself. And of course, taking the opportunity to go to Verona, to gaze up at the fourteenth-century residence with its tiny balcony overlooking a courtyard, which was said to be 'Juliet's House'.

But now, as he finished his coffee, he said, 'I can't believe that we're due to return home tomorrow.'

'I know,' she said. 'And we each have to do our own packing!'

He grimaced. 'Still, we didn't want servants around on our honeymoon.'

She laughed. 'At least we could be as carefree as we liked, and spend illicit hours in the bedroom.'

'Not illicit,' he protested. 'We're husband and wife.'

'You know what I mean. We didn't have to obey any social conventions.'

He reached out to hold her hand. 'It's been wonderful, thank you, darling.'

Deborah smiled across at him. All the hours they had spent together *had* been wonderful. She had tried, and most of the time succeeded, in subduing her concerns about the young boy in Wiltshire, wanting, longing, to think only of Theo and their passionate love for each other.

But now within her was rising a desperate urge to see the young Robbie again. Had it been her imagination that had turned a passing resemblance into something much more sinister? Gerard might have an obsession with the reputation of the Claremont name, but surely . . .

'A penny for them, darling?' Theo broke into her thoughts. 'You've drifted away from me.'

She was swift to reassure him. 'Not at all. How could I?' Deborah held out her hand for him to take. 'It's just that with us leaving tomorrow . . .'

When she hesitated, he said, 'What is it, sweetheart?'

'I just wondered whether we might be going to Felchurch Manor quite soon?'

Theo didn't answer immediately. Then he said, 'Is this something to do with that boy?'

She nodded. 'I need to see him again, Theo.'

'It would set your mind at rest?'

Again she nodded.

He lifted her hand to his lips and kissed it. 'Then that is what we shall do.'

Chapter Forty-Five

A week later, in Grosvenor Square, Gerard opened one of the drawers in his desk and, searching at the back for a particular document, felt the outline of the blank but sealed envelope. Since receiving it from Freddie Seymour as an insurance in case anything happened to him, he had so far left it unopened. But since Deborah's refusal to say whether or not she was going to reveal her past to Theo, Gerard had been fighting an underlying uneasiness. After a moment's hesitation, he picked up his paperknife and slit the envelope.

Inside was a single sheet of paper with the present address of the boy.

Robert Waters,
c/o Mrs Bagshaw,

No. 4, Bluebell Cottages,
Felchurch,
Wiltshire

Gerard stared down at it aghast, while the sheet of paper slid through unsteady fingers. Seymour had managed to secrete the child in the one village where Deborah could possibly encounter him! Whether or not Theo's home was close by was of no consequence. Gerard didn't want the boy to be even in the same county. Nobody was to blame, Wiltshire hadn't figured in the list of counties to avoid that he'd given Freddie; at that time neither he nor Deborah were acquainted with the area.

Fraught, Gerard rose and began to pace around the study. He could only thank God that he'd opened the envelope. It was imperative that the boy be moved. At least to another county, somewhere like the wilds of Northumberland would be even better. Panic was beginning to rise in him. What if there was any sort of resemblance? The scandal of that brat's existence could never be known. That blasted maid, Waters, with her threat of revealing Deborah's scandalous behaviour; her blackmail had lasted all these years. He'd made a huge mistake in telling her the baby was destined for the workhouse! And now the boy knew too much to be confined to one.

Opening the door, Gerard strode along the hall to the morning room.

Julia turned as he came in. 'Darling, it's not quite time for coffee, but shall I send for some?'

He forced a smile, shaking his head. He needed something stronger than coffee, but he would take it in his study. 'I was only wondering – did you say that Deborah and Theo are back from their honeymoon?'

She nodded with a smile. 'Yes. You know, Gerard, I miss her. It took some time, but I really think we have become friends. And I have you to thank for that, by suggesting that first trip to Paris. You are a clever old thing.'

'Not so much of the "old", my sweet.' His reply was automatic, while his mind feverishly continued to plan ahead. Already walking towards the door, he added, 'We should invite them to dine. I'll come and join you later.'

Julia smiled and was returning to her magazine even before he'd left the room.

Back in his study, Gerard poured himself a stiff brandy, and sat in one of the leather armchairs, trying to think.

Several minutes later, he rose to pull the bell cord and when the butler entered, said, 'Fulton, would you tell Cook I shall be dining at my club tonight.' And, he thought, every other night until I've spoken to Seymour. The man must act immediately. And if it took the threat of blackmail to give him the necessary impetus, Gerard was prepared to use it.

It wasn't until two nights later that Gerard, with a profound sense of relief, saw at the opposite end of the dining room the familiar features of Freddie Seymour. And it was only after suffering an agony of impatience that afterwards he managed to speak to him.

Glass in hand, he went over to where the young man sat alone in a quiet corner of the lounge. 'Good evening, Seymour, may I join you?'

Freddie looked up. 'But of course, sir.

Gerard sat in one of the brown leather club chairs. 'I trust you are well?'

'In the best of health, and yourself?'

'Indeed.' Gerard leant forward. 'I need to talk to you.' He glanced over his shoulder. 'I think we're out of earshot, and I'd prefer it to be here rather than at Grosvenor Square.'

Freddie nodded, but kept his voice low. 'I hope there isn't a problem with our arrangement?'

Gerard didn't answer. 'Tell me, what made you send the child to Wiltshire?'

'I didn't. The woman who took him had been recommended as an honest woman who wasn't prone to gossip. She was living in Dorset at the time.'

Freddie shrugged. 'I think there was some sort of illness in her family, and I was notified that she'd moved to a new address. Wiltshire wasn't on your list, so I didn't think it mattered.' He gave a sharp glance at Gerard. 'But obviously it does.'

Gerard stared at him. So Seymour hadn't yet made the connection with Theo and Felchurch Manor. 'It has significance, yes.' He paused. 'I need you to move the boy elsewhere.'

Freddie looked startled. 'I say, sir, it isn't that easy. I doubt Mrs Bagshaw will wish to leave her present location.'

'Then find someone else.' Gerard's tone was sharp. 'I don't care how you do it, use bribery if you have to. But you must take action immediately. Don't forget that we're in this together, Seymour. I'm willing to settle another of your gambling debts. But you'd best remember that I'm not a man to cross.'

It was shortly after they'd returned to London when Theo drove Deborah to Felchurch Manor. As well as fulfilling his promise, it served another purpose. Redecorating was going to begin in their new home and he had no desire to spend his precious weekend among noise and confusion. Bertie and Jennifer Manston had already invited them to dine on Saturday night, and as the car purred along the country roads, Theo thought that everything was working out really well. Except for one cloud on the horizon.

He glanced at Deborah, sitting quietly in the car. He thought he knew what was going through her mind. It would be the matter of the young boy. At least this time she would know what to expect, what to look for. In a calmer state of mind she would be able to study the child's features in more detail. Surely the resemblance she'd seen was simply a vague one?

Deborah's distraction was not about the boy, at least not at that precise moment. She hadn't forgotten Father Keegan's comment about Evan's political potential. And being enclosed in the car with Theo gave her the perfect chance to raise the subject. She was also aware that she needed to present Evan's case in a way that would impinge on his memory, even make him more likely to want to support him. After all, they were of a different political persuasion, but despite that she was certain that he would have the necessary contacts.

And so Deborah forced herself to dredge up the 'ugly incident'.

'Theo?'

'Yes, darling?' He slowed down and indicated right.

'You remember when we went to hear Evan Morgan speak at Battersea Town Hall?'

He smiled. 'Of course I do. It was our first outing together. I suppose one could hardly call it a date.'

She laughed. 'It wasn't what you'd call a romantic evening, I admit.'

'And your point is?'

'There is something I've never told you about him.'

'What is that, then?' His tone wasn't especially encouraging.

'He once did me a great service.' Slowly and carefully, her voice at times trembling, she related to him what had happened in that alleyway several months earlier. She heard his sharp intake of breath, saw his hands clench on the steering wheel, and after a moment's hesitation carried on, 'There was no doubt of the thug's intention, I was terrified, and if it hadn't been for Evan's interference . . .'

He reached over to grasp her hand. 'Deborah! Why haven't you told me this before!'

She shook her head, trying to clear her mind of the shock, her terror, her feeling of being defiled. 'At first I couldn't bear even to think about it. I never did have the heavy cold that prevented my seeing you, Theo. I was so ashamed, unwilling to let anyone see my bruised face because of questions.'

'You reported it, of course!'

'That was Evan's reaction. But how could I? The constabulary would have wanted my details, my address. I couldn't risk my true identity being revealed. Think of the scandal, the humiliation if it were reported in the press.'

'I see what you mean. And you were right, of course.' Theo's voice was tight with fury. 'I cannot bear to think of you being subjected to such an ordeal.'

'I just thanked God that Evan happened to be in the area. I tried to repay his support by finding him some employment.' She told him about the Colonel, adding, 'He feels that Evan could have a career in politics.'

'Does he now? Recalling how he held that audience in the palm of his hand, I think he could be right.' Theo drew up at a junction, then after pulling away said, 'I'll give it some thought. I'm certainly in the man's debt.'

A few minutes later, he said, 'What I can do is to mention his name to one or two people. Much as I hate to give any advantage to the Opposition.'

'I'm afraid success in life too often depends on having the right contacts,' she said.

'That's always been the case, no matter how unfair.' He

turned to smile at her. 'But let's see if we can open a door for Evan Morgan.'

She looked out of the window. In all honesty, should she admit to Theo the attraction that had lain between herself and Evan? Deborah didn't want there to be any secrets in their marriage, but surely a feeling, and that was all it had been, didn't constitute a secret? What if Theo didn't understand? Mentally she shook her head. No, it wasn't worth taking the risk.

Chapter Forty-Six

'I'm sure it was a good idea for us to come on a weekday.' Theo turned into the long drive that led to Felchurch Manor. 'The laundress is much more likely to be here. I expect she probably lives in the village and the boy comes to see the horses after school.'

'Won't the grooms consider him a nuisance?'

Theo laughed. 'If I know Harry, he will make use of him.'

'At least enquiring after the collie's welfare will give me an excuse to visit the stables.'

They were now approaching the house itself, and almost as soon as Theo drew up outside the front door, the butler came out to meet them, followed by a footman.

Theo was greeting them both when his father appeared, smiling.

'I can see married life suits you, daughter-in-law,' he said as he kissed Deborah's cheek.

'It suits both of us,' Theo shook his hand.

'I believe the Blue Rooms have been prepared for you. Come down for tea once you've freshened up.'

The young maid, Cotton, came forward to bob a curtsy, and led the way upstairs, opening the door into a large pleasant room, decorated and furnished in a style to suit its name. Another door stood open to an adjoining bedroom, although Deborah doubted Theo would actually sleep in there.

But welcome though the later refreshment was, she found it an effort to join in the conversation, her mind acutely attuned to the precious minutes ticking away. Now that she was actually here, within walking distance of possibly seeing Robbie again, her impatience was almost painful. It would be impolite for Theo to leave his father so soon after they'd arrived, but surely she could?

'Do you know,' she said. 'I'm feeling rather uncomfortable after the journey. Would either of you mind if I went out for a breath of air? I could take Emma with me.'

Theo turned to her. 'Not at all, darling. Shall I come with you?'

She shook her head. 'Thank you, but I'm sure you and your father have much to catch up on.'

She took the same route as before, walking around the garden with Emma trotting beside her, before turning towards the stables. As they neared, the retriever didn't gallop ahead, but remained by her side. A sign, perhaps, that the boy wasn't there and waiting to pet her?

And indeed, her spirits plummeted when she saw that the stable yard was empty, apart from a couple of grooms attending to the horses.

One turned as she approached. It was the same one who had previously remonstrated with Robbie.

He took his cap off. 'Good afternoon, my lady.'

She smiled. 'I remember you, but I didn't catch your name.'

'It's Les.' He nodded to the other groom. 'And over there's Jim.'

'I was wondering, Les, about the injured collie we rescued a few months ago. Have you any further news of its welfare?'

He scratched his head. 'Not really, you'd have to ask Harry that. He'll be in tomorrow.'

'I see.' Deborah paused. It was obvious the boy wasn't around. 'We'll be staying for a few days, so I'll probably see him then. Thank you.' She called the retriever to her and, keenly disappointed, began to make her way back to the house.

Theo looked up as she went into the drawing room, and she gave a slight shake of her head. 'I think I'll go up and have a rest, darling. I'll see you at dinner, Father-in-law.'

'I shall look forward to it.' His smile was warm, and she wondered what his feelings would be if he knew of her past. Theo might be understanding, but she doubted that his father would be quite so forgiving. His generation were even more moralistic than her own.

* * *

408

Friday morning dawned with the promise of good weather, and both Theo and Deborah were looking forward to a brisk ride in the country air. Instead of sending a message for mounts to be saddled, they strolled along to the stables themselves.

'Morning, Harry,' Theo called as they reached the yard. 'Lovely day for a ride.'

The stableman came over, smiling. 'Good to see you back so soon, sir. And good morning to you, my lady.'

'Good morning, Harry.' Deborah glanced over the well-swept yard. 'I was hoping to see you. We were wondering whether you had any further news about the injured collie?'

He grinned. 'Fallen on his feet, he has. A local farmer took him. He'll be well looked after there, I can promise you.'

'Good. Although it was a pity that young boy was disappointed.'

'You mean Robbie? Aye, he's good with the horses too. He'll be here this afternoon after school.'

'He comes every day?'

'Mostly, apart from weekends. He gives a hand to Mrs Bagshaw with her bundles.'

After Harry had gone to saddle their mounts, Theo said, 'Bundles? I thought we had a wash house here?'

'I'm sure you have,' Deborah said, 'but don't you remember she said Robbie couldn't have a dog because of the washing? She'll probably launder the heavy stuff here, sheets and towels, but take away delicate items for hand-washing.' She laughed at Theo's amused expression. 'As a child, I spent lots of time in the kitchen at Anscombe Hall. It's a wonder I didn't get fat, all the treats Cook used to give me.' Then her expression changed. 'At least we'll be able to see the boy.'

'Ah, thank you, Harry,' Theo said, as the horses were led over. 'They're both looking in splendid form.'

And it was indeed the perfect weather for riding. Warm with a slight breeze, blue skies above and surrounded by glorious autumn foliage. They put the horses to a gallop, eventually slowing down to a trot, then a walk, and eventually dismounted.

'What time do you think he'll be out of school?' Deborah asked. She'd been unable to forget even for a minute what lay ahead. No matter how often she tried to convince herself that she was mad to imagine such a thing, her whole being was suffused with nerves. They were standing before a massive oak tree to admire the view over sunlit fields. She turned to Theo in anxiety. 'I don't want to miss him.'

He bent to kiss her lightly on the lips. 'The bell will likely go at four and it's only a short walk. He'll probably run, anyway. Stop worrying, sweetheart. We can judge the right time to go, and I'll ask Harry's advice about horses. He can be a bit long-winded so that will help.'

She nodded. 'I'll probably find that I've made a fool of myself. As you say, just because I saw a marked resemblance . . .'

He turned and collecting the reins, cupped his hands for Deborah to mount. 'A steady ride back, I think. And then a delicious lunch.'

* * *

410

For Deborah, the hours and minutes after luncheon seemed an eternity. Theo and his father were quietly discussing local issues at one end of the drawing room, while she sat in a deeply cushioned sofa flicking through *Country Life*. Nerves were increasingly making her restless, and once she excused herself, only to go along to the morning room where she could pace restlessly unseen. When she returned, it was to find Theo alone. 'My father's gone up for a rest,' he explained.

'Did you remember to cancel tea?'

'I said we'd ring for some later.' Just then came the sound of the grandfather clock in the hall striking four. 'We'll just give him time to get here. And sweetheart, try and stay calm and level-headed.'

'You think I'm making too much of it, don't you?'

'Deborah, whatever you decide, I'll be by your side. Never forget that.'

Twenty-five minutes later, they left the house and began to walk along the path that led to the stables. 'So, the plan is,' Theo murmured, 'exactly as I suggested before. I'll engage Harry in conversation, which will give you the chance to talk to the boy.'

She nodded. And then they were in the yard, where immediately she could see a small figure in one of the stalls, reaching up to stroke the long nose of the chestnut she had ridden that morning.

'He's there', she whispered.

Theo swiftly glanced at him before Harry approached them. 'Good afternoon, sir.'

'Ah, the very man. I could do with your advice, Harry. We have a stable at our new house in London, and I'm thinking of buying a horse.'

As Harry launched into a barrage of questions and descriptions of horseflesh, Deborah, after listening politely for a few minutes, began to move away. She strolled casually along the row of stalls, until she reached the entrance to the right one.

Her breath stilled for a moment. She said quietly, 'Good afternoon. Robbie, isn't it?'

The boy turned and looked up.

Deborah's heart leapt into her throat. The resemblance was stark, just as she remembered. The same black curly hair, the slight cleft in his chin, brown eyes so like . . . She needed to see him smile. 'I have some milk chocolate in my pocket, would you like some? You can eat it now, if you like.'

His small face lit up and he stretched out his hand. 'Thank you, my lady.'

So he remembered her! She watched him remove the silver foil from the small bar of chocolate and eagerly devour it. 'Is it good?'

He gave a cheeky grin. 'Smashing.'

Deborah's heart missed a beat before beginning to race, her eyes hungrily searching every feature, every aspect of his face. And the small seed of suspicion, even hope, that had been buried in her heart, that she had struggled so hard to submerge, burst into leaf. But it couldn't be, it was impossible. Questions flooded into her mind, and despite Theo's warning not to reveal her interest, she couldn't help herself.

'How old are you, Robbie?'

He drew himself up. 'Seven.'

She caught her breath. No, she mustn't ask his birthday! But perhaps a more general question?

She hesitated. 'And do you have another name besides Robbie?'

'Waters, my lady.'

Deborah felt the blood drain from her face.

Chapter Forty-Seven

Deborah was stunned. His surname was Waters? It meant that that Myrtle Waters, her cold-faced maid, had stolen her baby . . . Stolen him! Fury rose in Deborah so elemental that she wanted to scream, to lash out. Because she knew without doubt that she was standing before her own child, her *living* child. She made an impulsive move towards him, longing to gather him in her arms, to tell him that she was his mother, and she would always love and protect him. But with the discipline instilled into her from childhood, Deborah forced herself to step back. In a strangled voice she said, 'I'm glad you enjoy being with the horses, Robbie.'

'I like all animals, my lady.'

Deborah glanced desperately along the stable yard,

wanting, needing Theo. To be able to spill out all her chaotic thoughts and be comforted. But he was still patiently listening to Harry. She was in such upheaval, she couldn't possibly act normally, go back and join them. She looked at Robbie again, reluctant to leave him even for a minute. Feeling as if her heart was split in two, she managed to smile at him and turned away.

Reaching the privacy of her bedroom just in time before the hot tears rained down her face, Deborah flung herself on the blue silk counterpane and wept. She wept for herself, for all the years of her child's life she had lost. She wept for Robbie, deprived of her love. All those years ago, when she was pregnant, it had broken her heart to agree to him being adopted – assured that he would be with a family close by, where she could at least see him grow up. Promised that he would be educated in keeping with his class. She had done it as much for his sake as for her own. Philippe would never have wanted his child to be thought a bastard and treated as such. And now, the sickening truth was that she didn't even know whether he'd been properly cared for. Her whole being was suffused with an anger she would never have thought herself capable of. Then there was the treachery. Was it possible that her own brother had colluded in the cruel deception? She couldn't believe even Gerard capable of such wickedness.

'Darling, are you absolutely sure?' Theo, who had at last managed to extricate himself from Harry's well-meant words, had joined her in the bedroom.

Deborah nodded and got up from the bed. Her voice quavering, she told him of Robbie's devastating answers to her questions. 'If only I had a photograph of Philippe to show you. Does a mother know instinctively her own child? I only know I felt some sort of recognition the very first time I saw him.' She paused, 'I put it down to the amazing resemblance, I didn't dare to think or even hope it could be anything else . . . but now I know the truth.' She gazed up at him. 'Theo, the boy is mine, Robbie is my son.' She looked at him in both despair and elation.

Theo drew her over to the window seat and sat by her side. His hands holding hers, he said quietly, 'So, tell me, exactly how you were told that your baby had died.'

Deborah's mind went back to that terrible day. She began, 'I was still in my lying-in period after the birth. Waters came in, crying, saying that the baby had died while with the wet nurse. That he'd caught an infection.' She clung to Theo's hands. 'She stole him, stole my baby! She stood and watched my shock, my grief, as all I could think of was that little warm body I'd held in my arms. How could any woman do such a terrible thing?'

'And what of Gerard? Did he come to Wales, to comfort you?'

She shook her head. 'He just wrote expressing his condolences, and saying that under no circumstances was I to attend the funeral. That the secrecy of the past months must be maintained.'

'So who arranged the funeral?' Theo was frowning.

'Waters, in accordance with his instructions, and Gerard

sent the money for it. At least that's what she said.' She looked at him in distress. 'I cannot believe now that I was so compliant.'

'You were nineteen, my love, and recovering from the ordeal of childbirth. You must never blame yourself.' Theo fell silent, and Deborah sat twisting her engagement and wedding rings. Then he said, 'So you never actually saw the grave?'

'Yes, of course I did, I insisted on it.' Her voice was rising in hysteria.

Theo turned to gently kiss her. 'It's alright, sweetheart. Take your time.'

She looked at him despairingly. 'I'm trying to remember. I know that Waters came with me and that dusk was falling.' Deborah looked at him, her eyes darkening at the memory. 'She took me to a small unmarked grave, saying arrangements had been made for a headstone once the ground had settled. I took a bunch of anemones from the cottage garden and replaced the ones already there, on top of the mound.'

Theo's expression was grim. 'Was that when you returned to London?'

She nodded. 'Waters was to follow once she'd attended to everything at the cottage. But she never did. Instead she wrote to say that she'd been offered a position with my Aunt Blanche and preferred to stay in Wales. I thought Gerard must have arranged it. Knowing what she did, it was safer than her being at Grosvenor Square, I was just glad to be rid of her . . .'

'And you never went back to visit the grave?'

Dismally she said, 'Gerard said it would draw attention to me.'

Theo drew a deep breath. 'Deborah, we need to think very carefully about all this. I suggest that I go down to the drawing room and order tea. We'll be able to sit more comfortably there.'

'I'll come and join you.' After he had left the bedroom, she remained sitting for a moment, then went to splash her blotched face with cold water before dabbing it with powder. Deborah stared in the mirror, scarcely able to believe that she was the mother of a living seven-year-old boy.

In the drawing room, Theo was trying to piece together the threads of what Deborah had just told him. Part of him wanted to hurry to the stables, to see the boy for himself, but he hesitated, not wanting to draw attention. In any case, Robbie may have already left.

It was unworthy of him, he knew, but Theo couldn't help some resentment that this had arisen now, to disturb the idyllic rhythm of their early married life. Was it selfish to want his new wife to himself? He almost felt that he had been superseded in Deborah's heart by this small boy.

But his overwhelming feeling was one of fury that she had been treated so callously. And for heaven's sake, child abduction carried a severe penalty. Had this woman Waters realised that? As for the supposed funeral, he doubted there had ever been one. The false grave Deborah had been shown?

A bribe to a gravedigger to dig a small mound of earth in a secluded corner of the graveyard.

And this woman, Waters. How had she been able to afford to raise a child alone, and have the veneer of respectability to do so? Someone must have financed her, and it could only have been Gerard. But why on earth had he got himself involved in a criminal activity?

Theo smote his fist into his hand. Blackmail! That must be the reason. Waters had wanted a baby and seen her opportunity. What if, once the baby was safely delivered, she'd threatened to reveal everything?

He turned as Deborah came into the room, noting that she was looking better, although there was no doubting the strain in her face. It was fortunate that tea, with tiny sandwiches and scones, had already arrived, so there was no chance of their being disturbed or a servant noticing that she had been crying. She would have hated that.

'Come and eat something, sweetheart. You'll feel better for it.'

Deborah forced herself to eat a sandwich and did indeed feel revived by the comfort of a hot drink. Then she looked across at Theo. 'What are we going to do?'

Her plaintive, bewildered question went straight to his heart. 'First and foremost, darling, we are going to find out the truth, what happened, and how it happened.' He put down his empty cup. 'And we both know that we can't do that ourselves. You can hardly go around asking self-incriminating questions. A similar restriction applies to me. But tell me, is your Aunt Blanche still alive?'

She shook her head. 'She suffered another stroke and died within six months of Waters going there.'

'So we have no way of knowing whether she actually went.'

Deborah frowned. 'There could be. I believe a distant cousin inherited, so it's more than likely he'd retain the staff.'

'Perhaps you could make a general enquiry about Waters' welfare?'

'Yes, I will. It's a start, anyway.'

Theo said, 'I think I'll go along to the study and make some notes while I have all the facts in my head.' He turned to look back before opening the door. 'And tomorrow afternoon we will go to the stables together. Do you realise that I've never actually seen your Robbie?'

Deborah leant back in the armchair, closing her eyes and hugging the last two words to her. He *was* hers. Whatever difficulties lay ahead, nothing could take away the wonder of knowing her child was alive.

Chapter Forty-Eight

It was raining the following morning, so instead of going for a ride, Theo took Deborah to see the nearby village with its broad high street and honey-coloured cottages. As they passed one or two thatched ones, she remarked how attractive it was.

'Wiltshire has a wealth of history too. We'll come and spend more time here next summer, and I'll take you to see places of interest.'

'That would be lovely.' But Deborah's response was an absent one. She just wanted the hours to pass quickly; for the late afternoon to come so that she could see Robbie again. And she was longing for Theo to see him. Would he detect any resemblance to herself? If not facial, then perhaps in a gesture or a fleeting expression? Also, her mind was in a constant whirl trying to forecast what was going to happen in the future. Deborah only knew that she had no intention of losing her son a second time.

'I wonder in which cottage the laundress lives?' She was scanning each doorway as if her son would miraculously appear. 'And where Robbie was beforehand? Do you think Waters has died?'

'Darling, I've told you, the right questions will be asked, but not by either of us. And no need now for you to make any enquiries about her. As soon as we return to London, I intend to hire a private investigator.'

She turned to him. 'I worry that I'm not being fair to you, thinking about this all the time.'

'There's no need, honestly.' Theo reached to take her hand for a moment. 'But I did miss making love to you last night.'

'I'll make it up to you, I promise.'

'Darling, I'm teasing you. Trying to distract you. Anyway, it's time to go back for luncheon. And one of the footmen mentioned Cook is making an apple pie.'

'Honestly, you men and your stomachs.'

'It's the way to a man's heart . . .'

'Perhaps I'd better learn to cook, then.'

'I like you just the way you are.' Theo laughed as Deborah blew him a kiss.

Yet again the afternoon dragged on, until at last the time arrived. Theo had gone up to the nursery and found in a cupboard a small box of lead soldiers, their uniforms still brightly coloured.

'The perfect excuse to go along to the stables again,' he said, when he brought them down to show her.

Deborah's heart was racing as they made their way there. She knew there were going to be huge decisions to make, but kept pushing them away, not wanting to face the obstacles that lay ahead. Her mind was still reeling with joy that the love she and Philippe had shared would live on in their son. Yet if she had never met and married Theo, she might always have thought her baby had died.

And so her expectations were high as they reached the stable yard. Her eager glance around didn't see him, but he was probably inside one of the stalls.

Theo called out to Harry, 'Good afternoon, glad the rain has cleared up. I have something to give that boy, Robbie, is it? My wife has taken a liking to him.'

'Aye, he's a good lad. But I'm afraid you're out of luck, sir.'

'He isn't here?'

Deborah caught her breath. Was he unwell?

'Nor will be again,' Harry said. 'I believe he's gone to live somewhere else.'

Deborah stared at him in shocked disbelief. It couldn't be true, where would he go, and why? Her feeling of loss was like a physical pain.

Theo's tone was casual. 'And the laundress, too?'

Harry shook his head. 'No, she's got a sick relative in the village. That's why she moved here in the first place.'

Deborah was stunned, unable even to think. Theo took her arm, his slight pressure warning her not to query further.

'Thanks, Harry,' he said. 'If you know of anyone who would like some toy soldiers, let me know.'

'I will, sir, and thank you.'

They walked back to the house in heavy silence. As Theo's father had gone to visit an old friend, the drawing room was thankfully empty.

Stricken, Deborah slumped onto the sofa. Theo went to sit beside her, putting his arm around her shoulders. 'Don't worry, darling. We'll find him.'

Her voice was tremulous. 'How? Why has he been moved?'

'Because someone is desperate that you and he don't come into contact.' His face was grim. 'Only he's too late.'

'But who?' Theo saw her eyes widen, as realisation dawned. The name seemed to hover on her lips and at last she whispered, 'You think that Gerard . . . ?'

'Much that it pains me to think he could betray his own sister, I can't think of any other explanation.' Theo related his theory that Waters had blackmailed him. 'He may not have been complicit in the scheme right from the beginning, maybe he did intend your baby to be adopted. But when he was born . . .'

'I do remember that was the only time I saw her expression soften. When she held him in her arms, she looked at him with such tenderness . . .'

'Do you think her capable of it? Blackmail, I mean?'

Deborah brushed away threatening tears. 'If she can steal a baby, she's capable of anything.'

Theo was silent for a moment. 'The boy's disappearance has changed everything. We don't have time for a private investigator now, we'll have to act ourselves.'

'What about the laundress? Could she help?'

'Too risky, it would reveal our interest, arouse curiosity. I'm convinced Gerard holds the key to all this.' Theo gazed into her worried eyes. 'Do you trust me?'

'But of course.'

He leant to briefly kiss her. 'Then leave it to me. I'll get the truth out of him, I promise you.'

Deborah was all for leaving for London immediately, but Theo dissuaded her, pointing out that they were dining with Archie and Jennifer Manston the following evening. 'They have invited several of their friends to meet you and my father is coming with us. I don't see how we can let them down.'

She stared at him. Surely it was more important for Theo to go to Grosvenor Square? 'They will find me poor company, I'm afraid.'

'No, they won't, darling. You'll look beautiful as always, and your natural poise and confidence will carry you through.'

'But we'll be able to leave on Sunday?' Her voice was sharp.

He shook his head. 'No, I think we should act as if everything is normal. Wherever Robbie has been taken, he'll be there now. Another day won't make any difference.'

Deborah drew a deep breath and asked, 'And if we find him, Theo, what then?'

Theo hesitated. 'Let's cross one bridge at a time.'

On Monday morning, they said goodbye to Theo's father, and set off to drive back to London. By mutual consent, any more talk of Robbie was out of bounds.

'At least for the journey,' Theo said. 'I need to distance myself from the issue until I confront Gerard tomorrow. That's what I do when I have a major speech to make in the House. It keeps the salient points and my strategy clear in my mind.'

For her own part, Deborah was desperate to stop her ever-circling thoughts about her young son. And so she forced herself to focus on their new house, imagining how the redecoration would look when they returned. And she did manage to distract herself, but only for some of the time. Her son was missing! Now that she knew he was alive, he was *her* responsibility. She glanced sideways at Theo, feeling guilty that she'd burdened him with all this. After all, they had only recently returned from their honeymoon, and he deserved a happy new wife not an overwrought one. But there would be no more crying. She had rediscovered her core of steel. The same one that had sustained her in 1918 when she'd lost the three people she loved most in the world. This time, Deborah thought, that won't happen. *I can't lose my little boy again!*

* * *

Theo wasted no time the following morning. His policy had always been to face a problem head-on. And so, at what he judged an optimum time, midway through the morning, he set off for Grosvenor Square. He didn't telephone beforehand, wishing to catch Gerard unprepared. Any military man would advise that a surprise attack gave the advantage.

When the door was answered, he stepped inside. 'Good morning, Fulton. I would like to see my brother-in-law. Is he at home?'

'The Earl is in his study, sir.'

Theo passed over his hat. 'No need to announce me, I know my way.' He strode along the hall, tapped, and taking a deep breath, opened the wide, mahogany door.

'Good morning! Not too busy, I hope?'

Gerard glanced up from behind his desk. 'Theo! I thought you were in Wiltshire.'

'And so I was. We got back late yesterday afternoon.'

Gerard's expression became wary. 'A good visit, I hope.'

'An illuminating one.' Theo indicated the leather chairs on either side of the fireplace. 'May we talk?'

Frowning, Gerard rose and slowly came to join him. 'Of course. Can I offer you any refreshment?'

Theo shook his head. 'I haven't come here for a social call.' He looked at the other man, noting again his cold eyes and thin lips. He had always considered that Deborah's brother was not a man he would choose as a personal friend.

'So, what is it you wish to discuss?'

'It concerns Deborah. As we both know, Gerard, she was

previously engaged to a certain French lieutenant, who was killed at Amiens. Also, that she found herself pregnant and subsequently gave birth to a baby boy.'

Gerard's eyes flashed with anger. 'I did not give her permission to reveal all this.'

'My wife is a person in her own right, Gerard. It was her decision to make, not yours.'

'Then I trust you will respect that confidence? I would not wish our family name to be tainted by scandal.' Gerard paused. 'But then, I would imagine that in your own interests, you too would hardly wish it to be known.'

Theo nodded. 'That is true.'

'And the point of your unexpected visit is? Come on, Field. I'm a busy man.'

'As am I. It is just that when visiting my father's stables, Deborah came across a seven-year-old boy, ostensibly the nephew of the laundress. She came back to the house in bewilderment, to tell me that this child bore a strong resemblance to the late Lieutenant Lapierre.'

Gerard stiffened. 'Really? These coincidences do happen sometimes.'

'My thoughts exactly,' Theo said smoothly and saw Gerard relax.

'But only at first. Because the next time she saw him, Deborah became even more certain of the resemblance. She asked him two questions. Would you like to know what those questions were?' Theo was trying to keep his tone even.

'I can't see what relevance—'

'The first was to ask his age. Which he gave as seven. Exactly the age that Deborah's son would have been if he'd lived. Strange that, don't you agree?

'Deborah's second question, was to ask his last name.' Theo paused. 'He said it was Waters. Now, wasn't that the name of the maid you sent to Wales with Deborah? The only person present at the birth?'

Gerard shrugged. 'Was that the woman's name? I cannot recall.'

'My wife,' Theo said, 'is now convinced that she was lied to when she was told her baby had died. That the maid, Waters, stole him, and that this boy is actually her own son.'

'Oh, for heaven's sake, that is pure hysteria,' Gerard snapped. 'We all know that women are emotional creatures.'

Theo's dislike of the man was increasing with every minute. 'Rather a generalisation, don't you think? I think that is exactly what did happen.'

'Then this is an appalling situation. I bear no responsibility for it, Field, believe me.'

'Don't you, Gerard? Who else but yourself could have financed this woman? She could hardly have carried out her crime without help. I would remind you that assisting an abduction *is* a criminal offence, carrying with it a lengthy prison sentence.'

'Nobody would believe such a preposterous assumption.'

Theo said slowly, 'I think Scotland Yard would listen to an MP, don't you?'

'And why, may I ask, would I become involved in this woman's scheme?'

'Blackmail.' The word hung in the air between them.

'I've no idea what you're talking about.' But now Theo could detect a note of desperation in his voice.

'What if Waters had always wanted a child? She finds herself in possession of a secret you went to great lengths to conceal from the outside world. With a young mother who is isolated. And a brother obsessed with his family's good name. Blackmail, Gerard. A threat to reveal what she knows. Or she takes the baby.'

'That's all fiction, and you know it.'

'Do I? Isn't it a brother's duty to protect his sister? Whereas you lied to her, told her the baby had died. Can't you imagine her anguish?'

Gerard glared at him. 'You have no proof of any of this.'

Theo nodded. 'You are right. I haven't. But I could easily hire a private detective to uncover the evidence.'

For a moment they sat in silence, then Gerard gave a thin smile. 'You would never bring this to the notice of the authorities. Because it would mean everyone knowing that you'd been stupid enough to marry not only a fallen woman, but one who'd given birth to a bastard. How would that affect your political career?'

Theo managed to resist the urge to punch Gerard in the face.

He leant forward. 'You are forgetting Deborah. Have you any idea of the emotional upheaval she's suffered? She's a strong-minded woman, as you well know. I'd have no power to prevent her going herself to Scotland Yard. And believe me, she will. She's lost her child once, she has no intention of losing him again.'

Gerard bristled. 'She would never do that to me, to the Claremont name.'

Theo waited a moment, then said, 'Did I mention the boy has disappeared? Suddenly been taken away? And not by the woman who was looking after him.' He looked directly at the man opposite. 'Judging by the ferocity of your sister's feelings, you need to tell us where he is. Otherwise, that is exactly what she will do.'

Chapter Forty-Nine

While Gerard had refused to reveal Robbie's present whereabouts, he had grimly agreed to Theo's demand that the boy should be returned to the laundress at Felchurch.

'But don't forget,' Theo reminded Deborah that night, 'he did warn it could take a little time.'

'At least we will know where he is.' Deborah raised Theo's hand to her lips and kissed it. 'You're my Sir Galahad, darling.'

He smiled at her. 'I'm afraid I failed to ride to Grosvenor Square on a white charger.'

She turned to him in their new luxurious four-poster. 'Well, you're my knight in shining armour, anyway.' Deborah said softly, 'And don't you think it's time we recaptured the magic of our honeymoon?'

He reached over to take her in his arms. 'My own thoughts exactly.'

Ten days later in Battersea, Evan Morgan was again the main speaker. Seated on the platform before being introduced, he was scanning the packed hall for one particular face. And as he hoped, the Colonel's niece was seated near to the front, her red hair covered by the customary shawl. As she looked up at him, they exchanged a swift smile. Geraldine would, he knew, not only analyse his words, but frankly express her opinion when she next came to visit her uncle. And these visits, as his employer had recently commented, were becoming far more frequent. Evan had tried to convince himself that this was because of her interest in the model railway, but instinctively knew that wasn't strictly true. There had been too many covert glances between them, an exchange of the silent messages only passed between people attracted to each other. And inwardly he groaned. Yet again he was attracted to someone out of his class.

And then Evan was being announced, and with his message crystal clear in his mind, began to speak about the continuing plight of the miners and other social injustices. His commanding voice rang out with sincerity and, on drawing to a close, the audience gave him a standing ovation.

'Well done, comrade,' said one of the union officials as he left the stage. Evan lingered to speak for several moments with other union members, and then said, 'I'll be glad of a pint, I know that.'

'Then please allow me to buy you one.' Not recognising the voice, Evan turned to see a well-dressed middle-aged man smiling at him. 'Sorry, I'd better introduce myself. Andrew Wilshaw, Labour MP.' He shook Evan's hand. 'It was a privilege to listen to you. Young man, you and I need to talk. How about we go for that pint you mentioned?'

Within fifteen minutes the two men were sitting in the lounge of a nearby pub. With pints of foaming ale before them, both took a long sip. Evan, feeling rather mystified, looked across the small oak table. 'What constituency do you represent, Mr Wilshaw?'

At the mention of one in the north of England, Evan gave a grim smile. 'So you'll have witnessed much hardship, then.'

'Unfortunately, I have. And life doesn't get any better up there.' He took another sip of beer. 'It was a fellow MP, Theodore Field, who advised me to come and listen to you, and I'm glad I did. He's a man I have a lot respect for, even if he *is* a Conservative.'

Evan could only stare at him in disbelief. He knew the name, of course he did. Deborah had married him. And didn't she say that he'd accompanied her to hear him speak at Battersea, just before the General Strike?

'I wonder, Evan – you don't mind my calling you, Evan?'

'Of course not.'

'Would you mind if I quizzed you a bit?'

'Please go ahead.'

A comprehensive list of questions followed, by the end of which Evan had related every fact about his background, army career, and political leanings, ending with a description of his employment at the Colonel's house.

The MP frowned. 'That sounds rather below your capabilities, if you don't mind my saying so.'

Evan spoke slowly. 'Finding a job is more difficult than it's ever been. I'd used up all my savings and needed to earn money. But I've never seen it as a permanent position.'

'Well, I think I can do better than that. The Labour Party needs men like you, Evan Morgan. And in the House of Commons. But a year or so of parliamentary experience would be useful before putting yourself forward to stand. As it happens, I'm able to help you, because one of my assistants is leaving in a couple of months. How would you feel about replacing him?'

Evan was stunned. To have the prospect of becoming an MP, of representing a constituency and the chance to influence government policies?

His reaction was instant. 'Full of enthusiasm!'

'Excellent. That's what I like to see, fire in a man's eyes. I think we shall do very well together. And I'm sure the pay will be better than your current salary.' He felt in the top pocket of his jacket and took out a small notebook. 'Give me your address and I'll write to you.' Minutes later, he drained his glass and stood up. 'A useful evening for both of us, I think.'

Evan rose and the two men shook hands. 'Thank you, sir.' Liking his straightforward manner, he watched the stocky figure leave. Then to celebrate he went to the bar and ordered another pint.

Carrying his glass back to the table, Evan tried to sort out his thoughts, excitement racing through his veins. For his name to come to the attention of someone with influence was beyond his wildest dreams. He would always be grateful for Deborah's thoughtfulness. And to think it all began with him rescuing her flyaway hat.

He decided to wait for the promised letter before explaining to the Colonel what had happened. Evan suddenly realised this golden opportunity could mean him losing touch with Geraldine! Would he only ever see her when he was speaking on behalf of the union, and then from the platform? The dismay that flooded him was startling in its strength.

But didn't this offer change everything? With the possibility of a political career opening up, he would no longer feel hesitant to reveal his feelings. He could volunteer to help the Colonel with the railway layout in his own time, and if Geraldine happened to visit . . .

Evan finished his drink, and threading his way past a group of men at the bar, couldn't wait to return to Greenwich and share his good news. He grinned, thinking how proud Aunt Bronwen would be when a letter from the House of Commons came through the letter box.

The following day, Theo and Deborah were relaxing in the morning room with the newspapers, when their new butler came in. 'There is a telephone call for you, sir.'

Theo rose and followed him into the hall. 'Do you know when the other extensions will be installed?'

'I believe it will be next week, sir.'

Within minutes Theo came to rejoin Deborah. 'That was Gerard. Robbie is back with the laundress.'

Deborah, who had refused any contact with her brother, was elated but wary. 'How can we be sure he's telling us the truth?'

'Because he has nothing to gain by lying.' Theo smiled at her. 'I won't sit down, darling, I need to look through some papers before I leave for the House.'

Deborah leant back and closed her eyes. There had never been a time, not even during loss, grief and the shock of discovering her pregnancy, when she'd been in such anguish. She'd spent hours wrestling with the problem of Robbie's future. She'd tried to ignore her own needs, instead concentrating on what would be best for her child. Because there was no escaping the word *bastard*. So she had shared a night of love with a brave man before he returned to fight for his country. Why was that considered so shameful, so wrong? And yet the world would stigmatise Robbie, the innocent child of that union. He'd probably been told that his father was killed in the war – true – and believed Myrtle Waters, who would undoubtedly have worn a ring on her third finger, to be his mother. So far he would have escaped that slur. But now it was up to herself, his real mother, to protect him.

Theo, bless him, had gently refused to discuss the matter. 'I don't want to influence you in even the slightest way. Whatever you plan to do, you know I'll support you.'

Deborah only knew that her love for Theo grew with every passing day. Yet she was acutely aware of what Robbie's permanent presence in their home would mean for her husband's political career. He would become the victim of whispers of ridicule and scandal, which was bound to affect his ambition to rise higher in government. Had she married him only to his detriment?

She longed with every inch of her being to have her young son with her, to make up for all those years of loss. Yet didn't Robbie have one other living relative? Someone who had every right to know of his existence. Could this prove to be the ideal solution? Deborah wasn't sure. But now that Robbie was within reach, it was time to explore the possibility.

'I'll be late this evening,' Theo said as later he came in to kiss her goodbye. 'There's an urgent debate in the House.'

She smiled at him. 'Take care, my love.'

A few minutes later Deborah went up to their bedroom and to her dressing table to take from a drawer the small leather box she sought. Once back in the morning room, she slowly opened it to gaze down at Philippe's signet ring with its family crest. Memories came flooding back, of how he had talked of his happy childhood at the chateau, with his beloved dog and horse. And how close he had been to his mother.

Now seated before the escritoire, Deborah drew towards her a sheet of headed writing paper and, taking the top off her fountain pen, began to write.

Dear Madame Lapierre . . .

Five years later . . .

Madame Lapierre, an elegant Frenchwoman in her early fifties, had welcomed her unknown grandson with open arms. She vaguely explained his sudden appearance, Robbie's strong resemblance to Philippe preventing further questioning. Twelve months later she confirmed him as her legal heir.

Robbie, known now as Robert, is happy, fluent in French, and the proud owner of a chestnut mare and his own dog. Deborah now owns a house in France, and on the pretext of being a friend of his grandmother, is able to see him quite often. The question of whether she will ever admit the truth is one she still hasn't resolved.

Evan, eventually selected as a candidate in a Midlands constituency, won his seat with an outstanding majority. He and Geraldine were married three years earlier.

Theo's political career flourishes. He has recently been appointed as Home Secretary, the youngest man since Winston Churchill ever to hold such a prestigious position.

Elspeth, with a capable assistant, continues to successfully run the agency, and she and Deborah remain in regular contact.

Deborah, blissfully happy in her marriage, is the loving mother of twin daughters and expecting her third baby. She goes occasionally to Grosvenor Square to take coffee with Julia, but apart from unavoidable social proximity, Deborah has determined never to speak to Gerard again.

Gerard remains childless.

Acknowledgements

First and foremost, my gratitude to my brilliant critique group for their perceptions when we meet each week overlooking the sea in Eastbourne. Our shared bond of writing and literature has led to much-valued friendships.

And as always to my loyal writing friend in Leicester, Biddy Nelson.

To my lovely agent Ros Edwards, of the Edwards Fuglewicz Literary Agency, whose support means so much.

And my special appreciation to the excellent publishing team at Allison & Busby.

ALSO BY MARGARET KAINE

Margaret Kaine

The
BLACK SILK
PURSE

Sent to the workhouse as a child, all Ella Hathaway can remember is a voice whispering, '*Dearie, promise you will never forget what you saw. Your ma was killed deliberate ... and someone oughter pay for it.*'

When young, wealthy spinster Letitia Fairchild witnesses Ella being ill-treated, she takes her in as a scullery maid. But as Ella grows up, she is determined to find the truth about her mother's tragic death and appeals to Letitia for help, revealing to her the contents of her only personal possession: a black silk purse. Intrigued, Letitia agrees to begin a quest to solve the mystery of Ella's past. But neither could have imagined the astonishing and dramatic consequences.

Born and educated in Stoke-on-Trent, MARGARET KAINE now lives in Eastbourne. *A Life of Secrets* is her third romantic historical novel set in the early twentieth century, following publication of *The Black Silk Purse*. Her debut novel, *Ring of Clay*, won the RNA New Writer's Award and the Society of Authors' Sagittarius Prize and was followed by a further six bestselling sagas set in the Potteries.

margaretkaine.com
@MargaretKaine